Desolate Places

DESOLATE PLACES

Edited by Eric T. Reynolds
with Adam Nakama

Hadley Rille Books
PO Box 25466
Overland Park, KS 66225
USA
http://www.hadleyrillebooks.com
info@hadleyrillebooks.com

To Ruth Colvin
1904-1997

Second Grade Teacher, Mulberry School, Eureka, Kansas, USA.
In 1964 she instilled the sense of wonder in this editor,
ultimately leading to the idea for this book.

Acknowledgments

"Tomb" copyright © 2008 by Z. S. Adani.
"Don't Leave, She Said" copyright © 2008 by Michael Anthony.
"Honeymoon at the Pearly Gate" copyright © 2008 by Tom Barlow.
"Red" copyright © 2008 by Paul L. Bates.
"All Quiet on the Vega Front" copyright © 2008 by Chris Benton.
"Ozymandias Redux" copyright © 2008 by Skadi meic Beorh.
"Bone Wars" copyright © 2008 by Brenta Blevins.
"Tenth Orbit" appeared in the April 2005 issue of *Jupiter*, Issue #8,
     copyright © 2005 by Gustavo Bondoni, reprinted by permission of the author.
"A Poor, Desert Planet" copyright © 2008 by Sue Burke.
"The Days After" copyright © 2008 by Jean-Michel Calvez.
"A Helmet Full of Hair" copyright © 2008 by Scott Christian Carr.
"Adrift" copyright © 2008 by Willis Couvillier.
"A Requiem for the Sons of Kings" copyright © 2008 by Jennifer Crow.
"Acid Rain Rocks" copyright © 2008 by Hazel Dixon.
"A Dream?" copyright © 2008 by F.V. "Ed" Edwards.
"Death and Love in Gehanna" copyright © 2008 by Sara Genge.
"Weapons of Mass Destruction" copyright © 2008 by Jude-Marie Green.
"The Ugly Ones" copyright © 2008 by Max Habilis.
"Someone is Dying" copyright © 2008 by James Hartley.
"It's A Dog's Life" copyright © 2008 by Shelley Savran Houlihan.
"Engaging the Idrl" appeared in the anthology *Glorifying Terrorism* in January 2007,
     copyright © 2007 by Davin Ireland, reprinted by permission of the author.
"Husk" copyright © 2008 by Meghan Jurado.
"Nor Winter's Cold" copyright © 2008 by Stephen Graham King.
"The Road" copyright © 2008 by Fran LaPlaca.
"Lucky Shot" copyright © 2008 by Gerri Leen.
"Gifts of Bone" copyright © 2008 by C. A. Manestar.
"Gray" copyright © 2008 by Paul E. Martens.
"A Wilderness of Sand" copyright © 2008 by Lyn McConchie.
"History" copyright © 2008 by Alex Moisi.
"End of Time" copyright © 2008 by Mari Ness.
"Flying Solo" copyright © 2008 by A. Camille Renwick.
"Blown to Dust" copyright © 2008 by Stephen D. Rogers.
"Empty Epochs" copyright © 2008 by Trent Roman.
"The Peach" copyright © 2008 by Shaun Ryan.
"What Doesn't Stay in Vegas" copyright © 2008 by Lawrence M. Schoen.
"The Last" copyright © 2008 by Cavan Scott.
"Honeymoon" copyright © 2008 by Katherine Shaw.
"Enlightenment" appeared in the September 2004 issue of *InterZone*, Issue #194,
     copyright © 2004 by Douglas Smith, reprinted by permission of the author.
"Geisterbahnhof Trinity" copyright © 2008 by Eric Vogt.
"Together—Nowhere" copyright © 2008 by Bill Ward.
Cover Photograph "Racetrack—Grandstand" copyright © by Erich Hernandez-Baquero,
     used by permission of the photographer.
Editorial assistance by Adam Nakama and Rose Reynolds is greatly acknowledged.

Contents

Introduction

The stories in this book illustrate how humans (and non-humans) survive in desolate places, reflect on their lives, interact and struggle with native life forms, try to solve the puzzles of escaping their predicaments, or cope with their lonely lifestyles. Many of the stories are about people's internal conflicts and how the absence of civilization's clutter allows for clearing one's mind and contemplating life's struggles. Sometimes they look forward to (if they can get out of there) better relationships when they return home. Many of the protagonists presented in these stories end up as better people in the end. Others are not as fortunate.

So what *is* desolation? Some synonyms might be: wasteland, barren place, emptiness, bleakness. Or depression, sorrow, despair. A desolate place can be one or all of these. However, isn't desolation also mysterious, challenging, unspoiled, natural, relaxing and adventurous? These were the words that came to my mind during a recent trip across California's Mojave Desert.

But does nothing happen in a desolate place? This book's cover photograph by Erich Hernandez-Baquero was taken in a dry lakebed of Death Valley National Park called The Racetrack where rocks separate from the nearby mountains and slide across the flat valley floor. This movement has never been witnessed, but is evident from the trails left by the rocks creating a local and unique mystery.

Our world has an abundance of desolate places, but in the early part of the twenty-first century as the human population passes six billion our cities grow more crowded and human settlements continue to expand as bulldozers push out into the wilderness. Areas that were once thought to be uninhabitable are now being converted through technology; barren tracts of land are bought up by speculators, divided and sold. Earth's desolate places are quickly becoming less common.

But desolate places exist elsewhere. In fact, *every* place beyond Earth is a desolate place. Shortly after Buzz Aldrin stepped onto the lunar surface in 1969 he uttered the words, "Magnificent desolation." Magnificent it was, for surrounding him was a land that had never been explored. And to think that the Moon—a mostly unexplored land the size of Africa—is just a tiny speck in a vast, desolate Universe.

These stories are rich in description and human introspection. Alone in a desert, stranded on an asteroid, adrift in space, and more. Individuals examine their lives, their relationships with those they left behind, their skills at survival, whether they have the right to intrude on whatever occupies the place (however subtle that may be), and their adaptability to the unknown. In some cases they've chosen to venture into these barren worlds. For others the selection was *not* theirs. They cope as well as they can, solving the puzzles presented by their new environments.

Eric T. Reynolds
Socorro / Very Large Array, New Mexico
and Overland Park, Kansas
Summer and Fall 2007

Flying Solo
by Camille Alexa

*B*egin Transmission

Dear Jack,

Well it looks like I'm not going to make it to the wedding after all. For that, I really am sorry.

I know you had your heart set on your sister being your best man. It did seem funny when we first thought of it. I guess you'll have to go the more traditional route after all. Ask Cindy's brother to do it; it'll make him happy. He thinks you don't like him, you know.

I was on my way, honest. I rented a two-seater and debarked from Earthside Station without a hitch. The hitch came later.

I know you told me I wasn't ready to fly solo and I guess you were right. It wasn't the flying I had trouble with actually, but the wormhole navigation; fried the ship's computers on the dismount. I hate it when my little brother is right.

I'm not sure exactly where I am: somewhere east of the sun and west of the moon. (Joke.) I actually got as far as the Dimotros moonbelt, I think. That's where I'm pretty sure I am now. You used to tell me about this place. I think I remember you said as many as one in sixty of these planetoids has breathable air. *A miracle there were so many*, you said. *A wonder of the Universe*, you said. Let me tell you, brother: one in sixty doesn't feel like great odds when you've got forty seconds to choose a rock and your ship's going down with nearly total engine burnout. Hah! I bet my chances of even surviving a crash landing were only one in . . . I don't know how many millions, but we'll call it a lot. And as for what happens next . . . .

Excuse me, Jack. I think I have to go throw up. I think I just now understand the full measure of my predicament.

Love,

Katherine

* * *

Dear Jack,

I'd like to say I feel better after a long nap. By the barely-functioning ship's chronometer, I slept for something like twenty-three hours. I feel like crap.

I did try going outside. I got back in here as quickly as I could. I know space is big, but when you're out there bobbing around in all that bigness, at least you're protected by the shell of your ship. It's like a floating, navigable, free-standing apartment. It makes all that vastness doable, you know? Gives you at least the illusion of some small shelter against the wonders of the unknown.

Gods, but I always hated even going out on that bloody deep-sea boat of yours back Earthside. All that rolling brown-grey water, stretching away forever and ever into nothing and nothing and more of the same. Forget sea-sick: I always stayed in my cabin the whole time because I was open-sick. Couldn't wait to get back to the safety of my high-rise loft in the Tower Cities. Couldn't stand all that unmitigated wind and air. It was like the sky was crushing down on my head the whole time. Too much weight for me.

I've transferred these letters into my palm-pad. This little two-seater ship was only equipped for a quick hop. With the computer fried like it is, I figure I've got about another day of power and no way to recharge. The palm-pad will last at least another Earth-standard week, maybe two if I don't use it too often, before I wear the charge out. This will be one hell of a letter, Jack. If it ever reaches you.

Love,
Katherine

Dear Jack,

Well I was wrong. The ship had about six hours of power left.

I feel quite clever actually, as I thought to fill the recirculation suit with the proper amount of water before the condensation stills quit. See? I remembered something from my pilot courses, after all. Not that they spend much time on crash survival training. It's only just now occurring to me that's because they don't want to explain how low the odds are of surviving. So I managed to pull off the miracle and land in breathable atmo. The double-miracle, really, because I'm still talking to you now. Well, *typing*, though these palm-pad keys are bloody small, Jack! I should have listened to you and bought the upgrade.

I won't ignore the advice of my baby brother again, I promise. No flying solo without the full pilot's license. No buying inferior products to save a few credits. No wasting my life behind closed doors. Actually, this last one seems to be giving me a bit of trouble, not quite working out for the best. But you see I'm taking it to heart. I'd better, as the ship's air pumps are off, gone with the rest of the power.

I've got the recirc suit on. I have the recommended amount of water in the bladders. I have plenty of food. Those syntha-meal bars do taste like a dog's ass, Jack, you were right. I thought you were just bragging. I still do not appreciate the mental image of the empirical data-gathering you must have done to arrive at such a conclusion.

At any rate, the meal bars will last way past the water; I've stuffed my pack and all the pockets of my suit. Before the ship ran down I calculated the location of this rock's claim beacon and typed brief descriptions of the topographical landmarks I should encounter between here and there. There aren't many.

So I'm steeling myself for a trek to the beacon to see if there's a way to send out a distress call or a message, maybe even this letter. If the ship's calculations were right I'm nowhere near Dimotros or its moonbelt, after all. I'm on some rock claimed by an asteroid mining company out of West Virginia: Aggregated Minerals Consortium. Class Yellow Planetoid D-Z1282, in case you're curious.

Right, Jack. Signing off for now. Stepping out into the unknown.

Wish me luck.

Love,

Katherine

Dear Jack,

No life behind closed doors here, brother! No life at all, so far as I can tell.

My gods, but this place is empty. Huge empty. Enormous empty. Forever empty. Emptier than empty.

Even the open oceans of Earth have movement and spatter and vaguely threatening shapes glowing beneath the murky surface just out of view. I know you told me they were buoys marking oceanbed strip-mines, Jack, but I tell you they still looked like the gleaming, bulbous eyes of massive sea monsters. And don't give me the speech 'bout how humans killed off the last living ocean creature larger than my thumbnail over sixty years ago. I've heard that particular speech too many times. You and your soapbox! Not everybody cares to live as you do, off in the wilderness of the under-charted extraterrestrial

17

frontier. At least Cindy is willing to be dragged about on your venture surveying expeditions. You've got a good woman there, Jack—better than I. I hope you appreciate her.

I know you've seen some amazing places on your journeys. You've described a few for me over the years. Let me try to describe this one for you.

I think I've already said it's big. Not big by planetary standards, I'm sure. But when I stepped out of that sweet, warm cocoon of synthesized glass and metal I shall henceforth affectionately refer to as my dearly departed ship—may it rest in peace—I felt vertigo.

You've been to my loft in Atmosphere Stratum Three Tower City, Earthside. Remember when the fashion was to have sporadic transparent wall programming? There'd be opaqued panels which would appear and disappear in the polarized exterior glass on a random cycle, so you could be walking to the bathroom and suddenly the wall would completely visually dissolve to your right? Or you'd be making dinner, and the glassite would suddenly become so clear right in front of you it was like the sink dangled off the lip of a cliff and you were about to plummet over the edge, glass of milk in one hand and dishtowel in the other? It was absolutely vomitous.

You laughed at me then; you can laugh at me now. I know I'm more a trend follower than I should be. You've always said so, and you're right.

But what I'm trying to describe is the first split moment of that feeling of unexpectedly falling over the edge of a high place without warning and with no thought but the panic spasming the muscles of your stomach. You want to grab hold of something, anything, and you fling your arms out to your sides, some dim part of your brain hoping to clutch onto the very air.

Imagine that feeling in your gut, low and tight, and that certainty in the portion of your mind beyond rational thought that tells you you're falling. That's how it was for me stepping out onto the plain of this desolate place.

Desert, I guess you'd call it. Cracked, mottled ground, dry and vacant. Nothing in sight to relieve the monotony of the landscape. There's nothing here, and it's the most horrible feeling. That sky is going to crush the breath out of me, it feels so heavy. Just the visual weight of it, Jack, bearing down on my mind.

I've chosen a random patch of parched ground on which to spend the night. The day/night cycle here is quite fast by Earth standards. I think it's just over eight hours light, eight hours dark. I've been wearing the suit's helmet even though the air's perfectly breathable. If I remove that last bubble of synthesized glass between me and this place, I'm afraid all that empty land will swallow me whole.

It's about to get dark. It's no gradual process here. I can see the shadow of night racing across the ground toward me over the flat plain, though it's still some distance away.

This palm-pad will last longer if I don't use the light function, so I'll tell you more tomorrow. Goodnight, Jack. I hope your pillow is softer than mine.

Love,
Katherine

Dear Jack,

It was incredible! The most amazing thing I've seen in my life! Why didn't you ever tell me what it was like to view a field of stars through atmosphere clearer than glassite?

There were neighboring asteroids up there of course, dominating the heavens. None as big as this one, I believe. From here, they shone like a loosely strung strand of huge baroque pearls in the night sky.

And the stars. I was totally unprepared for the stars. Like a blanket of diamonds, Jack! At night, that huge sky which felt so overpowering in the glare of day felt gentle, benevolent. It didn't seem like it was going to crush me into the ground: more like it was going to sweep me up with it to take my place among uncharted constellations. I've never seen anything so beautiful in my life.

The strangest thing: when I woke this morning the dust around my body had been disturbed, as though I'd been making a snow angel in the thin layer of ochre powder. Remember when you showed me how to make those, Jack? It was one of the better trips you dragged me on, to the snow preserve in Antarctic Glacial Global Park. I know it's gone now. I've always been secretly glad you convinced me to see it before it disappeared forever, though I know I complained something awful at the time. I tried to go once to that theme park they have in Nevada. You know the one, with the generated blizzards and simulated snow for skiing? I tried to lie down on the floor in the flakes and make an angel like we did that day, but it wasn't the same. Maybe the piped-in music had something to do with it. Distracting. Also, the mood advertisements scattered invisibly around the place, making one suddenly ravenous for Shmuggler's Pretzels™ or NearlyBeer™ or VileCorp Bail Bonds™. Quite off-putting, in my opinion.

Nothing theme park about last night! I had to take off the suit helmet to get comfortable lying on my back on the ground, arms out at my sides. I'm glad

I did. Somehow, filling my lungs with air directly from that massive sky without filtration or interference between me and it . . . . It was like nothing I've felt before. Or tasted or smelled or *absorbed*. I can see why you've become addicted to filterless breathing, Jack: makes your head clearer.

I left my suit helmet back there on the cracked soil where I spent the night. It was bloody heavy, anyway.

Love,
Katherine

Dear Jack,

It's been two local days since I've added to these letters. I've missed the wedding by now. I'm so, so sorry.

I hope it was beautiful. Did you kiss the bride? How did her brother do as your best man? I'm sure he was great. I bet in your tux you were the most handsome man on the planet. Certainly the handsomest baby brother I've ever had.

I don't want to say this, but I think I'm lost.

Writing it down like that makes it seem more real. Until now I've been pretending I was merely temporarily disoriented.

I've been studying the stars after darkfall to see if I can't remember which direction I was headed that first night and re-orient myself to the same trajectory. But it's no use. I'm not a natural in the out-of-doors. Not like you. You could probably find water in this desert with a forked stick, or tell the direction you wanted by licking your finger and holding it to the breeze.

Not that there are any sticks here, forked or no. Nor much breeze for that matter.

It is strange, but after my initial panic ebbed; after I fell to my knees and sobbed away gods-know-how-much valuable salt and water into this parched ground; after I slept another short night lying palms to the sky and waiting for the judgment of the heavens and the fates to rain down on me in a shower of those cold, beautiful stars; I felt at peace.

I barely recognized peace. I'm sure it's not a familiar feeling. But sitting here; the light from the local sun brushing my skin like invisible feathers of heat; the ground solid and warm beneath my legs; my lungs full of this slightly sweet, peppery air; I have nothing pressing for my immediate attention but existence.

And not a desperate existence, Jack. Not the scrabbling, driven existence of living in the Tower City in Stratum Three. Not the agonized existence of a person in pain or angry at herself or anyone else in the Universe for bringing her to this point.

I think for the first time in my life, I realize how sweet it is to draw breath. How beautiful the firm, gentle sound of one's heart beating in one's chest, pushing the blood though one's body. It is truly miraculous.

And it took this desolate place to show me. I think I must in some small way be grateful, at least for that.

Love,
Katherine

Dear Jack,

The dust angels have appeared every morning now.

It's almost alarming how quickly I've adapted to the short day/night cycle. During the day I make my way toward the ridge of hills I see in the distance. How far away they are, I'm not sure. It's one of the beautiful things about this place, and the most terrifying: that you can see what feels like forever in every direction, but have no true understanding of where the perimeters of forever *are*.

Don't worry I might be lonely, Jack. I keep myself good company. I can't remember the last time I had a serious conversation with myself, a rational one not full of blame or abuse or regret. There's no room for those feelings here. The simplicity and largeness of this landscape have no tolerance for petty thoughts.

I leave no footsteps. Sometimes I turn to look behind me, to see if I leave a trail stretching across that crackled infinity like the trail of a microbe slug on the leaf of a potted fern. But no: there is only hard-packed dirt, dry and waterless and of an ochre sameness that tires the eyes. There are patches of dusty areas, but those are irregular and thinly-spaced, though the ground less hard. It makes for a slightly better sleeping surface.

One of the lovely things about losing the drive to self-recriminate: you get to sit down right where you are, and close your eyes, and feel the warmth of an alien sun soak into you from above and leach up into your legs from the day-heated ground below. You listen to your heartbeat, and count your breaths, slow and even, to a thousand, or as close to a thousand as your mind lets you before it forgets its task and hums into a soft glow.

I wanted to tell you I've been noticing small things about this place. When I first stepped out onto this flat, cracked ground, I thought there was nothing and all was emptiness. That's not so. What I thought were mottled patches of dirt are actually lichen fields. It's across these sections my steps leave no trace. The growth is more resilient than it looks.

I know modified lichens are used in oxygen production on Earth, and when I lie on my stomach and press my cheek to the dry, nubby, miniscule curls of the stuff here, I'd swear I breathe easier. It is the origin of the mild peppery scent in the air, I believe, and what lends the dust its color. My suit has become covered in super-fine particles. I no longer stick up from this landscape like an enormous, sore silver thumb. I'm now an ochre one instead.

And the dust angels. Last night I stayed awake all night, or thought I did, not moving. I lay, dazzled by the brilliance of the starfield, soaking up the day's stored warmth from the ground beneath me and breathing the slightly peppery air. When daylight rolled across me a few hours later I rose and looked down at the patch where I had lain. I can only think I must have hypnotized myself with that huge beautiful sky, Jack, because I clearly had moved my arms and legs in the night to make a pattern on the ground. For now, it shall remain a mystery.

I believe I'm near the hills. I hope climbing to the top of the tallest peak will allow me to see either the direction of the ship or the mining claim beacon. It is toward this peak I head now. Perhaps I shall write you tomorrow from its summit.

Love,
Katherine

Dear Jack,
Nocturnal butterflies!
Not really moths, and I know you'll know the difference, brother.

Nocturnal butterflies crawl up from small fissures in the ground and crowd around my limbs at night. I hypothesize they are attracted to the water bladders in the suit, as they seem to congregate around the main arteries which run along my arms and legs.

I watched them last night by the light of the palm-pad. I shouldn't have run the power cells so low, but I know you'll forgive me. My drive to study my new friends must appeal to the scientist in you.

They seemed not at all bothered by my tiny artificial light. I wonder if they do not register its existence? I watched them flutter low across the ground and alight at my sides. Not so many: a mere few dozen. I watched as they performed a funny, dignified little dance; a solemn procession that beat against the hard soil, disturbing the layer of fine ochre dust along the outlines of my limbs in a radiating pattern.

And they aren't anything like the ones kept back home as pets. Someone gave me one once: a beautiful specimen with blue and gold wings. I gave it away the very next day. I couldn't bear to watch a creature I knew would live for such a brief time, and know it would spend its entire life in a glassite box. Is that what you meant, Jack? When you begged me to leave the Tower Cities of Earth? I think I understand better now than I did at the time.

Oh, and good news: I can see the claim beacon quite clearly from here. I reached the tip of this rocky hill this afternoon. Not the highest peak, as I had thought I would, but a perfectly adequate little ridge nonetheless. After my midday meal of thrice-drunk water and dog's-nethers bars, I shall make for the spire.

Love,
Katherine

Dear Jack,
My water's definitely getting stale.

I'm under no illusions about how the recirc suit works or where this water's already been, but a diet of recirc water and synth bars wears even more quickly than one would think. The suit's specs give it a full fourteen days before the water bladders need rinsing and refilling, and that's Earth standard days, not local ones. Either this particular suit is sub-par, or I've got considerably farther to go before I reach untenable quality standards. If my mouth weren't so dry, that thought would make me nauseous. As it is, it just makes me thirsty. Thirstier.

I'm quite pleased with my progress toward the claim beacon. I indulged myself by spending the rest of the day and last night atop the ridge. No butterflies up on the rock, I'm afraid. I was surprised to find myself disappointed at the lack of nocturnal visitors.

But I did mark my position by the stars. I lay on my back up on that ridge and studied this glorious sky. I never really understood the constellations that used to be visible from Earth. I'm sure it would make a difference if they could still be seen with the naked eye. From the Tower Cities, any natural starlight is far outshone by orbiting space-junk and abandoned satellites and free-floating garbage barges. I know there's been a push in recent years to clean up some of that detritus, but people are slow to change.

So I did as our most distant ancestors must have done: I marked the stars. Planets, I suppose they are, and suns. Everything is just a matter of perspective in the end, isn't it? Tonight I shall check my direction. I feel confident, Jack, that I shall have more of note to report tomorrow, which is only some eight hours away. Here unfurls the darkness across the plain, bringing with it my new friends the stars, and perhaps butterflies as well.

Love,
Katherine

Dear Jack,

However could I have thought this place empty? Vast, yes; panoramic, yes. Inhospitable even, perhaps. But not empty.

I've become accustomed to the shapes of the distant hills and the rolling plain. In this landscape, everything has a presence. The patterned soil, which I know must house my lepidopteran neighbors while they sleep during the day; the more distant rises, particularly the three distinctive hills I've come to think of as the Sleeping Giant, the Spire, and the Hook. Perhaps the Hook is actually a massive J? J for Jack. I shall henceforth think of it as your mountain, my brother.

Even the lichen tundra has distinct forests. Granted, these forests grow no taller than the thickness of the tough, rubbery skin of my recirc suit. But still, I've come to recognize the subtle variations in shade and texture which indicate the beginning of one forest and the ending of another. I am a giant, Jack; my long strides clear whole forests, whole ecosystems, whole continents. I am *invincible*.

Love,
Katherine

Dear Jack,

I cried last night, thinking of you.

A complete waste of water, I know, though the butterflies seemed to like it. They moved their strange procession from the ground near my arms to the area around my head. They never touch me, but several of them crowded close enough to my damp cheeks, I could feel the air moved by their tiny wings when I turned my head toward them. I wonder if my tears are the first rain ever to fall on this parched soil.

I hope you and Cindy are having a wonderful time on your honeymoon. It comforts me to think you are.

When I rose this morning, a looping halo had been added to the angel I left in the thin dust beneath me, where the butterflies had marched in circles around my tears.

Love,
Katherine

* * *

Dearest Jack,

My water has become truly foul. I won't tell you what the stuff causes in the way of headaches.

I have reached the claim beacon. I just kept walking toward the Hook; toward your mountain, Jack. I never let it out of my sight, and it led me to my goal.

You shall be so pleased with me when we see each other next. The beacon *does* have transmission capacities. I've already sent a general, pre-programmed SOS, that anyone might find. Until then, I wait.

It is a pretty spot here. Prettier than any other I've seen this whole adventure. And adventure this has been. I regret only that you had to hear about this lovely place second-hand.

Of course I can't say I wish you were here, because I don't. Not unless you had your ship with you, in full functioning order. If that were the case, I would love us to lie beside each other, our backs warm against this bright and beautiful plain. We'd breathe the peppery air, and watch the achingly brief days and nights roll across the patterned soil with a most gratifying regularity.

Time to send this letter. This and all the rest. I promise: when I return to Earth, it shall not be to spend the rest of my life in a glassite box. It's not good for butterflies, either.

Love always, your affectionate sister
Katherine

End Transmission

The Peach
by Shaun Ryan

Exactly when he had come to the desert, the old man could not remember. All he could say with any certainty was that it had been many years ago. His reasons for staying were enigmatic and he had long since ceased to ponder them. Why was a meaningless question and he did not care about the answer any more than the desert did.

That the desert had changed him was undeniably true; the desert changed everything, even its own face, though at heart it remained immutable in its brutal simplicity. The earth was an unforgiving anvil beneath the hammer of the merciless sun and the body and soul of anyone who stayed for very long was fundamentally altered, if they managed to survive.

In this place, he thought to himself as he trudged up the sandy bottom of the wash, every last bit of softness was wrung from a man like dirty water from a rag. The desert offered nothing in return but grudging wisdom or, more often, madness.

Most often, the only lesson the desert taught a man was how to die. He had not yet learned that final lesson, though countless enemies and more than a few friends had tried to teach him over the years, as had the desert. His body and mind bore the scars such single-minded instruction must always leave upon a man. He did not complain. There was no one to complain to.

He thought about the endless nature of the barren land he inhabited as he followed the strange tracks in the sand. He knew that it was not really without end of course. Had he not wandered down out of the mountains to the west in a former age? He thought so, but the man he had been before was less than a memory, a phantom that only rarely haunted his dreams. The mountains had receded from him as well, leaving only hazy, half-formed images in his mind. They were but ghosts now, winking halfheartedly at him through a shimmering mirage, which suited him just fine.

He, too, was a ghost in many ways. He had not seen nor spoken to another human being in many years and had lost the need for human companionship. The only words to fall upon his ears in that time were his own. That also suited him.

27

No, the desert did not stretch on forever, but it might as well have. If a man tried to make his way across that timeless expanse of sand and rock, he would be reduced to a dried husk before he made it half way, the water sucked from him by the relentless heat until he resembled a piece of jerky.

The old man resembled jerky himself and he chuckled in recognition of that fact. It was a harsh, guttural sound that rasped across the mummified landscape like rusty iron on stone, fading first to a whisper, then a memory. Like all things, it was swallowed by the bleak vastness around him and soon forgotten.

After a while, he paused to kneel beside one of the tracks, sniffing the air and then the earth itself before bending to examine it. It was inexplicable of course, but he had expected that, gotten past it. Any track that had not been left in the sand by his feet or those of the few creatures here was a mystery.

The old man loved mysteries, they gave his mind something other than itself to ponder. A mind that was always bent inward soon remained so, becoming twisted over time until it was incapable of coherent thought. But he also hated mysteries, for pondering them more often than not led only to more mysteries. A man could lose himself that way, becoming a shepherd of sorts, forever guarding what soon becomes a herd of mysteries wandering aimlessly through the tortured landscape of his own mind. Unanswered questions led only to madness.

Touching the edge of the strange track with the tip of one calloused finger, he watched as the crusted sand gave way, losing its shape and slumping into the shallow depression in a miniscule avalanche. The sand was bone dry, but the tracks had been made while it was damp, which meant they were at least a day old, left in the dry watercourse within a few hours of the rain that had fallen a day or so back. The estimate was close enough to suit the old man's purpose. Beyond day and night, time had little meaning.

He thought about the rain as he examined the track. It had been the first in many months and had not fallen for long. The mountains to the west gobbled almost all of the rain that made its way inland from the sea, leaving only pale imitations of clouds to straggle across the sky. They had made the desert. He understood how this could be in only the vaguest possible way, but knew that it was true. In another life, he had roamed them often. He did not miss the mountains; this was his home now. But he sometimes dreamt of green places. They always faded from his mind quickly once he woke and the desert reasserted its rightful claim upon his soul.

Green was foreign here, an invader that must inevitably shrivel and die. He had seen it happen only a few times during his years here. Perhaps once in a decade, rain would bless the land with its soft kiss. Not the fleeting shower that could be measured in minutes like that of the previous day, but real rain that fell for hours or, as he had seen happen only once, days.

When that happened, usually in the late winter or early spring, the dead land would suddenly explode with vibrant color. Any patch of ground that was not solid rock sprouted with green life. The flood plains became meadows of wildflowers containing entire rainbows of color. The shriveled brush that littered the edges of the dead watercourses sprouted with tiny leaves and flowers. The rocky hills became havens, holding the blessed rain in their cupped hands for a time, giving birth to a myriad of tiny creatures. Game arrived to feast upon the sudden bounty. The land was alive for a few short weeks, evidence of God's twisted sense of humor. Inevitably, however, the days would grow ever hotter, until the frantically blooming life withered to dust, leaving only the barren majesty of the earth's bones to bake in the furnace for another decade.

There was no evidence of that now. The pitiful bit of moisture from the brief downpour was gone, swallowed by the parched sand and broiled away by the sun.

He stood, shielding his eyes from the harsh afternoon glare, peering ahead at the tracks that made their way up the wash toward his sanctuary. He slowly lowered his gaze to the prints at his feet. They were the strangest things he had ever seen in his long years. Equal in length and depth to those of a large, heavy man, the tracks were inexplicably narrow, as though made by the skeletal feet of a dead man. The small depressions of five toes were obvious, a centimeter or so ahead of the larger mark left by the narrow ball of the foot that had made the tracks. But unlike a man's footprints they were apparently tipped with long claws like a dog's. The tiny dimples were there in the sand plain as day, undeniable. Of the heel there was but scant evidence, whoever had left the tracks walked on the balls of his—*its*—feet, only occasionally touching heel to ground.

It was a mystery, of that he was certain. The old man had not seen evidence of any living thing other than wild creatures since his mule died. That had been more years ago than he cared to think about. He missed the mule sometimes, had carried on many a one-sided conversation with the surly animal. It had been a good companion.

But that was irrelevant, he thought brusquely. He pushed the memory aside and went back to pondering the strange tracks that seemed to lead directly to his home.

He shrugged the makeshift pack higher onto his shoulders and resumed his slow trudge up the wash as the afternoon began to bend itself toward evening.

Home. Now there was a word that man had imbued with so much meaning that it had become ponderous. Unfortunately, that meaning was shifty and vague, at least for the old man. He had never known a home until coming to the desert, had spent his days wandering, toiling, fighting, and sometimes killing to survive.

He wandered still, eking out a lonely existence that others would shun. He welcomed the isolation. Here he was free. He continued to toil, such was the nature of life. No matter where a man found himself, he must sweat to live. But in this place he toiled in his own way in his own time for his own purpose and that made all the difference. He continued to fight for survival as well, but it was a different fight here. It was straightforward and simple, known with an intimacy rivaling that shared by lovers. A man knew his enemy here, for the enemy was the land itself. But it was also his home. Not the shelter where he slept and prepared his sparse meals, though the word applied, but the entire desert in all its harsh, beautiful, deadly glory. His home encompassed the land around him to every horizon for the simple reason that no one else cared to claim it.

Thinking about the strange tracks, wondering what sort of man or creature might have made them, he followed, knowing he would find out sooner or later, for tracks in the sand must inevitably lead to their maker.

He had been following the trail since early morning, when he came across the broken-egg thing out on the nameless flood plain to the south. He chuckled again, poking fun at his own thoughts. The plain was not really without a name, everything had a name. Humans were obsessed with names, sticking them onto everything they encountered, from the tiniest insect to the mightiest mountain range without regard to meaning or suitability.

There was no feature on the globe that had not been given some moniker or other. The plain had a name but if the old man had ever known it, he had forgotten. He too had once answered to a name. He had forgotten that as well. Even the desert had a name. It did not matter. Names were meaningless in this place. Landmarks were important, of course, but *The broken ridge with the notch in the west end* or *The long alkali flats north of the hills* were as good as any ridiculous name dreamed up by egocentric explorers or mapmakers and more accurate to boot.

The thing on the plain had instantly intrigued him. It resembled nothing so much as a huge egg shell—not oblong like a chicken's egg, but round, like a turtle's—lying broken and empty on the cracked earth, its contents baked away by the sun perhaps. The interior, which he could have sat comfortably in, was padded by some material he had never seen, soft to the touch but nearly invulnerable, as he had discovered when he tried to cut a swath of it away with his knife. There were odd markings and little glass studs scattered around inside as well, indecipherable and indestructible, respectively.

What it could be and where it had come from he could not guess; it was a mystery. But the tracks had really sparked his interest; they led from the space between the two halves of the broken egg-thing and away to the north. They also offered a hint about the egg-thing's purpose if not its origins. With nothing better to do, and headed in that direction in any case, he followed.

It had been slow going at first for the ground was baked hard on the flood plain and the tracks were but scratches and smudges visible here and there. He was also burdened by his pack, inside which he carried several tools and a few interesting bits of stone as well as a canteen full of water. Being in no particular hurry, he doggedly followed the tracks up into the hills.

The old man never hurried. Rushing to and fro could kill a man in this place. Every move and act must be carefully deliberated and weighed against the harsh reality of the deadly world around him. To do less would be to perish, caught in the open without enough water, tumbling from a trail in the hills after failing to consider whether or not it had been weakened by one of the infrequent rains, losing one's way because known landmarks had been swallowed by the shifting sands. The desert offered a million ways to die and but one to live. A man survived by molding himself to the wilderness around him, shifting when it shifted, altering his patterns of behavior to match the patterns of the land.

He had been young and strong and foolish when he first came here. Foolishness was cured early on. He thought about the hard lessons from the desert as he continued up the wash. He had learned them well, quickly grasping that the gaudy trappings and baubles of civilized society were worthless here.

Once, while he was setting snares for jackrabbits in one of the rocky mountain ranges, he had come across the corpse of a man who had simply keeled over in his tracks beneath a heavy pack full of sacks containing ore. The dead man had forsaken everything to carry as much gold as he could manage, even water. The spot where he lay was meters from an old water hole that had been dry for months. He had not known that of course, no doubt relying on information gleaned from some map or, worse yet, word of mouth passed on to him by some traveler who had not set foot in that place for years. Seeking wealth in the desert was a fool's errand. He had taken whatever useful items he could salvage from the dried husk that had once been a man and buried the rest without a word. He shook his head at the memory.

31

* * *

As he neared the head of the dry watercourse, the ground grew hard and rocky once more. The tracks reverted to indistinct scrapes and smudges, but they were easy enough to follow. He was nearing the stone hut he had built so long ago it had blended itself into the landscape. He had not been there for a few days now and was anxious to return. Such absences were not unusual for him, especially this time of year. The weather was good, the days not too hot and the nights not unduly cold. His excursions often took him away from his little sanctuary, but never far and he always returned.

He kept up his deliberate pace, still watching the ground as he walked, keeping an eye on the tracks. He wondered what the man or creature or whatever it was he followed thought about the desert. Had he come here deliberately or had he been stranded somehow? Would he be able to survive? Would he find water? Would he discover the old man's hut in the canyon ahead? Would he find the peach?

That thought sent a shiver down his spine, not of fear, but of excitement. He smiled at the thought of the peach.

It hung there on the little tree he had nurtured for so long it was like a child to him, nearly ripe and ready to devour. He had been anticipating how it would taste since he had discovered it one morning in the early summer. It was the only one, the only pitiful blossom to have survived the climate and been pollinated by some passing insect. He cherished it and lavished it and its mother tree with affection and attention, watering them deeply at least once a week, tying strips of tin he had found to the branches in order to discourage any marauding birds that might discover his prize. How he had known to do such a thing was lost to him; he simply had.

He had sprouted the tree from a peach pit discovered in a pile of rubble and dead wood left jumbled upon the rocks of the very wash he now traveled, marooned there by the surging waters of some flash flood or other. How it had come to be there he would never know and did not care to. He viewed it as a gift from the desert and put much time and energy into bringing forth the life it contained. He had prepared a bed of soil near the hidden spring in the canyon he called home. He had protected the sapling after it had sprouted from the earth with a fervor that bordered on obsession. He had cherished the green of its leaves as they burst forth each year, a bit more numerous and luxuriant than the one past. He had watched in fascinated awe as the tree began to blossom each spring and sobbed with despair when the blooms withered. The tree had given him something to look forward to as each passing day turned to years.

And now, the tree had borne fruit at last. He would savor it, every last sweet drop of juice and bit of pulp. Then he would plant the pit as he had that other, bringing forth more life, defying the desert with his little patch of green.

He wondered if that was foolish as he scrambled over the scattered boulders and slabs of broken stone into his canyon. It was a hidden place, a haven from the desiccated wind and glaring sun for most of each day. He smiled as the shadows cast by its towering walls enveloped him. He was almost home.

Perhaps it was foolish of him to challenge the natural order, he thought. So be it. Foolishness was every old man's prerogative, was it not? Even he must have his little treasure to cherish and the living tree he had nurtured was a more worthy icon than gold or silver had ever been.

Satisfied with his conclusions, he scanned the canyon floor ahead. The tracks were there of course, still heading on their unerring course toward his hut. How had this being known it was there? Did it smell the water from the spring he had taken such pains to develop?

The fact that he now regarded whatever had made the tracks he followed as "it" instead of "him" was not lost on the old man. He had decided that it was no man he followed. Whatever it was, he did not think any human designation applied. The thought filled him with both wonder and dread.

Part of him ached to set eyes on whatever had made these tracks, perhaps he would be the first man ever to do so. But part of him quailed at the thought of sharing his sanctuary with another, no matter what kind of being it was. He had come to relish the lonely nature of his life and did not wish for change of any kind.

Perhaps he would be forced to kill the thing that had made the tracks. He would do so without hesitation if it proved a threat to his self imposed exile. Perhaps it would kill him. That thought did not bother him much; he had faced death and did not fear it, though he shuddered involuntarily at the thought of the tree perishing in the heat, which it would inevitably do if he were not there to care for it.

He brushed these thoughts aside as he marched along, the tracks leading him toward his little haven among the towering stone monoliths that were the bones of the desert. He could smell the water now; it whispered in his head like a siren song, speaking of life and enticing him onward. He did not rush, but slowed his pace instead, cautious now.

The canyon narrowed, the stone walls leaning inward to block the sun's light that fell to earth in the west. He walked in shadow toward the narrow crack that he had discovered a lifetime ago. Beyond that rift, which was hidden from view by a screen of broken rock and dead brush, the canyon opened into a walled fortress, a courtyard of sorts, surrounded by sheer cliffs. The little piece of ground within, perhaps fifty meters wide and a hundred deep, was his secret place. There, against the overhanging stone battlements, he had built his hut of rock and mud. Next to his shelter was the spring that he had cleaned out and encouraged to flow with the infinite care of a mother tending her newborn child. Fresh, clear water burbled from the ground into the little pool he had dug, removing the sand until only the rocky bones of the desert received the life giving water, next to the pool stood his treasure, his tree.

The tracks led to the brush and rubble that hid the secret entrance and he followed. He made no sound as he eased through the screen and into the narrow passage beyond. His heart pounded in his temples as he cautiously navigated the twisting, bending slit through the rocks. He paused at the other end and peered warily around the stone wall into his sheltered hideaway.

The hut stood as he had left it, the door of planks he had salvaged from the wreckage of abandoned wagons and ruins of would be mining camps over the years firmly closed and latched. The spring burbled its song of life, the joyful sound unchanged from when he had heard it last. The tree stood at the side of the pool as it had. All seemed unchanged, but that was an illusion, he knew. Something was different.

For the tracks he had followed through the entire length of this desert day, the tracks he now struggled to make out in the growing shadows of evening with his aging eyes, the tracks that had been left upon the unforgiving earth by a being that he could not possibly fathom, led unerringly to the pool of water and the tree. Of whatever creature it had been, there was no sign but the tracks themselves. Nevertheless, a glaring discrepancy screamed in his mind like a mad banshee. The peach was gone.

His eyes closed as the pain of that harsh truth sank in. He blinked a few times and his bony hands clenched into fists at his sides. He shed no tears, for his body refused to give up moisture in such a wasteful way. But his heart quailed with hurt anger in his sunken chest. He slumped ever so slightly against the stone wall and paused for a moment longer before finally stepping into the open. He followed the tracks to the pool and saw where the being had squatted to drink. He pondered that for a while. So it was enough like a man to need water, he thought. That was no surprise, had the tracks not led straight to the nearest source for many kilometers around?

His gaze followed the tracks from the side of the pool, two short steps of those strange, clawed feet, to the tree. The thing had stood, no doubt staring in wonder at the defiant bit of life before it. The sand was dimpled where drops of that precious, sweet juice had plopped onto the earth as the peach was devoured. The tracks continued to the blank stone wall of the cliff and there they ended.

He closed his eyes as frustration and rage tried to overwhelm him. He quelled them after a moment. Such blind emotion could kill a man if he allowed them to rule him in this place, but it was hard, so very hard. He had toiled for years to nourish the peach into existence, pouring his love and life into the tree as he had never done for any human being. He had loved the tree and the peach it had bequeathed to him and they might have been the only things he had ever loved in his long, grueling life.

But anger would bring him nothing but more pain and possibly death, he knew. For deep inside part of him recognized it had been anger and the folly it invariably led to that had brought him to the desert those many years ago. It was not a conscious memory, only a vague, visceral knowledge that ruled him in a way he did not understand. There would be no sense in following the being that had robbed him of his life's greatest treasure with hate in his heart and his mind bent upon vengeance. And besides, what would he follow? The tracks led to blank stone and no farther. Had the thing simply climbed the wall out of the canyon? Would he find the trail up there in the dimming light of evening? For some reason he doubted it. Why, he could not say.

He opened his tired eyes once more and stared at the tree, then glanced down at the spots in the sand where the sweet juice had dribbled from the chin—did it have a chin?—of the thing he had followed to his hideaway. He felt violated. It would be a time before that feeling left him, he knew. But leave him it would, swallowed by the vast and empty land like all things human eventually were.

He would go on. There would be more blossoms, more peaches, more struggles and more pain. But there would also be joy. Watching the leaves of the tree shimmer in the errant breezes that found their way into his haven brought him joy. The wink of sunlight on the pool of water brought him joy. The bleak expanse of rock and sand and sun that surrounded him and held him to its unforgiving bosom brought him joy as well.

Sighing, he turned and trudged to the door of his hut. It was a one room affair, snug and dry, cool in the long days and warm at night as it gave back the sun's energy. He would build a cheery little fire in the stone hearth and roast the rabbit that hung aging from a rafter for dinner. He would ponder.

As he reached out his hand to unlatch the weathered door, his eyes fell upon a strange sight. There at his feet upon the slab of stone that served as his stoop sat a small bundle of what looked like some kind of cloth. Perched atop the bundle was the pit of the peach. His peach. He could see the shriveling tendrils of sweet flesh still clinging to its variegated surface.

Bewildered, he bent and picked up the bundle, stroking the drying peach pit with his hard fingers. He slipped it carefully into the pocket of his tattered trousers and cautiously opened the cloth bundle, marveling at how soft it felt in his hands. He peered with wonder at the object revealed within.

In the rapidly failing light, perched upon the cloth in his palm, sat a sleek, black object the size and shape of a hen's egg. He examined it closely, ran his fingers over its smooth surface, which was cool to the touch. He sniffed it cautiously, detecting a faint odor that reminded him a little of lavender. His mind did not identify the odor as such, but was reminded of something from his childhood, his mother perhaps.

It was a wondrous thing, the seed in his hand, for that was what it had to be: a seed of some kind, an offering left in payment for the peach, left in thanks. The old man marveled at that. Gratitude from one wanderer to another, a gift given in return for the life saving water and nourishment the being had found in this isolated sanctuary.

For the first time, he thought about the tracks and the broken-egg thing from which they had led in a different light, regarding them as not only a mystery to occupy his mind, but as a tale left for him to read upon the land. A tale that he now realized spoke of one lost and lonely in a strange and deadly place that was alien to him.

Him. The old man smiled as the anger left his heart to be replaced with awe and wonder. He stepped back from the door and lifted his face to the darkening sky, where the first stars were winking to life.

He gazed at the heavens above his beloved desert and came to understand that in many ways, the vastness above represented another kind of waste, one infinitely harsher and more unforgiving than his own. He marveled at the bravery and sheer will crossing that endless expanse must require. He wondered what might have motivated such a being to do so. He smiled at the thought. It made little difference. For good or ill, the land that had shaped him for so many years was now home to whatever being he had followed this day.

He lowered his gaze to the door and reached for the latch, already anticipating the joy he would experience when the first sprout from the strange seed broke through the crusted ground and reached for the life-giving light of the sun.

As he stepped across the threshold and into his cozy little home, he wished good fortune to the traveler whose tracks he had followed across the desert, hoping the stranger would find the solace that he had found.

The old man placed the two seeds, one peach and one not, in a jar upon the rickety table he had built with his own hands and stepped to the small hearth. Fumbling in the darkness, he located his precious cache of matches and scraped one across the stone, cupping his hands protectively around the tiny flame as it flared to life in the gloom. He touched it to the fire already laid within and stood, staring into the dancing flames as his fingers unconsciously stroked the cloth which had wrapped the seed.

Outside, the stars blazed in the firmament above a land that hid its secrets behind a mask of desolation, revealing them only to an initiated few.

A Helmet Full of Hair
by Scott Christian Carr

Dear Mom—

Well, I was never really privy to the specifics of our mission—none of us were—but I think that it's a pretty safe bet to say that we failed. *The Wormwood* exploded three days ago, just sixteen months out. We never even made it past the Magellanic Cloud.

I hate to say it, but I actually miss Kentucky. I miss Gasper Creek and those long Sunday drives out to Bowling Green to buy sausage for the gravy biscuits. I miss the weeping ferns hanging down and making a canopy over the gravel drive—the Sun busting through and turning everything golden, the wispy-white cocoons high up in the trees, the whisper of the insects, the thrum of life and the textured scents of a million types of pollen and flowers and hot apple pies drifting through the air. It's the outside things that I miss—the stuff you never think about when you're at home in the house in front of the Screen. The stuff that you never notice until you're gone.

I feel like I've been away for a million years, and in a way, I guess that's not too far off the mark. The best that I can figure is that in the days, weeks, months that I've been drifting in space, nearly ninety thousand years have passed back there on Earth . . .

Jeez—it's hard to comprehend.

The ship exploded while we were still inside the EPR effect, while we were traveling in that strange Einstein-Podalsky-Rosenberg spectrum that's at the same time faster than, and yet somehow *outside of,* the speed of light. Don't ask me to explain it. Just tell Dad that he was right—this whole damned thing turned out to be a disaster.

The rest of the guys on the mission—they're all dead. I'm the only one who made it out. Ryerson had his suit on, but he never made it back to the airlock. And, best I could tell, Captain Hardwick never even got up out of his seat. I don't think he truly realized what was happening until it was too late.

And the others—Byers, O'Brien, and Reeves? I don't know where they were or what they were doing, but their suits were still hanging on the rack when I dropped the bulkhead, blew the hatch, and catapulted myself out of the ass-end of the ship.

The *Wormwood* exploded just seconds later. There wasn't time to do anything, and if they were still onboard, there's no way that they could've survived. I'm gonna miss 'em. Even Ryerson, the big lug.

No one will ever hear this transmission. Not you, not Dad, not anyone. I'm still trying to wrap my mind around the idea that it's been a year and a half—my time—since I last saw you, heard your voice, smelled Dad's whisky breath and Old English cologne—and yet you've been dead now for nearly ninety thousand years. It seems like so much longer . . . than eighteen months, I mean.

Since I last saw you.

It's hard to believe that I'll never see any of you again—that I'll never see *anyone* again.

Oh, by the way, that doesn't sound quite right—Einstein-Podalsky-Rosenberg. It's more like Rosen*field*. Or Rosen*stein*. Rosen-*something* . . . But I guess it doesn't really matter anymore, anyway.

I've never been much of a writer, Mom. I don't have to tell *you* that. I've never had the patience for it. Or the skill. Maybe that's why this is so much easier now—speaking these letters to you into the tiny microphone set inside the neck of my helmet—knowing that you'll never hear them. Drifting through space with the stars shining in all around, and the black void filling in the cracks between them—it almost feels as if the universe is calling out to me, pulling the words from me. Begging me for prose.

Really. I can almost hear the stars speaking to me—calling my name. Urging me on.

"Come on, Donald. Bring it home!"

I remember the first time that I ever saw Phileas Gantry on the Tube—his wild mop of Groucho Marx hair and his thin goatee. He seemed likeable enough. He seemed sincere, and *determined.* You could actually *see* the stars in his eyes when he gazed skyward and lamented over how much he wished he could make the journey himself. His face lit up when he implored his viewing audience to take just a moment to share his vision, help to realize his dream, and to acknowledge its practical reality—to reach for the stars.

"And Sponsorship," he had implored, the word itself magic when he spoke

it, "*is the secret to it all, our key to the stars. With sponsorship we can build a starship, we can develop faster-than-light travel, we can make theoretical EPR physics a practical reality!*"

Sponsorship, both corporate and private: Companies and conglomerates would fund research and development. Hence the gaudy and objectionable vanity naming of newfound stellar objects—the *Zagnut Cluster*, the *Vegas Quasar*, the *Dow-Jones Nebula* and *dot-com Binary*.

But out here, all alone in the empty infinite reaches . . . the stars have no names.

Did you ever really understand why I did it, Mom? I know Dad didn't, that's for sure, but I really wanted you to understand.

I think what really drove me out into space was the Earth. It was as much about getting away from our world as it was about finding new ones—as much about leaving the familiar as it was about charting unexplored territory, reaching for the stars, if that makes any sort of sense. It's the whole attitude these days that rubs me the wrong way—this idea of looking inward instead of outward. It's been nearly a century and we still haven't gotten past that post-Star Trek™ mentality of looking out at the universe and saying "been there, done that" when in reality we haven't even come close. I guess that's what a hundred years of syndication will do to a culture.

But then, it's been eighteen months and ninety thousand years now. I suppose it's possible that things have changed.

I've been trying to remember exactly how it all went down—the explosion, that is—but it's difficult. It all happened so fast. And timewarp does funny things to the memory—things that Einstein, Podalsky, et al, never could have predicted. And you have to have timewarp in order to break the speed of light. Or is it the other way around? You automatically enter timewarp when you exceed the speed of light? Either way, it's all relative, I guess.

Suffice to say that we were traveling very fast, at least from our perspective. But time was also passing by very fast outside of the ship. So, from your point of view, we were probably moving pretty slow—considering the fact that it took us nearly ninety thousand years to get as far as we did (which in the scope of the mission wasn't very far at all). But then *we* did it in only eighteen months. It's all very confusing.

But the point I'm trying to get at is that, in timewarp, it's sometimes hard to remember things. That's a side-effect of EPR, I suppose, though I never really talked about it with the other guys. We never really talked all that much about *anything*, really, other than routine ship functions. Especially in those last few months. Odd, now that I think about it—but then, maybe it was just me. I always was the quiet one. Maybe the other guys whooped it up and talked about all *kinds* of things when I wasn't around, and I just never noticed. I don't know.

Anyway, like I was saying, timewarp makes it really hard to remember things sometimes. Not *hard*, really—but *weird*. It's sort of like trying to remember around a curve, if you can imagine. That's the only way I can think to describe it.

Our days on the *Wormwood* were initially divided into duty shifts—twelve hours on and twelve hours off (not that there was a whole lot to do in the off-time other than read or sleep or eat) with two one-hour breaks for meals.

Not that there was much to do in the *on* time, either—by the end of the first month, we were all pretty much ignoring the shift changes. ALICE and the autopilot pretty much kept things running smoothly. We slept when we were tired, ate when we were hungry, and worked on the increasingly rare occasions that there were things that needed to be done.

Don't get me wrong, there were *always* things that needed to be done. Only most of them just weren't worth doing or important enough to do right away or the right way. Things like cleaning the cargo hold, Pledging the aft windows, and dusting the computer consoles. Technically, these things needed doing; they just didn't get done. By the end, the *Wormwood* was a stinky, cluttered, coffee-stained mess. More akin to my old college dorm room than a state-of-the-art interstellar ship. It smelled like a locker room and looked like a tornado had swept through it. Stuff was everywhere—dirty laundry, used food containers, sweaty socks, tools, magazines, and crud.

Fiberglass and insulation littered the main corridor and hung from the ceiling where Ryerson had torn down the walls between his and O'Brien's quarters in a claustrophobic attempt to make a rec room. They'd welded a spare bulkhead to the floor and used a couple of heat shielding plates and a #46 ball bearing to try and invent a zero gravity ping pong table. It hadn't worked.

The *Wormwood* reeked. To be fair to the guys, though, most of the perishable trash—the uneaten food and leftover meals, not to mention bodily excrement—was blasted out into space, rather than strewn about the ship. Three weeks into the mission, Ryerson had had his first drunken tantrum and ejected all of the bio-bags (which were used to collect all of the biodegradable trash: excrement, food, and garbage to be recycled) as well as O'Brien's mattress, the Captain's cherished catcher's mitt, and my dinner out of the dorsal air lock.

We were in EPR timewarp at the time—traveling faster-than-light—so it's a goddamned wonder he didn't get us all killed and end the mission right then and there. As it is, our trash, dinner, bio-bags, poop and pee, catcher's mitt, and O'Brien's mattress are probably scattered across half the galaxy by now.

We'd since had no choice but to follow Ryerson's example and (having no bio-bags to contain it) start ejecting *all* of our perishable garbage from the ship. Of course, we were careful to make sure that we only opened the dorsal airlock when we were traveling at sublight speeds. And even then, only after it had really begun to reek. We didn't consider this to be littering.

Ryerson would argue tooth and nail whenever any of us used the term "litter"—he insisted that we were actually doing the universe a service by dumping our trash.

"It ain't like we're polluting, man," he'd insist. "It's not like back on Earth where you don't got no choice but to dirty your own pond. We don't *have* to live with the stuff way out here—we *shouldn't* have to live with it way out here. Once we dump it, it's *gonzo* . . . " He licked his teeth—since he'd started drinking heavily (right around the time he went ballistic and sent O'Brien's mattress, the bio-bags, the Captain's mitt, et al, hurtling faster-than-light from the back of the ship—*Gonzo!*), he'd stopped brushing them. His halitosis, if not his unpredictable rage, was enough to convince the rest of us to keep our distance. To not argue with him, in the hopes that he might not breathe in your direction.

"It ain't littering," he insisted. "The universe is *big*, man. Space is *big*. A few specks of rubbish aren't going to spoil the scenery. Besides, eventually all that garbage'll find it's way into a gravity well and burn up in some planet's atmosphere, or drift into a star. *All of it.* Even Earth might drift into the Sun someday, if it hasn't already," he clapped his hands together, "*Gonzo!* End of pollution problem. End of every problem." He leaned in close, exuded a sharp breath of Jack Daniels, and whispered, "Entropy, man. *Entropy.*"

During his more philosophical and sober moments Ryerson explained that we were actually doing the right thing by setting our garbage adrift in space. If there *is* intelligent life anywhere in the universe, he explained, then the best thing we could possibly do would be to leave behind as much evidence of our own existence, and passage through space, as possible—on the one in a trillion chance that they might stumble upon it and realize that they are truly not alone. "Besides," he added soberly, "If there *ain't* any intelligent life out there, then who the hell will notice?"

I once asked Ryerson why he'd joined the mission. He told me that it was the only way that he could be sure of respecting his ex-wife's restraining order and not kill her.

There's lots of junk from the ship floating all around me now. I had a head start when I escaped through the air lock, but now some of the debris is beginning to catch up and pass me. I can twist around and see more behind me, too. Not just our garbage, either—there's lots of wreckage and huge pieces of the ship. Wires and circuit boards, broken plasti-glass, and thousands of diamond-shaped heat-shielding tiles and solar panels spinning and sparkling in the starlight. I can also see a large chunk of the engine. It's huge—at least as tall as a four story building and just as wide. It's still glowing from the heat of the explosion, and jagged vents and torn conduits poke out all around it. A small haze of debris surrounds it like a cloud of gnats.

I pass through a field of shattered glass, probably the cockpit windows. I'd seen it in the distance, a sort of shimmering fog, and I didn't know what it was at first. But as it drifted closer I could tell that the window had splintered into a million tiny shards. Passing through it was not unlike driving through sleet or hail—I could hear the *tinkle-tinkle* of shards' impacts, and feel their tinkling vibration as they hit my faceplate, more than I could actually see them. And then I'm through it and all is silent and motionless again.

It's strange—I can't even tell that I'm moving. The stars are so still and immovable in the distance. It's only when I look back at the ship debris that I can even detect any sort of movement at all. The Oahu Nebula, directly ahead of me (the ship must have twisted around in the moments before the explosion), is much larger than it seemed from the Captain's window—however long ago that was. Time has ceased to have any meaning out here.

The nebula is silent and vast, stretching across the stars, tranquil and ominous.

A lot of debris is drifting slowly past me now. There's a bulkhead. There goes O'Brien's bunk. Oh, there's the Captain's locker—I cans see ice crystallizing on his sneakers.

It's hypnotizing, just how quiet it is out here. Only the hollow sound of my breathing breaks the moment, and even that seems somehow muffled and distant. There's an echo-like quality to it, no doubt due to the face-mask that brings in air from the lower part of my suit. I can hold my breath, and it seems for all the world as if the universe has gone to sleep. As if time has stopped. As if I've found a new life within the moment, forever placed inside a picture postcard.

*   *   *

You'd be amazed how much unauthorized crap we'd managed to smuggle aboard the ship!

Little things: cigarettes, booze, T-shirts, magazines, snacks, a carton of freeze-dried bananas. (As I understood it, Ryerson had some sort plans for smoking the freeze-dried peels in the event that he couldn't get the marijuana seeds that he'd also smuggled onboard to germinate. He actually *did* get them to germinate and grow, in a tract of potting soil he'd planted directly on top of the *Wormwood's* hyperdrive—the effects of the strange EPR time-shift on the plants was staggeringly psychedelic, he'd claimed. But none of us would go near the stuff.) The Captain had smuggled aboard his mitt. And O'Brien's pillow and comforter certainly weren't the same stiff, scratchy regulation sleep accoutrements the rest of us used. Come to think of it, neither was his mattress . . . Come to think of it, I was the only one who hadn't brought along anything non-regulation for the voyage.

Ryerson had also stowed away an enormous coffin-sized crate of cigarettes. I have no idea how he got it onboard, past the inventoriers, and he wasn't talking. Whenever I think of Ryerson now, I picture him with one of those Reds dangling from the corner of his mouth. His scruffy beard stained yellow with nicotine. Dark circles and raw pink rings around his bloodshot, sleep-deprived eyes . . . He was constantly smoking those unfiltered cigs, at least two and a half packs per shift. In just the first few weeks of the mission he'd made a sizable dent in his coffin (as he called it), and by eighteen months he'd smoked his way through almost a third of the enormous crate. The ship reeked of tobacco, and when I concentrate, I can even imagine I can still smell traces of it clinging to the inside of my suit.

Blue tobacco smoke drifted in clouds all throughout the *Wormwood,* stretching and massing in strange ways whenever we shifted in EPR.

Yeah, Ryerson was constantly smoking, and if any of us ever broached the idea that he cut down, that he was slowly asphyxiating us all, he would calmly counter that ninety thousand years had gone by, Earth-time, and by his math that was barely one cigarette a decade . . .

O'Brien's mattress was another of the smuggled luxuries. Man, did he love that mattress. It was too big for his bunk, but rather than set up on the floor, he'd crammed it onto the boxspring above Ryerson. The edges of that mattress—it must have been twenty centimeters thick—hung over the edges of the bunk and drooped down slightly, like cheese sticking out the sides of a sandwich.

It raised O'Brien that much closer to the ceiling (for me it would have been uncomfortably high and claustrophobic, but then, I've always been a bottom-bunk kind of guy) but he didn't seem to mind. He even hung a curtain (another smuggled commodity, no doubt) around the perimeter of his sleeping area, and at night we'd hear him counting or rocking himself to sleep, or see the muted glare of his flashlight as he stayed up going over his star charts.

O'Brien was our navigator. He was allegedly some sort of mathematical genius—a real prodigy with numbers and faster-than-light EPR equations. As such, he spent the majority of his time working with ALICE (he'd logged more hours, certainly, than any of the rest of us, just sitting and talking to the computer), and as little time as possible with the rest of us. When we did see him he was quiet and reserved, reclusive and guarded, never one to start conversation. He'd usually just answer any non-ship-related question with a blank stare. He was more interested in his star charts than he was in the rest of us. And he was always counting.

It drove Ryerson crazy. Not just the counting, or the flashlight to all hours, or the gentle, monotonous creaking of the bunk as he rocked himself to Dreamtown—what bothered Ryerson, I think, was the very fact that O'Brien had closed himself off from the rest of us, both physically and mentally. That he had created a private area in which to do private things. Ryerson wouldn't have it, and took to poking at the mattress above him in an effort to annoy the reclusive mathematician. Of course, the mattress was too plush and O'Brien never even noticed, but this would only aggravate Ryerson even more. He took to calling O'Brien the *Princess and the Pea*. As in, *"Hey princess and the pea! Shut the hell up, up there!"*

After the poking and prodding and yelling proved futile, Ryerson began holding his cigarette lighter (a stainless steel Zippo with *The Sunshine Boys* engraved on the side, along with the crude etching of a fiery Sun sporting a toothy, grinning skull set into its center) under the mattress until the material began to char and smolder. Aside from the thick, acrid smell of burning polyurethane that filled the cabin, gagging and choking the rest of us, there was no noticeable reaction from above. Sealed in his nightly cocoon, O'Brien was oblivious to all around him. He'd effectively sealed himself in and the universe out. Only his muffled counting and squeaky rocking found its way through the labyrinthine tangle of sheets, around the mattress, and past the folded curtains to fall softly and annoyingly upon our dozing (or trying to doze) ears.

"Twelve . . . twelve parsec-C . . . twelve omega-A . . . beta alpha niner . . . section one fortyniner . . . Thirteen . . . "

I think it was the endless counting, as much as it was the alcohol, that finally put Ryerson over the edge. I wasn't there when it happened, I was in the cockpit with Captain Hardwick when it all went down, but Byers tells me it was quite the thing to see.

Ryerson was struggling with one of the biobags, trying to attach it to the recycling node, when it tore open and splattered him with five day old chili, rotting banana peels, and human waste. Reeves and Byers fell silent, afraid to laugh as the dripping giant stumbled backwards, gagging on the smell and spitting vile filth and profanity. All was quiet but Ryerson's angry, choking curses and O'Brien's eternal counting.

"Thirteen... beta-niner... thirteen parsec-D... thirteen omega—"

"Goddammit!" Ryerson exploded. He lunged across the room and dragged O'Brien (mattress and all) from the top bunk and onto the floor. In a whirlwind of fury, he'd scooped the corner of the mattress under one arm and the industrial-sized roll of biobags under the other and stormed off to the rear of the ship. And the rest is history.

How the Captain's catcher's mitt came to be involved is beyond me.

If I hadn't stumbled upon Ryerson down in the bowels of the ship's hyperdrive with his time-irradiated plants and one of the ships radio transceivers quietly singing old tunes—*cuz this voice it keeps whispering in myyyy ear, saying I might never see you again . . . and I gotta peaaaaceful, eaaaasy feeeelin'*—to the ex-wife and baby daughter he'd left behind on Earth . . . Well, if I hadn't seen that I would've thought he was a complete monster.

I was with Captain Hardwick when it all went down. He was waxing philosophical like he tended to do towards the ends of our twenty-six hour shifts, and complaining like he was apt to—about how he was sick of the mission, sick of the crew, sick of the food, and tired of all the bullshit. How he hated space travel, didn't know what we were trying to accomplish, and how no one on Earth even cared, anyway. The usual. I guess you really had to know the Captain to get where he was coming from—he complained a lot, and he wasn't the quickest to get things done, but he was a *good* Captain; he never gave any of us a hard time, and he did his best to keep things casual and make life aboard the *Wormwood* as easy and tolerable as possible. He wasn't a stickler for rules and regulations, that's for sure. In fact, I don't think I can remember him ever actually *giving* an order after the first week of the mission—and by that time, we'd all five of us sort of settled into our own routines, anyway. Believe it or not, there's really not a whole lot that needs to be done on an interstellar ship. Well, not on the *Wormwood*, anyway—and if there've been any interstellar ships since ours, I imagine that they're run the same way.

Mostly, everything was automated, and the things that needed to be done were for the most part obvious. And if anything urgent did come up, it was usually ALICE that let us know about it, not the Captain. But more often than not, if something really big *did* come up, ALICE would just take care of it herself.

No, Captain Hardwick never really gave too many orders. Sometimes he talked about his strange philosophies of life, travel, and outer space, but mostly he just complained.

So it's not surprising that that's what he was doing when the ship blew up—philosophizing and complaining.

"You have to step back from it all sometimes, Dewitt," he was telling me. We were talking again about our reasons for taking on the mission—that's one of the things about faster-than-light travel—with the peculiar tricks that timewarp plays on the memory, you can often have the same conversations over and over again, and not grow tired of them. They seem new and different each time. It's strange. Maybe that's why Captain Hardwick's endless complaining never seemed to wear on me. Because, even though he was complaining about the same old things, it somehow seemed like he was experimenting with newer and more interesting topics of complaint.

"You've got to get some distance on things," he was saying. "At least I do. I go crazy when I'm cooped up."

He waved his hand towards the dazzling array of stars that seemed to hover just beyond the window behind him. They seemed to be as large as softballs. Thin tendrils of the Oahu Nebula reached into space and seemed to entwine the stars in their grip along the left side of the window. The heart of the nebula was currently out of sight, hidden halfway behind the bulkhead wall next to the window and halfway behind the Captain's head. But we'd all seen it from the cockpit, and the *Wormwood* was moving slowly (or quickly, depending on your perspective, Mom) towards it. The heart of the nebula was a fiery crimson, tinged with unnatural brushstrokes of green and yellow, and marked with silent, violent electric flashes of bluish white energy discharge. It was almost beautiful.

We'd been staring at the nebula for what seemed like months, but was in fact only days. That's another peculiar side effect of EPR travel—whenever you adjust your speed or change direction even slightly, your perception of time goes all haywire, stretching and compressing so that things seem to drag on endlessly or fly by in the blink of an eye. Even your thoughts seem to slow down or speed up, while your perception of your surroundings remains constant.

And there were physical effects, too—the ship itself seemed to buckle and bend with each minor course correction. With the cockpit door opened to the main corridor, looking straight back down the entire length of the ship and into the dorsal cargo hold, you could actually see the *Wormwood's* rear twist away out of sight every time we turned, or stretch nearer or farther whenever we sped up or slowed down. It was unnerving. We kept that door closed after the first week.

Anyway, we'd been staring at the Oahu Nebula for what seemed like such a long time that it had become more aggravating than anything else to look at it.

But from the Captain's quarters, the bulk of the nebula was out of sight—just the ends of its wispy arms were evident in the window behind him. The thin tendrils were a pale, translucent pink, barely discernable against the brilliant light of the stars.

They seemed to be reaching out toward us, those tendrils, wrapping casually around Captain Hardwick's head, playing doggedly with his wild mop of hair as he spoke, teasing and pulling and curling. The Captain was working up to some sort of point, in his usual roundabout, complaining sort of way, though I'd be damned if I could guess what it might be.

"Think about it, Dewitt—everything that we see of the universe is funneled through the pinholes of our eyes," he was saying. "We can encompass whole solar systems, entire galaxies, in our pupils. It's no wonder that those poor fools back on Earth are mesmerized by their computer screens. There's a world of wonder in there too. It's an artificial one, but how are they to know the difference? By the time things are funneled through your eyes and into your brain, everything is pretty much the same size. The solar system is no bigger than the television screen when it hits your eyes—hell, take a picture of the solar system and it'll *fit* on the TV screen! How can anyone truly know what's important to look at, and what's not, when the universe is so damn huge and our eyes are so damn small?"

I just shook my head. He was on a rhetorical roll, and only he knew where he was heading.

"Do we look through the microscope or the telescope?" He held up each hand as if balancing two weights. "That's the question! The window or the computer screen? *Perspective,* Dewitt, it's all about *perspective!* Well, perspective and putting yourself in the proper surroundings. To gain the proper perspective on things, you've *got* to put yourself in the proper surroundings. That's why *I'm* here," he smiled.

I thought you hated it here, I thought.

"In space there's nothing to put under the microscope. In *space* you can fit it *all* in. The Earth, every living creature on it. The entire damned *Internet.*

49

Every atom of every planet in the solar system and every other solar system in the galaxy. Even other galaxies! It's all out there, and from out *here* it all fits into the field of vision."

He pointed out the window toward a distant cluster of stars. The constellation reminded me of Dad's Buick convertible, don't ask me why. "Earth is out that way," the Captain said matter-of-factly, pointing. "It's nothing more than a miniscule, microscopic speck, but it's there, all right." He moved his pointing finger slowly to his temple and tapped at the side of his eye. "And it's all in here," he said.

I nodded. Ryerson and Byers were planning chili again for dinner, and things were unusually quiet from down near the galley—usually you could hear their bitter arguing and bickering as the steam-kettle tension slowly built and Ryerson worked himself up towards a tantrum. After the fiasco the last time he had attempted chili, the silence now was beginning to worry me.

"That's what pisses me off about people, Dewitt. *Everyone*. The dopes back on Earth and the dopes on this ship—not *you*, but the rest of them," he tilted his head and indicated the rest of the ship with his bony chin. "Nobody *gets* it. It's all out there, it's so obvious, but people would rather choose to close their eyes and be stupid. Rather than take a long look at the beauty of everything around them."

Only Captain Hardwick could so masterfully weave philosophy and complaint. He leaned back, and placed his arms contentedly behind his head. "All things in perspective, I suppose." He sighed. "Learn to see the forest for the trees, when to look closely, and when to step back. That's the secret, Dewitt. Only then will you see the true beauty of the Universe. Only then can you truly learn to appreciate." He turned and looked longingly out the window. As he did, his elbow absently brushed a panel of buttons on the arm of his chair.

"I swear, sometimes I think even the walls of this ship are too—*Omigod!*" A shrill electric squawk sounded from the arm of the chair. The Captain jolted as if he'd been shocked.

Lights started flashing and klaxons began to blare. ALICE's soothing voice announced the we had exactly seventy seconds to evacuate the ship before it exploded.

Yeah, I remember it now. I was with the Captain when it happened.

It's hard to describe the feeling of life aboard the *Wormwood*. I don't know if it was a side effect of existing for so long in timewarp, or just how it is on a big ship with a small crew, or even if it was maybe just me—but whatever the case, time just seemed to bottom out on itself. In a strange way, hours seemed to go by almost quicker than minutes, months flew by faster than weeks or even days, so that we were constantly scrambling to get things done. And all the while we were dying of perpetual boredom and the monotony of it all . . .

Life on the *Wormwood* was inside-out. The ship itself seemed vast and endless to the five of us. We could go hours or even days without seeing one another, and yet there was a constant feeling of being exposed to the universe and the stars—stifled under the claustrophobic weight of their gaze, like so many protozoa caught under a magnificent galactic microscope.

It really wears you down after a while. All that space, all that time, just going by in the blink of an eye—stretching all around the ship and flying past— slippery and ungraspable—forever ahead of us, and lost behind us in a blur of momentum and Einsteinian theory. It can make you seasick.

I've been thinking a lot, Mom—I've had a lot of time to think—and remembering things. I remembered something that you once said to David when he and Susan first found out that she was pregnant. You remember? It was two or three months before the wedding.

You said to David, not to worry about a thing. *That's the secret of life,* you said, *just accept every new challenge as if you had chosen it yourself.* That's really good advice, Mom. I may not have followed it when I was home on Earth, but I'm sure going to follow it now.

I am going to accept my current predicament—my current *situation*—as if I had chosen it myself. No matter what the universe might still have left to throw my way, I'll look it full in the face with confidence, optimism, and acceptance. I'm taking life by the reins and rising to the challenge. Just like you taught us to do. I've got a new attitude and a sunny perspective on things. A new lease, as Dad might say . . .   Life is what *I* decide to make of it. There's no such thing as bad situations, just bad attitudes.

So here it is in a nutshell:

The *Wormwood* exploded three days ago. I escaped in an environmental star suit. I'm positive that none of the others survived (and, being unable to establish radio contact, I must assume that they did not).

I am approximately ninety thousand light years from Earth, and drifting (along with several large pieces of debris) towards one of the edges of the Oahu Nebula.

Oh, man . . .

The good news is that there is enough compressed air in the redundant filters on the back of my suit to keep me breathing for another sixty years. And there's enough vitagel solution to feed me intravenously for twice that length of time. So as long as I do my exercises to keep my muscles from atrophying, and unless I die of boredom, it looks like I'm in for the long haul.

That is, unless I get sucked into a sun or drift into a planet's gravitational well.

As for the *Wormwood*—the explosion was totally unexpected. It had something to do with those buttons on the arm of Captain Hardwick's chair, I guess. That much seems to make sense. Especially with the way Ryerson had jury-rigged and cross-wired every system on the ship these past eighteen months.

The Captain's elbow hit them while we were talking—he just sort of turned to point at something outside the window, and he brushed over them with his arm, depressed them with the noop of his elbow—and that's exactly when the sirens started blaring.

The buttons were older, mechanical rather than digital (a lot of things on the ship were—most of the ship's secondary systems had been salvaged from old NASA shipyards or donated by Lockheed or Lear)—*radio buttons* I think they're called. The same sort that you used to see way, way back on old-fashioned telephones and switchboards. Like in the movies. Little clear plastic cubes—lit from the inside with numbers printed on translucent tape pasted to the tops. Yellowed with age. You know the ones I mean, one was always depressed, and it always popped up whenever you pressed another one—so that only one could ever be pushed down at any given time. There were six of them there in a row, all along the arm of the Captain's chair.

Well, when he brushed them with his elbow, he must have hit them funny—in a way that they were never meant to be pressed—because right when the alarms started going off I could see that *two* of the buttons were actually pressed down, jammed together and stuck. And try as he might, the Captain just couldn't get them to pop back up.

He was still tugging on them, trying to pry them up with the zipper of his jacket, when I jumped up and made a run for the dorsal airlock. I imagine that, right up to the bitter end, he was trying end to unpress those buttons.

I've been thinking about it a lot—none of the other chairs had buttons like that. Just the Captain's. And I can't for the life of me figure out what they could possibly have even done. I can't imagine what they could have been used for—what purpose they could possibly have served. Other than to blow up the ship, I mean.

*   *   *

But I was going to try and explain to you why I did it, Mom—why I joined this godforsaken mission in the first place. What I saw in the *Star Reach* program. Why I decided to leave it all—the Earth and my family and my life—behind.

Well, Mom, I don't know if I can really answer to all of that—not in any sort of simple, easy way. It's complicated. But I guess I've got more than enough time on my hands to at least try and sort it all out. I *know* that I can *try* to sort it out. Just like I know that as long as I keep talking I can postpone going mad and panicking from loneliness and boredom and fear. As long as I keep broadcasting my thoughts out into the empty universe, I think that I can keep the hysteria at bay. God, I *hope* I can keep myself from panicking.

I'd hate to lose it out here.

The radio in this suit was only ever meant to broadcast back to the ship during short-range space-walks and external repairs. I guess we all figured that it *might* be strong enough to reach the *Wormwood* in orbit from a planet's surface—not that we ever really expected that we'd stumble upon a planet hospitable enough to support a surface excursion. But I guess we had to be prepared just in case.

In any event, the radio signal from my suit sure isn't powerful enough to make its way back to Earth—not by any stretch. And even if it were, it would take it well over a million years to get there. That plus the ninety thousand years that you've already been dead. And the eighteen months of the mission. And the four days that I've been adrift in space. Jesus Christ.

No, I don't expect this signal to make its way anywhere or be heard by anyone. I'm just talking now to keep from going mad.

I know that even if somehow I could miraculously transport myself home to Earth, that ninety thousand years would still have gone by. Everything I ever knew would be gone.

It's hard to wrap my head around that. So, I'll just stick to my own perspective for now—that only eighteen months have gone by. It's easier that way. And, unless I *were* somehow able to get home and actually *see* the passage of the years, from my perspective things *are* still on the up-and-up. Sort of. I think Schrödinger proved that. Or maybe it was Heisenberg. I guess it really doesn't matter.

Schrödinger and Heisenberg—Einstein, Podalsky and Rosen—they never had to deal with the scruffy itchiness of a new beard growing in the sweaty confines of a starsuit, didn't have to live under the constant worry of suffocating in a helmet full of hair while drifting, endlessly and forever through the boundless perpetuity of space . . .

In any case, I'm content to think of you there at home, just finishing with dinner, sitting and looking at the computer and wondering how I'm doing—and on my end, I'll do my best to think about what it was that I wanted to tell you—my reasons for joining this crazy mission.

I'll think about it really hard while I float through space.

Adrift.

Alone.

All the way out here in the middle of the goddamned universe.

History
by Alex Moisi

Fifty years have passed since I last looked at the sun. Six hundred long months of solitude spent patrolling the corridors of the Citadel, the last human haven in this world. Yet despite the self-sustainable perfection of this last human conclave, I feel trapped in a dark mausoleum. Often, in this artificial cell, I have longed to break my research cycle and return to the surface, to the pale sunlight and the warm breeze. A dangerous temptation I must resist. Order, patterns, that is all I have to keep my sanity. The tiniest detail can make the difference between survival or complete breakdown and failure, and I cannot fail in my mission. I simply cannot.

The elevator speeds up towards the safety hatches as I check the sensors in my hazard suit once more. I know there is no reason to, but every small detail counts or at least I must make it count. If I want to survive I must give a deeper meaning to everything I do. I must create rituals, otherwise there is nothing left but routine and mindless routine will drive you insane. I smile as the well-rehearsed mantra unfolds itself before my eyes: "Everything has meaning; meaning is everything."

I feel nervous as the lift jerks to a stop and the doors to the quarantine room slide open. I always feel nervous before leaving the Citadel. Trend analysis can predict what the surface should look like but it is never certain what changes await beyond the solid walls of my confinement. After a few seconds the computers identify me and the massive metal door slides open. I am blinded by the sun. Sensors click as my mask grows darker with UV protection. Finally, I can look at the world in front of me again.

The sun, as pale and yellow as I always remember it, shines high above the dusty city. The whole scene is an ancient charcoal sketch. Muddy colors merged in a desolate, crumpled brown. Jagged lines stretch around buildings and abandoned cars, twisted pipes and bent street lights. The whole city is a pile of dirt, dotted with the desolate gray of abandoned skyscrapers.

I glance back at the dome-shaped exterior of the Citadel. For the most important building in human history, it looks depressingly plain: thick cement walls covered by a modest cupola, one simple door and a hand scrawled graffiti that reads: "The ark."

My sensors are registering every dent in the massive construction and I will later read the data looking for any cracks or weak spots. I must check, although I am certain everything holds perfectly. After all, ever since it was designed, the Citadel was meant to be eternal. Unfortunately the city it overlooks does not share the same perfection.

The doors of the ancient building open into what was once the most majestic central plaza in the world. Only ruins are left. I step on once beautifully crafted white tiles, now merely a mosaic of cracks and patches of yellowish grass poking from underneath. A decorated marble slab with an illegible message lies, broken, at my feet. It is the first time I cannot read the sign. It used to proclaim the immortality of human ingenuity. It is gone, just like everything else, in a mound of dust.

In the center, a solitary mermaid still pokes towards the stars. I recognize its stone features from long ago. It's just a decoration for a small fountain, a final human artifact pointing towards the heaven, but heaven is far out of reach.

To the left lies what was once the City Archive Center. Built centuries before we left the surface, it was marvelous. Even more, as everything built in the last decades, it was a masterpiece of utility. It spread a global wireless web we could all tap into and use to connect with each other. By the time it was built most humans were already connected with each other through implants but the Archive center worked on frequencies that did not require any implants. The new connection was deeper and more pure. Its completion was the beginning of the new era, an era of unprecedented collaboration among all humans.

Now, long after it changed the way we existed, the archive center remains just a pile of old bricks and dust. Patches of genetically engineered grain are already covering it up. In another ten years all trace of the most significant human revolution will be gone, consumed by time.

I smile at the irony. It is this very building that made it possible to create the genetically engineered crop that is slowly covering it, crumbling its structure. Just like in a few centuries it will crumble the ancient city completely. After all, there is nothing that should stop the genetically modified crop brand number 23 from claiming this city as its own farmland; not since we left the surface. We made sure of that when we created a plant that could mutate at phenomenal rates and survive in nearly any condition.

The deeper connection provided by the Archive Center's powerful computers allowed us to reach unexpected levels of concentration. It was for the first time in human history that we started reaching decisions as a race instead of individuals.

Even more, we were able to use each other and our common computing power to tackle each major problem we faced as a species. Our common fear of death was probably the major instigator in the early phases of our connection. We eradicated crime and most major diseases first. The empathy we felt for each other made it impossible to ignore issues of poverty and famine. GM#23 was just one of the many genetically modified plants we used to eliminate global malnutrition. It was just another perfect solution, a stroke of genius, genius that became all too common in our last days as a species.

Suddenly I notice a sliver of yellow as a newspaper floats away in the afternoon breeze. It twists on a weak current and I watch it fly into a broken display window. I barely recognize the once-familiar facade of the Commerce Center. Since the last time I saw it, the old building has been crushed under a small forest of oak trees. Roots twist through and around glass and bent steel. The whole second story has collapsed on itself and metal frames hang from branches slowly growing around the concrete. The combination is breathtaking. I must suppress a flicker of pleasure knowing I am the only one who will ever lay eyes on such a marvel. I must maintain my role. I cannot get involved. This is only research, only a duty I must fulfill with perfect focus and dedication.

I start towards the trees and the collapsed center. I want to see more of the destroyed building and its strange symbiosis. Besides, I have always started my search in the commerce center. It is a pattern I cannot avoid.

I grab the fluttering paper and read the headline. "The Future is Here!" it proclaims in massive font. I try to turn it and read the article but the paper crumbles in my hands. The yellowish dust floats away and I'm left staring at the empty plaza. A strange feeling of nostalgia and sadness overcomes me. I must fight not to return to the safety and comfort of the Citadel. The Commerce Center suddenly seems dark and uninviting, grotesque with the over-sized roots covering it. I look around making sure everything is safe. The screen in my mask blinks as the many sensors within my bio-suit flash green. Everything is safe, despite the cold chill I feel on my spine, so I continue.

I squeeze between a metal beam and a thick root still thinking about the old newspaper. We stopped printing newspapers decades before we entered the Citadel. There was no need for news anymore. Knowledge was distributed perfectly and uniformly. Every death, every birth, every flicker of originality, everything was shared equally. It was the future one prophetic news editor promised us in large font when the era of connections was just beginning.

It must have been such an exciting moment in our history. Truly a shame not all of us understood what was happening. Most humans were still struggling with the potential in the first prototype of the network: the World Wide Web.

Alex Moisi

The barbaric connection through external computers was the first step in a long journey and the one with the most visible impact. Barriers of speech, geography and culture became obsolete for the first time. The very first open communities of shared knowledge, huge encyclopedias open to everyone to edit, as well as the first common research projects, using personal processing power or volunteer collaborations were created, changing the way we looked at knowledge and interactions forever. Implants and later on the Archive Center were just minor steps considering the mental revolution of these first years of connectivity. It must have been an exciting era to live in indeed.

When I finally enter the Commerce Center it takes a few seconds for my sensors to readjust to the dim lights. The room looks much like it did fifty years ago, save for an unnerving coldness. I know my suit would protect me from any temperature change but it cannot protect me from the coldness running down my spine.

Simply cut mahogany desks still stand in their places, except dustier and much older than I remember. The large glass windows are now completely covered by roots and dirt on the outside and sickly looking mushrooms on the inside. Somewhere in the distance I hear water slowly dripping and as I glance around I realize why I feel a cold shiver, even inside my suit. The whole room is an ancient cavern. We ceased using myths or religion as a guide for our lives long before the pure connection was reached, but images of the underworld flash before my eyes. I chase them away with a forced smile: "Even the underworld is void of humans." Yet the feeling of uneasiness lingers and I twitch nervously before I convince my feet to continue moving.

I head towards the center of the building, carefully avoiding the maze of moldy desks. My feet sink deep in the thick layer of dust as I approach the sensors I placed here long ago, when I was just starting in my mission. The tiny computers gather data about the temperature, humidity and light conditions. Somewhere in my suit another computer connects with the old sensors and they exchange data about everything that happened in the last fifty years. I wait while the machines trade the information and then I move on, towards the core of the building.

I approach the main elevators and glance into the empty shaft. The last time I was here I recorded a bat colony nesting in the elevator. In the mean time its safety cables have failed and all that is left is a twisted cabin at the bottom of a narrow, black well. I feel strangely relieved that my sensors cannot detect any organic matter in the shaft. The bats must have left the center before the elevator failed. Maybe they moved close by, in another part of the building and I can record their presence again.

As I turn around my hope dies and I cannot fight the sinking feeling in my guts. I realize why the room seemed cold and void of life. It is. There is a deep silence all around the center. Never before had the whole place seemed so eerily quiet. I check my sensors again, this time searching for insects, mammals or reptiles. The screen in front of my eyes stays empty. It is because of the heavy concrete that my scanners are limited but even so I can tell that for a radius of twenty five feet in each direction, there is not one living animal. I turn the sensors off and look around the room again. It seems even emptier and darker now and I feel a burning urge to get out.

Every year when I visited the Center there were red eyes staring at me in curiosity, descendants of our laboratory mice. There were spiders hanging in their intricate webs and small lizards running away as fast as their short stumpy legs could carry them. Not once was the place abandoned, empty and dead like this. I get out as quickly as I can, wondering if there is anything alive in the old, ruined city.

Outside, the sun is still shining, yellow and pale, but in my eyes everything has changed. Over the centuries I grew used to a place with at least some traces of life and movement, but this time I am reminded of the empty corridors of the Citadel. Nothing stirs in the perfect silence; not one bird swoops down from the sky, landing with precision on a rusted lamp post. Not one stray dog chases happily towards my solitary figure, licking my hands out of some ancient instinct. Nothing moves in the pale afternoon sun except for the yellow patches of grain slowly turning in the wind.

I quickly make my way towards the northbound highway passing empty, ruined buildings covered in ivy and moss. Avoiding large patches of collapsed roadway covered with tall grain, I skirt around manholes without covers and twisted benches. I jump over a crushed water tower and land on the other side in a thick patch of grain. In front of me the highway stretches barely a few kilometers before it's covered completely by the genetically modified crop. I suddenly realize how much the world has changed since the last time I saw it and I am speechless. There is nothing but grain as far as I can see. There is no patch of grass, no tree, nothing but a giant field of grain slowly moving in the warm breeze.

Crashed, with my back tight to the ruins of the ancient water tower, I stare in disbelief. Cold sweat breaks on my forehead as I know I have broken every research pattern I carefully constructed over the years, but I must know. It doesn't matter what the consequences will be. I must know for sure.

I check my sensors again from the top of the tallest building I can climb but I know the answer before they finish scanning. As far as I can see in any direction there is nothing but grain. It makes sense; the plant was created to survive in any conditions and be resistant to all types of pests—a silent, unstoppable force, always advancing. Yet I had never expected it to multiply so fast, to survive the increasing levels of sodium or to resist the chemical boundaries placed around cities, just in such a case. Not even the computer predictions could estimate the majority of animals and plants would be eliminated by a single crop so soon; I expected at least another century of green grass and colorful birds. I was wrong.

I know my sensors will automatically gather data so I lay down on the rooftop. It might very well be the last time I can still visit the surface, at least the last time there will be anything to see besides grain. Although I know I will regret it, I cannot pass the opportunity of a lazy afternoon in the pale sun. At my feet the city stretches empty and I am tempted to remember a time when it was much different, a time before the great sleep.

The first stages of the connections brought forth remarkable changes and breakthroughs; however we were still deeply selfish and concerned only with ourselves. This was the achievement of the Archive Center, a perfect network that would eliminate these individual flaws through a connection much deeper than we expected. The Internet and similar networks through artificial implants opened the way and set the standard but the connection based only on ourselves as transmitters and receptors brought a new meaning to our lives. We became one. We all shared feelings, knowledge, intuition and abilities and we were more powerful and content than ever. Mindless distractions became obsolete as we united under one goal, perfecting ourselves. Depression, envy, misunderstandings and greed disappeared virtually overnight. We could all see what a valuable part of our common mind each individual was. Complete peace overcame our souls as we fought to eliminate the most resilient human problems. We had reached peace. We created our own heaven.

After that it was only a question of time and focus. The complete force of our common mind was finally free to create at full potential without petty distractions and problem. Illnesses, death, anger: all were eliminated leaving a perfect human being. We were completely content with our new world. As a united entity we could do anything. We could experience everything. We had achieved perfection, but perfection came with a high price. There was nothing left to improve, nothing left to explore. Our brains could predict all the possible actions for the next decade. Not even art attracted us anymore. After all, everyone shared the same view point, what was there to express? The incentive to do anything slowly dissipated. We ran out of problems to solve.

For centuries we tried colonizing other planets, creating virtual realities, even developing other intelligent creatures, but in the end the inevitable caught up with us. Nothing was really that interesting anymore. We were bored and apathetic. Why should we bother when we could predict the result, the next generation was never going to judge us and death was unlikely? There was nothing left to experience in this reality. And nothing happened. The sun continued to shine and the earth continued to turn and we grew more and more distant from the world.

In our darkest moments as a race, during the medieval ages, we were never so depressed. It was then that the religions we deemed useless and obsolete came back to haunt us with promises of afterlife. Death, an outdated concept, was more distant than ever and maybe therefore extremely desirable. In our common connection the thought of a grand ending came back more and more often. Global suicide seemed dangerously appealing. If we wanted to save our species we had to act.

The decision was taken in seconds; anything was better than the constant boredom of omniscience. We wanted to experience the only state we had yet not explored, the lack of existence. We decided to enter cryogenic sleep, deep and eternal nothingness. We did not require rest anymore, but the cryogenic slumber was far from sleep. Our consciousness was going to be virtually eliminated. What was left, if anything, was as close to the afterlife as anything we could imagine. All our research showed it was nothing but eternal void, but if we were wrong, this was the only way to know without killing ourselves.

It was almost a millennium ago that we turned off the last lights in the world and entered the Citadel—a perfectly self-sustaining building designed to store our bodies during the eternal sleep. Almost a thousand years passed since we answered the question:

"Why do bad things happen to good people?"

"To keep them entertained."

Almost an eternity passed since I started on my mission. A mission I knew full well was going to last until the end of the world as I knew it and probably much longer. An end I did not expect so soon.

The first time I recorded information from the surface, the city was still perfect. Animals had not inhabited it yet and the perfectly white tiles stretched for kilometers, clean, waiting for their owners. I remember it well, walking through the deserted streets, expecting to see another human turn around the corner so I could connect and greet him.

Since then I have seen animals pass through, destroying years of work. I have seen trees break the concrete and bring down houses. I have seen rats nest in expensive suits and crows lay eggs in broken servers. Slowly our world decayed and I witnessed its passing, reuniting with nature, until today.

The grain must have absorbed most of the water, killing the larger animals and the strict diet of fibers must have done the rest. Brittle bones and shorter life spans were just a few of the known side effects of a restricted diet. Eventually the damage to the genetic material was irreparable and with the precarious cycle broken species must have died one after another. By leaving the surface back in the hands of nature we condemned it to a slow, inevitable death. A deep feeling of sadness spreads through my body as I stare helpless at the last dying green trees in this world.

I eventually climb the fire escape, heading home. My sensors have collected enough data and the sun is almost setting. It is time to return to the Citadel. I must make sure the data transferred correctly and check it in the main computer. After that I must inspect the cryogenic capsules and make sure they are still sealed shut and safe. Then, I can return to the main archive and go over the data I collected and read the predictions for the next years.

I approach the old metallic door and punch in the release code. The hatch hisses open and my sensors adapt to the artificial light inside the Citadel. I glance back one last time, at the empty market square and the small patch of grain growing near the main fountain. I miss the days when water ran from the mermaid's mouth and the sky above was blue and the streets were crowded and I could feel my fellow humans around me. But this was the only way we could make sure the program would never fail. We could not take the risk of a malfunction. A short circuit in the solar panels or a minuscule computing error could lead to catastrophic consequences. I volunteered to remain, after humanity entered their eternal sleep, the only archivist of this world. The last safety check, I would make sure the chambers were secure and I would run the computer programs over and over again, checking every time for mistakes. Looking at their faces, frozen with hints of a smile, I know I am barred forever from the void or the heavens that wait beyond the darkness and a bitter sweet sadness overcomes me, but we all have to take sacrifices and I took mine. I am the voice of a dissolving race. I am the last historian and witness to the life and death of this small blue planet lost somewhere in the infinite universe.

—*Dedicated to Cat for all her love and faith in me.*

Death and Love in Gehanna
by Sara Genge

Queen Beyali was running out of food. It had been six days since the Emperor's exile order had landed her on the penal continent of Gehanna, and the sea was nowhere in sight. Whaling season had started and there should be boats hugging the south coast. That was her only chance.

She gathered a pinch of sugar from her pouch and thrust it into her mouth with a handful of snow. It would have to do for now. The warmworms crept up from her neck, seeking out and neutralizing the cold in her cheeks. The Emperor, in His Wisdom, had given her provisions for a week.

Afterwards, His Will would be done.

The queen trudged ahead, scanning the horizon for signs of the pantiger. Nothing. Not that it meant much; the animal was bred for camouflage. The glacier rolled on for as far as she could see. From the distance, the landscape looked flat, but close up, there were cracks ready to catch her foot and twist it, chasms into which to fall and boulders that bared slivers of icy teeth. It seemed to her that nature conspired to carry out the Emperor's will. Even the pantiger, wherever he was, fit in His Holy Design.

The queen panicked for a second and took three short breaths. I'm running out of food, she thought, I know this, and this is all I know. From the corner of her eye, she caught the shimmer of her aura. She sighed in relief; it was still blue. She dreaded that her anguish would make it flash red, attracting the predator. A single bitter thought, a moment of anger and her aura would flare up for the pantiger to see for kilometers round. She kept her eyes open but directed her concentration inward, feeling the tender places of resentment and denial in her soul and soothing the creases of distress. The pantiger had been conditioned to attack her aura, no doubt about that. The Emperor's punishments were the stuff for legends.

Day after day, she walked.

Her heartbeat spread out to match her steps. Occasionally, she stamped her feet, a warning to the warmworms that her toes were starting to freeze.

Was it a sin to try to make her way south? The Emperor had sent her here. Was it heresy to try to escape His divine will? The thought of thwarting the

Emperor was hilarious. It made her laugh each time she thought about it. But still, she would try to reach the coast. No use wondering about the Emperor's plans. His will would be done whether she succeeded or not.

At dusk, she unfolded the tent and watched it puff up into shape. Then she started packing snow on top, preferably grahina, windblown, since it was the best insulator and she didn't have to use her knife to get it lose.

Finally, Beyali crawled into the tent, snuggled with the warmworms and slept. She had nightmares of palaces and balls, strung along, one after the other like sausages. In her dreams, she saw her own gold-coated arms reaching out in worship, and the Emperor Himself bowing to kiss her wrists.

The most dangerous part of the day was dawn, when she woke up and had to dig herself out of the snow. She was tempted to stay inside the tent. It would have been easy to doze off and let lack of oxygen claim her when the air-recycler gave out.

Every morning she cursed herself as she dug, but by the time she'd retrieved the deflated tent from the tunnel and gotten her bearings, she was anxious to keep on south, towards the coast.

On the eleventh day, there were still no signs of the pantiger.

The warmworms burned with the energy they stole through her skin but the parts of her body that they didn't cover were freezing. The wind curled around the hem of her skirt. In the distance on her right, she thought she saw something flat and grey.

Water!

Her pace quickened. After a few hours the grey line had expanded slightly. She didn't dare stop. From time to time she stamped her feet hard and wiped the tears from her eyes to keep them from freezing shut. Each time she removed her goggles the wind bit the sensitive flesh around her eyes.

She walked for hours while the sun crawled towards its zenith. When her legs gave out she seemed no closer to the coast. It was so like the Emperor to let her come this far, only to die here.

She fell onto the snow. It was gehnamin, soft and firm. Of the thousand types of snow, on gehnamin was where she would die.

In Gehanna, death was a maiden with a white sleeve and scythe. That's all that could be seen of her in the dark. Beyali wished that the wind would pick up and end the ordeal, but the breeze ploughed on with a gust of metronome, teasing her flesh without biting it.

Time slowed to the yawn between heartbeats. That space the ancient yaratoris identified as singleness, the empty space between the crevices of the soul. She stretched her consciousness to fit the new clock. Waiting was forever, death was only now. She begged her flesh to give out.

Soon, she was a statue.

Pain woke Beyali. Pain licked at her toes, tortured the soft flesh beneath her calluses. It was mobile agony, fast and tingling. She felt warmth on her face. If she hadn't known better, she would have thought she could smell smoke.

Fire! She gasped for breath and the hands pummelling her chest retreated.

"She's alive," said the one that had been massaging her heart.

"Damn you, Shaida. Damn you into the crevices of hell." The second voice carried venom in it and threw her into full consciousness. "She cannot stay."

"The Emperor save us." It was a female voice. Its owner sounded irritated and a little sarcastic. She could feel the speaker's breath on her cheek and the soft pressure of a human body against her side. She tried to move away but her head hit a wall.

"Everyone knows that," the voice continued. "You cannot stay while your pantiger is still alive," she told Beyali. "You always state the obvious, Claude, maybe that's why the Emperor got sick of you." The woman's fingers explored Beyali's face. She tried to open her eyes but a warmworm sat on her face and pressed them shut. She reached up to remove it, but the woman held her hand.

"Let it be. Your eyes were badly burnt, even the goggles aren't enough in sunny weather like this. Let it do its job."

"You'll get us both killed," Claude said bitterly. "The Emperor Who-Knows will not allow this." His voice came from somewhere close to her feet.

Shaida muttered a curse and turned around so that her face was close to Beyali's feet. Then the woman took the Queen's boots off and started to rub her feet with snow. Beyali hadn't expected the pain and groaned.

"She's only a girl," Shaida said. "You told me so. You can't leave someone to die on your own doorstep." Beyali howled in pain. The friction was warming her feet too fast.

"Stop, please stop!" she cried.

Shaida let go of her foot, felt her way up Beyali's legs with her right hand and shook a reproachful finger without turning her head to look at her. Beyali lifted the warmworm and squinted in the dim light. She could hardly see the finger and the woman was a blur at her feet.

"It was easy to give up, wasn't it? Well, this is what happens when you give in to frostbite, you've gotta get unfrozen afterwards and it hurts. Gea alive! Didn't they teach you anything wherever you came from?"

"Gea worship is heresy," Beyali recited. It was clear this woman believed in the thousand incarnations of Gea. A little spiritual anguish was small retaliation for the pain she was making Beyali feel.

"Hush, girl, your aura! The pantiger will be upon us in a second if you keep that up. We're underground but that never stopped a cat before."

Beyali looked around. "Cave" was inadequate for this place; "crawl-space" was more precise. The fire crackled close to her head and the hard-packed snow ceiling was too low to sit. The tunnel widened at the end, making space for the fire. Moonlight came in through the smokehole. There was barely enough space on her right for a person to crawl by to tend the fire, and Shaida was occupying it. Beyali breathed in the salty warmth of human breath and smoke. Shaida grabbed hold of her feet and dragged herself down to inspect them. Beyali gasped.

"You've lost a few toes. Nothing a hot broth won't fix." Shaida turned her head back towards the girl and flashed an awkward grin staring at the fire just above Beyali's head. Beyali gasped at the sight of the woman's eyes. The white around her pupils had turned red and an ugly liquid fell down her cheeks. The woman felt her way to a bundle near the fire and handfed Beyali a meaty paste.

Farther away, Claude muttered something about wasting food.

"How have you survived?" Beyali asked.

"We are white," the man said. "We don't have souls."

"Ha!" said the woman. "What we don't have is auras. The cat cannot find us without them. That is, if we're smart and keep out of sight. He can also see, smell and hear just fine. Our own cats are long dead. But each time they bring a newbie like you it starts all over again. We have to watch our tracks. The cats may be conditioned to one victim but when they're hungry . . . " she shrugged.

"What did you do?" Beyali asked.

Claude sighed and dragged his fingers through a white mane of hair.

"Nothing," he said. "What did you do?"

"Nothing."

"Ha!" Shaida cackled. "We did something all right. We did what we had to do. In fact, we did all we could do. I warned the Emperor against the Scion alliance." They all fell silent for a few minutes. The Scion had broken their pact two years after the treaty was signed and allowed the tenth regiment to be decimated by foreign elements. Beyali mulled that over, filling the chinks in her diplomatic knowledge.

"He didn't exile you when he signed the treaty, right? He killed you later, when the Scion rebelled because you were right and he was wrong, and nobody can be more holy than the Emperor."

Shaida nodded, head pressed against Beyali's feet. The girl could feel the woman's breath torturing her toes but it did not distract her. She had hit upon something important. Something that might unveil the mystical secret of His Holiness, the God among men. She felt a warm drop fall on her ankle. She would have sworn it sizzled on her skin. A tear felt hot because she was cold, she was only human after all. Only the Emperor could judge the absolutes.

"I warned him," cackled the old man. Beyali lifted her head to look at him. The flames put every wrinkle in relief. "I warned him not to take that woman for a wife. She was a queen in her own right, she had too much of her own mind. He was enthralled by her beauty. He fastened gold chains on her feet. He did it himself! He, the Emperor, touched the feet of a woman. He draped precious stones around her neck until she could hardly move; only sit frozen on his throne. He shone the light of myth on the pools of her navel and wrists. He is a God but he worshipped her! No, he did not wait for me to be wrong before he sent me here." The old man coughed something deep and moist. "I wish I knew what came of that," he muttered.

Beyali threw her head back and rested.

"Why don't you leave here?" she asked. "I know the coast is close. If you can light a fire, you can stay warm until you get there."

"We may be traitors, but we are not heretics," the old man said. "We accept the Emperor's punishment."

"Ha!" Said the woman. "He sends new cats when we try to leave. Some say he lives in those cats, can see through their eyes and control them."

Beyali was shocked by the woman's irreverence.

"The Emperor is wise," Beyali said softly. She wondered again if she wasn't doing something terrible by trying to reach the coast. She decided not to dwell on the thought so as not to disturb her aura.

"Yes, he is," Claude said.

"He loves all of his traitors," Beyali said. The woman whistled but the man nodded in agreement.

"He leads our way." The whistling became intense and for a second she was afraid it might attract the pantiger. Then she relaxed into a meditation trance. *What must be must be, I know this and this is all I know.*

"Once upon a time," she said, and felt the old man tense with anticipated pleasure, "there was a woman covered in gold."

Shaida rocked from side to side, warming Beyali's feet with her breath.

"Gold chains tied her feet to a throne."

Shaida kissed her feet.

"Precious stones crushed her to the floor."

The old man gasped.

"The Emperor himself kissed her wrists and promised her she would never grow old."

"What happened," Claude whispered.

Beyali's voice sounded weary in her ears.

"The Emperor was strong; his aura was so clear. His aura shone through the door before his holy presence appeared. He could have done it; he could have kept her young."

"What happened?" It was Shaida who asked.

"She refused. He would have upset the order of creation for her, but the order of creation will not be upset for anyone."

"So he sent you here?" Claude said.

"Yes, he could not stand the thought of seeing me aged and ugly."

"He would rather see you dead!" Shaida said.

"Such is the will of our Emperor!" the old man bellowed.

Beyali thought of reprimanding Shaida for her lack of faith, but she was tired and the darkness welcomed her.

"Did you love him," the man asked.

Beyali felt a surge from a well of bitterness she hadn't known she possessed: "Yes! I loved the Emperor. A hundred thousand sycophants, sixty billion grovelling subjects cannot love him as much as I did."

The man gasped and Shaida started a prayer to her Gean deities. Beyali waited for the pantiger with the peace of what must be. After a while her mind started drifting.

"You cannot stay." It was Shaida's voice. "You still have an aura. The cat will come for you. You cannot stay." She heard it just before she sank back into unconsciousness.

Wind lashed around her. It was the girwind, only a blizzard. It wasn't wayuma, the baby-killer wind that snatches newborns from their mother's breasts and hurls them upwards to the land of God.

The Emperor never deigned to catch them in his arms.

She plodded on southwards. When it was too much, she buried herself in a drift and waited until her body and warmworms heated up the hole. Claude and Shaida had taken her tent in exchange for food. She was glad they had left her the warmworms. Then she slept, and dreamed of being bathed in gold and painted in stucco for the world to see. She swallowed back bitter tears and thought of what the Empire had given the world. Her anger floated away from her as a whisp of red silk, a butterfly to be torn and frozen by sleet.

She heard the growl on her thirteenth day in Gehanna.

The pantiger had found her. The Emissary of God had found her at last. She shed a single tear of joy. Her ordeal would be over soon. Her body would offer a last service to God.

That night she buried herself shallower than usual, hoping that the beast would get her while she slept. She awoke surprised at being alive and better rested than she'd been since she'd left Shaida and Claude. The weather was good these days and she knew the beast could hear, smell and see to his liking. Her aura alone must be visible for kilometers. It had become the barest whisp of blue but feline senses were sharp.

The growl came again at odd moments when she was walking. It was an intimate sound, a rumble from the depths of the beast.

She was no longer afraid.

On the fourteenth day, the sea flew up towards her in icy embrace. She stood on the glacier's peak, two hundred meters above water level. In the distance, she saw fishing boats with small dolls on the masts, insulated men and women on the lookout for ice-monsters that could break the hull of the ships that plumbed the riches of the Sweet Ocean.

Beyali sat on her peak and watched them go. One, two, three. She didn't wave or try to signal. The hunter had found her. It would be wrong to try to avert the punishment of God when it was so close.

She heard him come up behind her, unsheathed claws gently scratching the ice. She did not dare turn around. The queen could hear the rhythm of his breathing, sense his doubts. He came slinking, hugging the shadows in the midday sun. She knew that if she turned she'd see the great contour of the cat against the snow, camouflage or not. She did not turn until she felt the warm breath on her back.

He had the body of his panther ancestor but his fur was white with the slightest grey stripes to camouflage him in the uneven color of gahn snow. Now that she saw him up close, she realized she had seen him many times, a distant blur crouching against the ice, watching her.

She was so surprised that she wasn't afraid. She looked to the side and couldn't see her aura.

Damn the Emperor's tricks! She thought, trying for a red flare. Nothing; she still couldn't see her aura. The cat stood motionless as if she weren't there. No, as if she weren't his prey.

"Come on, eat me!" she shouted. Even an ordinary predator should react to that. The pantiger lowered its massive head, whiskers tuned onto her and waited. She understood why this was God's Emissary. His stance was noble and his eyes intelligent. She was sure the Emperor saw through those eyes.

"Come on!"

He leaped and she sighed in relief and in fear. His jaw clamped loosely on her throat. It took her a couple of seconds to realize that he wasn't biting, just holding her and dragging her across the ice. Ice beat upon her back and the cold made it hurt even more. Thousands of years of tectonic pressures had shaped the glacier into snags, rifts, and mountains. The great cat dragged her down the slope, secure of his grip on her throat.

He dropped her and muzzled her trembling wrists. The pantiger didn't leave until she used the flares to call a ship. Then it leapt onto the next icy rift, licked at the drops of blood that his teeth had coaxed from her neck, and paced until she boarded.

Yes, she had loved the Emperor. And the Emperor, in his own small way, had loved her too.

Bone Wars
by Brenta Blevins

D reams of publications and tenure floated through Eric Gordon's mind as he stepped over a clawed forelimb. He walked through the interior of the moon, light years from Earth or any senior exopaleontologists. After a decade of infrequent employment, he thought his luck had finally changed. Despite the loneliness of months working in solitude, he felt cheerful. He couldn't have planned a better exopaleontological site if, eons ago, he'd baited and murdered slews of aliens, depositing their skeletal remains for later "discovery" on this ancient moon.

Grave robber. Eric's mother's words echoed in his mind as he walked out of the mine to check on his chargers. The pink sky carried enough radiation to maintain power for his equipment. *I'm no archaeologist, no Howard Carter. I don't work with human remains,* Eric had protested, those years ago as he'd started his graduate study. *No superstitious curses afflict exopaleontology.* But the longer he'd been in the field, the more he'd wondered about his assurance to his mother.

He'd already inventoried *hundreds* of distinct species throughout the abandoned mine—carnivores, herbivores, omnivores, and creatures with mystifying digestive processes. Mapping, documenting, excavating, and stabilizing fossils in secret deep within the mine was precarious, but doing so had yielded unique spiked vertebrae, barbed wings, chitinous exoskeletons, and weirder ossifications—for Eric's credit alone. He wouldn't abide another ultracompetitive exopaleontologist stealing his research again. Even though it had branched out into space, paleontology hadn't grown beyond the rivalries of Earth's nineteenth century, when the field's first scientists had exceeded professional boundaries to lie, cheat, and steal, to discover more and more sensational finds than their peers.

Through the mask of his environment suit, Eric gazed across the empty landscape, bare of any vegetation to relieve the intensity of the red iron surface. Without the chargers and the oxygen generators, a human couldn't survive the isolation here, and Eric guessed that some of the alien species he'd discovered couldn't without assistance, either. He'd stored bizarre fibers that might have been alien environmental wear. He wondered for the thousandth time what had brought them here. He'd never determined what might have been mined here; he'd found no traces of valuable elements or fuels, nothing to explain what would draw and bury so many aliens. But he didn't dwell on the question for long before he wondered how many journals he could submit his findings to and contemplated whether he could have a paper prepared for the exopaleontology conference coming up in a year on Mars.

Eric switched out batteries in the chargers. He had to do everything—cooking, maintenance, and science—be as self-sufficient as a sole human could be here, especially since he hadn't told anyone where he was, so fearful that any of his communication might be intercepted, revealing to another exopaleontologist where he would be doing field work. In fact, as Eric ran a quick inventory of his food and water stocks, he wondered if the moon had ever supported life. But if it had never supported life, he wondered why the mine held so many skeletal remains.

He'd been lucky to be in the right place at the right time—not on the moon, but in a space station bar where he had been supporting himself as a bartender and loader. A drunk, angry prospector had unburdened himself, dumping his irritation at the counter by complaining bitterly about an unpopulated moon he'd found. He'd been so excited about the site when his ground-penetrating radar had revealed tunnels deep into its interior, tunnels that he had hoped would be a mine and that it could be his and his alone. The prospector had landed, praying to find a mine that hadn't had all its resources excavated, but all he'd found were bones. And everyone knew bones were worthless unless they'd turned to jewels or fuel. He'd tossed a thorny molar on the bar in disgust. Eric had picked it up, examined it, and realized he'd never seen its like in any journal. He'd quietly swept it into his pocket, then asked the prospector for the moon's coordinates, begging the man to save him from the wasted opportunity of exploring the "worthless" moon. Eric had then used all his savings and took out loans to fund his ship rental, supplies, and travel to the site. But after everything he'd discovered, the trip would be worth the expense.

Only when Eric had consumed enough food and water from his ship to store the crates of stabilized bones would he leave the moon. He switched out the batteries on his scanners and returned to the mine to search a new room he'd just found.

He walked the kilometers back through the darkness, following the paths he'd memorized, branching off tunnel after tunnel, then into a room. He walked to the far side and angled his flashlight through a crack in the wall to peer into yet another chamber.

He gasped. Already, he'd found the richest and most diverse exopaleontology source ever, but even this room revealed new fossils. A lattice-structured "femur" protruded from the ceiling. Rising above the floor urchin-like crystalline spines glimmered like an exopaleontologist's petrified fantasy. A jawbone gaped in an eternal scream. Bizarre samples, unknown in any of the literature—and they were his and his alone on this desolate moon in the middle of an unpopulated solar system.

The new chamber was supported by internal pillars, likely cave formations, as it appeared unspoiled. He reached in, scraping the arm of his suit against rock, making the suit's skin vibrate. Not for the first time did he wish he could remove the suit and directly touch the material. Instead, he ran his radiometric scanner over the crumbling fossiliferous sediment, then frowned. These specimens had been entombed millions of years *later* than the ones at the surface, in an unusual stratigraphic time-scale inversion.

He stood up and grabbed the jackhammer he'd left in the room. Hammering the opening, Eric tried hypothesizing why such diverse species were preserved *in reverse*, 1,500 meters below the surface. The usual field sites included sinkholes where animals fell, becoming trapped in quagmire, or watering holes turned buffets where predators stalked victims. But here? What would bring such a diversity of alien life to this remote location?

What could explain this bizarre exo-cemetery, populated with one specimen older than the moon itself? An alien burial ground? A galactic gladiatorial coliseum? Eric imagined grotesque creatures fighting, then roaring in mortal agony. It was no wonder his mother had, at his last graduation, deemed him "Doctor Death." But it was a question so puzzling that he would churn out publications aplenty after completing his dig; papers, conference presentations, books, and speaking events. He'd get a tenured position that his luckier, more ruthless classmates had already received.

With the opening just large enough, he stopped the jackhammer and crawled over the fragments he'd chipped from the wall, wriggling his shoulders through the gap.

Halfway in, he heard something above snap.

Dust rained down. The air rumbled and shoved him to the floor. Rubble pelted his suit like a desert sandstorm, the impacts booming and cracking. A stone smashed against his hip, cracking his pelvis.

Eric's scream of pain was stolen by thunder roaring through the mine, echoing, rolling. Boulders exploded as the sandstorm whirled into complete collapse.

When the cascade ended, Eric struggled to move, but found himself encased in agonizing weight. He blinked grit, but he was blind. His flashlight had been ripped from his broken fingers. His mask was cracked; he gasped, and choked on dry sand.

He was completely trapped. Entombed. Just like all the other—

A hypothesis finally crystallized in his mind. What if some species that lived for millions of years had an ambitious exopaleontologist competing for research? Might he be driven to create a honeypot to entice alien fauna to enter his trap and trigger their own demises?

A sob shook Eric's body. He'd never publish. He would appear in someone else's conference presentation—as only a desiccated skeleton.

I'm no grave robber, Mom. I dug my own.

Together—Nowhere
by Bill Ward

They walked over trackless waste; he with eyes fixed on the horizon, she with sorrowing regard for him. With each day, each empty league, he had slowed, losing strength and confidence in the face of the limitless nothing of the barren earth. Now, weeks out from the City, he dragged his feet and stumbled and once or twice fell heavily to the parched ground in a cloud of dust. She waited, unwilling to risk his ire with speech. He regained his feet with effort and continued their course, the skin of his lifesuit gray with dead earth. And so they walked on together in the twilight beneath a weak white sun.

"Caon, please listen, you cannot go on much longer."

He bent to pick up a stone and, with no malice, flung it at her head. It arced through her, landing with a soft *pfft* in the dust beyond.

"Please, Caon, I won't watch this anymore." It was the first he had seen her angry since she appeared at his side ten days ago.

"Then don't watch, I don't want you here, you aren't real," Caon said over his shoulder, walking on.

"Just let me call the City, it will send a flyer—"

"No."

"You will die out here!"

"No, Eré."

Had he been watching he would have seen the slight tick of the head, that subtle acknowledgment of the unexpected, that marked Eré's surprise. It was a gesture he had seen many times—the half-speed blink and the slight dip of her chin that had punctuated their talk. Here was the unadorned gesture, free of exaggeration or self-conscious display or the ready obscurement of laughter that had colored its many moods and uses. Here too was the reason Caon would not look at the simulacrum of the woman he had known so well.

"At least you are using my name again," the image of Eré said.

He moved determinedly ahead, toward nothing, not looking back.

City had told them the world was eons dead, but Caon was not prepared for this. Around him in all directions stretched a featureless plain, a flat, brittle expanse of stone and sand. At first it had seemed a challenge, a few empty leagues around the black crystal dome of City itself, a landscape designed to discourage citizens from leaving the protective enclave of Lasthome. But with each step away from City Caon had learned doubt, and his conviction that the stories of the dead world had been cruel lies had weakened. Still he had moved with deliberation, and even as hope died in his chest, even as the tall dome of City had receded behind him like the setting of a black sun, he had clung to his stubborn need to be right. To be justified.

"We should stop and make a glow, Caon, it's already getting cold," Eré said, gently.

How could she know it was cold? Caon wondered, and continued walking, following the long shadow that stretched before him. Night came, and still he walked, and once or twice sucked a thin stream of water from the recyc tube in the lifesuit's breather. There were no sounds in the world and the night felt emptier than anything Caon had experienced. In City, in the dense and busy world he had been born into, there had always been sounds. Even in the snug quiet of a City night, alone in the womb of a slumber cell, the warm hum of City's vibrating bones staved off silence.

True, absolute silence was a frightening thing. The worst kind of isolation.

When he sensed Eré was about to protest again he stopped and searched the ground with his glovelight. Finding a suitable stone he flipped it over to show its flattest side, and set the glow strip upon it. It was his last strip, and heavily flecked with dark spots, nearly as dark as the others had been when they finally guttered out. He flicked the end of a friction rod over the strip and it blossomed with warmth and dim orange light.

Eré sat beyond the glow, looking concerned. Looking like Eré.

Once there had been a moon, a pale lantern that had been man's companion in the dark. Now only the night and the brittle stars remained.

"How long has it been since you've eaten?" she asked, and not for the first time.

He had refused to discuss it. The truth was he had not eaten in weeks, in all the time since he left City. He had left in a frenzied rush to get outside, to get away from City's watching eyes. He had slid into the ancient suit and blown the locks on the hatch and ran into the wasteland, sure that he would find an unspoiled wilderness somewhere on the forbidden surface. Somewhere out of sight of City, a garden paradise more beautiful and more wild than the tame and tailored environs of City's parks.

"The suit won't let me die," he said quietly as he lay down on the hard ground. The suit was everything; it preserved him, locked him in, protected him from the nothing world of dead earth. He was a closed system; his waste recycled, returned to him; his needs anticipated, artificially provided. As he lay there willing sleep to come his suit obliged with a chemical lullaby. It was older than the oldest man, older even than City, and for uncounted years the suit and others like it had hung empty, without purpose. Now Caon's purpose was its own.

He awoke stiff and cold to the early morning radiance of the decrepit sun. A sickening mix of sensations assaulted him—hunger, fear, slow dying—only to be banished by a symphony of synthetic hormones provided by his suit. He was up and moving in seconds, his purpose clear, the frizzled remains of his glow strip forgotten. Eré hurried along beside him.

"Let me call them," she begged.

Caon stopped, turned to look at her as if considering her offer. They had been ten days together, ten days and a lifetime if he considered her the same person as the woman he had grown of age with and made art with and learned love alongside in their long, safe years together in City. He had loved that woman. They had planned their escape together as a romantic adventure, a promise that they were each other's universe. Had she shone last night beyond the fading flicker of the glow? Shone with a light that was entirely her own?

"Why haven't you just told City to get us? Why did it bother with you to begin with? It could have me by now." Caon said slowly, precisely.

Eré shook her head, her dark hair sliding over her shoulders. She wore her work clothes, the beige singlet he had last seen her in, an unflattering and unadorned outfit in which he had nonetheless always found her most appealing. "City does not coerce," she said simply.

"Does not coerce!" he flared, lumbering toward her with arms flailing. He fought the urge to swing through the empty space of her image, to batter the idea of her. "It sent you to torment me, didn't it? That's not coercion?" His voice rolled away over the oceanic emptiness of the waste, an insignificant disturbance in the still air.

"I asked it to Caon!" She held her hands out imploringly, desperately. "This is a mistake, I know what City knows, Caon. It didn't lie, the world is gone. It's dead, the whole world is like this. I had second thoughts before but now I *know*. There is nothing beyond City, nothing but the corpse of a dead world!"

"Eré . . . " Caon said quietly, his voice breaking. He reached for her, wanting to dry the tears on her cheek. "But how can I trust you Eré? You're part of City now, a hologram. You aren't real."

"But neither am I a lie, Caon. You know that. I'm like any of the honored dead, like any simulation of the ancestors you'd care to speak to in the archives or anyone brought back for the Remembrance Ceremony. I'm a true memory, Caon. I'm Eré."

How many ancestors did City have stored away in its mind? How many ghosts lay in crystalline storage, the record of their lives listed in minute detail? Caon could see them all, stretched backward to infinity, enough spent lives to fill the waste around him. It was another kind of emptiness, and now Eré was a part of it. She was a part of it because of him.

"If you are Eré then you hate me. And if you don't, than I can't forgive you for not hating me. Not hating me at least as much as I hate myself," he said, his voice trailing into a whisper. He turned from her and walked, each leg pistoning out stiffly like the parts of an old machine. The suit walked for him.

With the sun came the mild heat of the day, and a white glare. They walked in silence; he with eyes fixed on the horizon, she just a step behind. Caon stalked along on limbs he no longer felt, toward a goal he no longer believed in. Only the ghost in his mind, at his side, kept him moving forward. Behind him, he knew, Eré wept. The suit knew his needs, and did all in its power to meet them. Throughout the long day they moved together, without speech, going nowhere. The waste moved endlessly beneath their feet, league upon league of it; the crumbling, monotonous shell of a dead planet. Sometime before nightfall Caon collapsed, and did not get up.

Eré was at his side, radiant in the darkness. "I don't hate you. I could never hate you."

"I know," he whispered, nodding as best he could.

Caon did not feel the cold of evening, or the need for sleep. He urged Eré to speak, and throughout the night she called up the warmth of their former lives, spoke of things known and intimate and joyous. Spoke of love and, at last, forgiveness.

"I'm sorry, Eré." Caon sobbed sometime near dawn. "So sorry . . ."

They had planned escape together, like any work of art or shared performance. But when it had stopped being a game their paths diverged, and Eré had tried everything in her power to get him to see reason, pleading with him until the end. On the day of his leaving she had yelled at him, fought with him, tried to restrain him. But he was wild and desperate with the fear of getting caught, and the heavy dread of leaving the city without her. He had grown mad with the fear, if only for a moment, and he had killed her without ever seeming to choose to do it. But he had killed her just the same.

"So sorry . . ."

"I know, Caon, it's over now, it's over," she wept. "I won't leave you again."

The sun limped above the horizon, lent its wan radiance to the borderless waste for another day. Two figures moved beneath it, flotsam in the sea of stone. One staggered jerkily forward, head lolling, no longer alive except for the suit that guided his movements. The other cast no shadow, but was instead herself a kind of shadow, a trailing memory. The world was long dead, and they were part of it now.

It's A Dog's Life
by Shelley Savran Houlihan

He lives with her in a godforsaken place. All rock and mud where there used to be water and trees. They sent him there four years before with a group of other people who were deemed inconvenient for the government. Some would say he's not gotten a bad deal, given the state of affairs elsewhere in the world. After all, so many people died, so many continue to die from the scourges they fashioned centuries ago. Women suffer the most, he's told, due to the ways the world has become animal.

She likes calling him a dog, but he has only two legs and opposable thumbs. He doesn't roll around in his own waste, but he pisses in the entrance to their cavern, marking it.

He's at the very edge of the coast of what used to be Florida. They say it was beautiful before the war. He's seen pictures, but they tell him pictures don't do it justice.

There were oceans then instead of stagnant expanses of damp. There were trees and grasses and edible fruits. The sky used to be blue some of the time, and the temperature used to be reasonable. There used to be fish. Tomatoes. Eggs. Tastes people now can only imagine.

When it's safe he walks outside on what used to be a beach. Sometimes he picks up a relic. A seashell. A bone. He found a patch of cloth they say was probably from a piece of clothing, and he can still see traces of a leaf painted on it. He's told it's a palm frond, but he doesn't know if this information is correct. If there was a museum left he could donate the shred of fabric. That's how rare it is. Right now it just sits on a piece of stone in his cave and mildews, which isn't good for a relic. He keeps it in case he needs it. For bartering. A life or death situation. Anything less would be wasteful.

Flies, cockroaches and lice survive, as do snakes and one breed of goat. Dogs, of course, but not lap dogs. Those were eaten by larger dogs in a spirited chain of canine cannibalism.

Seagulls were the only birds to survive, and this has not been scientifically explained, as most of the scientists perished. The government delighted in the execution of fate. The weak did not inherit the earth.

There's not much of an ecosystem yet, and some say there'll never be again. The seagulls screech and dive when he brings his rations home from the caged and guarded place the government has sanctioned for them. They're allowed two bags of chemicals, only enough to mitigate hunger. There's not much more to eat than that. Try as he might, he searches for something else, something that might grow in the cracked earth despite all that's happened there, though the dogs usually find it before he does—they've had many generations to hone skills people can't master. Smell. Persistence. Survival. The gulls pick at corpses after the dogs are done with them. Everyone has a turn.

Bands of men approach the cavern sometimes with makeshift weapons, and it's not unusual for them to kill for the thrill of it with their own arms and teeth, like monsters. They have little else to do. She hides in our cave most of the time, afraid. Fear is her survival instinct. She only comes out at night to watch the sky, hurrying back inside when the dogs howl or we hear another person approach.

Nobody's safe. There's nothing to own but many who covet. She knows it. That's why she stays with him. He's her amulet, but he doesn't feel used; he feels needed.

She peers out at the dogs that roam around them. Dogs look much like they say they always did, but their tails have changed. Their tails provide the only whimsy left in this world, curled as they are like decorations against the steely sky.

They hear the dogs all times of the day and night, especially after a fresh kill. She admits that scares her. The only time she clings to him is when she's scared. He appreciates it when she's scared because, more than anything else, he doesn't want her to leave. Most words have vanished from disuse after all the destruction. There seems so little to say.

He can't tell her he loves her. He's not sure she wants to hear it. She stays there because she's protected by him, because their world is hazardous and cruel and because he has that small piece of cloth to protect them.

Herb's wife Estelle bought him that tropical shirt with the palm trees the day she died. He never could have predicted that a tattered piece of his clothing might save someone else's life many years later. If he'd known that, he might have felt that he died with dignity, for a noble cause, instead of in a stupid sonic boom that sank much of the world into itself like a fulminating boil.

The day Estelle died was hot and humid, typical for Florida then, in the summer. She left the mall with the Hawaiian print shirt; she saw the storm clouds gathering above. She thought she'd make it home before the sheets of rain came down, but she didn't. All of a sudden it was dark, and the windshield was layered with thick sheets of rain and hail. She couldn't see, but didn't stop. She wanted to get home. When the truck hit her on the driver's side, her car traveled horizontally along the glazed road and rolled over like road kill, looking more like a dented tin than a Buick. They tried to save her.

Everyone told Herb not to visit the car. It was too gruesome they said, but he couldn't help it. He needed to see it, the last space his wife had lived. It was only then, amid the dusty, broken cars at the lot, that he saw the shopping bag still lying on the backseat. He wore the shirt almost every day after that. It made him feel as if Estelle were still alive.

Herb was an old man for a very long time. He never thought he'd live as long as he did, especially after Estelle died. He never predicted he'd die because of a war, along with lots of other people who didn't deserve to die just then. He'd never have predicted that the one thing he'd accomplish, merely by owning it, would be a piece of clothing that refused to dissolve when everything else around him did.

It would be as foolish to say the treasured square of fabric joins the two men together any more than the two worlds are joined together. There is simply the passage of time.

Engaging the Idrl
by Davin Ireland

I

The desert here is pink and rocky and shrouded in darkness for much of the day. The excavation site is slashed with grey spills of rubble that could be collapsed towers or random seams of granite. To the east, great clouds of mortar dust boil across the plains, scouring the arid landscape, depriving it of fresh growth. Only the Idrl remain. Oblivious to the wind, seemingly blind to the desolation, they drift through the emptying topography like azure phantoms, the robes that stain their hides a deep, lustrous blue snapping petulantly in the breeze. They refuse to talk to us or communicate in any way, for they consider our troops to be an army of occupation.

Our generals are therefore left to draw their own conclusions about what went on before mankind arrived on Serpia Dornem.

Grue says he knows. After listening to his story, I am inclined to agree with him. The Idrl did not build these ruined cities. Nor did they occupy them. They are instead a separate nomad species, periodically emerging from hibernation to roam the land and take whatever sustenance their dying world has to offer. The mysterious Constructor Race, however, strove for greater things.

II

A transport carrier arrived unannounced this morning. Its harried crew whisked us away to a salt flat fifteen hundred clicks east of base camp, and dumped us there to await further instruction. None came, and when the adverse weather conditions disrupted our communications equipment, some of the younger men grew visibly anxious. Grue himself appeared towards the end of afternoon, tiny reconnaissance craft bobbing and groaning against increasingly heavy turbulence. The perpetual scream of mortar dust had whipped itself into a sandstorm of vicious proportions, yet the latest intelligence took precedence over all.

"We depart at eighteen hundred hours," the corporal announced, and took shelter on the leeward side of the craft. He would say no more and prohibited further discussion between the men. Forty minutes later we took to the skies.

"Right beneath us," Grue cried above the shriek of the engines. We had been in the air for maybe a half hour at the time. "Tell me what you make of *that*."

I looked down. The pink and grey shelf of desert that followed us everywhere we went had suddenly vanished, only to be replaced by what turned out to be forty-thousand square kilometers of unfettered parking space—an asphalted lot of such grotesque proportions that it extended all the way to the horizon in three different directions. And not a motor vehicle in sight.

Who were the Constructor Race, I ask myself. What made them do this? Precious little evidence remains beyond the cities themselves, and these have been stripped, razed, and abandoned in a way that suggests the destruction was thorough and wholly intentional. By the look of it, the only exception is a parking facility identical in character and composition to anything one might have found outside a conventional strip mall circa 2010. With the exception of size, of course. This thing dwarfs anything Earth had to offer by several thousand orders of magnitude.

Tomorrow we will learn more. For the remainder of this evening, we'll kick our heels and wait for the survey team to complete its remote sweep from orbit. Naturally, the Idrl sense that moves are afoot. They have ceased roaming the sterile plains and watch us cautiously from distance. The calm dignity these beings exude stands in stark contrast to their magnificent trailing robes, which ripple and flutter incessantly on the gritty air currents. A displaced show of emotion, perhaps? We may never know. Meanwhile, certain members of the unit already exhibit the first signs of battle fatigue, though we have fought no war.

III

Tang and Spritzwater, two of my best, are refusing to go on. They shed their laser carbines shortly after dawn this morning, and now stand with their backs to the spent orb that is this system's sun, shadows trailing before them like tired ghosts. They say there is something wrong with Serpia Dornem. They say the planet is haunted. I am beginning to believe them. When we performed a perimeter sweep at 2300 hours last night, rocks, pinkish sand, and lazily flipping dust devils were about the extent of it. As the false dawn colored the sky, a monstrous city loomed in the east.

My men blame the natives. Even those of us who retain a degree of objectivity are becoming unnerved by their austere presence, which grows by the hour. During breakfast I counted eleven Idrl gathered about a cluster of the spiny-leaved plants that cling in the cracks between the parched rocks. By first inspection their number had swollen to seventeen. They filter down from the arid hills to the south—gaunt, weary, faces expressionless yet eloquent as pantomime masks. This is not uncommon for a race subjected to prolonged oppression. A spectacle is unfolding here, and the spectacle is us. We have found the one city the Constructor Race overlooked—or perhaps *it* has found *us*—and now we must investigate.

Later.

The nearer we get, the greater the extent of the challenge. In the swirling wastelands between base camp and city, we spied a dead tree. It stood naked and branchless in the wind, sand-blasted for what may have been centuries, the very last of its kind. Oloman was dispatched to investigate, and returned minutes later in a state of high agitation.

"You have to look at this," he said, tugging at my sleeve, "you have to see this right away."

We deviated from our game plan just long enough to verify the lieutenant's claims, which were irrational in the extreme but perfectly justified. The tree was not a tree at all, but a roadsign: a rusting iron pole pointing the way to a city with an eerily prophetic name. Venice Falls. The words were still legible despite the corrosive effects of the wind. There could be no mistake. Out here in a region of the galaxy visited by no human, there exists an urban settlement large enough to accommodate the entire population of New York City.

And it has an English name.

The Idrl appear unmoved by our discovery. They form a serene gathering to our wind-choked huddle, steadfastly refusing any attempt at dialogue, even though the surreal possibility exists that we may actually speak the same language. Nye has tried to tempt them with extra clothing and with food, but all is ignored. Even when an older female, badly undernourished and clearly hypothermic, allowed her eye to wander in the direction of the rehydration kit, her fellow tribal members closed ranks about her. We have not seen her since.

IV

Much as I suspected but dared not mention for fear of spooking the men further, this metropolis is a full-scale reproduction of an Earth city circa 2010, faithful in every detail except one. There are no people here. None except us, that is. We wander the empty streets in aimless fascination, weapons drawn but pointed at the ground. Sand dunes clog the intersections. Erosion blights the shopfronts; but any wear and tear is incidental, a tawdry gift of the elements. I stare at the red-brick apartment buildings that line the sprawling avenues, at the reproduction brownstones with their salt-stained walls, at the magnificent steel and glass towers that pierce the gloomy sky—and wonder again who the Constructor Race were and why they should have built this place.

Were they intending to populate it with immigrants from our own planet? To forcibly humanize the Idrl for their own ends? To create a holiday resort? Such notions strike me as absurd. The dying sun, the alkaline soil—a bleaker aspect is difficult to imagine. And yet they *must* have had a reason for such folly. Acquiring enough knowledge to make a balanced judgement on the subject would take decades of investigation, and we only have weeks at best. In the meantime, the men are determined to make a start. Without my consent, Oloman used the butt of his carbine to smash a movie theatre window and thus gain access to the sealed lobby. Inside, our flashlights revealed plush red carpets, a ticket booth, even a hot dog stand advertising various brands of popcorn and ice-cream. None of the food on offer was actually available, but that didn't detract from the authenticity of the moment. It seemed so real that I half expected an usher in a velvet suit to emerge from a side door and escort us to our seats.

But not everyone shared my enthusiasm.

"It doesn't smell right," Oloman complained, "like fresh paint and new carpets shut in for thirty thousand years."

"And no movies," agreed Nye. "Look at the poster frames: they're all empty."

It was a pattern that was to be repeated throughout the city. Bars with no liquor, trash barrels without garbage, corporations bereft of employees. And beneath it all, lurking at the very edges of perception, the unshakeable conviction that we were being watched.

"Of course we are," I declared in exasperation, "the Idrl are everywhere. The fact they choose not to show themselves doesn't mean they're not around."

But my words failed to allay the unit's increasing sense of unease, and in the end we retreated with weapons raised and hearts aflutter. Venice Falls is an unsettling place.

V

Tang and Spritzwater are gone. We arrived back at base camp an hour ago to discover the radio damaged beyond repair and half our stock of rations missing. This is not the work of the Idrl. If the men are to believe that, however, we must locate and capture the deserters before the spiral of suspicion and paranoia becomes too great. Already some of them are starting to question my authority.

The search begins immediately.

Ranging through the powdery foothills beyond the city, we encounter the entrance to one of the stately Idrl burrows. The rock-lined tunnel leading down into the ground is high enough for a man to stand upright during his descent, yet from just a few feet away it appears no more conspicuous than a natural fissure in a seam of granite. We enter, calling out the names of the missing as we navigate these labyrinthine corridors. Occasionally we find signs of occupation but no actual occupants. These people have nothing. The few oxen-like beasts that survive on this desiccated globe are reared and worked to exhaustion underground, never to see the light of the pale sun. The lapis lazuli the Idrl mine for their own personal use—the one commodity this barren place has left to offer—we would gladly take off their hands in exchange for food, water, and crops engineered to survive the inhospitable conditions. But that would be dishonorable, it seems. So instead they survive on a diet of insects and the coarse spiny plants that thrive out here in the desert, taking hope from the knowledge that, quite incredibly, they are almost there. The Constructor Race is gone; we could very well be next. Freedom, at any price, is almost within their grasp.

I wonder what the Idrl will be left with once we return to space?

An answer of sorts has arrived from an unexpected source. The search for the missing men having proved fruitless, we withdrew to the surface in pairs, myself and a soldier called Gosling bringing up the rear. Just prior to breaking the surface, Gosling angled his flashlight at the ceiling. The scalding white torch beam revealed a long niche carved into the rock along the top of the cavern walls, and here, stowed like so much excess firewood, lay the mummified remains of countless generations of deceased Idrl. Intrigued by the discovery, we retraced our steps, following the dusty seam of corpses to its source. The oldest, driest specimens were stored at the heart of the burrow, nearest the fire pit, which is where the Idrl sleep, cook and keep warm. It made sense for their carbon store to begin here, nearest the flames, where the dead could do their bit to sustain the living. No wonder we never found a burial site.

Back at the entrance to the burrow, we made another discovery. Huddled next to the freshest addition to the line of shriveled corpses crouched a juvenile female—shivering, barely alive, no larger in my estimation than a six-year-old girl. Hunger had collapsed her face, preternaturally enlarging the eyes. But already she had learned her people's way. When I offered my coat, her gaze drifted to the rock wall opposite and she was lost to me. Almost. But then an idea struck me. The chocolate bar was freeze-dried, vacuum packed, and perfectly fresh. When I broke the foil package and waved it beneath her nose, the child's nostrils quivered spasmodically, and a tremor of anguish seemed to travel through that pitifully slight form. For a moment, just a microscopic sliver of a moment, her eyes betrayed all of the misery and the suffering and the longing in her tiny heart. Then all of the fight, all of the emotion, seemed to bleed out of her, and she was lost to me once more.

"Move out," I whispered to Gosling, and we broke the surface together in uncomfortable silence. But at least I had confirmation of that which I had suspected all along: the Idrl are not the empty vessels they pretend to be. They feel, just as we do. They hurt; they hope.

VI

Tang and Spritzwater are now officially missing. I reported their disappearance this morning when a second transport carrier dropped by with news, supplies and a fresh radio. After consulting the high command, it was decided we would make one last sweep and then return to headquarters for the final assessment—the one that will decide the fate of our entire mission. Already Serpia Dornem is being discussed in terms of a washout, and that suits the men just fine. I myself retain mixed feelings on the subject.

I think I understand the nature of the problem now. I honestly believe I am starting to comprehend the size of the dilemma the Idrl face. They are a dying species on a world that will soon expire. They have spent the last thirty-thousand years subjugated and occupied by a race who were at best indifferent to their existence, and who at worst may have enslaved them. Perhaps they no longer understand the meaning of compassion. Their lives are brief and cruel and filled with all the bitter harshness of winter, even in the warmest of months. Perhaps they need someone to show them that not all visitors to this place are hostile, and not all outsiders are to be viewed with distrust.

All I need is a chance.

We continue to follow the winding pathways through the foothills to the south, but few believe the deserters—if deserters they truly be—would seek refuge in exposed outlands when the corrupt monolith of Venice Falls squats so predominantly to the east. They are much more likely to be drawn by the prospect of shelter and the comforts of home, no matter how strong their initial reluctance. Still, we must be thorough and we must be sure. And the search has not proved a complete waste of time. Bit by bit, the land is giving up its secrets. We discovered a deep quarry veined with countless fractures and many millions of the tough, spiny plants upon which our hosts depend. We also discovered a broken loom near a deep, natural well. Attached to the loom was a cup filled with powdered lapis lazuli. So now the picture is somewhat complete. The Idrl eat this plant, feed it to their livestock, weave its sinewy fibres into robes that are subsequently stained blue with the crushed lapis. If you add in the not unreasonable amounts of geothermal energy generated beneath the surface, you have an entire ecosystem right there.

Returning to the city at noon, the men are somewhat cheered by the knowledge that the approaching storm will not hit until we have completed our projected sweep, and are on the way back to base for our final pickup. As we draw nearer, Oloman's behavior becomes increasingly erratic. So great is his distraction, in fact, that word of it filters up the column to me, and I am forced to drop back and confront him. The last thing I need right now is another Tang or Spritzwater.

"What the hell is going on?" I demand. "Your attitude is making the men restless."

In lieu of an answer, Oloman turns on his heel so that he faces back the way we came, finger jabbing in the direction of our dusty tracks. The dry soil here is heavy with iron oxide, and our footprints describe a pinkish-red arc that trails all the way back to base camp. He then flats a hand in the direction of the old signpost that marks the way to Venice Falls. It stands perpendicular to our position, about a kilometer distant, and I can just make it out through the murk of late morning.

"We've got company," Oloman informs me, and then narrows his eyes. "But not Idrl."

Another species, perhaps? My field glasses are useless against the membranous skeins of dust that drift lazily across the intervening plain. I therefore make a decision based on instinct. Oloman may have his weaknesses, but foolishness is not one of them. "Collect Gosling and Nye and follow in my wake," I tell him. "Send the rest of the men on into the city."

We reach the signpost just as the last of the forward party melts into a decaying business district on the edge of town. The little girl is no more forthcoming than on the previous occasion we met, though her whole body betrays the incredible risk she has taken in coming here. A pronounced pulse-beat bangs at her throat, and her overly large eyes dart frantically to and fro in their sockets. Not another species, then: just a smaller version of same. Now, at least, I can begin the process of redressing the balance, of showing a little kindness where before cruelty reigned supreme. Dropping my carbine in the dust, I produce the uneaten chocolate bar from my flak jacket and offer it to the girl. There is no hesitation this time: she snatches the confectionary from my hand, consumes it in six diminutive bites—chewing, swallowing, unable to disguise the terrible need that lives inside of her.

"Rations," I mutter, and four packs hit the dirt. There is no longer any point in offering, I merely load the pockets of the girl's robe with food, and pat her gently on the head—all too aware, as are we all, that it is at such moments history is made.

Recalling the notion that the Idrl may actually understand something of English, I call to the girl as we depart. "Tell your family we are their friends," I cry. "Tell your tribe we mean them no harm. We are not here to hurt you; we can help. Tell them soon."

My words are lost in the rising moan of the wind. Perhaps it is for the best. Perhaps the gesture alone should speak for us. As long as we march towards the city, the little one remains in place—watching, waiting, possibly savoring the taste of our friendship and the notion that not all strangers are aggressors. One can only hope.

VII

The storm is almost upon us. Angry thunderheads roll in from the horizon; purple-white lightning veins the clouds. We do not have much time. Sensing that the end is near, we fan out through the streets, the names of the missing echoing back at us from abandoned buildings.

I cannot stop thinking about that little girl. With one simple gesture, one overt act of kindness, the relationship between Human and Idrl may have changed forever. If they come to us for more, we will accommodate them as best we can; if this entire people requires refugee status, we will provide it. The hardy crops and other supplies initially offered as trade items will be granted as gifts, part of a larger goodwill package that will grow in size until the Idrl can no longer deny the sincerity of our motives. We will not rest until freedom and democracy are established in this barren arm of the galaxy.

I am already dreaming of petitioning generals and world statesmen on the Idrl's behalf, when a call goes up from the next block. The cries are eerily faint against the overwhelming groan of the wind, but reverberate hollowly among the glass-fronted towers. I race down the sand-clogged avenue, past homely little Italian restaurants with generic-sounding names, past lofty investment houses with grandly-furnished reception areas, past diners and hardware stores, supermarkets and coffee shops—all of them empty, none of them dead because they were never alive. They are stillborn, unborn, aborted.

Tang and Spritzwater are cowering in a walkdown when we find them. They claim to have fled into endless blank acres of parking lot after we left them yesterday morning, only to awaken hours later in the very heart of the city with no memory of how they got there. They have been trying to find their way out ever since. The story sounds contrived, I admit, but their fear is only too real. No matter. I drag them up to the sidewalk by the hair and shove them in the direction of base camp, my anger at their behavior tempered only by the knowledge that our time here is coming to an end.

VIII

Trudging back through the gloom and the gathering winds, we find ourselves veering inexorably in the direction of the signpost that marks the way to Venice Falls. Is it curiosity that draws us on, or a deeper need to confirm, one final time, that this is not some vast illusion? The men are excited. Certain of them discuss the snaps they will take of themselves with the city in the background; others express a wish to take the sign home with them as a souvenir. The mood is upbeat and euphoric, and remains so despite the knowledge that we are under scrutiny from the south. For at the summit of each foothill stands a lone Idrl, robes swirling, posture unreadable. The sky has turned the color of an old bruise, and the resulting light tinges the ground beneath their feet an ominous purple. Lightning flickers at our backs, illuminating those austere figures but revealing nothing of what resides in their hearts.

We encounter the girl one last time. She is still in the same place. The pockets of her robe still bulge with untouched ration packs, a brown smear of chocolate still decorates that delicate mouth. As ever, the blue stain of her garments flutters endlessly on the strengthening breeze. One of the men—I think Gosling, but it could just as easily be me—allows a horrified moan to escape his throat. It appears the natives have found yet another use for the spiny plant they rely on so much. Its platted fibres creak gently back and forth as the little girl twists in the wind, the weight of the ration packs grossly elongating her already slender neck. Once and for all, the Idrl have answered our gesture of kindness with an unequivocal statement of intent.

Only now am I beginning to comprehend our predecessors' motives for leaving this place after investing so much in it for so very long. Victory is not a question of superior firepower, it seems. It is not even a matter of right and wrong. It is simply a matter of conviction, and of belief—and who would dispute that the Idrl's is far, far greater than ours could ever be.

Lucky Shot
by Gerri Leen

Lieutenant Sirella Nacleth breathes in green dust and tries not to cough. Her feet feel too heavy to move, but she forces herself to walk on, ignoring the heat that blasts down and around her, heat carried by winds that do nothing to cool the air from the sun above. This planet is a harrowing furnace, and she is bound here for the rest of her life—or until her people find her.

Or until her enemy's people do. She glances back, sees that the Vermayan has finished filling in the deep grave he put his crewmates' bodies in. She is assuming the Vermayan is a he. It's hard to tell from where she stands, and she doesn't intend to get very close if she can help it.

If their ships hadn't crashed almost on top of each other, she might not have seen him for days, if at all. But their ships did land nearly twisted together, and the bodies of the crews are strewn all over. She has to get closer to him than she likes just to retrieve her dead.

She is the only one on her ship who survived the crash. Her left arm is broken, and her right ankle wrenched. Her back feels strained and her head hurts. But she is alive. She is alive and burying her dead, shoveling one handed and pulling her crewmates behind her as she limps from body to hole, body to hole.

The Vermayan is way ahead of her. There are no rust-colored bodies strewn over the plain anymore, while so many of her own dead still lie waiting for her to reach them. The green sand blows over the bodies as the blazing wind lifts stinging grit and flings it at her, making her eyes hurt and her lips crack. She will help her friends; she will give them rest. But not soon. She is only one person. And she is tired. So tired.

The Vermayan has sat down. He is watching her as she limps toward the next body, which is halfway between where she has dug her hole and where he is resting. Glancing at his rank, she sees he is the Vermayan equivalent of lieutenant. He has taken his weapon out of its holster and is playing with it—no, he is checking it. She laughs bitterly. If it is built as poorly as hers, it will be clogged with the fine green grit of this damned world. And since his ship didn't perform any better than hers, why should his gun?

"It won't work," she says, unsure why she bothers. He won't understand her, and talking will only make the dryness in her throat worse.

He gets up, closes the weapon, and aims at the ground. The gun sort of clicks as he pulls the trigger, but it doesn't fire.

"Nothing like fine Vermayan craftsmanship," she says, laughing as he drops the weapon on the ground. Obviously, the Vermayans went with the lowest bidder, too. She is sorry she laughed when her throat begins to itch. Soon she is coughing, and she imagines her lungs are filling up with green dust.

He stares at her, and she stares back at him as soon as she gets the coughing under control, wondering if she should challenge him to a hand-to-hand duel. They are enemies: the Revirian Confederation is at war with the Vermayan Union. Surely they should fight?

She moves on. She'll fight him later. When her arm doesn't jolt with pain each time she moves it wrong. When she can actually move gracefully again on her ankle and not feel like a crippled old woman.

When she's found some water. She's almost out of the small amount of water that she salvaged from the wreckage. She'll die without water.

But first, she has to finish burying her dead. She cannot leave them in this blistering heat, cannot face them if she abandons her duty. She will imagine their accusing faces. She will see them look over at their enemy and note that he has buried all of his dead—what is wrong with her?

She sighs and drags the body of the navigator back to the hole it took her all day to dig. She cannot settle him gently into the hole as she did the others; her broken arm refuses to cooperate any longer with such foolish demands. She ends up rolling him into the hole, easing him over the edge with her foot.

The sound of his body landing on the others makes her wince. She hears another sound, whirls and sees the Vermayan dragging the medic's body toward her. She reaches for her knife, and he stops walking and stares at her. Their eyes meet, and she tries to read what emotion has prompted him to help her, but his dark eyes are barricades she cannot see past.

He says something in a language she has never been taught. His tone is guttural, harsh. He sounds impatient.

She sees that his water carrier is half empty. Why is he helping her when he could be out looking for water?

She holds onto her knife but does not pull it out of the sheath. The handle of it is comforting, familiar, and makes her feel stronger. The Vermayan also wears a knife; its ornate hilt is carved with symbols and inlayed with some kind of golden metal that shines in the bright sun. Following her gaze, he sees that she is studying his weapon. He smiles—it is not a pretty expression. She wonders if he meant it to be.

Easing the medic down, he walks off, and she watches him go. He is collecting the captain now. She does not want his help with the bodies, but she cannot face the idea of trying to drag them all to the grave herself, not when just easing the medic up enough to get her to the edge of the hole is such torture.

The Vermayan gets closer this time before he sets the captain down. Something falls, and she realizes it is part of the captain's weapon. The thing has shattered, but the Vermayan collected the pieces and carried them back with the body. He crouches down, touching the pieces of metal. One of them is sharp, and he holds it up, a questioning look in his eyes.

She nods. He is right. They should keep it as a knife.

When did she and the Vermayan become they? Frowning, she reaches down to pull the captain toward the grave. He is lighter than he should be, and she looks back, sees that the Vermayan is helping her move him. His eyes are wary as he stares her down, but she is too tired to tell him to let go.

They ease the captain into the grave together, his body settling gently, not landing hard as the navigator and medic did. She is glad; the captain was good to her, made her feel welcome when she was a green recruit. She does not want her last act for him to be one of desperate disrespect.

Turning, she marches slowly across the sand to the last of the bodies. Her black uniform is greenish, as if covered with pollen from the trees that line the streets back on Doala. There are no trees in sight, and her home world seems very far away. She is not even sure what planet they have crashed on—maybe it is not a planet at all; maybe it is a moon. This area of space is a wasteland; their ships fought in the middle of the astral desert, and it's just possible they were lucky enough to crash on what passes for an oasis in this sector.

As oases go, it's pretty dismal.

She leans down and sees that the body she has approached is Justina's. Her friend is lying at an odd angle, broken, shattered inside. Sirella was in the back of the ship—it was probably what saved her, but she is not sure she is glad she was saved.

She wonders if the Vermayan would have buried her, too, if all of his enemies were dead instead of just most of them.

He is already dragging the engineer back to the grave. Justina was assistant engineer. She was in love with the ship, more than she ever had been with any man. This was supposed to be the start of a long, adventurous life. Life is rarely long during wartime though, and Justina must have known that on some level.

Sirella brushes her friend's hair from her face. Her skin is unmarked. No sign of the trauma that is written in the crooked way her bones lay. She is still so beautiful, still so young. She will be young forever.

Sirella reaches for Justina, using her bad arm. Pain erupts, and she cries out. She looks to see if the Vermayan heard her but thinks he is too far away. Panting for a moment, she presses her throbbing arm firmly against her body, then drags Justina with her good one.

The Vermayan walks past her, the engineer already in the grave. She sees his eyes drop down to where she is cradling her arm against her stomach, but he doesn't stop as he heads back to the main wreckage of his ship.

The walk to the grave seems even longer, or maybe it is just that her back is aching more, the strain made worse from pulling and lifting. She ignores the pain, finally gets Justina to the edge and whispers a silent apology as she pushes her into the hole. Her friend's body lies just as crookedly on the top of the pile as it did on the fine green sand.

Sirella pushes herself up with a groan, picks up the piece of wreckage she used to dig the hole and starts to fill the grave in. The Vermayan comes up, but she refuses to stop. She is not sure how she managed to climb out of the hole with a broken arm when she first dug it—she can barely remember digging or pushing the first bodies in. She must have been in shock. She may still be in shock, but she does not dwell on it because she is not a medic and is not sure what she should do. She is a tactical officer; she shoots things.

If she had been a better shot, maybe her ship would not be lying in pieces behind her?

Maybe the Vermayan would not be helping her move dirt into the hole that is filled with her dead friends? Maybe he would be the dead one?

She tries to lift the dirt, but her strength is giving out, so she starts to push it toward the hole. She feels the Vermayan touch her arm and shrugs off the touch. She will finish this.

He touches her again, and she ignores him. He touches her a third time, and she pulls her knife out and turns on him.

His eyes show emotion now. They are confused—and angry. She has cut him and his hand drips blood. A hand that is holding a sling out to her.

They are frozen, staring at each other, his dark eyes piercing hers, his frown deepening as he holds his hand over the cut to stop the bleeding. It is not deep; she struck out in rage, not with any real intent.

He pushes the sling out to her. His blood is red like hers, and it has soaked into the fabric. She takes the sling, slipping it over her head, trying to get her arm in it. She can tell by his eyes that she is not doing it right, but he makes no move to help her. She gives him credit for not being stupid.

Putting the knife back, she moves closer to him and looks down at the sling that she has twisted so badly. "Help?"

The word cannot possibly make sense to him, but her tone does, and maybe the look in her eyes. He tears a piece of cloth first from his uniform, tying it around his hand before reaching out to adjust the sling. Once it is in place, he steps back, picking up his own version of a shovel, which he dropped when she cut him. He moves away from her, to the far side of the pile of dirt.

She feels bad. She has hurt her enemy's feelings, and she feels bad. She also feels stupid for feeling bad.

She should not hurt his feelings; she should hurt *him*. She should kill him.

She goes back to digging. Moving closer to him as she works, she says, "I'm sorry."

He looks over at her. Pointing to his hand, she then makes a face. She hopes it is the same expression that conveys regret in his culture. He nods, seems to understand. Or else he is just being agreeable because she is an unpredictable woman who stabs those who try to help her.

They go back to shoveling, and soon the grave is covered up, and she can stop working. She drinks sparingly from her water container even though her throat feels dry enough to cut her if she swallows too hard.

The Vermayan lifts his own bottle and shakes his head. He says something. She has no idea what it means, but then he mimics filling the bottle. He starts to walk off, his walk sure, as if he knows exactly where to look for water on this terrible world.

She watches him go. She wants to lie down in the small shade offered by one of the big pieces of his ship. She wants to fall asleep and never, ever wake up again.

He barks something out to her—it sounds just like the captain ordering her to fire, so she follows him until he slows and waits for her to catch up. He doesn't look at her as they walk, his gaze is fixed on the ground, on the sand that shifts as they move, making her ankle hurt even more.

They walk and walk and the sand turns into something less fluid. Leaning down, he picks up two small stones. He seems to be rolling them in his fingers, as if checking them for smoothness. Then he pops one in his mouth, seems to be rolling it around in there, too.

Does his species eat rocks? He sees her look and smiles, then opens his mouth. The stone is still there. He closes his mouth, goes back to sucking on the rock, motioning for her to do the same. Her enemy wants her to pretend the smooth yellow stone he found is some kind of sucking candy. He is clearly insane, but she slips it in her mouth anyway. They will go insane together.

At first, the rock tastes only of dust and a lifetime spent lying in the sand.

The dirt does not taste green—she wonders what she thinks green should taste like. She swirls the stone around some more and realizes that her mouth is less dry. She looks up at the Vermayan, and he nods, then turns and walks on.

She follows him as he heads down, always down, and she remembers that water is usually in low-lying areas. He still has his shovel, and she realizes she does not have hers, but he did not tell her to bring it. With her broken arm, she is not much of a digger.

The sun beats down on her unmercifully, and she tries to tear off some of her shirt to make a wrap for her head, but she can't do it with one good hand. Grabbing her knife and using her bad hand to hold the fabric, she cuts into it to start the tear. The rest is easy.

He watches her as she wraps the strip around her head, then nods as if she has done something very smart. He is soon wearing his own version of a turban.

She realizes there are no animals on this planet—or none in this area at least. Other than the sound of the relentless wind, there is nothing. No hum of insects, no faraway screech of birds, no rumbling or roaring that would mean something larger. They are alone here. It would be easier to find water if they were not. They could follow the game trails. But there is no game here, no predators. Only the two of them.

They were game to each other just a day ago. Their shiny ships attacked like two great beasts thundering toward fatal collision, fighting until they fell out of the sky.

The Vermayan makes a sound as if he is excited. He rushes to something that looks like any other piece of ground they have covered except that there are more of the short, spiny bushes that seem to be the only form of vegetation. Kneeling, he begins to dig down into the sand with his hands.

The sand is no longer dusty green. Where he has uncovered it, it is a dark, wet green.

She thinks it is the prettiest green she has ever seen.

He stands up, begins to dig with the shovel. He moves quickly, which is good because the water wells up rapidly and then begins to soak back down as soon as he stops digging. Dropping to his knees, he fills his container, motioning for her to hurry.

By the time she has her bottle undone, the water is gone again.

He holds his hand out for her container, and she stiffens. Water is life. More than their useless guns, their knives, even their wits and will to survive. Water is life, and he wants her to give him her only way to hold it.

On the other hand, if he wanted her dead, he could just walk away and leave her to try to dig it up herself. She hands over the container. He begins to dig again with his hands, and as water wells up, he dips her container in, filling it. There is sand in there now too, but she can live with that. Or she can filter it out with more of her shirt.

It occurs to her they will probably need the fabric from the uniforms of their fallen comrades if they are on this world for very long. She knows she could never have taken them, though. Just as well they lie buried, out of reach. She wonders if the Vermayan could have taken them from his crewmates. Studying his face as he digs again, then uses the water to wet his turban, she thinks he probably could not have.

She pulls off her turban, lets it fall into the water. He moves it around for her until it is sopping wet, then hands it back.

It feels blessedly cool when she winds it around her head again, and the sensation of water dripping down her face makes her smile. He pushes the sand back into place, then stands, and she follows him back to the broken ships, to the graves, to the spot where their two lives came together. Whether they wanted them to or not.

Digging around in the wreckage, he pulls out what looks like rations. She does the same, comes up with more than he does—the rations were kept in the back, where she was during the crash. She ran back there to try to get the auxiliary lasers online after the primaries had shorted out. She didn't expect the ship to take that final hit, to virtually ram the Vermayan ship as it, too, reeled out of control. She didn't expect both ships to tumble down until they hit the surface with such terrible force. It was probably only because she was strapped into the padded targeting seat of the auxiliary station that she wasn't crushed like her friends.

She's still not sure she's the lucky one.

They have been on this hideous world for three days now. Their rations are half gone. Their water supply holds up, but only with daily trips to the place the Vermayan first found them water. For two days, he has led them out in other directions, hoping, she thinks, to find an area verdant with plants and not just this endless expanse of green sand and rock. But they have found only more dust, more wind, and no water.

Her arm hurts less now, but it seems to be healing crookedly. She knows if she was rescued today, the medics would re-break it. They did it to her leg when she broke it in training, out in the Doalan woods with her squadron.

She can still remember the sound of bone sliding against bone. There was no pain—they'd given her something to numb that—but that may have made the sound worse. She was not distracted, could focus on it fully. The sound of her bones being split apart then eased back together was the only thing she knew, and her focus gave her an unnatural presence in the now.

She feels that here, on this world. That she is unnaturally present. Water and shade have become her world. There is so little of either, and she feels a sense of panic every time the Vermayan sets out to explore. Why leave this place? Somewhere else is just somewhere not here, and here is safe . . . and somewhere else may not be.

She looks over at the Vermayan. He is dozing in the late afternoon heat. Tomorrow, he will lead her off in the last direction, the one opposite where they found water. He is like that: regimented, disciplined.

She does not think she is that way at all. If he were not here, she would have taken her knife and opened the veins in her wrists. She would have let her life drain away into the sand. Green and red make brown—her blood would have finally turned this awful dirt the right color.

But he barks orders at her in his strange language as if she was a member of his crew, and some follower part in her does not want to disappoint him. He has appointed himself guardian of their safety. She cannot get in the way of that.

He holds out a ration to her—they both prefer his food to hers—and she takes it. Then she realizes the pile they've been working through is gone and tries to hand it back. They are enemies; she should not eat the last of his food.

He pushes it back to her, smiles a bit, and now that she has gotten used to the fierceness of the expression, she finds it comforting.

He says something that sounds like, "Vrenden Kai." His tone is not forceful; he is not ordering her to do something. He points at himself, then says the words again slowly.

His name is Vrenden Kai.

"Sirella Nacleth," she says, pointing to herself.

He nods and closes his eyes again. She wonders what prompted this exchange of identities. They've been together for three days; why does he choose to share now?

She looks at her own pile of dwindling rations and thinks that perhaps he is losing hope. They have one direction left to explore, and unless they find something they can eat, they will starve to death when her rations run out.

She has seen people on hunger strikes, people who were demonstrating against the war back on Doala. They did not die, of course. They collapsed and were taken to the hospital where their generally rich parents paid for private rooms and nutrient supplements. She and Vrenden Kai will not be so lucky. They will not be rescued before hunger closes in. They will die slowly.

Painfully.

She wonders if they would consider killing each other for food. She does not think she would; but she has never been hungry enough to face the question. She doubts Vrenden Kai has been either.

Vrenden Kai. She doesn't know which is his surname. "Vrenden," she says softly and he opens his eyes. "Vrenden?" she asks.

He shakes his head. "Kai."

Kai is his first name. She touches her chest. "Sirella."

"Sirella," he says softly, his harsh voice doing strange things to the vowels. They are less clean in his mouth, less fluid. It is as if he has laid a fine coat of dust over her name. Suh-rull-uh.

He closes his eyes, is asleep quickly. The first night, neither of them slept much. She dozed but was afraid to let go, afraid of what he might do. When she glanced over at him, saw him looking back at her, she realized he was afraid, too. Somehow that made it worse, harder to let go.

The next night, she was too exhausted to care what he did to her. He could have her body, could even kill her. So long as he let her sleep through it, she did not care.

Tonight she thinks they will both sleep deeply again. Exploring this world is exhausting and her whole body aches. Lying on the hard ground is not the relief she might seek if she were back home—or even on the ship—but she is not home, nor on the ship. She is here. On this wasted world. With her mortal enemy who gave her his last ration when he could have kept it for himself.

She studies him while he naps. He looks completely relaxed, but she knows he will get up again just before the sun goes down and lead her to the water, and they will fill their containers and the spare bottle she found in the wreckage of his ship. They will wash the dirt off their faces and drink greedily from the ground. There is not enough water to take a bath. They both smell bad, and she knows they will only get worse. She used to pride herself on her looks, on her long brown hair that was so clean it shone in the sun. It may still shine, but if it does, it is because of the oil and dirt that coat it now. She is filthy but at least she is still alive. She knows that should be worth something.

When they are done with the water, they will walk back to the wreckage in the light of the setting sun and long shadows. As the temperature goes down to something nearly as uncomfortable as the daytime's heat, they will huddle under the emergency blankets that he found in the wreckage of her ship. They would build a fire if they could, put it between them so they could shiver next to warmth. But the spiny shrubs go up like a flash, and there is nothing to sustain the fire. Unless they can find something like real wood, they will have to resign themselves to shivering until dawn comes and the sun rises and the cycle of blasting heat begins again.

She pulls out her knife, sees him stir, then sit up. He is watching her as if he cannot decide why she has unsheathed her weapon, and his hand goes to the place she stabbed, where the skin is healing slowly under his fabric bandage. His eyes are not as hard as they were that first day, but there is something there. Something dark and unsettled, as if he is fighting some demon just by trusting her.

She realizes that he is as afraid of her as she is of him. Even though he was the one to reach out first, he is still afraid. She sets the knife down on the blanket she is using as a cushion and looks at him.

He pulls his dagger out, too. Lying down on his stomach, so his head is closer to her, he moves the dagger so that the golden tracings catch the light. She smiles and he smiles, too.

"Merelven mostic," he says, and she has no idea what it means. He touches the symbols, saying more nonsense words as he goes over each one. She thinks maybe he is trying to tell her a story, or maybe his history is etched into that knife hilt. She waits until he is done, then smiles softly.

He smiles back, the look making it clear he knows she did not understand. "Sirella," he says softly. Then he shakes his head and puts the knife back into its sheath.

He rolls to his back, closing his eyes again. His breathing shifts into that of sleep as she sits and watches him. Playing with her knife, she wonders what stories she could tell him of her life, or of Doala or the Confederation. There is nothing etched onto her knife; the handle is made of some utilitarian blackish material, slightly sticky so that she won't lose her grasp on the weapon if she sweats—or if her hand is covered in blood.

Her hands are already covered in blood. Her crewmates lie below her a short distance away. Buried in a heap, their bodies broken because she missed the shot that should have been easy.

"Sucker shot," the captain said as he'd grinned at her as the Vermayan ship pulled into range.

And it should have been—should have been a sign that their luck had finally turned. A sucker shot—lucky for them, not so lucky for the Vermayans. But it had not been easy at all. The shot went wide.

She missed. She missed, and her friends died, and their blood covers her hands, but this knife will not slip. Ever.

She knows she could move now, one quick burst and she would be over the Vermayan. She could bring the knife flashing down, bury the blade in his body, down low where his kind keep their heart. His eyes would fly open, and he might reach for her hands, try to pull them away. Or he might grab his own dagger and strike out at her. She does not think she would try to stop him if he did.

She looks down at the knife. She should kill him—despite this strange union of desperation, they are enemies. She has a duty to kill him.

She slips the knife back into its holder, then leans against the wreckage and closes her eyes.

As she suspected, sleep comes easily.

Sweat pours into her eyes, and Sirella pulls off the head wrap, wringing it out so that it will again catch some of her perspiration. It feels hotter today than it has the three days before. She wants to sit, but there is no shade, and resting in the sun is barely rest at all. The Vermayan is ahead of her. He seems to have less trouble making headway through the shifting sands, but then his ankle is not hurt.

At first, he did not appear to be injured at all, but she has seen him hold his side, and he has burn marks on his left hand and arm. His right knee is bruised and cut—she noticed it the night before, when he tore off more of his uniform shirt and wet it and used it to fashion a makeshift brace for his knee.

He turns to look back at her, waits for her to catch up. He surprises her by kneeling down and pulling up her pant leg, his hands surprisingly gentle on her swollen ankle. She is not sure what he expects to accomplish, but when he stands back up, he is nodding. "Silvesh." He smiles at her.

She hopes it means "better" and not "infected and about to kill you." Although maybe that would be preferable to slogging around the desert in search of vegetation they can actually eat. The spiny bushes are inedible, and there is nothing else around the immediate crash area.

As they walk on, she scratches her arms; red bumps cover the skin. She has seen no insects on the planet, but something is eating them alive while they sleep. He is covered with the bite marks, too. She scratches harder, and he barks out something as he slaps her fingers away from her skin. "Stop it," is easy to understand in both their languages.

He glares at her, then heads up the rise. The terrain is growing rockier in this direction, and it is growing more interesting in other ways—the rises look like hills, and she sees small clumps of some type of grass growing.

"Kai."

He turns and she points to the grass. He is so focused on leading them ever onward that he missed the grass. He crouches down and studies the shoots, then looks up at her and smiles. "Machrin." It is the same word he uses when he hands her a ration bag. Food. They have found food.

"Not much machrin," she says, motioning to the few clumps, miming picking them, then looking for more.

He nods. Not enough food. He marches on and she follows.

They have become adept at this strange form of sign language. They act things out as if they are both mimes. In a sense, they are; they share no common words. They can talk as much as they want, but they will just be babbling. But their hands and faces and bodies can make pictures, and words and ideas come to life as they play survival charades.

They top the rise, and she gasps in pleasure. On any other world, the sight of a few trees and more of the grass would not be cause for celebration. Here it means food and probably water to spare. They walk to the trees—they are short and spindly like the bushes, too squat to sit under. But they will burn. She touches the bark reverently and looks over at him. "Fire," she says, holding her hands out as if warming them in front of a roaring blaze.

He smiles, holds his hands out, too, obviously looking forward to a night with some warmth. He begins to test the branches, trying to break some off easily. The tree is having none of it. She knows she will do no better one handed. She looks pointedly at his knife, but he pulls out the piece of the captain's weapon that he first identified as a possible cutting tool and begins to work on the branches. Soon, he has sliced through enough to break off some pieces. They leave it in a pile to collect later, and continue to explore.

He leads them to the lowest area and digs for a moment with his hands. The sand is wet. He has not brought his shovel, but it does not matter. Their other water hole is still giving them what they need. But an alternate source for water will be good. They cannot afford to be too dependent on any one thing. She knows it is why he pushes on again, toward some low hills. The grass may be seasonal or may contain little of nutritional value; they need other sources of nourishment.

The low hills turn out to be higher than they appear. There are large rocks clustered at the base, some areas of true shade finally. And some new plants, thick-skinned like succulents she's seen on some of the hotter worlds of the Revirian Confederation. She points to one of the bigger plants, mimes for him to cut a leaf off. He does and quickly turns the leaf upside down so that the fluid inside won't run out. He tastes it, nodding to himself as if giving it the all clear, but she knows the most he can do is determine that it tastes all right. If it is poison, they may not know until he falls ill. But she notes the liquid is clear not milky, something she remembers as being important from the brief survival training the Revirian recruits got. He drinks more of it, then hands the leaf to her.

She drinks it, too. It tastes sweet, an unexpected sensation. Smiling, she hands it back, and he scores the skin and then peels it off, exposing the pulpy flesh. He bites a piece off and chews carefully. Again he nods, as if he is a walking bio lab, and she laughs. At his look, she mimes eating happily until she clutches at her throat as if she can't breathe. He does not laugh, but his lips curl up in an unwilling smile.

He thrusts the leaf at her, pointing and then clutching at his throat. Obviously, he's not going to die alone.

She eats. The flesh is less sweet than the liquid, tangier but still full of fluid. She moans, then hears him laugh at her sound of pleasure. The flesh is surprisingly filling. Her stomach was rumbling earlier, but now she feels good— she supposes the plant's flesh is very rich, hopefully teeming with vitamins and minerals they will need to stay healthy.

He cuts off another leaf, and they share the juice, but she lets him eat the flesh while she sits watching him.

"How did you survive the crash?" she asks.

He looks at her curiously.

She mimes something falling out of the sky, crashing to the ground. Drawing out a rudimentary spaceship in the sand, she then puts a mark near the back, where she would have been sitting. He leans over, puts a mark even farther back and points at himself.

She pretends to crawl into the weapons seat, drawing protective belts around her, pulling the top over her head. She acts out firing a huge weapon, then hitting against the sides of the seat but bouncing back. She tries to convey the idea of padding.

He nods, pretends to fire, too. Then he makes the sound of laser blasts. Bing bing-bing-bing. She laughs. It is too rich. They are the cause of this—they and their bad shots.

She wonders if he thinks his hands are covered with blood, or if he is more accepting of his role in all this.

He pretends to have the target lined up, and she knows it is her ship after she missed the sucker shot. He narrows his eyes, squeezes off the shot. His hand shows the trajectory, straight and straight and then whipped off the side. Another sucker shot wasted.

After they missed each other, there were a few minutes of false peace as both of them scrambled to correct their targeting systems. Then there was nothing but streaks of bright light and the eruptions of damage as the ships battled. The barrage was costly; they lost control, both ships drifting toward each other as the primary systems shorted. That was when she raced for the back, to the auxiliary weapons system. She was about to fire, waiting only for the system to come online, and it did, but too late. She could still feel the impact as the ships collided, could imagine her lasers tearing his ship apart, even as his own secondary lasers probably engulfed her ship.

They fell to the surface like two insects mating.

All because of two bad shots. She looks at him, and he smiles a bit sadly and draws out something around the ship she's marked in the sand. They look like lines of interference—some kind of field, perhaps. She nods. Yes, blame interference. She'd rather not think it was solely her fault that everyone who trusted her is dead.

"Sucker shot," she says, and he looks at her, his eyebrows drawn.

She cannot think how to act out that concept, so she just shakes her head and shrugs.

He finishes the leaf then leans against the rock, enjoying the shade, in no hurry, apparently, to head back. It is getting too late to press onward. She watches the sky, wishing not for the first time that a bird would wheel overhead, or an insect she could actually see would buzz around her. She never thought she'd miss insects.

She wonders why this world has no life. If they walked long enough and far enough, would they run into some other climate zone? One with surface water and animals and noises all day and night from the life around them? Pursing her lips, she closes her eyes, forcing herself to listen as hard as she can. She can hear his easy breathing. She can hear the wind as it whips grains of sand against the rocks. She can hear her own heartbeat if she listens even harder. But nothing else. She relaxes her mouth, realizes that her lips don't hurt, don't even feel as chapped.

She touches them; they feel softer but also a bit numb. As if something in the liquid has made them stop hurting. "Kai?"

He opens his eyes, looks up at her. She awkwardly cuts off a small leaf and reaches for his left hand. He pulls back.

She mimes spreading the liquid on her skin, points to the burns on his arm, then to the gel. Then she touches her lips, breathes out loudly as if in relief.

He slowly extends his arm, and she squeezes out the liquid. He watches her as if he is waiting for her to rub it in. The liquid starts to run off his arm, so she does it even though she feels repelled. He is different than she is in more ways than just his rust coloring. His skin feels tougher, more wizened than hers, but she doesn't know if that is how all Vermayans are or if he has spent too much time in climates like this one.

She can feel his eyes on her as she rubs in the liquid, but she doesn't look up. She hears him sigh and realizes that he must have been in great pain but was hiding it. Pulling her hands away, she studies him. He looks more like her than not. Two arms, two legs, facial features similar if more pronounced on him. His skin might be leathery, but it is still skin. She was taught in training how to kill Vermayans, so she knows that his internal organs differ from hers in function and placement. But the differences are minor. She would have to aim lower to deliver a fatal blow to the heart, aim higher to hit his liver and poison his whole system slowly. But the Vermayans reproduce the same way, eat and eliminate what they eat the same way. They need water and air and sleep to survive. They are not so different. He is not so different.

Especially since he is a shooter, too.

"Sirella?"

She realizes he is looking at her curiously as he eats the pulp of the leaf she cut for him.

"We are enemies," she says, but she is not sure if she is confirming it or questioning it. She knows he is waiting for her to explain, but she does not feel like trying. A question comes to her instead. "Are you alone?"

He cocks his head at her. She draws in the sand again. Simple figures, two tall, one smaller. She pantomimes rocking a baby, and he seems to understand. He points to the tallest figure, nods. Then to the other two and shakes his head. His palm turns upward, a question for her. Is she alone too?

She nods. "Just Sirella."

It seems to translate, because he nods sadly. His face becomes bleak, and he looks away from her.

"Kai?"

He looks back at her, and she is surprised to see anger. He glares at her, and she shrugs helplessly. What has she done?

He points again to the larger of the two figures in the sand and this time says some other name.

"Not Kai?"

He repeats the name. Then he draws in a smaller figure in the arms of one of the adults. He pretends to fire at the drawing, pulling the trigger four times, then he points at her.

She meets his eyes, even though she doesn't want to. Was this a brother? A friend? She sees his anger fade. He shakes his head, as if regretting what he just did. Pushing himself to his feet, he kicks at the dirt, rubbing the picture out altogether.

"Sirella, jarsten." It is clearly an order. One that sounds like, "Let's go."

She pushes herself to her feet and follows him to the pile of wood. Without speaking, he grabs most of the wood and sets off walking, not even looking back to see if she is following. She loads up the rest of the branches, awkward with her one arm in the sling. A piece of wood shifts, almost falls, and she catches it before she drops it. It pokes into her arm; it hurts. She ignores the pain.

Walking slowly, she follows him to their camp. He never looks back at her, and she doesn't even try to catch up.

They've all lost someone in this war. He's not the only one to have friends or family ripped away. She could name some herself, loved ones who've fallen for the cause.

The cause. What is the cause, exactly? When she was on the ship, it was so easy to believe in all the reasons that the Vermayans were evil, why they had to be stopped. But here, on this world so harsh that everything is scrubbed down to the most basic level, it is difficult to remember why they are fighting.

He is waiting for her when she trudges into camp. Taking the wood from her, he piles it near the rest, within arm's reach of their sleeping area. She sees he has laid the fire, has put the wood on the bottom, spiny fast burning bush on the top. All it needs is to be lit. It will be a great fire.

He is watching her, his eyes sad.

She points to the fire he has readied and tries to smile. "Good."

He nods, repeats it back, "Good," as if seeking connection. Then he picks up their water bottles and heads for their usual digging hole.

For the first time, she does not follow him.

He does not seem to care.

The fire crackles, and Sirella watches as Kai lies with his eyes closed, pretending to sleep. She knows he is pretending because his breathing is too soft. She has heard his almost snores since the second night, when they had both finally relaxed enough to sleep. She heard them and registered the strange, soft noises—realized they came from him and not from someone or something trying to sneak up on them in the dark of night—before falling back to sleep.

"Kai?" The word is a whisper. She is not sure what she wants to say to him. Just that she should say something.

His breathing stutters, but he does not open his eyes.

"I'm sorry." She looks away from him. She is sorry. But she does not know who the people he lost were. She does not know if they were innocents or not. She does not know why they died, only that someone from her side killed them. She wishes he had not lost people he loved. But he would have died if her shot had not flown so damned wide. And then what? Would some other Vermayan have sat with some other person from one of the nations that make up the Revirian Confederation, and drawn out in strangely colored sand how Vrenden Kai was killed?

Vrenden Kai would have killed her if his shot hadn't also gone wide.

They are in the middle of a war. Killing is part of that. She cannot feel bad about it.

She must not feel bad about it.

She feels bad about it.

"Sirella?" Kai has turned over, is staring at her, and she wonders how long he has been watching her.

"I've lost people, too, you know?" Her tone is as abrasive as the sand-laden wind.

He frowns. He does not understand her, and she will not act it out for him. She is tired of this, tired of drawing in the sand or playing charades. She wants to talk, wants to laugh at a joke, or cry at a sad story. One she understands in words—not one drawn in the sand by her enemy.

She rubs at her eyes, forcing the tears back. She does not want to weep over his tragedy. Or that she is stuck here with him. Or that she missed such a damned easy shot. Why didn't she check for interference?

Why didn't he?

Why are they alive when no one else is?

He sits up and stares at her, and his dark eyes seem even blacker in the night. She can see the fire reflected in them. He adds more wood to the fire, and the flames flare up, in his eyes and between them.

"Good," he says, using her word and trying a small smile on her.

She wonders if he understands what she was conveying with the word, or is he just seeking to reconnect with her. With the only other living thing on this awful world?

"Good," she says, trying to smile, too, but she can feel that the expression is forced.

She does not want to be here with him. Somehow, the fire is making it worse instead of better. It reminds her of all the things she has lost, is bringing up memories that razing wind and green dust could never evoke. She can see the fire in her brother Cahl's large oven, the one he uses to make bread every morning for his restaurant. She wonders if he thinks she is dead, if Confederation officials informed him of the tragedy out in the wasteland. Maybe he's grieving and making bread in his fiery oven for some post-funeral meal.

She can see flames flaring in a fire pit on the vacation world of Scaloth. She imagines her and Justina's friend Moren crouching down by the pit, warming his hands as he stares out at the sea. He will cry for them. He is sensitive and soft, and she loves him for that. He opposed the war, begged them not to go, to stay on Scaloth with him and let the ship go on without them.

Justina laughed at him; she loved the ship too much. Sirella was tempted to stay on Scaloth, but she knew that Justina would always be first in Moren's heart. He might take Sirella as second best, but would she want to be that for him? Not that she loved him, or at least not that way. But she didn't want to be anyone's consolation prize.

Right now, being a consolation prize on that beautiful, soft world with that beautiful, soft boy sounds wonderful.

"Sirella?" Kai's rust skin looks bronze and hard and alien in the firelight, and she looks away. She does not want grizzled bronze. She wants soft yellow skin like her own. She wants Moren's or Cahl's, or anyone's but Kai's.

She turns away, more to stop the flow of hurtful words she can feel welling up in her than because she cannot face him. She can taste the bitter things that are fighting for release into the air between them, things that she'll never be able to take back even if he understands nothing she says.

He will understand the tone. He will understand the look on her face. He will understand hatred. Anger.

And loneliness. Sheer, wrenching loneliness caused by his beautiful, roaring fire.

She holds her hand out to the flames, closer and closer and then in them. The fire burns, and she clenches her teeth to stop a cry of pain from escaping. She will feel this—she will feel this instead of all the other things she is afraid to feel.

Kai grabs her wrist, pulling her hand out of the flames. Her skin is red but was not in the heat long enough to burn badly. "Basla?" His eyes are confused. And worried.

She does not need a translator for that. "Why?" he asks her. And she has no answer other than that she is a coward and a failure and his enemy.

He touches her hand gently, looking at her quizzically as if checking her reaction. She hisses as he hits the part of her palm that took the brunt of the heat, and he pulls his fingers away. Shaking his head, he lets her hand go. But she notices he is watching her carefully, as if to make sure she will not do it again.

She studies her palm, touching the red area until he frowns at the way she is poking it. He says the thing he said to her when she was scratching the insect bites. His voice holds impatience but also worry.

She holds her hand up, palm facing him. "It hurts," she says, as if that is a good thing. As if it will be a focus now, one that can take the pain and anger and fear that might have come out of her in cruel and cutting words, and transmute the bad things into something good. Something the two of them can use to survive.

She feels stronger; the pain makes her feel stronger.

He holds up his left hand, lays the back of it against her palm, his burn against hers. His skin is cooler than hers, and it feels good against the raw flesh. She looks at him, feels tears begin again. He reaches out with his right hand, as if he will wipe her tears away, and she shakes her head.

His hand stops midway to her.

"Don't." She is holding herself together with only the pain from the flames. His touch, if it is gentle and sweet and forgiving, will undo her, will send her into some place she does not want to explore.

He drops his hand.

"I'm sorry," she says, pulling her hand away from his.

He does not say anything, just looks away and puts more wood on the fire.

She lies down, staring into the fire until the flickering of the flames puts her into some other state and she can finally look at him again. He is sitting up, watching her as she rests.

Watching over her.

The gentleness of his expression threatens to destroy the control that pain gives her. She stares back at the flames until she can finally close her eyes and go to sleep.

Sirella wakes and stretches, immediately regretting the move as her back threatens to cramp. The sun burns down brightly, pushing away the coldness of night, making it difficult to feel the sadness that overwhelmed her in the dark. Her hand throbs where she burned it, but she holds on to that pain for it is the feel of survival, the pain of getting on with life. Her skin may burn, but it is no hotter than the sun beating down on her, than the winds that blow as always.

"Sirella."

She turns. Kai is there, holding several of the succulent's leaves. She did not realize he wasn't in the camp, wonders how long he has been gone.

He says something long and complicated, his face concerned. She thinks it is a lecture on keeping her spirits up, a lecture he is giving her because she has not reached for a leaf. She takes one of them from him, squeezing the juice onto her hand. The relief is immediate, the scorched feeling replaced with wonderful numbness. She wonders where loneliness and bitterness are located, wishes she could pour the juice on them, too.

Kai turns away, grabbing her water container and the spare. He already has his looped over his shoulder. She notices his water is half gone. He looks at her curiously, as if unsure whether she will want to accompany him after not going the day before. Nodding, she motions for him to walk on. She keeps up with him this time, her ankle no longer hurting as much as it did. Her arm still throbs when she forgets herself and turns it the wrong way—she keeps the sling on just to remind herself not to overdo.

The winds whip even more strongly, and she turns to look back the way they came. Their tracks are already blown away in a frenzy of small green cyclones. She is glad they know the way back by heart.

Kai sighs and rubs at his eyes. She notices they are red and watering. He is more sensitive to the gritty winds than she is. He will rinse his eyes when they get to the watering hole. And for a few minutes, while he kneels low to the ground and rests his eyes, he will be at peace. But as soon as they start back, his eyes will begin to water again. She has seen it happen for five days now.

She watches him as he walks, judging whether his knee is hurting him. He is walking fine, and she thinks his knee is better, that his injury inside it was much more mild than the cut on top of it.

He seems to sense her eyes on him, glances over. Rubbing at his eyes again, he makes a face. She tells him to stop it in his language—she's heard that word enough to learn it. He smiles.

She pats her knee, then points to his, hand turned up as she shrugs to ask him how it is. He nods, his smile grows. It is fine. It is good. She motions to her side, points at his. He makes a face, dismissing her concern. She decides if he had internal injuries, they would know it by now.

She can tell by his walk that he feels good, that his body is strong and not hurting. But she can also see tiredness in the way his eyes seem to be extra sensitive to the blowing grit, in the way he yawns repeatedly as they walk. How long did he keep watch over her?

He looks at her again, another question in his expression. She points to him, makes their sign for sleep. He rolls his eyes—a gesture he picked up from her—and she laughs. She is not sure what it means to him, but it amuses her that he probably intends something sarcastic. That it is her fault he is tired, perhaps? That he does not know what she expects him to do? Does she think he will sleep during the day when he should be working to ensure their survival?

Still grinning, she stops inspecting him, secure that he is in better shape than she is. The juice is starting to wear off, and she wishes they had a way to make it more portable. Maybe she can find another container in the wreckage. Even something small would be sufficient.

Kai says something and she looks up. He is pointing up, his face pinched as he tries to see. She follows his gaze, realizes a ship is coming down to the surface.

It is one of hers.

He realizes it too. Glancing at her, he takes a step back. "Sirella, kosha."

She wonders if that is the word for home. "Kai . . ." She is not sure what else there is to say.

The ship is Revirian; he is not. This is very simple. He is a Vermayan, her enemy. And now he is her prisoner.

He looks at her. His hand slips down, to his knife, but he does not pull it out. "Sirella?"

She feels her throat lock up. How do her people treat prisoners? It is not something she has ever had to ponder. It was her job to shoot, so she shot, and ships either blew up, crashed if they were in a planet's pull, or they were disabled, floating in space until boarding parties loaded those aboard into detainment shuttles and sent them on their way.

On their way to where? Where will they send Kai?

"Sirella?"

She hears the sound of metal sliding on leather; he has pulled his knife from the sheath. She turns, sees his eyes. They are black and empty for a moment, as if he could really do it, could bring his knife, which he has raised so high, down and down and into her flesh.

She cannot move for a moment, stops breathing and just waits. It is only fair, really; she stabbed him first. She meets his eyes, sees them change, the darkness in them giving way to something sad and hurt and unsure. He stares at her, blinking as water streams from his eyes. Then he smiles. A frightened and slightly apologetic smile.

She inhales; the hot air feels good suddenly. The dust against her face feels good too. She does not want to die. That fact surprises her.

Maybe it is just that she does not want to die at his hands?

He sighs, and looks up at the ship. His expression is one of grim resignation. He mimes a sign for captive, his hands held in front of him as if tied.

She shakes her head. "No. I go. You stay." She makes a sign for hiding, which is stupid because there is no where to hide here. If she hurries back to the site, she can beat the ship down. She can say she was the only survivor. She turns to go.

"Sirella," he says, and she turns. "Water." He has learned the word from her.

And he is right. She will need one of the bottles to keep her story up. He tries to hand her the spare, but she shakes her head. He will need it more.

She looks up, the ship is in slow descent—the winds must be making it hard to stay level. And, of course, there is no need for it to hurry. She imagines her people expect to find only bodies and wreckage. She wonders if Kai's people are also on their way.

He turns his knife, holds it carefully by the blade, offering it to her. "Pa Sirella."

She is about to refuse it, but something in his eyes tells her she should not. She pulls her own knife out, hands it to him. "It has no stories. It has no past. Nothing but your blood."

He doesn't seem to want her to try to act out what she has said, just nods and sticks the weapon in his sheath. The knife is a little too big, sticks out more than it should, but he smiles as if it is a perfect fit. "Derne Sirella."

She shoves his knife down into her sheath where it fits with room to spare. She touches the gold tracings, then looks up at him. "Goodbye, Kai." Now her eyes are watering.

He holds his hand out to her, and she takes it. Her burned palm protests as he clasps her hand tightly, but she does not try to pull away. He says something with many words and in a voice so soft she can barely make out the tone. Then he lets go of her hand and lopes off into the burning desert, away from the camp.

He will be fine. She must not worry. He has been the one who kept them alive. He will be fine.

She turns and walks back to camp as fast as her hurt ankle will let her.

She has enough time to hide any evidence of Kai, to make it look like she has used all the blankets, to be sitting on the pile of them, watching as any lingering footprints disappear from the green sand—the rush of air the ship is bringing up as it lands is finishing what the winds started.

Kai will be fine. He's a survivor. She must not worry about him.

Her people are here. She can go home. Or at least be with her own kind and talk and laugh and probably cry a little.

Isn't that what she wanted?

The ship is landing, and she recognizes the type. A search and salvage shuttle—they will be here for a while. She will just have to make sure they don't head toward Kai and the watering hole.

He will have no blankets at night. How will he stay warm?

He will find a way. It is immaterial now. The door is opening, and an officer who outranks her twice over is stepping out. He looks startled to see her.

She forces herself to her feet, stands at attention. "Lieutenant Sirella Nacleth, sir!" Her posture is perfect, her salute regulation, her voice that of the well-trained soldier. She is Doalan, after all; they are known for their soldiering skills. Loyal, brave, cognizant of their duty.

She would never let a prisoner escape. She would never give succor to the enemy.

"Captain Rejehr." He gives her a pleased look. "At ease, Lieutenant. We didn't expect to find anyone alive."

"I'm the only one, sir." She manages to put everything that means into her voice. Sorrow. Guilt. Loneliness. Fear.

He walks closer to her, wrinkles his nose. He is Doalan, too—the epitome of fastidious. "There's a shower in the ship, Lieutenant. Go use it."

"Yes, sir." She does not want to go; she wants to stay and make sure they don't find any trace of Kai.

"Now, Lieutenant."

She nods, heads to the ship where another officer is stepping out. As she passes her, she sees her make a face at the smell.

"Nacleth?" Rejehr says.

"Sir?" She turns, afraid he will hold up some personal item of Kai's.

He is not holding up anything, he is merely staring at her, a strange look on his face. "You buried their dead, too?"

"They were starting to smell, sir."

He nods; that is easy to understand.

Sirella turns back, tries to give the other officer a wide berth. "Shower?"

The woman smiles. "Come on. I'll take you. I'm Commander Trabeli." Leading her down the hallway, she takes Sirella past other crew working to make the shuttle ready for lift-off, past the salvage crew gearing up to take anything of use from what is left of the two ships. "You must have been through hell, Lieutenant."

"Yes, sir."

"Well, you're back among the living now." Trabeli smiles again, the expression true and generous.

Sirella is touched. Her people, her language, her life. All back. "Thank you, sir."

Trabeli looks out toward the grave Sirella filled with Kai's help. "All those people dead. And you had to bury them? With a broken arm?"

Sirella nods. "I was in shock."

"I believe that." The woman's expression clears, and she goes to a storage cabinet and pulls out a pair of coveralls. "Not an officer's uniform, but it will have to do. Go get cleaned up and then ask someone to take you to the mess."

"Thank you, sir."

She waits for Trabeli to walk away, then ducks into the shower. Dialing for cool water, she lets it hit her body for a long time before using the cleanser to scrub the dirt off. The water as it drains is green, and she scrubs harder, working at her skin until the water finally runs clear. Then she turns off the shower and gets out, staring at herself in the mirror. Her skin is darker, burned brownish-red from the harsh sun. Her nose is red and her lips chapped. There are dark circles under her eyes, and her skin is so dry that she looks older. Much older.

She touches her skin, finds some lotion in the bathroom and spreads it on. Hearing a yell from outside, she feels a shiver go down her spine. They didn't find Kai, they couldn't have. He stayed away, surely?

She pulls on the coveralls, not bothering to comb her hair as she rushes out. There is no sign of Kai. Only a few of the salvage crew, whooping over something they've found in the Vermayan wreckage. Trabeli looks at her curiously as she stands in the entrance, and Sirella realizes she has started to shake.

"Go get some food and sit down before you fall down, Lieutenant. That's an order."

Sirella turns back into the ship, finds her uniform and shoves it into a refuse chute. She buckles the knife around her waist. Let them ask her about the dagger. She will say she needed a replacement for her own, and one of the dead Vermayans was wearing this one. It was pretty and very sharp. It was only efficient to take it.

And greedy. They'll think she's a little greedy to have stolen it from one of the enemy dead. But greed's allowed when it is also efficient. She is not so sure they would understand her saving a Vermayan from the grave—or from them—even though that too was efficient. He was her only chance for survival. And later she owed him her life.

She doubts they will care. She would not in their position. So she will not tell them. They can all rest easy—she with her secret, they with their ignorance.

Sirella sits in the back of the shuttle and watches as the surface drops away. They have been on the moon—she was right, it was only a moon—for barely more than a day. The salvage team was quick and there was little to take back.

They dock with the larger ship—the captain's true command. She sees the numbers on it. Revirians don't name their ships as she knows Vermayans do.

Rejehr invites her to the bridge, and she stands behind his chair as they start to pull away from the moon, ready to make their way across the wasteland.

Trabeli is the pilot, which surprises Sirella for some reason. She frowns slightly, watching something in the screen at her station. "Incoming ship," she finally says.

The ensign at tactical confirms. "It's Vermayan."

Kai's ride home has arrived.

Rejehr leans forward. "Ready weapons."

"Weapons ready," the ensign says.

Sirella walks over to him. Watches as he does exactly what she did. "Sucker shot," she says under her breath.

"The enemy is charging weapons, sir."

She can see it all over again. Her ship will shoot and they will miss. Then the Vermayan will shoot and they will miss, too. And then, while they try to reconfigure their sensors to compensate for the interference, they will drift dangerously close. The shots, when they come, will be too much, the damage too heavy. They will crash; they will die.

She thinks she should just head for the auxiliary station now. Belt herself in and wait to see if she can survive a second crash from her padded cell.

Trabeli looks over at her. "Just like old times?" Her grin is sympathetic. She has told Sirella that she's been approved for leave as soon as they make it back to Revirian-controlled space, probably did not want Sirella to see combat this soon after trauma.

"Just like old times," Sirella says.

The ships will collide, they will crash, and all these people—these fellow Revirians who are just trying to fight the best war they can—will die. And so will all those Vermayans.

She leans over the tactical officer, begins to compensate for the interference.

"What are you doing?" he asks.

"Giving us all a chance," she mutters as she looks over at Rejehr. "Fire?" she asks, knowing she is completely out of line taking over this way.

"Fire," Rejehr says, obviously not caring any more than Sirella does about protocol. But then he and Trabeli have heard her story of what happened on that other ship.

Her shot strafes along the side of the Vermayan ship. They fire back but miss by a wide margin.

"Interference," Sirella says, and hears the ensign make a sound of understanding. She compensates again, her fingers working fast enough that she thinks the younger man can't follow what she is doing. "Fire," she tells him.

He fires. The shots strafe the other side. She thinks that the damage looks worse than it is, but she hopes that the tactical officer won't realize that.

He doesn't. "Good shot."

She laughs softly. "Lucky shot." Turning to the captain, she says, "Still too much interference to get a good shot, sir. I'll try again."

"No need," he says, pointing to the screen with a disappointed look.

Kai's ride is running away.

"Shall we pursue?" Trabeli asks.

"No. Let's go home." Rejehr looks over at her. "Is that the right answer, Lieutenant?"

She tries to smile; she should be eager to go home. "Sir, yes, sir." She watches the Vermayan ship disappear. "Do you think they'll be back?"

"Why would they? They must know we got everything of value off the planet." The captain is already programming something into a data module. Probably a report of the encounter. She wonders how he'll write up her role. "There's nothing on that planet they'll want."

She doesn't argue, suddenly is overcome with tiredness.

Trabeli looks over at the lieutenant at comms and says softly, "Why don't you show Lieutenant Nacleth to guest quarters?"

He gets up and leads her through the ship, to the habitat area. Her room is small, but she doesn't mind. It is hers. And she can be alone.

The way Kai is alone now. Alone with all the dead—his and hers. The Revirian dead weren't worth salvaging. It's a pragmatic thing; they were buried after all. Never mind that they lay one on top of the other, or that strange green dirt filled their noses and mouths and eyes.

They have left their dead behind. She does not think the Vermayans will do that. Any people that carve stories on their knife handles will go back for their dead. Maybe they'll wait until they are sure it is safe, or until they fix the damage she did to their ship, but they'll go back. They'll go back, and Kai will be safe.

It's a fantasy; she knows that. But it's the only one she has to hold onto.

The little skiff bucks in the harsh atmosphere of the moon. Sirella knew when she rented it that it would be a handful, but she took it because the owner was one of the few people interested in loaning his ship out for a joyride to the wasteland. She holds onto the controls, is jerked a bit from side to side.

Her arm barely twinges at the motion. The medics did have to re-break it. The sound was just as bad as that time on Doala. The pain reminded her of Kai.

The ship finally touches down, near their camp. She rushes out, yelling for him.

He is not there.

She checks the camp, sees that the blanket she hid for him when Rejehr and the others weren't looking is spread out in their sleeping area.

He was here. He must have made his way back as soon as the Revirian shuttle took off. Did he sense his ship up there in the sky beyond his ability to see? Did he know that she saved and doomed him both?

"Kai?" She screams it, then breathes in too deeply, her mouth filling with the green dust she hoped never to see again. She forces herself to breathe shallowly.

There is no answer. She walks to the water hole, afraid that she will find him dead. He is not there. She walks to the place where they found the succulents. He is not there, either. She tries using the scanner on the skiff, but the dust and winds block anything more than a few meters away.

Night falls and she beds down in the skiff. She has to believe his ship came for him. Even if the Vermayan dead are still in their grave, his ship still came. She can't find Kai because he is not here. He is home. Safe. Happy.

She sleeps fitfully, waking at each change of the wind, thinking it is him. She cannot stay here long. Her leave is short. She has a new assignment: tactical officer on Rejehr's ship. He was impressed with her, and the ensign was due to transfer off, anyway.

When morning comes, she walks back to their watering hole, digs down and dunks her hands in the rapidly retreating water. She closes her eyes, tries to block out the sun and the wind and the harsh loneliness that fills her.

Kai was not her life. Kai was her enemy. They were thrown together by circumstance. They looked out for each other, that was all. She saved him because she owed him. Not because she was his friend. Not because she liked him.

He is the enemy.

Pushing herself to her feet, she walks slowly back to the camp. Kai will know that she was worried about him. Kai will know that she would come back to look for him. She does not know why she believes that, but it is a certainty, an in-her-gut knowledge that won't be denied.

Kai will know she has come back for him.

She takes his knife and a piece of material from the inside of his ship. It is soft enough to score, and she carves the number of her ship into it. Then she pins the message through the blanket and to the ground with the dagger.

With a last look around, she smiles. This part of her life is over. It is time to rejoin the living. Time to rejoin her own people.

Time to rejoin the war.

She flies the little skiff back, barely making it into the docking ring before the engines give out. The owner yells at her about damage and green dust wearing delicate systems down, but she pays him and leaves, ignoring his whining as if he was speaking Vermayan.

She reports to her new ship the next day, settles in to a routine that seems strangely easy. Life on that moon was hard. She cannot turn on a water faucet without thinking about digging for water. She eats the meals in the mess with far more gusto than anyone else, remembering when plant pulp was the only delicacy to look forward to. And she talks to her crewmates in ways she never did when she and Justina traveled in that other ship.

People are precious. Communion is precious. Life is precious.

Which does not stop her from taking it. War does not end just because she thinks life is precious. After she destroys a Vermayan warship, the first thing she does when she gets off duty is throw up. Over and over and over again.

The second thing she does is cry. What if that was Kai's ship?

In time, she does not cry any longer. She has to believe he is okay.

She is off duty now. Walking with Trabeli to the habitat area when a courier drops a package in her hands. She shrugs at Trabeli's look, but is unwilling to open it in front of her because, while the package is addressed to her, her name is spelled strangely, as if by someone who has sounded it out.

Trabeli just smiles knowingly and leaves her alone. Sirella locks the door and unwraps the package with shaking hands.

It is her knife. And wrapped around it is a piece of paper with the name "Morascan" on it.

She looks it up in the database. It is not one of the ships that has been obliterated by the Revirian fleet. She knows from memory which Vermayan ships she has destroyed.

There is something else written under the name of the ship. In a careful hand, in a strange, stilted form of Doalan, as if he looked each word up in the dictionary and laid them out according to Vermayan logic, Kai had written. "The war lasts not forever. Meet when over on world of green."

She smiles. They will meet on the dusty green moon when this is over. And she will take a Vermayan-Doalan dictionary with her.

Now all she has to do is stay alive until then. She feels sorry for the Vermayans that come up against her ship. She feels just as sorry for any of the

Revirian fleet who take on the Morascan. Both she and Kai have something to fight for.

Not a cause. Not something abstract. They have something to fight for that actually makes sense.

She smiles. Once again, he has found a way to ensure their survival. She soaks the paper in her sink until it disintegrates—there must be no record.

Picking up her knife and pulling the sheath out of the closet, she slides the dagger home and buckles the holder around her waist. It looks right there, and her hand goes down to touch it for comfort before she goes to join the others in the mess.

Trabeli eyes her knife as she walks up. "Is that what was in the package?"

Sirella nods. She told her that she lost the Vermayan one on leave. Trabeli didn't question it, was sympathetic at her loss of such a fine trophy.

"Not as special as your last one."

"Not as pretty." Sirella touches the black handle gently. "But still special."

Acid Rain Rocks
by Hazel Dixon

The white speck streaked across the turquoise sky and faded into the vastness of the firmament. Alone. Just me, my collection of large tin boxes and the wide plain. There was nothing to mar the unbroken plain, no trees, no green of any sort, just beige in lighter or darker shades. Nothing moved. No wind, no sound save my own breathing and that of my feet. The ground was not just dry, it was baked and cracked into a hard cobbled surface not the type to create dust; the rounded cobbles compacted under the weight of my boots with each step I took.

The contents of the boxes were a mystery; they were all marked with obscure stenciled codes. I took a guess that my new home would be in some of the larger ones. I found the roof and all four walls before the floor; I knew it was the floor because it said so and had "place on base" stenciled on it. The nearest thing to a base I had were the pontoons that the boxes had been floated down on.

I had half my new home built by that first nightfall. I spent that night huddled within a circle of my boxes with a couple of pieces of the yet to be constructed wall as a roof hoping the work I had done would not collapse in the dark. I did not want to use fuel for heating so it was cold and uncomfortable, but sleeping, cocooned in the parachutes, in the thin air was not difficult; I was tired.

For my first breakfast I had the luxury of real eggs, two of them, on toast. Then it was back to the building. The roof proved to be the most difficult, until I mastered tying a rope through a couple of the fixing points then throwing the rope over my house, hauling the roof piece up then anchoring it by fastening the rope to some of the heavier boxes which freed me to clamber up and bolt the roofing piece in place. That night I slept in a bed made from an upturned box, the parachutes and a sleeping bag. It was questionable which was the comfier, the bed or the ground from the night before.

I was light-headed the next morning. Sometime during the night my supplementary oxygen had run out. There was enough oxygen in the air to breathe but not quite as much as the human body was used to. And the gravity at only three quarters of what I was accustomed to had interesting effects too. I spent that second day putting the finishing touches to my home. I had been provided with kits for a rudimentary table and chair, a basic kitchen, waste and water recycling plants, a small generator and enough supplies to last three months. Ideally the shuttle would return at the end of each month to collect my work and resupply me. It only took a quick inventory of my supplies for me to know just how frugally I would have to live.

I was also aware that being resupplied depended upon me having done the work and enough of it, so I began my appointed task. Using my hut as a center point I walked ten meters due north then took surface samples every ten degrees from north, bagging and labeling as I went, then marked the spot with a circle of spray paint. Each sample looked consistent: granular once extracted from the irregular shaped formations and the same shade of beige. I had not been supplied with any tools other than those with which I could make the most basic observations.

There was no moisture in the air yet fine white clouds gathered over the distant hills throughout the day. Once the giant orange sun dropped behind the horizon, night fell rapidly. It was cold, dark with only unfamiliar stars and eerie silence for company. I decided not to waste fuel by burning it for light once I had dined on a hot meal and so retired for the night. This was to become the pattern for my days.

By the end of the month I had completed a 360 degree circle around my hut, I had seen no other living thing but occasionally I had come across a trail in the ground as if something heavy enough to crush the tops of the cobbles had been dragged over them. They led nowhere and stopped abruptly without any visible reason or object that could have been used to make them. But who would make them and for what purpose? Granted it was unlikely that I was the only person on the planet, but for as far as I could see in any direction I was alone in this bowl shaped valley.

Two weeks after my arrival the shuttle returned, in advance of its schedule as I knew it, and in exchange for the sample collection left me with a small corer and rig and supplies for a further two months. I also had been given new instructions: subsurface samples from the same spots as the previous samples had been taken from, (now the instruction to mark them became understandable), to a depth of three meters.

And still those clouds rolled over the distant hills, growing ever more in number and depth of grey but without spilling a drop of moisture on the ground below, as far as I could tell.

The equipment was cumbersome so I packed it in one box and dragged it those 10m to the north. The box left a wide, clear trail in the otherwise unmarked ground; it was like someone had flattened the tops of each of the small cobbles to make a narrow road, like a wider, deeper version of those I had come across previously.

The first three core samples had an almost identical appearance to the naked eye, granular in construction getting more compact with depth and a constant beige in color. The fourth was more interesting; there was a slight deepening in color just below the three-meter mark. I had gone deeper than I should have; I'd been watching the increasing greyness of the clouds and way they rolled as if a storm wind was stirring them instead of the gauges. I decided to go on to the six-meter mark. On a whim I split the sample and kept the second half, all correctly labeled, for later. Each night I left the equipment at the last bore site and carried the collected samples home; it had not taken long for me to come to think of that crude metal hut as home.

The sixth sample contained a distinctly darker, less granular layer at the 3.5-meter mark that looked as if it could be a layer of silt. But there was no water that I knew of anywhere near here. I prepared the top three meters of these samples for collection and kept the second sections with the deeper sample I had accidentally taken. Due to the time it took to reach that depth these were the only three six-meter samples I collected at that time and each one had that curious darker layer in them.

As I neared the southern portion of my sample circle I came across more of these trails: whatever had made them had been traveling in relatively straight lines but as to exactly what or who it was I had no clue.

Upon my return to the nineteenth sample bore I found it blocked by the first true stone I had seen. I knew the hole had not been blocked when I had left the day before but there it was wedged in the top of the bore. I fished the stone out, collected my equipment and continued on to the next marker. The stone was still in my pocket when I returned home. I sat it on my table, got on with the task of logging the samples then ate a simple meal. As darkness had fallen I lit a candle so I could have some light to complete my ablutions. I could not remember just how near the stone the candle was when I lit it but the stone was right next to it when I came to snuff the candle out.

That was the night I first heard the scratching, like little scuttling feet dragging something around. The next morning I discovered my pen on the floor and put the noises down to that, but I could not account for how or why it should have moved. Each night the scuttling continued, sometimes in the mornings I would find something had moved—my empty mug, a few papers—

yet never to the point where I could be positive I had not imagined it; I knew I was feeling the effects of working in the new atmosphere and those of my meager diet, until the day I found the scorch mark on the table top. That had most definitely not been there when I had retired. It had the appearance of an irregularly shaped acid burn that had eaten through the corner of some papers I had left out and down into the wood. I had not spilt anything; I had no acid.

By the time I had completed the second traversing of the sample circle, fingers of cloud had begun to stretch across the open spaces above my home: the initial thin whips that marred the perfect blue were thickening as the shuttle put in an appearance. They took my samples and left new supplies and orders; cores of subsurface materials to the depth of six meters to be collected from all previous sample sites.

I was dreaming in green, of green grass and green leafed trees, when a loud clatter woke me. It had come from inside my hut. And I was the only one there. I lit a candle then the proper lights. Having made a thorough search I concluded that I was alone, just me and my rock, which sat on the table. My tin mug however was lying on the floor in a small pool created by the very last dregs of coffee. I made sure the door was secure, returned my mug to the table and went back to my now ellusive dreams.

I had left the boxed rig at the northern most collection point. There were several new trails heading in straight lines either to or away from the hills. They were most definitely new as they traversed the marks my own boots had left the day before but again they seemed to begin and end without visible cause. The only difference was that the formation at the end of the trail was slightly deeper into the ground than those around it, and one trail started with a hole.

The clouds over the distant ring of hills were truly rolling and there was a faint smell of lemon drops in the air as the depth gauge neared the six-meter mark. Acting upon a whim I decided to continue drilling to the nine-meter mark. By the time I had completed the third sample the hills had turned dark brown. As the ground was softer here than further south, I managed to collect two additional samples that day and was dragging them home as the tide of brown crept from the foothills and onto the plain. The aroma of fresh lemon drops had also increased.

I had taken the sample cores into my hut when the first large drops of rain landed on the parched ground. I left the parachute I had used to drag the samples back where it was and closed the door. Darkness came even swifter that day; for the remainder of it I prepared the samples, stored the extra cores and then dined. I had become accustomed to the hiss of the storm when I detected a scraping sound, as if someone or something was pressing against the wall of my hut as it slowly moved along it. The sound seemed to come from low to the ground, so I put it down to a condition of the storm and stayed encased within the warmth of my sleeping bag.

The crack of something landing on the floor of my hut startled me from sleep. Somehow my rock had fallen from its usual place on my table, I left it there, blew out the candle once more and went back to sleep.

As I had breakfast I pondered upon the appearance of a second scorch mark, this time on the floor of my home and in close proximity to the table. My rock, I discovered, had some how managed to roll under my chair.

The storm had not truly reached me; just a scattering of heavy drops had come this far and had stained the ground a dark brown. As I toured the exterior of my home I followed a trail of crushed earth; this had most definitely not been there before, but just like before it ended suddenly without revealing its creator. The parachute was where I had left it; as I was gathering it up I noticed it had worn, or so I at first thought, into holes in a number of places. It was as I inspected the holes that I realized they looked more like something had eaten through the material. I did not gather samples that day; the line of darkness swept across the plain bringing with it a haze of low-lying lemon drop scented fog.

From my doorway I watched the rain devour the parachute then turn the ground into a heaving quagmire that gave off clouds of vapour. My nostrils stung from the effects of it. I closed the door and prayed to whatever gods or demons were in charge for my roof to remain intact. I was marooned for three days.

I gifted my world a day to dry out then, on the fourth, I ventured out. The distant hills had taken on a strange orange glow as if someone had dusted them with rust. Patches of lichens had sprung up everywhere. I collected some and left them on my table while I went to inspect my home for damage. The instructional labels, "wall" etc, had been stripped off my home as had the paint on the supply boxes I had left outside. Fortunately none of the goods in them had been reached and so contaminated by the rain.

The mysterious trails were everywhere; one cut a bare swath partway through a patch of lichens then stopped dead in nothing more than a perfect circle. As I circumnavigated my home I found a large stone had become wedged into the corner created by the output pipe and the external part of the waste recycling plant where the makeup of it created a small overhang. Other than the things I had brought with me the rock was the largest object I had seen so far in my time there. This stone's presence elucidated the scraping sounds, I concluded. I dislodged the stone and went inside.

My rock was sitting on my table but the samples of lichen were nowhere to be found. It was while I was searching for them that I noticed a faint pinkish red line around the base of my rock. The only explanation I had was that this was where it had come into contact with the floor when it had fallen. I collected several more samples of the lichen, but the lichen disintegrated soon after collection, or so it appeared. That fine line expanded around the flattish base of my rock over the next few days, then began to traverse up its center line. As the line neared the base again, I went in search of the stone I had freed, but it was nowhere to be seen. There were more fresh trails but still no sign of what was making them.

The rain, I discovered, had washed the old markings away from my sample collection points and filled the boreholes with soft silt. Having to clear the silt slowed my work down, and I was lucky if I collected two new samples a day for as the silt hardened and dried it turned into another of the cobble formations.

Fortunately when the shuttle came I had sufficient samples to fulfil my obligations. They left me with wood for extra fuel and three pots of a viscous black substance that had to be heated then painted over the roof and external walls of my home. I found pouring and spreading it worked faster than trying to paint with the stuff. Consequently I had some wood left over once the task was completed. This I fashioned into a crude but effective sledge that could carry my core samples back to my hut.

As I neared the southern arc of my sample circle I constantly had to free stones from my boreholes. This was annoying as not only did it mean that up to the first 30cm of the shaft was no longer a good fit to the corer but there was a possibility of sample contamination.

At eight meters in depth, just ten degrees short of due south I hit an extremely hard layer of rock. The corer juddered to the extent that I slowed the drilling right down in fear of damaging the equipment. Once I had extracted the sample I discovered a four-centimeter layer of white quartz type rock. This rock was much harder than the layers it was sandwiched between and twinkled beautifully in the light. With the exception to the dark, granular layer of silt, it was the first change in the samples I had seen. I separated the core sample into two halves, labeled them and put the deeper sample to one side as I was only supposed to be drilling to six meters. The next three samples also contained this quartz type rock at, or close to, the eight-meter mark.

*　*　*

To celebrate my birthday my rock and I lit a fire with the left over scraps of wood, fried the steak and my two precious real eggs, then washed them down with my one bottle of beer. These luxuries I had especially requested before I embarked on this venture. It was a feast. The wood popped and crackled and sent showers of glowing golden sparks into the sky. The colors in the flames and those of the sparks were a treat for the eyes. Only as the fire began to die did I become aware of the sounds around me, like the clack of a pebble against another in the roll of the tide. The noises came from in the darkness surrounding me. Leaving my fire I gathered my rock and my crockery, retreated into my home and locked the door. Were the sounds I heard that night the effects of good food and my first alcohol for a year in the rarefied air and lighter gravity? I was hoping so, until I opened my door the next morning.

In the ashes of the fire stood a circle of rocks: big ones, small ones, all beige with pinkish red lines running around and over their surfaces. There had not been a single rock in the vicinity when I set that fire. When I returned with four more core samples the rocks were still there, but when I went out as the long night arrived they had gone. In the band of light that spilled from my doorway I examined the ground. Some of the stones simply appeared to have disappeared; others seemed to have been moved as there were trails in the ash, but where they had gone I had no idea.

That night as I washed there was a scrape and scuttering sound then a brief whiff of an acidic odor. I turned to find my rock sitting huddled next to the candle and right on the edge of the table. I moved them both and somehow managed to burn my finger but not on the candle. It was after I had soaked the wound in the water that I noticed the third scorch mark. It was bigger than the other two and was exactly where my rock had been sitting.

I was working in the eastern quarter trying my best to ignore the throb of my finger as I eased the first sample of the day from the ground when I heard a noise much louder than I had ever heard before. I looked all around but could see absolutely nothing that could be making it. The sound continued on and off all day. When I returned home I discovered my supplies and logs had fallen to the floor. I assumed the sound was the effect of some subterranean movement.

The next day I only collected two samples while listening to the spasmodic outbursts of noise. When I began to return to my home in the last of the daylight I found there were a large number of trails all heading in the same direction and all ending directly at my home. Everything loose was on the floor and the biggest stone I had seen lay partly buried at one corner of my hut. The stone, I know, had not been there before. Some of my precious water had escaped from the recycling plant after one of the seals had worked loose.

Cursing the loss I made the necessary repair.

I was sitting in the shadows cast by my single candle pondering how the stone came to be there as I waited for the water for my coffee of the day to boil when the scuttling, scraping sound came again. This time I saw its source. My rock was moving. The only thing I could ascertain as I examined it was the faint lines it had developed had now faded away and that it felt slightly heavier than I remembered, but that could have been my imagination. It just looked like a rock. But it had moved.

It was that night that what I first presumed to be an earthquake struck. I spent that night clinging and hoping as everything around me shuddered, aftershocks continuing through out the night. My world appeared to be most serene the next day. The hills were their usual beige, the clouds over them rolling and white with only the slightest hint of grey, but my sledge was nowhere to be found.

It took me an extraordinary length of time to reach the spot where I had left my equipment, set up and ready, and in perfect condition. I collected two samples, packed and left my equipment ready to be moved to the next sample point and set off for home. As I crossed the plain I became aware of something sitting on the distant ground; it became clear that it was my sledge. Close to it was a darker, burnt patch of ground. There were many trails here, some much bigger and deeper than others, many intersecting others but all traveling in an eastern direction. Dragging my samples on the sledge I continued on; perhaps my steps had been shorter, my pace slower for the sun was slipping behind the distant hills in a blanket of grey cloud as I neared home. The trails were leading me there. When I reached it there was a semi circle of stones around my home.

Just as the sounds had continued all day the disturbances continued throughout the night. At first I was sufficiently disturbed not to settle; it was on one of my perambulations that I opened the door and watched as the cobbled ground appeared to creep away under the pontoons that my hut sat on. To ascertain whether I was seeing things I stepped away from my front door and my home only for the movement to be confirmed. I managed to get some sleep despite the constant commotion and spent the next day moving the metal boxes containing my additional supplies to my new location. Bigger stones had joined the collection and by the time darkness fell my home stood on a low plateau overlooking the valley.

Due to the additional time it took me to reach the sample collection points I only collected two cores that day. Upon my return home I discovered my supply boxes missing; I followed the trails and found them surrounded with rocks by a shallow cave. I pushed the boxes under the overhang, as that was where the rocks seemed to want them then went to dine.

I had not given time to examining the build up of clouds so was surprised to see how grey they had become that next morning. The plateau was covered in rocks of all sizes; moving between them was difficult. I was considering how to extract my sledge from the forest of rocks when the tide of dark brown began racing across the hills and down into the valley. I retreated into my hut.

It rained—for that is the only thing I can call it—continuously for the next two days. The smell of lemon drops was ubiquitous. I am glad to say my roof remained intact. The valley floor had turned into a black steaming marsh under the onslaught and an acidic lake formed in the center of it.

Once the rain ceased and I had ascertained that my supplies where quite safe in their small cave I explored the higher ground as the valley was still quite wet. The rocks stayed on the plateau until the return of the orange lichens signified that the ground was beginning to dry.

I discovered another variety of lichen that bore a small colorless flower. The rocks seemed to consider this variety a delicacy and devoured it with great relish. Out of curiosity I brought my own little rock to a patch and watched as a set of six legs somehow unfurled from inside the hard exterior. The only creature I could compare it to was one I had seen in pictures, an old world crab. Once my rock had eaten its fill it scuttled back to me and hugged my foot; it seemed I had been adopted.

There was another valley on the other side of the hills. Like mine it was featureless but almost in the center of it stood a hut. I waited until the valley floor was dry enough to traverse then set out to meet my neighbor but at I approached I saw the true state of the hut. The roof and walls were marred with rust; sunlight twinkled through the holes where the rain had eaten through the metal. There were drag marks where the rocks had attempted to move the hut to higher ground but whoever lived here had not appreciated their help; all around the hut were shattered hollow corpses of rocks. They looked like the discarded cases of boiled eggs; the sight was so distressing I was glad I had decided to leave my rock at home.

I called out and pushed the door open. My neighbor was at home but not in a state to receive visitors; huddled on the bed was a picked clean skeleton. I decided to salvage his table and chair and anything else of use and to stop complaining about the increased distance I would have to walk to collect my samples. Once my valley dried out, having acquired a layer of fine black silt, and I began my work again.

The distance is such now that I only collect one sample a day from the western quarter of my sample circle. I do not begrudge that distance, nor the drudgery of taking the samples to the shuttle's landing zone and retrieving my supplies.

For it is only in the distance that the land raises from the perpendicular. That smooth roll of hills looks to be within a day's walking distance, but here distance is deceptive. Clouds will gather over the softly rising mounds, they'll roll and darken, promise sweet rain—not that they will ever bring such sweet deliverance to the parched ground that stretches before me. My steps have left an indelible mark on the planet's surface; who can say how long they will last? A week, a day, a year, until the next storm, forever?

And what of me? One year of service here is worth three incarcerated should I survive. Is that a fair price?

Nor Winter's Cold
by Stephen Graham King

The therm in my suit is starting to go.

I could tell from the faint click-wheeze I heard when I powered up the cycler. Great. Means when I get back, I have to dig through every backup system to scrounge a replacement. I ran the diagnostics out of habit, knowing they would come back green, but also knowing that my ear's a better judge. When your life depends on a therm suit, you learn how it works, what it sounds like when it's at peak and what it feels like when something's not right. Because if it fails on the surface, you'll be frozen before you realize you're dead.

Once I'd checked all the seals, I stopped and just let the suit tell me what shape it was in. I listened to the steady inhale-exhale of my own breath, then filtered it out. I flexed the suit's joints, heard the rustle reverberate inside my helmet. There was definitely still enough give in the articulation points for me to work. Finally, I focused my hearing, and just listened for any anomalous sound, anything out of place that might cause the suit to fail out there on the empty ice. Nothing.

Rotha always japes me, calling me the "Suit Whisperer." I had no idea what she meant at first, but she eventually explained it had something to do with horses. Then she had to explain what horses were.

Sometimes I actually hope I'll feel something wrong, find some flaw in the suit that will keep me off the ice. That I'll find some little thing to keep me inside where it's warm, where I can hear people laugh and shout and talk. Where I can smell sweat and choc and food cooking. Where I'm not alone.

But on those days when the storms come through or my suit fails and I have to try to beg or borrow another one, or try to find the parts to fix mine, I just get cranked, because the transceiver array is my responsibility. Collecting the download is up to me. I have two backups trained, but sending them out means pulling them from their regular work. So I mostly just bite the bullet and go. Lesser of two evils, I guess.

"Central Con, this is Mailman requesting permission for airlock open for the daily collection. Is there a skip ready for me?"

The returning voice of Bren, the logistics officer on duty, bounced around

135

the inside of my helmet. They must choose logistics officers for their voices. Bren's could calm pretty much anyone down. "Number Two's charged and has been assigned to you for the day. Be careful out there."

I smiled. They gave me Lola, my favorite. I don't know what it is, but Lola never gives me trouble out on the glacier. Any of the others and I'm jury rigging something on the fly to keep it running. Not Lola. She's sweet as a lickstick and always gets me there and back. I climbed onto the skip, settled into the seat and hit the power-up sequence. While the batteries came online, I strapped myself in. I got knocked out of the seat once, by a freak ice squall. I was just lucky my suit didn't hole or I wouldn't be here to entertain you with my ramblings.

When the engines went green, I tightened the muscle in my jaw that activated the comm system. "Central, I'm powered up and ready."

"Confirmed. Scrubbing the air out of the lock."

I felt the vibrations of the main pumps as they sucked the air out of the skip bay and into the storage tanks, causing a mumble to go through the floor, up through Lola and into me. My teeth were just starting to rattle when the pumps stopped.

"Opening Airlock," Central said in my ear.

The lock began to turn, a metal on metal grind. Even the best synthoils we have tend to freeze in this atmosphere. We have lube crews running pretty much 18/5 just to keep the mechanism from seizing up and it still sounds like the airlock is tearing a hole in the wall. As the circle of metal rolled away, an arc of light appeared at its edge, growing like the end of an eclipse and the last remaining moisture in the air huffed away in a cloud of ice crystals, like the sharp exhalation of breath when you come.

Before my helmet could polarize enough to cut the glare my vision turned white. My eyes were only just starting to adjust, but I hit the accelerator pedal anyway. Central wouldn't have cleared me if there had been anyone in the way, so I was already in motion when I could finally make out the sea of white ahead of me.

Thule is on the edge of a glacier, carved into the guts of a mountain that only shows its top tenth above the Frozen Sea, the rest plunging too deep into the ice for us to live in. It took us almost two years to drill down far enough to tap the scant geothermal energy this small planet has to offer, but we tamed it eventually. We had no choice.

The array is about eighty k from the base, on top of a stable ice shelf, so high that what we laughingly call atmosphere on this rock is nothing but an afterthought. It's all we have to keep us connected to the other communities we have tucked away in the unforgiving crannies of the galaxy. Without them, we'd lose what little information exchange we have. The quickline transceiver keeps us connected with each other at speeds far beyond the speed of light. It allows us to remember who we are. Who we used to be.

"Central, this is Skip Two. I've cleared the base and am beginning Traverse. ETA at the transceiver is two hours, ten minutes."

"Copy that, Skip Two. We have you on the grid. Looks like a nice day for a drive out there. Forecast is clear and cold. Did you remember to wear your warm undies?"

"Damn, they're in the wash today. No wonder my balls are frozen. Are we expecting anything special in the queue today?"

"Looks pretty standard," Bren answered. "Lots of personal mail. Nice new batch of entertainment. Looks like someone managed to upload a personal collection and it's finally making it our way. Oh, and the usual hush hush stuff."

"So what you're telling me is I need to get my ass in gear, empty the cache and decode the spurt in a hurry, eh?" Not that I wasn't going to go at best speed anyway. Transceiver downtime is a morale killer. The beds in the infirmary tend to fill up fast when people don't get their mail fast enough.

I goosed Lola's engine a bit faster, to make a bit better time. The gravs sent up a halo of ice crystals and it was like driving through a mist of diamond dust, every mote bouncing light in all directions. I shivered, fighting the false impression I was cold. It's hard out here on the ice to remember that your therm is set to keep you alive and at a comfortable temperature. The sheer volume of ice, combined with the knowledge that it goes down deeper than the oceans of Earth, just makes you feel cold. In your bones kind of cold, you know?

The glacier is so white, so flat and vast that some can't handle it. They can't come out here, to this immense emptiness without cracking. They work inside to grow food or monitor the geothermal tap to the core. They have acclimated to the rock walls and the emptiness out here scares them. Never had that problem, me. I'll take the extra pay and rations any day. I can handle the empty for an extra cup of choc with my dinner.

Someone told me there was some culture back on Earth that had over a hundred words for snow. They must have lived somewhere like Frostbite, somewhere where your eyes learn to see the difference between that many shades of white. Some corner of their world that no one else wanted to go.

This is what The Flense left us, these inhospitable places where no sane human wanted to live. Until we were forced into them.

They came from the black, from somewhere far beyond our colony worlds, the new homes we terraformed for ourselves, or the habitable planets we made our own. We're still not sure where they came from, really. They never bothered to tell us when they came on our screens that first time. They were just an armada of ships so advanced they made our most sophisticated jumpships look like toys. They destroyed the envoy ships we sent, cut them to pieces without even a word. We were insects in their path.

Of course, I've only ever seen insects in downloads from the transceiver. They have them on some of the other sanctuaries. From what I've seen, I'll take ice over insects any day.

Anyway, once we humans knew we didn't stand a chance against The Flense, we did the only sensible thing. We surrendered. But The Flense weren't interested in our surrender. They wanted our worlds. Once they were done demonstrating that we were nothing to them, they handed us our eviction notice. Any worlds that fell into our habitable range, they wanted. We were to leave them immediately. Some tried to defy them, to hold onto their homes in the face of this enemy. Botany Bay was the first. And the last. The Flense scoured the surface with their beams, transmitting the images on every Human frequency. Columns of red fire, each as wide as a city itself rained down on Botany Bay, razing every building flat. When every living thing on the surface was dead, they boiled away the atmosphere took the planet apart piece by piece, reducing it to elements and slag.

So we evacuated our homes. If we didn't manage to get everyone clear in time, The Flense burned all that were left, scouring the surface even as our ships were breaking atmosphere. Maybe they felt our presence tainted those warm, lush worlds. Maybe we were just parasites to them. No one knows what they do with the worlds we left. None of our remaining ships can get close enough to see.

They didn't wipe us out. In fact they showed no interest in us at all, as long as we stuck to these worlds, these too cold, too hot, too dark worlds outside our habitable range. We are allowed our tiny enclaves of thousands. We are allowed balls of ice, or deserts so hot that plastic melts in the sun, or worlds of water dotted only with islands smaller than Thule. As long as we stay in our corners, away from the worlds that The Flense want, they let us live. They let us have our ships and our quickline communications. They let us talk to each other and share what little we have of our old culture. Better than being dead.

I could see the ice shelf in the distance, just a line of blue-green along the horizon. You can barely tell that it rises higher into the frigid atmosphere than even our home does.

"You're coming up on base comm limit, Mailman. Blackout in two minutes." Bren's voice tells me.

"Roger, Central. Confirm comm blackout in two minutes. Chat you on the return trip."

Once the comm goes silent, there's nothing to do but watch the shelf grow in my vision. Lola and I are making good time, but she always likes it when I push her a bit.

Out on the ice, there's nothing but time. Lola's my baby, but she's not build for speed. She'll get me there in one piece, and that's all I really need her to do. The pressure of my hand on the accelerator is constant, I don't have to think about my grip. I could probably drive the route to the transceiver with my eyes closed. The white inside my eyes isn't much different than the white outside them. It's kind of meditative. If I were the type, that is. Only time I come close to meditating is in a hot shower.

Not much changes out here. When there's a storm, sometimes the surface gets rewritten and Frostbite gets a new face, but even then, it's only noticeable to someone like me who sees it every day. I know this piece of our world well; can feel it when the winds change. I notice the stuff that the others miss.

When I get closer to the ridge of the ice shelf, I can see the lines of blue, shot through it like lightning frozen solid in mid-strike. Like a tether of electricity connecting the ice and sky, or a rain of steel knives. The shelf is a good four kilometers high and it fills my vision as I near it. It runs almost the width of our world, disappearing to the edge of the horizons in both directions when you're standing underneath it. When you're standing there at the foot of it, it's like standing at the walls of heaven, if heaven were made of glass.

I nudge Lola into her niche next to the elevator and plug her in to charge for the ride home. I can't help but give her a pat on the grav cowling before I turn away. "Enjoy the rest, my girl. We're halfway done." My voice booms in the silence of my helmet.

The elevator is nothing more than a metal cage, just big enough to hold three or four people or one and some equipment for repairs. It has no walls, just bars of ceramic and steel that make a token effort to hold you in as you're rising above the glacier. One tiny cage on a skimtrack with its supports driven five meters into the ice and molecule bonded in place. One thin path to our link to the sky.

I ran the diagnostic on the drive, just to be sure. I don't need the elevator failing with me halfway up the ice shelf. Control would send someone after me when I missed the deadline, but a lot can happen in that time. The mechanism checked out, so I unloaded the collector from the skip and secured it in the elevator with the holding web. I double-checked the web to make sure the collector was securely in place. There's a lot riding on that hunk of circuitry, so I don't take chances with it. Only when I was sure it was secure did I attach my own safety line and hit the control to start the ascent.

The elevator gave a shiver as it rose, and when I looked down, I could see broken frost falling to the ice in fragments. Free again, the ride smoothed and my little metal frame ascended up the wall of ice.

I like this part. More than the ride out here. I can see over the curve of the world as I rise, the Frozen Sea dropping away. I feel unencumbered by anything as I am carried higher and higher, to the array that is my work, my destination, my reason and my role. This is what I do. The other hours in my day all lead up to this.

It's only a short walk to the array from the top of the elevator, but every time I'm up here, I find that the last five or ten paces with the collector make my muscles start to burn. The warmth is more than welcome, even though I'll pay for it later.

The array is a wide, concave disc of a dark burnished metal that is stark against the blue-white ice. It's covered with black transceiver cells, like a field of gemstone eyes, all turned outward to the night sky. They're so dark that it always makes me think they're bits of space that have broken off and fallen to the ground. And now they're just watching and waiting to find their way back home. Listening for us is all they can do until then.

All there is to do now is line up the collector at the link and activate it. A single point of fiery red light signals me that the collector is downloading, and suddenly I am holding people's words in my hands; holding dreams people dreamed long ago and managed to record for a posterity that has finally come. I am holding pain and love and art between my hands, fragments of what we used to be. Pieces of what The Flense took from us. Pieces we snatched back when they weren't looking.

Then it's done and the collector cycles down into passive mode and starts to decode the quickline spurt. The plain case gives no hint of the treasures inside as I carry it back to the elevator and strap it in once more, maybe just a little more carefully this time. One of my hands is resting on it as I begin to descend.

The Flense took our worlds, broke apart everything we had built, left us only these barren corners to live in. But even here, scattered in the dark, we found each other. Even families light years apart. We talk to each other in the night. We share what we have created. We share what we have learned and what we had forgotten we knew. Even on our tiny worlds of jungle and desert, of fire and ice, we found each other again and forged a link.

In my tiny cage of metal, suspended over a sea of frozen white, I close my eyes and for a moment, I can almost imagine I'm free of this ball of ice. I can almost believe I'm flying.

Tenth Orbit
by Gustavo Bondoni

Winter.

There is no motion. The feeble energy arriving from the distant star is not enough to support motion, yet move I must. Survival is dependant on movement, as winter does not allow sufficient energy accumulation to survive the night. To survive means to feed, and to feed means to stay ahead of the planet's shadow. Even that will not be enough in another fraction of a revolution. Then, the energy will only be sufficient if I stay aligned with the motion of the planet in such a way as to constantly absorb the noontime sun.

Ironically, this would be impossible without the cold itself. I cannot feel cold, yet it is a concept that I can clearly sense in the very crystalline structure of the planet. It is much easier to move through the crystal in the cold of winter. In winter I can move halfway around the planet in an instant.

But not without expending energy. Precious energy. And I cannot stay within the crystal more than the instant used to move. I need to be above the surface to feed from the star. All energy that reaches the surface is lost to me forever.

This is winter. Periods of feeding followed by desperate movement to a new feeding ground. Even my size diminishes as I consume the energy stored during better times. The area I can cover shrinks to the point where, at times, it stretches only the distance between two or three depressions on the surface. In winter, I wither.

Ah, for the glorious days of summer! In summer, I could easily rest for a night, and still have energy to expand the following day. I could stretch out and reach to the small moon in orbit, far from the surface, tracing its contours with the edge of the energy field that defines my existence. It feels different from the planet. It is more difficult to move there, as if the crystalline matrix is somehow imperfect.

In winter the moon is like a dream. I can sense its position, and its dimensions, and its motion, but I cannot stretch out and actually feel it. It is simply a question of insufficient energy.

This is also winter. Unable to act or move except for that movement which is necessary for survival, I must be content with merely receiving information from my surroundings. In winter, I must pay attention to all that transpires within my sphere of consciousness. It is the only way to avoid sleep. Sleep that is inaction. Sleep that is death. Only in summer, an eternity hence, dare I sleep.

I sense the star. Unimaginably distant, yet, at the same time, the center of my existence. It is the source of my nourishment, my life. It is also the compass for my perceptions, for I can sense only that which occurs inside the elliptical orbit of my planet. Is there, can there be anything outside my orbit? Logic would indicate that there is, for, often, the planet on the ninth orbit will move outside the ellipse, and disappear from my senses. Is the whole system just a product of my imagination, simply disappearing when the orbits are not aligned in accordance with a capricious set of rules? I think not. Over the long winters, I have come to believe that I am somehow linked to the star and that the universe has two halves: everything between my physical self and my source of energy, and everything else. I can only perceive that which transpires within my orbit.

Today, I only sense the star out of habit. There was a time, countless revolutions before, when the star was the only thing to which I would attune my senses. My consciousness was not as developed as it is now, and my only recollections of these winters are sharp sensations of fear and hunger. Hunger from the lack of nourishment available, combined with the fear that something would happen to the star. I would check the condition of the star. Upon finding it in good health, the fear would fade, only to return just moments later. My memories from the summers of the same period are sensations of joy and movement and exploration. It seems that, even then, I was able to forget about survival when more important pursuits presented themselves.

And, in hindsight, I find it understandable to have ignored the rest of the system. Of what possible use were the planets in the first four orbits? Little more than enormous balls of rock circling the star, they held no interest for me.

The sixth through ninth orbits held a small amount of promise, but, alas, unfulfilled. Similar to the star in composition, the energy they emitted was insufficient to complement the nourishment from the star. After a cursory glance, I had lost interest.

And the fifth! A sad, empty place devoid of the planet it should have had. The potential of the site was unlimited; a planet could form similar to either type of its brethren. But no planet had accreted here. It is a wasteland of small stones, none larger than the moon I dream of in winter.

It had been many winters ago that a small incongruence of energy on the planet of the fourth orbit had called my attention to it. Tiny, inconsequential, but different. A pulsing I could feel within the very core of my being, as if it called out to me. I could even feel it in the summer, when I would normally be more concerned with the exploration and the joy of unlimited, unworried movement. I tried to answer the call, but, as always, the moon was as far as my energy could go. That summer was the first time this restriction had seemed an unbearable burden. I wished to cross the barren space and join in the pulse. It became my new reason to exist. My fear and hunger were replaced by desire.

For many revolutions, it was thus. My longing grew and grew until all I could think about was how to cross the empty expanse. And I could feel the signal growing fainter with every passing moment. My urgency increased.

And the pulsing stopped. In the final moments, it had felt strained and weak, as if losing a monumental struggle. The very reason for my existence had ceased to be.

I have no recollection of the following winters. I am not sure how I survived, or even if I survived. Perhaps I simply ceased to exist, only to reappear at a later time. I recall nothing except that on one winter day, the pulsing had returned in a different guise. Somehow, impossibly, it had relocated to the planet of the third orbit, and was throbbing with a strength that had never been exhibited by the pulsing on the planet of the fourth orbit. It felt somehow victorious. It was like the difference between a summer day and a winter night.

The longing returned, stronger than before. A searing, uncontrollable urge to join the pulse, to immerse myself in it and to consume it, overcame my routine, honed over the ages to survive. Forgetting all caution, I accelerated to great speed over the surface of the planet, partly in celebration and partly to feel that I was doing something, anything to achieve my goal. But it was winter, and I had expended energy I couldn't afford. I almost didn't manage to escape the shadow, and when the winter finally ended, my size was the almost too small to feed effectively.

But I was content. The meaning of existence had, once again, moved beyond merely insuring the sufficient absorption of nutrient energy from the star. There was purpose.

And my hunger grew. As the strength of the throbbing increased, so did my hunger match it. And the strength increased continuously, revolution after revolution. I was barely in control. I would sometimes find myself trying to use the motion of the moon to fling myself in direction of the third orbit, to no avail. I would course down the crystals of the planet, deep into the core in an attempt to shut it out. But also, to no avail.

The throbbing grew ever stronger.

* * *

Winter.

A temporary respite, this object. It is obviously foreign to the planet, not part of its surface. The energy it absorbs is given freely, radiating outwards. It is here, and only here of all the surface of the planet that I can feast. This object has never been here during previous winters. The crystalline structure is different, much different from that of the planet. Even in the heat of summer, it is a joy to course easily through its tubes and walls.

It had arrived in the summer, this vehicle. It would never leave.

Many revolutions had passed, and the thrumming had grown subtly different. More complex, more intricate, somehow more purposeful. And ever louder. It was as if a tiny, faster pulse had been set over the original, which threatened to drown it out, but never did. My growing hunger was now joined by a curiosity, a fascination, which was new to me. What did it mean, this great concentration of pulsing energy? Why was the third orbit, with its short seasons and large rocky planet special in a way that the fourth orbit had not been?

Slowly, the second pulse grew, overtaking, and in some cases diminishing the original throbbing. With time, the planet on the third orbit came to be dominated by this new addition, and it seemed from my distant vantage point that the first pulse existed only where the second pulse allowed it to. The balance of power had changed, and I had no idea what it meant. But my hunger had not abated, it had merely changed focus. I would not be able to rest until I could consume the second pulse.

The planet in the third orbit began to change. This was not unusual in itself, but the rate of change threatened to overwhelm. There had been a time when it was sufficient to monitor the progress of these pulses every winter or even every two winters. While it was impossible for me, having become attuned, to drown them out, concentration was still required to grasp the subtleties, the details.

The rate of growth was incredible. Even when the pulse was just starting on the planet, the growth had not been this great.

But, one winter, the pulse broke away from everything I had expected. The first great shock came when the third planet began to emit energy. While feeble, this was the same type of energy that came from the star. Was this radiation, coming from such an unexpected direction, to be my next source of energy?

And then part of the pulse left the ground. It was as if it had split a tiny part of itself off and sent it far over the surface to rejoin the main body at a distant point. How could this be possible? And, as I watched entranced, this happened again and again. Could this be the way for me to reach the pulse? I tried to split off a small part of my energy field.

Success! But my excitement was short-lived. The energy I had split off had simply drifted onto the surface of the planet out of my control, and been lost to me forever. It was destined to be another winter of hardship. But what fascinating distractions!

The pulse split once more, differently now, and a small portion of it moved to the large satellite orbiting the planet. It remained there for what seemed like just a few moments, before rejoining the main mass, but it was distinct. Before summer was fully upon me, the process had been repeated a handful of times.

It never happened again until the following winter, although I watched anxiously, every waking moment of the longest summer of my life, trying to move the pulse simply through strength of will. I felt that if it could reach the moon of the planet, then it would come to me. To be devoured. To add its energy to mine.

And the time did come, the following winter, when the pulse surged outward from the confines of its planet. First, to its moon. Did I dare dream that it would try to leave the third orbit? Could I hope that, in time, it would come to me?

Yes. At the end of that same winter, tiny fraction moved away from the third orbit, on a course towards the silent planet of the fourth. Having left the main mass of the pulse behind, I could sense this small portion that much more intimately. I can still remember my shock upon realizing that it wasn't a small portion of a larger mass, but several individual pulses. Different, but almost imperceptibly so.

Upon realizing this I had eagerly returned my attention to the main throbbing, still on the planet. With my newfound perspective I could discern hundreds, thousands, billions of throbbing, pulsing, individual sources of energy. And, finally, some of them were coming to me.

Their progress captivated me for many cycles. I watched as they slowly approached the fourth orbit. I suffered when the signal from their energy became strained, reminding me of the pathetic final days of the pulsing from the fourth planet. I agonized as the individual sparks went out. I despaired when all pulsing finally disappeared. They had made it less than half way to the fourth orbit.

But they didn't give up. In short succession, two more groups of individual pulses left the planet from different points on the surface. A third followed soon after. All were headed for the planet of the fourth orbit, as if in a race. Two of the groups arrived on the planet. The third perished in the emptiness of the space between orbits.

The groups on the surface eventually set out on the return journey. Only one arrived on the planet of origin. By this time, however, a number of new groups had set out to cross the vast expanse. Many of them arrived on the fourth orbit, and several of these stayed on the planet through various revolutions. The pulse had gained its foothold and was growing in a completely new environment. It had crossed the great divide.

Would they come to me? My hunger knew no bounds. But I was patient. I had been there before the pulse, and I could wait a while longer to consume it.

I watched as the pulse continued to expand, gaining footholds in each orbit. In every case the pattern was the same. The first faltering steps followed by the wholesale covering of the surface by the pulse. The pulse was absorbing every orbit. The second. The fifth. The moons of the planet of the sixth orbit. The seventh. The eighth.

As the first tentative visits of the ninth orbit began, I knew fear for the first time since my earliest memories of winter. What was this unstoppable force that was absorbing the system? Could it be, as I had thought, a new source of energy to consume and feel the glory of it coursing through me and allowing me to grow beyond my wildest dreams? Or were they coming to consume me, as they had consumed every other orbit between myself and my star?

Only one thing was certain: I would soon find out.

The pulse was coming. I could sense the trajectory. My eternal wait would be over the following summer.

Winter.

Regret is unnecessary. I have learned that patience is the way to reap rewards. I will have my opportunity once again. And, then, I must use my patience to control my hunger. I have learned.

The shadow is approaching, and it is with some remorse that I leave the vehicle to find a safer place to feed. I have known what it means to be sated and have been punished for my greed. For now, I will move with the energy of the star. But I know I will grow again. I must only be patient. Over countless revolutions I have learned to wait. With deliverance so near, I must now put that knowledge into practice.

The landing of the vehicle had been a violent event. The sheer energy in the deceleration. The heat. I huddled deep in the crystalline structure of the planet and watched, my fear dueling with my hunger. How I wanted to move to the surface and absorb that energy! Even what little reached me at this distance was more energy than I had ever felt. More than I believed possible. What I could achieve if only I could consume it.

The vehicle finally stopped moving. I could sense two distinct pulses moving within. I moved closer slowly, afraid to reveal my position to these representatives of the force that had devoured the entire system. Only the desperate strength of my hunger pushed me towards the twin pulses. At this range, the strength of the throbbing was incredible. I inched closer.

And I could sense the pulse for what it really was. I retreated in disgust.

The pulse was not pure, clean energy, as I had so long imagined. It was encased in a physical body. Just like a rock. Or the moon. But the energy of the pulsing was intricately woven into the physical matrix. The pulse was the body, and the body was the pulse. The energy was corrupted, tainted.

But it was also infinitely seductive, calling to me, stirring my hunger. Despite my revulsion, I moved slowly closer. The body of one of the pulses had left the vehicle and was moving over the surface of the planet, interacting with it physically. Two protuberances supported the torso and aided in locomotion. I edged to the surface and extended my senses, fascinated.

At this range, the energy of the pulsing was almost irresistible. I hungered to absorb it, to make it mine. I forgot about the taint and moved towards the pulse. Only my fear kept me from closing the distance in an instant. Closer, ever closer, dreading the moment when I would be detected and devoured like all the planets of the other orbits. Would this be my fate?

Closer. And closer still. I could not move due to my paralyzing fear of this monstrosity, yet I could not bring myself to stop.

And closer still. And suddenly I knew it had detected me. The figure straightened and stood still. And then the pulsing increased in intensity. It radiated reflected fear and desperation. At this range, I could almost read the thoughts behind the web of energy. And the figure began to move towards the vehicle. It was afraid and was going to leave me forever. I would never experience what it was like to absorb this glorious new energy form. It moved quickly, desperately, towards the vehicle.

But not quickly enough. I crossed the crystal matrix of the planet's surface that separated me from it and flowed into the body.

And absorbed the pulse.

An eternity drinking the energy of the distant star had not prepared me for this. It was as if I had expanded to ten times my normal size. I flowed around the planet effortlessly. I expanded my size and enveloped the moon. The whole moon. I was more powerful than I could have imagined. The energy coursed through me to the point where I could actually affect the physical surface of the planet. I soared.

But, too soon, the energy was spent. It was gone. The desolation of its absence tore at my very being, agony such as I had never felt before. I would absorb the second pulse.

But this was impossible. I watched powerless as the top of the vehicle separated from the rest and moved off into the void, out of my reach forever.

Winter.

I must avoid the temptation to feed excessively. If I am small, I will not be detected.

They will return, and I will board the vehicle. I will feast on a different orbit, leaving the tenth forever. Will I be closer to the star that was my only companion for so long? Or even further away, on an unknown orbit with longer revolutions and harsher winters? No matter, for the pulse will provide me with more energy than I can expend.

But I must be patient. They will return, and I will be here.

Waiting.

A Wilderness of Sand
by Lyn McConchie

On the fringes of the great desert the story is still told. It is perhaps not truly a Toureg history, but it is they who tell it and their clans that claim the Queen as one of their own. She may well have been—since many bloodlines mingled to create the Toureg of today. But time passes, cities crumble into nothing and truth vanishes into mist and myth. No one will ever know for certain how Hanin died, but this is the tale as it was handed down.

A small foot stamped. "I will not leave my people to wed him. Besides, he isn't kind."

The old nurse, I'sha, nodded slowly. "That everyone knows, but he is rich and powerful."

"Rich on the backs of his starving people. He is powerful with their blood hot upon on his hands. They call him The Hyena, and they hate and fear him. I have seen it." Her own face twisted in fear and I'sha gathered her gently into strong arms.

"You are so beautiful," she crooned. "I am sure you would find favor in his eyes. You could teach him to be kinder to those you love?"

Hanin shook her head. "To him all women are unfit even to have opinions. I could be chief amongst his wives but I would have no voice he would hear." She shuddered suddenly. "I have seen his wives and I say it is better that I die than become one of them." Outside, a horn blew a long rich note. "It is time for me to sit in judgment. Pray the Hyena loses interest in me else we may all be doomed." The bead curtain swished as she passed through.

I'sha stood, her broad face troubled by her thoughts. It did not take a seer to foretell that danger approached her people. She stepped to the doorway to watch as her nursling sat on the stool of judgment, claimants seated before her. For a moment it was as if the child melted under the hot sun. She saw the delicate skull turn on the neck bones as a skeleton hand gestured gracefully. I'sha moaned in pain. No! She fled to the sacred hut that housed the spirit of the Moon her people worshiped. Let the Goddess tell her it would not be as she feared.

In the open air Hanin listened to both sides of a difficult case. The faces about her were serious—but in the eyes of those who sat there, love and trust for their Lady showed. Unlike the rulers of surrounding tribes Hanin had been raised to believe she served her people. Her mother had died at Hanin's birth and Hanin had been cared for by I'sha, ex-slave and Wise Woman. In one of the endless forays by other tribes Hanin's father had been killed and the girl had become queen. She had grown up with her subjects, played with many while she was yet a child. She knew them—and had love done greatly, but he had died young and she walked alone once more. Yet with I'sha's wisdom to guide her she judged carefully and with common sense.

In the hot air she wore a loincloth, as did her people. Her only other garments were the tanned lion skin that lay across the top of her shoulders, symbol of the Ruler, and the bright strings of beads that gleamed against her dark skin. Finally, she rose to seek the shade of her hut and it was there that I'sha came to her again. Hanin glanced up affectionately and saw the pain and sorrow etching the loved face so that she cried out in horror. I'sha nodded.

"Listen, my love, my nestling. What the Moon has shown me cannot be altogether averted. But if you have great courage our people may yet be saved."

The young head lifted proudly. "For my people I will have courage. Speak!"

I'sha bowed. She sat, telling swiftly of The Hyena, his hunger for a queen and her fertile lands that he could make his own.

"This I know."

"Peace. Listen." The story continued. Until now Hanin had not known there had already been two attempts to steal her away. She gasped.

"I foresaw and spear-women were ready. If that were all I would not yet have spoken. The Hyena is hated and feared, but his desire for you has become known in his lands. Now, here and there, laughter grows amongst his people. Such a great King, so powerful, yet he cannot even grasp the woman he desires." Her voice dropped to a murmur. "I have foreseen again."

Thus it was that when tired, dusty warriors trotted into Hanin's city of reed huts where she was waiting.

Tall and straight she stood in her lion-skin cloak. "I know why you are come. Go back to your Lord and say I must consider wisely before I give my answer."

Later, in a guest hut, the warriors ate musty maize porridge as they drank thin, sour beer. They muttered, to be sharply told by a serving woman that this was the best the tribe had. The rains had been late, she complained, and the hunting poor. If the best was not good enough then let them return home the more quickly. Outside the door she listened as the guests grumbled. She fled to share the overheard complaints.

"They believe us poor and hungry, a waste of time."

Hanin smiled. "Thank you. Go now, and see they have more beer." She turned to her nurse. "Will this buy us time?"

"A little. N'gombi will be slower to make war if there is no profit but an unwilling wife. Warriors are deep in the swamps preparing places where our people may hide. Much of our food and wealth is now stored there." She reached out, her face sad as she hugged the slender figure. "The day will come when you have no more choices, Hanin, but there is time yet."

As the weeks drifted by, Hanin forgot her fears by sinking deep into the lives of her people. She played with the children—and if there was a toddler with whom she played more tenderly, more often, none of her people commented as she shared gossip with their mothers.

With her spear-women she hunted, running fiercely, laughing over her kills, sharing the meat amongst them in friendship. Behind her eyes she was haunted by the knowledge that this time of peace ran out for her. She savored the breeze on her soft skin, the warm red dust under her bare feet. And always she smiled when not alone, a mask pasted into place so her people should not know her fears.

The warriors of N'gombi, known as the Hyena, came again. Hanin listened before retiring to talk with I'sha.

"There is no longer any choice. He will take my land, and me and my people. If I refuse they die. If I accept they will die, but more slowly. There is no hope for any of us."

I'sha held the quivering girl in strong arms. "I have seen a hard path, if you take it, our land and people may live."

"And me? Is there no hope for me?"

"I begged the Goddess for that but saw nothing. Perhaps She would have you save your people, and trust Her for yourself."

Hanin shook her head slowly as she freed herself and straightened. The long beaded plaits swung about her shoulders, tiny bells at the end of each plait tinkling cheerfully.

"No. Blood pays for blood. Yet if I must spend mine I will have a price for it. Go, have my people prepare. Their Lady goes to a wedding." Her eyes were bright with tears, her mouth twisted in bitterness. "Tell them I buy their lives with my duty."

The older woman shook her head. "They know why you do this. There will be no rejoicing." She dropped to her knees to crawl from the Queen's hut; she had orders to give. Behind her Hanin wept for the land she must leave, for

151

the people she loved, and for whom she feared greatly. And for herself also, that love was forever denied her now.

To the Kingdom of N'gombi she came with her lion-skin about her shoulders, while plumed warriors guarded her. Servants bore gifts to the Lord she must wed. Behind his hand the King smirked triumphantly at his Chief Advisor.

"She has come. I will gift you as promised once I wed her."

He waited until Hanin knelt at his feet and leaned out to raise her. His hands grasped her shoulders and he felt her tiny wince of disgust at his touch. He smiled, and spoke softly.

"You will feel differently once we have lain together. My wives do not complain." He saw sickness rise in her and giggled. A high-pitched tittering that chilled. "I will teach you our ways."

Around the throne the people had crowded closer to hear the words of their Ruler. Hanin knew it must be now. She stepped back, wrenching herself free. Her eyes met those of her warriors and they were gone, fading back with the servants. The gifts lay heaped in the compound while her people fled silently. Hanin's voice was strong and clear then as she spoke, not only to the King and his Advisors but also to the entire crowd who listened.

"King, who would wed me, your messenger said you would murder all my people if I did not come to you as your wife. But you also swore on your secret name that none would be harmed if I did, and I came to save my people. Do you now keep your word, O Great King?"

N'gombi swung his head to one side, hiding his smile from her. The woman was ignorant; once wed she had no rights here. No promise he might make to a mere woman was valid. Hanin did not know their laws. He nodded as his amusement at her folly grew within him.

"Before the Gods and upon my secret name I swear, may they devour me if I lie. Wed me and your people shall be neither injured nor slain."

Hanin bit back triumph. Now, for the other part of the plan I'sha had made. It would mean her destruction, but her people would survive. Her voice lifted more loudly, the tone sharpening, edged with sarcasm.

"You forced me here with threats. Your messengers say you are a great King? I say you are a man who must use rape to bed a woman." She watched as his face went ugly with rage. "Will you rape me before your people so they may see you as a man? Or will you have your guard hold me so you need not fear the lion's claws?" N'gombi stood, bellowing incoherent fury—but her voice cut through his outcry. "You who cannot find a willing woman. How will you rape me once we are wed?"

All about her she could hear the murmuring, see the mouths of his people fall open in shock at her defiance. A laugh bubbled within her as the King gasped and gasped again, so angry that he was unable to find words for a reply. It must have been very long since he had been openly defied. About them the crowd's voices swelled in chattering gossip, goading the king to madness. N'gombi found his voice in a shriek.

"Witch! I would not rape you though my people came to ask it of me. We will wed, yes, and I will wait then. I will lay no hand on you until it is you who crawl to lick my hands and beg for my touch."

She saw the sudden horrified look on the Chief Advisor's face and leaped in swiftly before him to speak again.

"Before the Gods and upon your secret name you have sworn my land and people should be unharmed if I came to wed you. Do you now expect me to believe you swear this to the Gods also?" The scorn and disbelief in her tones slashed like a keen knife. Before he considered his words the King was on his feet, bellowing so that all could hear him.

"I swear. Until you come to me upon your knees to beg my touch I shall not use you in any way. I swear this upon my life and secret name also and let all the Gods witness my oath!"

He sat again, panting from the force of his fury. Behind him his Chief Advisor groaned. He was ignored as the wedding proceeded. By sun-high Hanin was wed and the great feast had begun. The King lolled on his throne and smirked at her. She'd come to him once he took a few of her people. She would do anything for the rabble she ruled; she had already shown him that. He retired with his advisors, the chief of them wringing his hands in anguish. N'gombi stared at him when that continued.

"What bothers you, old fool? Hanin will crawl to me as soon as we lay hands on a few of her guards."

The Advisor wrung his hands again. "Great King, her guards are long since fled and if you touch one babe of her people the Gods will devour you. You yourself invoked them."

"Idiot! We are wed. All she has is mine."

"But Lord, you are not legally wed until she is bedded. She has tricked you."

N'gombi stared. "Tricked? Not mine?" His hands fastened on the advisor's throat. "I'll take them anyway." The Chief Advisor husked a word and he loosened his grip a little. "What?"

"I said, Great King, that the Gods heard your oath. It is they who will judge."

He was freed as N'gombi considered that danger. The Gods made no allowances even for Kings. His fat face broke into a vicious smile as a thought came.

"I swore not to harm her people or to rape her, but there are other ways to persuade a woman. You will find them for me but," his finger lifted in warning, "no one else shall have her, nor is she to be marked." The advisor bowed before vanishing hastily.

That night armed guards escorted Hanin to an isolated and hidden hut where she was kept in darkness as the king attempted to break her will. Day and night were all the same to her as time passed, but a King may not stop his people's gossiping. In the weeks that followed her disappearance their voices rose. The king punished those whose talk was overheard, but he could not altogether silence the whispering. He would have forsworn himself but he feared his Gods who were both bloody and unforgiving. Finally N'gombi had waited long enough.

"Break her or it will be your neck which is broken."

The Chief Advisor shivered at his feet. "Great King, I am forbidden to rape or to scar her. Three times have we starved her until she could not stand. Twice have we refused her water until she lay unconscious in the heat of the hut. We have not allowed her to bathe or to wear clothing since she was taken and her arms are twigs, she stinks—and still defies us."

"You boasted you could break her. Fulfill that boast or I will have you staked out on the Hill of Vultures. Go!"

The Chief Advisor slunk out to meet with his slave. "You said you might have a way to break the witch for the king. Succeed and I shall make you rich and set you free."

The slave nodded. "Master, she shall crawl to the king's feet by the dawn."

The Chief Advisor tottered off to report to the king. If this plan failed he would take poison. If it succeeded he'd poison the slave, and then wealth and the King's favor would come to the advisor. N'gombi listened and rejoiced.

"Do this and I will fill your hands with gold and salt. Tonight I feast. Bring her to me at first light before my people."

Two men approached the hut and the filthy pitiful figure faced them. Pride was still in her bearing though she flinched from the light of flickering torches.

"We ask one last time, woman. Will you go to the King willingly?"

"Let him have my dead body. He shall not have me alive."

The advisor turned to nod to his slave. Together they held her while the slave forced a drug into her mouth. She felt herself go limp though still she breathed, saw, heard. Feeling had left her body so that she no longer noticed the chill earth beneath her. They moved about her, filling her ears with soft wax, covering her eyes so completely she could see nothing of even the flaring torches. Then they left her in the secret place where she was captive.

"You are certain this will work?"

The slave smiled grimly. "It will. She lies in darkness, she can feel nothing, see and hear nothing, and it drives many mad after a time. One who is left for a few hours this way will do anything not to be left so again."

In darkness Hanin lay. But it was a silence and darkness of body alone. In her mind she filled the night with torches and the laughter of friends. She talked, smiled, and sang as around her clustered those she loved. In her mind the night was full of color and song. Sometimes a smile flitted across the wasted face as she moved deeper into the world she made. The hut that held her body became less real. Within the place where her spirit laughed and feasted Hanin looked up as one approached. With a cry of joy she flung her arms about I'sha.

"It is so good to see you at last. So wonderful to be free here." Her face clouded. "Must I return? Please, I'sha, must I go back?"

Over the bowed head I'sha's eyes sought the Moon. Her ears caught the fleeting silvery whisper and she smiled, a slow savage smile. She had watched in a gourd of clear water as the girl she loved had been tortured. She had seen the attempts to break Hanin's spirit founder on the rock of the girl's knowledge of how her people would pay if she yielded. The Goddess was fair; she had answered as I'sha hoped.

She released the girl gently. "Stand, little nestling beloved. Walk with me." Away from the others she spoke, "I told you truth when you left. You buy the lives of your people with your own pain but the Lady is fair. You shall have both justice and vengeance. Do you wish to remain here?"

Hanin smiled over her shoulder to where one who had feasted and danced with her waited. Love glowed in his eyes. Behind him her father placed a choice morsel of meat in the mouth of a beautiful woman. Hanin smiled at her mother before turning to look at I'sha.

"I wish to remain." Her hands flew out to seize her nurse. "But what of you? Must I lose you if I stay?"

I'sha smiled back lovingly. "No. I too shall stay here. That is my choice."

She swayed gracefully to her knees, with her powerful arms stretched upwards in prayer. "Hear me, Goddess, Spirit of the Moon. I choose to remain with those I love. Let that too pay the price required."

Moonlight covered her. It gleamed, sparkling on long silver chains that stretched from the waists of I'sha and Hanin. From the feasters a man came forth. Hanin laughed as his hands caught her up. His mouth lowered to hers as she waited. With light-silvered fingers I'sha stretched out her hands to take up the links. Her own chain broke easily. Then between powerful hands she took up Hanin's chain and her muscles leaped and writhed as she tore at it. Beside her, lips touched—as Hanin's chain broke.

Outside, the first light of dawn showed above the hills. Within the largest hut N'gombi still ate and drank deep. He boasted that soon Hanin would lie in his arms. About him his human jackals fawned in false admiration.

To those who are worthy and unworthy the Gods give what is due. From the secret place where Hanin had lain, a gift, bought and paid for, came creeping. One by one those feasters it touched died until only the King was left. Then he too died, his body lying where it fell, but the still death continued. The lands of the Hyena turned brown. Streams vanished leaving only dying trees. Sands drifted in to become great dunes that covered what had once been fertile lands. Now they were desolation, a wilderness of sand where nothing would ever grow again.

Before then those of his people who were the less guilty and who had been permitted to wake in time had long since fled, escaping into other lands with the tale. At last all the lands that had once been ruled by N'gombi were barren and the Goddess was satisfied. Death withdrew.

The people of Hanin wept. They sought her body until finally the tiny wasted form was found in the hut where she had been held. That remnant they placed in a stone tomb with the body of I'sha at her feet. One by one her people came forward before the tomb should be closed forever to throw into it some small thing that was precious to them. Even the children came; remembering their games with Hanin and offering loved toys.

Another Ruler was chosen in a time to come—Hanin's own daughter, the child of her youth by the one man she had loved—or so the tale goes. Hanin's people prospered after that, inter-bred, and half-forgot the tale. The land changed as the long years eroded it into different contours, and reed huts—even a city of them—leaving no traces. Those who came later would not count Hanin's city as a city anyway, nor would the story be believed.

But in the tents of the wanderers the tale would last as long as the great sands move, while their girl children would wear Hanin's name with pride. The Toureg say that in that other place she found, Hanin laughs and sings forever, dancing and feasting with all those she loves about her yet. I'sha ever at her side, milk-mother, wise-woman, nurse, and payer of one half of vengeance's price. Content that her name be forgotten so long as that of her nursling is remembered. At least—that is the story told in the black tents of those who claim her blood.

Tomb
by Z. S. Adani

Silent and cold, hidden beyond uncharted space and harboring dreadful secrets, Tomb danced between the uneasy concord of two stars.

Commander Tivor Corlin had argued against physical ground exploration after he saw the alien structures and the remains of bodies from orbit, but he was in the minority. He shook his head and turned off the shower. And stopped. Snatches of whispers drifted from their room. He plastered his ear to the prefab door and listened, dripping water on the plaz floor.

"Have you disabled it?" He heard Anna's voice. "Purge the EI's memory and transmit only the data I left you."

What was she talking about? Anna Rengar, senior xenobiologist of the ground crew, was his life mate. Why was she whispering? They shouldn't have secrets between them. Instead of switching on the dryer, he grabbed his skinsuit and pulled it on. The smart machines sandwiched between the bucky weaves soaked up the moisture.

"Be careful, we don't want the NP commandoes down here."

The tension he heard in Anna's voice made him stiffen, heart pounding. One hand clumsily fumbled with his suit belt, while the other one grabbed his wrist unit. The EI, a Cloned Human Brain Cell Nanoelectronic Enhanced Intelligence aboard the *Celestis* automatically sent down the Nano Patrol if the data it received contained even a hint of a biohazard.

Corlin pushed the door open and entered the room they shared. Anna turned and flicked off the 3D image, but he had seen enough.

"Tiv, I thought you already left." She reached for her suit, fingers trembling. The limp grayish skinsuit conformed to her body as she slipped it on, turning flesh color.

She had been talking to Kate, a junior xenobiologist, but he asked anyway, "Who was that?"

"Just Tom, he, he was checking if we needed any supplies."

Anger suffused him. Anna had been acting strangely for the past few days, but he had never caught her lying to him before. Corlin was tempted to remind her that the ground crew was essentially cutoff from the starship. All the landers had flown back two weeks ago, even before the construction robots finished erecting the base. Instead of starting an argument, he sealed the head flap of his suit and left her standing there.

He consulted his implant and ran through the checks: air-handlers, visuals, interfacing nanites, suit integrity. All functions appeared in green on his visual field. He hurried through the long corridor of the residential complex and turned into the supply shack. A small float pallet detached from the rack, and he slaved its simple system to his wrist unit, then piled on a handheld analyzer, a vibraknife, and a queser gun.

He was about to leave when his wrist unit projected a flustered image of Zephan, the senior medic. "Commander Corlin, please come to the science complex; I'm in the sickbay."

"On my way," he said, swallowing his annoyance. Normally, each department functioned on its own, collected and analyzed specimens. Then every night they collated the pooled data, discussed it, and transmitted everything to the *Celestis*. But the archeological site on Tomb was far from normal; it stretched their individual and collective expertise to the limit.

Before the ground crew had landed, orbital surveys and surface probes confirmed the remote probes' data of the alien ruins and the remains of a humanoid race. Though the small settlement and its many oddities bothered him from the beginning, the most recent find undermined his faith in Coalition technology. None of the probes had shown the bones Mara had found in the central structure yesterday.

How did the probes miss them?

He left the supply shack and hurried across the frozen plains. Tomb was slowly slipping into an ice age. Remote and isolated from Coalition space, it was in the region of the Mantus Nexus, the newest wormhole. The Mantus station was still in the process of assembly when they had passed through the Nexus, and the Neumanns had just finished constructing the CoalNet Sats. The *Celestis* was the nearest ship, just one wormhole away when the probes' data had reached the headquarters of Exploration and Survey Corps at Mars.

Corlin looked at the orange sun rising above the serrated mountains, limning the ice plains into an illusion of saffron warmth. Through the containment field, the landscape shimmered slightly, lending it a sinister specter.

He quickly entered the science complex. Portable lab units lined the central passage, each one with its own containment field. When he saw the shimmering field encasing the sick bay, his stomach lurched. The field detected his suit and allowed him to pass through.

"How's Sam?" he asked the medic.

"His spinal cord fell apart during the night," Zephan said. "Four of his vertebrae show spots like these." He stabbed a finger into the diagnostic screen that hovered above the autodoc containing Sam. It was a smooth buckyglass resembling a coffin, resting on a mobile sled and humming quietly.

The screen showed a dark, star-shaped smudge and four lacy vertebrae that seemed like delicate spider webs rather than solid bones. Sam had broken his back three days ago while eating dinner. With the medchines in his body working properly, there should have been some improvement.

"The trouble is," Zephan continued. "The autodoc doesn't know what's causing this. According to the analyses, his immunites are working, so it's not viral or degenerative disease. The autodoc's disassemblers can't even crack that cloud surrounding the anomaly. Look at this."

The image changed, displaying the nucleus of a nerve cell. Chromosomes appeared, like chewed clumps of yarns amidst a silver cloud. The view panned and individual genes unfolded.

"See those shiny snowflake shapes? We can't image them sufficiently, but I'm guessing they're flywheels, though they look different from ours." Zephan pointed to tiny twirling machines that seemed to move with purpose. "They're generating the fog."

"So what's the fog?"

Zephan looked distressed. "Well, the fog, I don't know. You can barely see the flecks, the flywheels that manufacture them. But that's not important." He flicked a wrist in a dismissive motion. "I'll put Sam in stasis, because it's spreading."

Corlin nodded, stifling a stab of fear.

"We must get him up to the *Celestis*."

"We can't."

"We must." Zephan grabbed his arm. "The medical bay aboard the ship could reassemble his spinal cord and vertebrae."

"Do you see any landers?" Tivor sneered, gesturing outside the building. Frustration boiled in him, and he lifted a hand to forestall further arguments. "No lander would come. Nothing goes up until we're finished here and cleared by the Nano Patrol."

"This is an emergency," Zephan said in a pleading tone.

Corlin turned away, unable to meet the man's eyes. He felt like a monster as he said in passing, "Put Sam in a stasis unit, then activate an individual containment field around it."

The door slid shut behind him. He kicked at the frozen ground, scattering ice chips around. What had he seen in there?

When he reached a designated port site at the edge of the base, he consulted his implant. The base system reacted and formed a bubble in the shimmering side of the containment field. He slipped inside and stood patiently until an individual containment field built up around him. His implant informed him that he could step through.

He shivered but not from the cold. Zephan's anxiety was another indication that Tomb was getting to them. For a medic to risk breaking quarantine when a stasis unit would keep his patient stable indefinitely didn't bode well for morale. Face set in hard lines, Corlin took long strides away from the base.

He would be remiss in his duty as a senior xeno-archaeologist if he didn't check the remains Mara had found yesterday, and though he should be thrilled at such a find, he felt his initial fear growing.

"Tiv, wait for me," Anna said through his wrist unit, running after him. "I want to take tissue samples of the bones."

Her black eyes sparkled and held a devilish gleam, a slight reddish tint caused by her containment field. Rarely was such extreme caution necessary; the skinsuits the ground crews of ESC used were normally more than sufficient protection on alien worlds. Not on Tomb, though. Her small float pallet trailing behind her reminded Corlin that he had left his in the supply shed.

"Going to the center, aren't you?"

He nodded and took her hand reluctantly, still upset about her secret talk with Kate. "I didn't sleep much, kept thinking about Mara's find."

"I was actually tempted to sneak out last night."

"We better not start breaking rules." He gave her a severe look. "No night excursions on this world."

She shrugged. As if dismissing the dangers, Anna waved at the alien ruins. "Some members of the crew still hope we could get Tomb approved for colonization. The planetary engineers could fix the ice age. Between the two suns, this wouldn't be such an awful place."

"It's not worth the resource expenditure. The red star is receding; Tomb will get colder and colder. Be content we're allowed to study the ruins. This place will never be another colony." The star system of Tomb was a physical binary of a K8 orange dwarf and an M10 red dwarf. Tomb was the second world of the orange component, and Tomb Guard, the large gas giant, the third.

"Dex has a viable plan to reengineer the deep core drillers. The Neumanns could incorporate his designs and in a year or two we'd have enough drillers to heat a continent," she argued, but her voice sounded hollow.

"Tomb is at perihelion now. Let's just take one day at a time, Anna. We're all desperate to find another world to colonize, but I'd rather err on the side of caution."

"And forgo an earthlike planet."

Corlin chose not to argue. He was glad they arrived at the edge of the alien site, a circular maze of streets and buildings constructed from a fused material that the analyzer registered as some form of carbon compound bonded by an unknown force. It was not buckyglass but perhaps something even more enduring. Considering the age of the settlement, over seven hundred millennia, it was in good shape.

He pushed aside the crumbling gate and walked along the curving street. Hues of cinnamon and henna streaks, akin to marble, made up the walls and stairs. Rubble stood in heaps here and there, collapsed roofs and fence-like structures moldering under the alien sun.

"Commander Corlin," he heard from his wrist unit.

"Go ahead, Kate," he said.

"Is Anna with you? Her com is turned off."

A flash of fear crossed Anna's eyes before she said, "What's up Kate?"

"The EI is finished with the new analyses."

"About time," Anna said, giving him a sidelong glance.

"Yeah, well, the EI got confused." Kate gave a nervous laugh. "The result is shocking; it could've addled its brains."

Corlin deduced by Kate's prattling that she must be perturbed, so was obviously the CHBC EI.

The probes had already determined that the alien colonists had *not* originated on Tomb. The cellular structures of the local marine life differed considerably from the one tiny creature whose bones lay naked outside the settlement, which they had designated Site I. The other 407 bones inside the settlement, Site II, were humanoid, covered by a greenish glassy substance that the probes' disassemblers couldn't penetrate.

"Vex you, Kate," Anna said. "Just tell me what the EI came up with."

"Fine, but you're not gonna like this. I ran it twice to be sure. There are three different types of genetic structures at Site II, even though the bones all look the same. All three types match the human genome to ninety-six percent."

"What?" Anna stared at the image of Kate, eyes full of disbelief.

Corlin felt his stomach lurch. Even aboard the *Celestis*, before they landed, he dreaded this. He had known when the shapes of large ribcages, femurs, and skulls first appeared on the probes' data. They were so obviously human bones. Despite its earthlike atmosphere, liquid water, and lack of microbes in the biosphere, he knew something dreadful happened here.

"Yes," Kate said. "The EI can't even analyze the other four percent. Its main theory is that they could be super genes. The Chief Science Officers are in conference with the captain."

Anna swallowed before she said, "Thanks, Kate. I'll get samples from the specimens at Site III. Finish collating data on the marine fauna."

Corlin flicked off the view from the tactile control in his glove. He sensed Anna's fear. Whether caused by the possibility that the mission might be terminated before they finished or something else, he couldn't tell. What he had overheard this morning was treason, Anna asking Kate to purge the EI's memory. And what did she want disabled?

"What do you make of this, Tiv?" Anna hastened along the maze, following the curving structures.

He shrugged, disturbed by her behavior. She must have found something important she didn't want to share with the other departments. Professional jealousy was not unheard of among ESC crews. Exploration has been clearly the playground for the xenobiologists, because most worlds didn't have ruins. ESC had found some derelict human settlements on marginal or hostile planets, abandoned by early colonists of the "Ark Ships" era, but those were barely millennia old. He always felt that even the probes neglected xeno-archaeology, programmed to seek only earthlike planets. Regretfully, his chosen field was considered a minor branch of science.

Until Tomb.

Corlin found it hard to fathom that human bones had moldered on this world for over seven hundred millennia. Or nearly human, he reminded himself. Where did they come from? Parallel evolution was out of the equation; besides, nothing else on the world supported it. But he said nothing about his thoughts. "Let's see what info the other bones yield."

"Right," she said in a tone of contrition. "Too bad we can't use the gravbelts."

The alien field that partially covered the maze and its environs interfered with the mechanisms of the gravity belts. Instead of risking accidents, he had decided not to use them. "Be glad the float pallets also have wheels."

Most of the tenement walls were intact in this section, laced with frost. Fluted columns adorned large gates. Balconies and tongues of slabs extended from the top stories.

Geo-imagers had shown a large chamber hundreds of meters below the ice, and the robots had started digging yesterday. A drilling robot churned inside a concave cavity, its upper chassis and shovel arms glinting orange with the rising sun as it threw out piles of ice. Analyzer units sifted through the sludge and recorded its composition.

As they neared the central complex, Corlin slowed imperceptibly. They paralleled the curving avenue and turned at the final junction. He found this route the shortest to the inner compound, but now he wished it were longer. His heart pounded and he looked around fearfully, eyes searching for the growing webs that had started in this ring of the maze.

He called up a grid image of the maze, slowly turning it, checking for any spread. Though he had run a quick surveillance at the base last night, he wanted to be certain. Some of the sensors they had placed inside the structure disappeared during the past few days.

"Wait up," he called after Anna. She was already at the edge of the path that bled into the central plaza. In a quick bound, he was at her side. "Don't rush this, Anna. I mean it."

"Sure, Tiv," she said and halted.

He read tension in her rigid shoulders, and urgency in her voice. They crossed the frozen ground in silence and reached the least damaged section of the alien energy shield. It was the color of a brown dwarf star, and it ebbed and flowed. A little farther, it fragmented into sharp ebony cracks, then thickened to murky brown corroded sections at the bottom.

Corlin turned away, his eyes smarting. They passed an amalgam of mechanical and biological jumble. Large pieces of machinery were fused together by filaments of barely seen webs, glinting with crystalline sheen at places, and then abruptly jerking into coarse black surfaces that seemed to suck light out of the surrounding area.

Anna entered a grisly tunnel, corrugated and lumpy. It seemed to undulate at their passage, like an esophagus of a large beast struggling to swallow them. According to the experts, it was a trick of the senses, because none of their sensors had ever registered any movement. When the tunnel ended, they ducked under a shiny blue arc.

He consulted the map grid again. "Below us to the left," he said and pointed across the large chamber. Anna activated her light and it bobbed up in the air. She hurried after him.

Gossamer strands of crimson and violet fluttered at their passing. From his peripheral vision, they looked like they would touch him at any moment. When he turned his head, they became still again. It was a nightmare scene, obscene and wrong. None of the disassemblers was able to analyze any of the samples they had taken thus far from the maze.

Tivor found the marked spot and felt his gorge rising. As his fear was a constant embarrassment, he appreciated his containment field for more than just protection, it also covered his skin flushes and palings and edginess.

"This is it." He stared at the wall. A mosaic of thick olive slime, wet fur, red pulsing sphincters, wrinkled yellow hide, and sharp spikes covered it. The entire tapestry looked like an experiment in biological outer coverings. Only the bodies were missing. They had passed it several times on previous visits, keeping well away from it, but Mara had stumbled and fell through yesterday.

"Come on," he said and grabbed Anna's hand. He closed his eyes and they stepped into the wall. Corlin couldn't help shuddering at the sound of sucking noises and moist embrace, but they passed through.

Large machines littered the chamber. His suit enhanced the images while he recorded everything for further study. The scene became even more disturbing, flowing into fractal patterns of chimerical shapes, playing havoc with his neural implants as his eyes strained to fit them into some perspective. Almost like a span of caterpillar thread, a ribbed wheel, and cranes with serrated mouths marched at the edge of his awareness. Sections of the machines had liquefied and then froze after the cold penetrated the settlement.

With a sigh, he moved his dating scanner in a wide sweep. The data downloaded automatically into his wrist unit.

Glancing at the device, he said, "Background dating only, a little over seven hundred thousand years old."

He approached the crystallized bones timidly, vaguely aware of Anna shuffling beside him. A sense of unreality gripped him at the sight. Preserved by whatever the glassy casing was, the white bones radiated an ancient warning. They were the partial remains of humanoid figures, giants of at least two and a half meters tall.

Corlin stood there and stared, palms slick with perspiration until his suit absorbed it. The bones were not just humanoid; they were human.

But the time, the time, the time, it echoed in his mind. The time factor was all wrong.

Some of the skeletons were nearly intact, others covered by purple mossy growths. A humerus lay detached from a shoulder bone, the green casing cracked. The skeletons were dotted with brown holes from which violet tubular structures burst out in clusters. A ribcage leaned sideways, poking curved bones skyward, as if imploring the heavens. Between the arcing bones, bundles of oyster-colored masses protruded. Corlin moved closer and squatted, adjusting his vision.

He gasped and scooted back, landing on his rump.

"You all right, Tiv?"

"Fine," he said after his suit adjusted to his rapid breathing. He stood up and approached again.

From the glistening globs, tiny faces glared at him, mocking human faces. He blinked and shook his head, but the vile scene remained. Some of the glassy coverings showed fractures and the faces underneath those looked like shriveled prunes.

He stood up, legs shaking, and started recording each of the sixteen bodies by moving his wrist unit over them. His hand trembled. Corlin didn't blame Mara for having neglected to take visual records last night; she was a greenie. He was not, but this place touched something primordial in him.

"Let me," he said and reached over his shoulder, removing the specimen gun from Anna's float pallet.

She stood in silence and stared, too paralyzed to protest the usurping of her work.

Corlin crouched next to the least damaged giant figure and pressed the specimen gun at the large femur. It punched through the pale green crystalline sheen that covered the bones and took a few grams of tissue sample. He checked the stasis window on the gun and saw it blink green, preserved and isolated. The question rose in his mind again: why were the probes unable to obtain tissue samples?

"Let's find the Hall of Statues now," he said.

"Mara said that's even worse." Anna walked before him but kept glancing back. She shrank away as they carefully wove their way below the hanging mucus and gossamer threads, ducking their heads to avoid contact.

Seven more skeletons lay at a short distance, barely recognizable through the layers of petrified organics and frozen crust that entombed them. He ran his analyzer over them, and again, it didn't register what the material was.

"We could've done this by using the VR program and we probably should have." He couldn't help the reproach in his tone, as Anna was among the scientists that had argued for landing.

"A physical survey always yields more answers. There's always something the drone sensors miss. Besides, the probes couldn't take tissue samples."

"Don't you find that odd? We're using the same tissue guns the probes did." A chilling thought occurred to him, so ominous that it nearly paralyzed him.

"Maybe the probes got damaged."

Corlin nodded, but he couldn't suppress his gnawing suspicion. He routed the data to the EI of the *Celestis* in mechanical motions. The physical specimens would be analyzed by the portable EI at the Base.

They walked through an arch, then a short tunnel, and finally stepped into a chamber. *The Hall of Statues, this must be where Mara had seen the standing figures.*

Barely discernible fractal patterns played on his retinas. The hovering light seemed to dim a fraction. The figures were a variety of shapes, all exceeding three meters. Standing upright and nearly jet-black with a faint luster of viridian and wine, like oil on water, they presented a menagerie from hell. The shine skidded across the hard surfaces of long knobby appendages that had five joints and looked like gears. They were undamaged and seemed full-fleshed. No bones showed.

Misshapen large heads displayed deeply set ruby eyes that he could've sworn were animated by malice. All had long hair, but the way it hung in neatly coiled fleshy tassels gave the impression of slim tentacles. Two had four arms coiling around their torsos, and one sprouted clusters of pincers from a human-looking mouth.

The fourth had six legs, but two of those dangled in the air. Its head was only a protoplasmic blob, folded and creased like a swollen brain, from which scarlet cilia sprouted. Some were connected to a round black disc.

Heart pounding, he reached over slowly and tried to pry away the disc. It didn't budge.

The grisly statues stood in a rough circle. Some had tails with metallic-looking spikes, and others were covered with round mirrors. He tried to guess the function of the overlapping blue flat organs covering a triangular head. Corlin gave up as they drifted past each one. Some sported tiny black clusters of eyes sprouting from shoulders, abdomens, and backs.

He took the tissue gun again and pressed it to a leg. And pressed it again. It emitted a shrill sound, but the covering of the statue remained unbroken. After he checked the stasis window, he tried another one. Nothing. He circled around the chamber and repeated the procedure, but the hard casing didn't yield to his tool.

"Looks like we'll have to skip these specimens," he said. "Let's go, there's nothing more we can do here."

He guided Anna across the hall and then through the slimy wall. They hurried toward the exit, taking long strides in doubled up positions. He could've sworn the filaments hung lower, fluttering at their passing and extending barely visible strands to reach them.

"So what do you think?" Anna's voice trembled.

"Something from space attacked them."

"Or they could be runaway replicators engineered by the colonists."

166

"No, it's more like a tailored swarm or some especially virulent replicators, something to kill the colonists." He wondered why she argued her point when the evidence was against it. "Perhaps they were refugees, fleeing from an enemy. And the enemy found them."

None of the native life suffered the same fate. The marine sediments and crust samples showed no great extinction in the timeframe when this happened. The ancient colonists were killed by a plague that had *not* originated on Tomb. Analyses showed that much, even if their instruments couldn't decode the structures of the pestilence completely.

Corlin called Dan and said, "Allocate four robots to install sensors in the new chambers Mara found."

"Right away," Dan replied.

Corlin ate dinner in the science complex, sitting by the portable bioanalyzer and munching a clish sandwich that Anna had brought him from the mess hall. Impatience gnawed at him, and he silently cursed the strident protocols of quarantine, slowing down the analyses considerably by adding numerous safety algorithms.

Disturbing scenarios crossed his mind. *What if the central complex was a testing site?* An ancient battleground where a molecular battle had been waged, subsuming foreign agents, decoding secrets, and forging alliances by wielding molecular armies within the silent tombs of each encased bodies.

The shrill sound of the alarm almost made him choke. He dropped the sandwich and jumped up, coughing, then blinking at the blurry image his implant generated. *The Nano Patrol,* he thought, and a chill exploded in his stomach. Silvery red forms stormed the corridor of the residential complex, stunners and blasters glinting with cold intent. They shoved crewmembers out of the dorms.

The seasoned crew fled instinctively, but some of the greenies milled around, staring, until one of the NP commandoes barked at them. Another one of the commandoes pointed a finger at a room, and a containment field formed instantly.

"Biohazard in room six," said the base system. "Residential section is presently—"

Another image popped up, showing Captain Norris aboard the *Celestis*. Distress lines marred her face. The curses and grunts emanating from the residential section nearly drowned out her voice. "Commander Corlin, the Nano Patrol landed. It's an auto response to a biohazard."

He stood in numbed silence, looking stupid with his mouth hanging open.

Finally, he said, "It's Rob's room."

"Yes," said the captain. "From the images we've got, it looks like something's replicating in there. It started from the tissue gun he used at Site II. He took one of the EI units into his room."

Corlin swallowed and felt his heart turning to stone. He didn't understand how this could have happened. The sealed systems were nanoimmune, hacker-proofed, and heuristic.

His earlier fear returned. The plague that infested the alien colony was not nano-based. He remembered Sam's bone cells and how those giant machines churned out millions of miniscule ones inside his genes.

He barely heard the captain's voice, "The NP will investigate if there might have been a human mistake. They'll examine the analyzer in—"

It happened silently. Rob's room buckled and turned vermilion, as if lit from within. Liquid fire oozed and burbled as it consumed furniture, walls, and equipment, melting them rapidly. The NP commandoes were backing out, their cyber arms spitting more thermnites into the residential building.

Corlin ran outside, yelling to people, "Get back! Clear the area." His eyes frantically searched for Anna, while he questioned the base system, "Where's Rob?"

Four commandoes stood outside now, pelting the residential complex with thermnite pallets.

"Is everyone out?" Tivor yelled. "Anna." Then he saw her angling toward him, whispering urgently to Kate. "Where's Robert?"

"Rob was in his quarters," said the base system.

Corlin felt like a punch in the gut.

He ran to the confused crowd and herded them toward the science complex, wondering who else might have remained inside. They were halfway across the open field when the residential building began to glow in intense ruby. The plaz walls swelled outward, bubbled and frothed, emitting a deep rumble until the entire structure began to collapse. The crimson goo kissed the ice with a loud slap, oozed and sizzled for a few seconds, then slowly crackled into pewter ash.

Four large figures stood in a ready stance around the inactive thermnites, cyber arms running analyzers over the ash. The sun stood high in the sky, etching their shapes into caustic shadows.

No one talked about Rob's death the following day, but some people looked cowed, others stoic, and the majority seemed neurotic, eyes shifting left and right. Anna and Kate looked guilty.

A small crowd gathered behind Dimitri in the science complex. He wore an interface design cap, its glistening convoluted surface like an extra brain, flickering with blue sparks. Corlin walked over and glanced at Dimitri's slowly turning 3D image. It showed a tubular, yellow object with blue spikes and barbs arranged around its outer surface. It looked like a cylindrical brush.

"It's a new disassembler he designed," Eli whispered. "He's running a final check, then we'll test it."

Dimitri had developed the disassemblers that traced some of the plague's structures. But his machines had halted at a certain stage.

"All right," Dimitri said and snatched off the interface cap. His black hair was matted but his eyes sparkled with enthusiasm. "These might do the trick. I just routed them to the sealed specimen container that has the bone tissue from Site II."

The image showed Dimitri's large yellow machines swimming to the site of chaos. Silver flywheels spun in a blur, spewing out snowflakes. Or at least they looked like snowflakes. They watched in silence, as Dimitri's machines started rotating also, snagging some of the silvery flakes.

People began to cheer halfheartedly.

The yellow nanomachines attenuated some of their spikes, but they seemed to be quivering. Clogs built up rapidly, and the tool arms stiffened. After about thirty minutes of struggle, they just circled the alien particles in a vague disorder, quickly losing their functioning abilities.

Dimitri zoomed in on one of his machines. It was covered by millions of snowflakes, busily winding filaments around it. When the snowflakes stopped spinning, his machine looked like a moth cocoon, the greenish substance similar to the casing of the bones.

"God, we're all going to die!" Carrie screamed. She began to cry, covering her face.

Corlin rushed over and led her away from the group. "Calm down, Carrie, we'll be fine," he whispered. "We have the best suits, plus the containment fields." Her body shook with great sobs, and she tried to shake off his arm. He felt sympathy for the greenie scientists. Tomb was a cruel blow to their illusion of grandeur, that humanity could do anything.

Mark, one of the medics, appeared at their side. "I'll get her a tranq," he said and led Carrie away. Corlin shot him a grateful glance and returned to the group, gauging the reaction of the others. They milled around nervously, glancing covertly at Dimitri's cocooned machines.

"Blast it," cursed Dimitri, as if unaware of the commotion. "I know the plague eats protein, carbon, and even necronites." He looked down at his boots.

"But they don't react to Tomb life," Ryan said. He was with the marine biology section. "We've just tested them on tissues and bones of several sea fauna."

Dimitri looked up. "Thanks, you've just given me an idea."

"It's been a long day," Corlin said and slapped him on the back. "You can start fresh tomorrow."

"Twenty-one hour days," Dimitri snorted. "Not long enough. I couldn't sleep anyway, so I'll run some combination programs of the Tomb life and the colonists'. See if I can design something new."

Corlin left and walked to the supply shack, their quarters since the destruction of the residential complex, wondering if the system would allow Dimitri to design hybrid disassemblers.

Anna lay on the airbed the robots had installed, wearing only a white shift. Though not as comfortable as the variforms that conformed to bodies, an airbed was better than the bare floor. Ground crews weren't too fastidious. She looked up from the image she was scrutinizing, then turned it off and gave him a careworn smile. "You look as tired as I feel."

While he removed his clothes and suit, his disturbing conclusions kept running through his mind. He lay down next to her and said, "Our probes activated the plague."

"What's that?" Anna looked away. She fiddled with the cover, hands shaking.

"The interstellar probes that ESC sent through the Mantus Nexus activated the plague particles."

"Oh," she said, and still didn't look at him.

"The probes couldn't take tissue samples from the bones; they've been sealed by that greenish substance, but they reactivated something dormant. It reacted to our own disassemblers, some recognition subroutine. Whether it's a lure to get us here physically or just an automatic recognition algorithm I don't know."

"You're saying it was premeditated, but I can't believe that." Her voice sounded false, and when she finally looked at him, her expression held fear.

"If someone wanted to infect us with the plague machines, they couldn't have gone through the probes. They only transmit *data* to the Coalition. They had to get us here. Our curiosity did the rest."

"Tiv, if what you're saying is true . . . . " She looked sheepish before she buried her face into his chest. "I'm so sorry." She began to sob. "We knew, Kate and I, from the initial samples. I ordered her to falsify the data sent to the *Celestis*, because—"

—you were afraid. Her body was shaking, and he pulled her closer.

"I, I suspected since the Site II samples that we were dealing with femto-scale replicators." She pulled away and wiped her eyes with the blanket.

"Dimitri may design something useful." Corlin embraced her, feeling his body responding to the warmth of hers. He didn't want to talk anymore, so he covered her mouth with his own.

They made love, then without the aid of their implants, they fell into a natural sleep.

Corlin woke up rested. After they ate a couple of cold ration bars, they went to see Dimitri.

A bustle of activity greeted them at the science complex, visual fields flickering with data loops, portable analyzers humming. A few stasis capsules passed them on floating sleds. He vaguely wondered why they were being moved when he saw Dimitri sitting alone and staring at a holoscreen.

Anna shook her head slightly, and he gazed at the images, trying to swallow his disappointment. Dimitri's hybrid disassemblers didn't work either; they just sat at the edge of the sub cellular structures of the ancient colonists.

"Commander," he heard from behind them. Eugene Thomas, the geophysicist waved at him, his voice filled with trepidation. "Please step over here."

He dashed to the other end of the room, Anna behind him.

"Something's tunneling through the ice." Thomas pointed to his visual field.

The base with its flickering containment field and the alien site above ground was rendered in color. The images below the ice looked a ghostly monochrome, but he could clearly see a bullet-shaped object heading in their direction.

"What is it?"

Thomas shook his head. "It's coming from here." He pointed to the central construction in the alien maze. A convoluted passage began below the ice, moving even as they were watching, not fast but relentlessly.

"Site III," Corlin whispered. He told the base EI to track the progress of the object and work out probable locations of its emergence.

"I am tracking and fully prepared to isolate the intruder," said the EI.

"Keep an eye on it," he said to Thomas and left.

The containment fields had been borne out of the Plague Years centuries ago, a brutal span of eighty years during which billions of people died and thousands of ecosystems were ruined. Everyone had worn them outside their communes and enclaves back then. As the plagues reorganized themselves and adapted, people invested more and more in field developments.

He opened the general com and said, "This is Commander Corlin. Everyone suit up and activate a personal containment field. This is an order."

The eye symbol, a classified reply to his earlier message, appeared on his retinal screen at 1400 shiptime. In a cold dread, Corlin blinked away the icon and left the science complex. Walking behind an ice rover, he activated the security program through his implant. He closed his eyes, hoping the scientists aboard the *Celestis* disagreed with his assessment. When he opened them, he gasped. DATA RECEIVED NECESSITATES A LEVEL FIVE BURN. BETWEEN 2000 AND 2400 HOURS. PREPARE CREW.

Tomb lingered in the wan sunlight of its orange primary before slipping into the long night. Corlin gazed out the plaz window of the science complex, between the jagged mountain peaks at the mauve sky, and dreaded the sparks that would soon appear on the horizon.

Anna was awake somewhere, but the rest of the ground crew slept. By regulation, they should be as well, perhaps dreaming about the future and a tomorrow. But he couldn't bring himself to sleep through the coming Burn.

A guardian of dreams now rather than a Commander, he grimaced and stood up, heading to perform his last duty. The prefab plaz door moved aside at his approach, and he stepped into the makeshift corridor. Robots had turned sections of the science complex into a dorm, partitioned them into tiny cubicles after the contamination of the residential building. A futile gesture to keep up morale, for they could have slept anywhere or nowhere for the short time, but ESC Quarantine Law was specific.

He stopped at the first door and interfaced with the base system. The occupant was in deep sleep. Marie Holt, planetary geologist, the image of the woman appeared on the holoscreen before him. She was young, thirty-six, and this was her third ground exploration. Corlin felt the guilt eating at him, but he had to remind himself that they had all signed the ESC contract.

I'm sorry I ordered your death, Marie, he thought and passed the sleeping woman's cubicle. The bare stone and plaz mixture made hard sounds under his boots. So much effort had gone into unraveling the mysteries of this world.

At the next cubicle, he called up the data, then closed his eyes to blot out the images. The memory of Dimitri's grinning face twisted his heart. He was the youngest member of their team, barely out of Space Force Academy, his very first exploration of an alien world.

172

The scene showed that Dimitri kept working until Corlin had released the sleepnites into the compound. Interface cap on his head, Dimitri slouched in the chair in front of his data streams, face lax in sleep like a child's.

He hung his head as he left Dimitri's door and proceeded to check the next one. From here on, he did them automatically, just making sure they were in deep sleep, then onto the next crewmember. By the time he finished, he was exhausted and emotionally drained.

Anna waited for him by the door of the supply shack. He walked slowly, trying to clear his head of the anxiety of waiting.

The Burn was a rarely mentioned topic among the crews of ESC, but it always hovered below the surface of their consciousness. A subliminal monster, it was the ultimate cure for a plague.

The low hum of the field generator barely penetrated his awareness when he passed the compact machine. They could even turn the force field off now. But then again, they had more power than they could ever use. A bitter laughter escaped his lips.

"You all right?" asked Anna. She held their suits.

Corlin shook his head. "No, I want to go outside and see this world with my naked eyes."

Her full lips tightened into thin lines, but she nodded. "I suppose it doesn't matter—"

He looked down, unable to face the despair in her eyes, though grateful she didn't state the time. He didn't want to know, needed to pretend for a while yet that these were not their last hours. They had agreed after he recommended the Burn, which he shouldn't have told her, that they wouldn't act, speak, and think morbidly. "It's over, it doesn't matter now, we're dead," wouldn't enter the remainder of their lives. But the words crept in more and more as the hour neared.

Anna shoved the suits into the supply shed and took his arm. He avoided looking at the two contained alien substances, baleful red domes protruding a meter above the ice and glimmering faintly. The containment field was fighting a losing battle, visibly dimming as the alien disassemblers rendered it useless.

When they reached the edge of the main field, Corlin asked the base system to form an aperture. Alarms rang through his implant, informing him that he needed a suit. The 3D schematic of the base was stitched with red blinking lights. Then all the pre-designated exit sites fused, and a biohazard sign hovered before him.

"Damn," he cursed. The stupid system thought there was still something worth protecting. He consulted the main program and found the override algorithm. From there, he shut down the field generator.

Beginning at the top of the coruscating dome, the containment field slowly etiolated, then flickered once. In the next instant, the field shimmered up again, sizzling as its energies singed the atmosphere of the world. It wavered above their heads for a second, and righted itself.

"Shit," Corlin cursed again. "The backup generator, I forgot about that."

Anna's hand slid up his arm. Her eyes filmed over for a second as she sent the command through her implant, then she said, "Fixed."

The field shuddered. Its rainbow colors rippled and lost coherence, turned red, and the field bled into the bruised sunset of Tomb.

He hesitated and looked back at the building that housed the sleeping crew. For both Anna and him, the next landing would have been their hundredth on an alien world. Neither of them would achieve that now. Not in this body, he knew.

A level five Burn, Corlin thought. He imagined the planet bombarded by thermnite missiles, consuming the atmosphere, the ice, and the ocean, liquid fire circling around. Dirty missiles would follow, exterminating whatever remained and thoroughly wiping away any chance for life for the unforeseeable future. A pang of sympathy stabbed through him at the thought of the native life, but then the full horror of *their* predicament hit him.

He gritted his teeth to hold his fear and led Anna from the base, lacing her arm through his. They walked in silence. The clouds had parted before the spilled ink of the sky, salted generously with stars. The wind tugged at them with icy claws. Tomb had no moons, but Tomb Guard, the gas giant next out, shone bright, its light flickering above the jagged teeth of the frosty mountains. Corlin sought calm by counting their steps.

Slowly, reason started nibbling chunks out of his fear and the tapestry of his life appeared in his mind's eye. He had woven that by threads of hard work, ambition, accomplishments, love, and even courage. How would all that reside in a new body?

As if reading his mind, Anna said, "I wonder how the Replives feel. You know, when they first realize . . . . "

"Maybe they don't know." *Or maybe they're not allowed to know.*

"We won't remember this." He detected motion from her body as Anna spread an arm to indicate the world.

He couldn't stand voicing that their new bodies would be robbed of the events on Tomb. He felt cheated. He dug his nails into his palms as a silent rage swelled inside him. He blamed ESC, but mostly Defense and Intelligence, because they had enacted the Quarantine Laws and carried out the, the . . . .

What, what was he thinking?

Murder.

Except they had all signed the consent forms and left tissue samples in stasis and memory records on file at ESC headquarters. Murder with consent, then.

"It's the price we pay for traveling between the stars," he said finally.

"Well, it seems the universe is exacting a steep price for expansion." Anna sounded resigned, her voice inflectionless, words falling on the darkness like stones.

Corlin wondered if he'd be happy being a cocoa farmer, or a corporate executive, or a virch designer, or a historian.

"What if we'd gone through a Burn before?"

"We could have." The possibility had occurred to him recently, because he had never seen or talked to a Replife before. There were ways that ESC could alter individual records and keep the identities of Replives classified.

"You think the Johannists are right?" Anna sidled closer to him.

"About what?"

"Our souls, that they're embedded in quantum packets of the universe."

He didn't put much credence in the Johannists' claims that some of them tapped into the inter-dimensional cracks and read the soul-memories. He wasn't even certain he believed that souls went into another dimension. But for Anna's sake, he said, "They've published enough *True Human History*, so it's quite likely."

"Our souls will wander around for some time before the *Celestis* reaches Coalition space. It'll take time to grow the clones even with the accelerators, then more time to imprint them. I wonder if our souls will recognize our new bodies." Her voice sounded distant, as if she was preparing for a long journey.

They stopped by the rise of a low hill and sank down on the ice. Their thermal clothing would protect them long enough not to freeze.

"I would've liked more time to study the sites since . . . . " Anna shuddered. "Perhaps not, because we don't know how long it would take to end up like the bones."

Worse than that, whatever killed the colony could still be out there among the stars. He regretted that they would never know why a race of super humans died on Tomb seven hundred millennia ago. Fear clawed at him again. How could the Coalition defend humanity against a threat like that?

Corlin was glad that he had slipped a small dose of tranq into Anna's coffee at dinner. She seemed calmer than was possible under the circumstances. He pulled her closer, and she leaned into him. Her even breathing calmed him eventually.

The wind stopped tugging. There was stillness in the air, as if Tomb held its breath. Abruptly the sky lit up with tiny red sparks, growing into fireballs, and then into a sheet of plasma.

A feeling of déjà vu gripped him as he stared, mesmerized. The next instant, pain seared through him as the heat slammed into them. Corlin held Anna in a melding embrace and felt their bodies blistering.

Captain Norris watched through the view port of her cabin, blinking to stem the flow of tears, useless moisture that didn't wash away the pain. Crimson worms crawled over the world as the thermnite missiles landed, expanding into blankets of fire. The oceans boiled as the nuke-tipped missiles ruptured Tomb's crust, throwing up steams of cloud and dust.

She turned away, wiped her face, and prompted her implant to file her report, "Celestis Log, Inner League date March 8, 1427 (3821), 2310 shiptime. Successful Burn at Coordinates: MNX-006485979. Interdiction filed, see data attached." Number nineteen on the list of interdicted systems, she thought. But the scourge must be contained. During her long career in Defense and Intelligence, Captain Claire Norris had watched four other worlds going through a Burn, though not in this cloned body. Despite the enormous expense invested into opening the Mantus Nexus, the wormhole would be dismantled.

Tomb, a world that should never have been named, has been named. A scourge that should never have been awakened, has been awakened.

Honeymoon at the Pearly Gate
by Tom Barlow

Hesperina wondered if she would ever again be able to enjoy making love back home, now that she knew the pleasure of one-sixth gravity. Here on the moon, Santiago moved into her as gently as a new mother opening her baby's fist.

Afterward, they lay in the Earth glow, wearing only their new wedding bands. Hesp caught Santiago staring at her.

"What are you thinking?" she said.

He laced his fingers between her toes. "I was thinking how lucky we are to be young and rich. Those old, rich people in the lobby? The mooncap told me they pay more than a million a year to live here year round, in rooms no bigger than this one."

"What do you suppose is so wonderful about their lives, that they'd move to the moon just to prolong them a few years?"

"Maybe their lives on Earth were so terrible this seems like a dream by comparison."

"There are dreams," she said, "and there are nightmares."

"Which is this?"

"If I woke up and found out this was a dream—that would be my worst nightmare."

Their reservation for time in the swimming pool came up the next morning. Hesperina stood so long on the edge of the diving platform, those waiting behind her began to mutter loud enough for her to hear. She took one last look at the stark black and white landscape surrounding the view bubble, then launched from the platform into a simple swan dive.

She fell so deliberately she could count her heartbeats while in mid-air. The water parted gently at her entry, and when she kicked back to the surface, the splash of her impact was still falling around her, like the tickle of waterfall. She wanted to float on her back, drinking in the crescent Earth overhead, but another diver was already on the edge of the platform above her, poised to dive into the small pool.

She and Santiago sat at the poolside cabana through two bottles of Pernod and a light lunch, watching others frolic in the water.

"What will you remember most about our honeymoon?" she asked.

"I thought it would be different," Santiago said. "I never realized there would be so much waiting. It's as crowded here as the São Paulo train station at quitting time. And all the old people. Instead of The Honeymoon Hotel, maybe they should have called it the Lunar Extended Care Facility."

Hesp noted the delay before he remembered to add, "But most of all, the honeymoon. Of course. I was right, wasn't I? That things would be better once we got away from our families for a little while? How about you? What will you remember?"

"Gravity."

"We call it the Pearly Gate." The voice came from the table behind them.

Hesp turned. At the next table an old man sat by himself, a reading tablet on the table in front of him.

"The hotel," he said. "We call it the Pearly Gate."

She tried to dismiss the old man with a smile, but Santiago chuckled. She bit her tongue, reminding herself she'd promised to overlook her husband's annoying habit of talking to strangers, anytime, anywhere. The old man took his reply as an invitation to continue.

"Ninety percent of the people working in this place are over a hundred. Not that you would know it. They put the kids on the front desk. They're . . . perky."

Hesp looked the old man over, trying to gauge how to take what he said. Recent weight loss, she thought, his skin hanging in loose folds down his neck. His milk-pale skin was covered with freckles or age spots; she wasn't clear about the difference. She could see a change in slope of his nose, where the bony edge tipped over into cartilage.

"One hundred and thirty-one," he said, meeting her eyes.

Santiago seemed oblivious to her sense of intrusion. "How long have you been up here?"

"Since they opened. Nineteen years, seven months, eleven days. Tariq Lowenstein, by the way." He raised his glass to them.

"Why'd you come up?"

"My wife wanted to live long enough to see our great-grandchildren grow up."

"How did it work out?" Hesp asked.

"She died a year ago. Now, nobody ever calls," Tariq said. "When you move up here, families back home eventually forget about you. Maybe they think we're close enough to dead that they don't need to stay in touch. Unless you have a big estate, of course."

"If you could prolong your life by moving here, would you do it?" Hesp asked Santiago as they snuggled into their bunk that Earth night.

"I suppose it depends on what kind of life I had," he said. "My first wife's grandmother could probably have afforded it, but she wasn't interested. She said the thought of living a second lifetime with her husband was more than she could take."

"So she let herself die?"

"She tried, but my wife's father and his priest had different ideas. Her body's still alive in a nursing facility near São Paulo. They visit her twice a year. To tell you the truth, I think he wishes now he would have let her die."

"Still, as long as she's still breathing they can hope for a miracle, right? That's worth something."

Santiago laughed. "That's what I love about you. You could find the bright side of a pitch-black coin."

Hesp put her hand over his mouth. "New topic. What sightseeing did you sign us up for?"

"None, yet. The travel agent said we shouldn't plan on sightseeing the first couple of days up here, but she wouldn't tell me why." He moved his hand up the smooth skin of her inner thigh. "I know why, now."

They ran into Tariq again at dinner. He was dining with a woman of a similar age, as thin and pale as a new moon, with white hair that stood out from her head like a corona. Hesp gritted her teeth when Santiago asked Tariq if he and Hesp could join them.

Tariq waved them to the open seats and introduced his companion, Esther. "Her husband John and I were poker buddies," he said. "We came up on the same shuttle, nineteen years ago."

Hesp paused before replying, to allow Esther to add to the conversation, but she only stared at the placemat.

"Esther can't speak, since her stroke a year ago," Tariq explained. "Just after John passed away."

Hesperina was relieved that the waiter interposed with menus while she tried to think of a polite reply.

"What do you recommend?" Santiago asked Tariq.

"It doesn't matter. If you eat with your eyes closed, it all tastes the same. They vary the color and shape, but it's all mush. Try the filet mignon. It's the chewiest mush."

"Do you always eat here?" Hesp asked as the sommelier poured glasses of wine.

"Not much choice, is there? I'd kill for a few falafel off a street cart, but we don't have those on the moon; too spicy for most of us. Most of the time I eat by myself." He nodded toward a table of not-quite-so-old-looking people across the room. "The youngsters are afraid to eat with me. They're afraid death might come here looking for me while I'm in the restroom, and take them instead."

To change the subject, Hesp asked Tariq which tours he would recommend.

"The Alpine Valley is nice. So is the Cape. You could climb Mt. Hadley, if you're into that sort of thing. Of course, everybody gets their picture taken next to the flag over at the Apollo 11 site—that's the main stop on the tram. The "Gateway to the Stars" memorial isn't too far from here. The thing about the moon is there isn't a lot of variety. There are only so many ways to pile gray rock and dust."

"How about the Schröter Valley?" Santiago said.

Tariq drained his wine, pulled the bottle from the cooling tube, and refilled his glass. "That's not a good honeymoon tour," he said. "I wouldn't recommend it."

Esther nodded in agreement.

"Why?" Santiago said. "I watched my father's holos; the ones of the canyon are stunning."

Instead of answering, Tariq said, "I might be able to get you on the Cape tour. The guide is seated behind you. Give me a second." He excused himself and walked across the room to the one table of young people. He talked to an attractive young blonde woman. She nodded.

Tariq arrived back at their table just as the waiter brought their meals. "You're set. Tomorrow, 1100 hours, at Attaturk gate. 400 Creds each. That's not a problem, is it?"

Santiago chewed his Nutribeef. "This trip was a wedding gift from my parents. They can afford it, believe me."

"If there's one thing better than young love, it's young love and rich parents."

"You talk like somebody with experience."

"Yes, I was a rich parent."

"Where did you send your children on their honeymoon?" Hesperina asked.

"They all asked for money, instead."

"We took care of that, huh?" Santiago said, giggling and looking at Hesp.

"We asked for both."

Hesp kept her eyes on her plate, methodically cutting her meat-like substance into smaller and smaller pieces.

Given the crowds everywhere they went, Hesp expected a large group for the Cape tour the next Earth day, so she was surprised to find only eight people, including the blonde guide.

The guide appeared to be about the same age as Hesp, but gifted with the grace of movement she had always lacked and the sultry, Levantine face that reminded her of Santiago's first wife. She introduced herself as Sarah.

Her assistant, a man who looked closer in age to Tariq, fitted them with suits. Hesp chose one with a jungle pattern, vines with green elephant-ear-size leaves and cones of orange ginger-flowers. Santiago chose a pin-striped New York Yankees suit.

Sarah talked them through the controls, how to work the shortlink suit-to-suit radio, and how to limit their transmissions to private conversations. She was unable to keep a tinge of boredom from her voice. Hesperina took comfort in that boredom as an indication nothing unexpected ever happened. Santiago asked Sarah to help him adjust the tensioner straps on his suit.

Hesp took a seat next to the bulkhead. The guide entered next, taking the aisle seat.

Santiago entered last, wiggling into the center seat between them. "Kind of cramped in here, isn't it?" he said.

"When we're busy we pack ten seats to a shuttle," Sarah replied. "That's tight. This is much better."

As Santiago settled in his seat, Hesp was pushed toward the sidewall until a small bulge in the fabric stabbed into her butt cheek.

"It's like sharing a coffin," Santiago said to the guide, turning slightly away from Hesp. "You pilot the shuttle?"

Sarah pointed to the panel on her sleeve. "Autopilot. One button." She took his hand and pulled it toward the panel, pressed her finger on his. "You do it. Push this button, once, then hold on. We use a ballistic boost at the start, so you'll feel some acceleration. Make sure you're not leaning against anything that might poke you in the back."

He pushed. They heard the maglev kick in. The shuttle shot up the long inclined trough.

The pressure of acceleration died out quickly. Through her portal, Hesperina watched the moon surface fly by, dark gray rock, sharp shadow. They were just high enough to see the oval mouths of small craters in the Mare

Imbrium as they passed. The horizon looked unnaturally close. Every few minutes, the engines fired briefly to regain altitude.

After a couple of futile attempts to claim a place in the conversation, Hesp tuned out Santiago and Sarah's chatter as best she could and stared out the portal.

Half an hour later, Sarah announced the shuttle was beginning its landing approach. Hesp was the first to spot the landing trough ahead. The shuttle settled into it, sliding smoothly to a stop against the dock. Santiago let out a big breath as the deceleration dissipated.

Sarah helped them unstrap and climb out of the shuttle. She lined them up on the dock and checked their suits, helping Santiago pull down his visor against the glare of the sun.

"Single file, please," Sarah said, clipping a line from one to the next until they were all connected like Japanese lanterns. "Please don't walk outside the walkway boundaries. There are soft spots in the soil."

Hesperina was reminded of her school trips as a child, holding onto the rope as the teacher instructed, to keep them from wandering off. They all fell into a shuffling walk.

For as far as she could see on either side of the trail the ground was covered with footprints, wandering like those of a dog in a dump. The footprints were widely spaced, lighter in color than the undisturbed surface.

After a few minutes, they reached the crest of the crater and confronted the Cape Agassiz.

"The Cape Agassiz," Sarah said, "marks the end of the Alps, where they terminate in the Mare Imbrium." She talked on, full of bits of geology and astronomy that went over Hesp's head. When Sarah began to point out places in the rock face that resembled the profiles of famous entertainers, Hesp tuned out, content to watch the light move slowly across the cliff face. Unlike back home, there were no gray patches; shadow disappeared in the sun as though caught in a spotlight.

Sarah led them down the slope into the Mare. When they reached an area near the base of the cliff that was relatively smooth, she allowed them to untether.

"This is a good place to try out your moon legs while outside," she said, pointing to the field before them, covered with footprints. "See how far you can hop, if you want to. Just be careful, please. Start easy. If your heart rate spikes, your suit will lock its joints until you calm down, so don't panic if that happens. Breathe and wait a minute."

Hesperina and Santiago spent the first few minutes broad jumping, pogo-hopping, playing leap-frog, and running with such broad steps she felt like she was flying. Sarah joined them. At Santiago's request, she demonstrated how to execute the Lunar double back flip from the top of a waist-high rock.

Hesp held onto his hand through the entire return trip.

Tariq joined Hesp and Santiago again for dinner later that day, as though it had already become their custom. This time he was alone. They were eating early, in order to attend the formal ball later.

"How did you like the Cape?" Tariq asked as he took a seat at their table.

"Fantastic," Santiago said. "I felt like Superman, running around out there."

Tariq nodded. "It is fun for the first year or two. The first year I was here, a few of us did a hike from Eratasthenes to Mt. Caucaus. 500 klicks in three days. It still might be the longest walk on record here; I'm not really sure."

"You don't walk outside anymore?" Hesp asked.

"As you get older, you find fewer and fewer reasons to go outside."

"Is Esther going to join us?" Hesp said.

"No," Tariq said. "She won't be joining us today. It's just me."

"Oh. I'm sorry," Hesp said. "I hope she's not ill?"

Tariq shook his head. "No, not really. I may be joining her later."

"You should bring her to the ball tonight."

"I'm too old for dancing," Tariq said.

Santiago caught the waiter's attention and ordered a bottle of Möet Champagne. He turned back to Tariq and said, "Any other tours you'd recommend?"

"Tranquility Bay is always popular. My wife's favorite was chasing the sunset."

"Chasing the sunset?" Hesp said.

"The moon rotates so slowly that, if you hustle, you can keep up with the line between night and day. There's a tour to the Sinus Iridium—the Bay of Rainbows? You can walk along in the dawn, watch it light up the Jura mountains in front of you. Or you can take the same tour later in the month and chase the sunset."

"Once I had a rainstorm chase me for ten minutes," Hesp said. "I could hear the raindrops behind me as I walked. When I had to wait to cross a street, it stopped, too."

Tariq nodded. "It's a strange sensation, knowing you're walking exactly as fast as the moon rotates, like you're keeping pace with the sun. Or the dark. I suppose it's a glass-half-empty question, whether you chase the light or the dark."

The sommelier delivered the champagne to their table. Santiago slowly poured Hesperina a glass. They both giggled at the grape-sized bubbles in the wine.

"I'm was sorry to hear your wife died a year ago." Hesp took a long sip of her champagne. Santiago immediately refilled her glass, and topped off his own.

"Why did you move to the moon? This is a great place to honeymoon, but it doesn't seem like a great place to live."

"She would have died years ago if we hadn't."

"But you could go home, if you wanted?" Santiago asked.

"Everyone that comes to the moon has to buy a round trip ticket. That way, if you run out of money, the hotel can dump you on a shuttle. Once you've lived on the moon for years, though, going back to Earth gravity is a death sentence in itself." He looked Santiago up and down. "You weigh, what—80 kg, Earthside? Suppose you woke up one day and you weighed 500 kg?"

"So was it worth it? Leaving Earth?"

"Some days yes, some days no. It depends on the weather."

When Hesp and Santiago didn't respond, Tariq said, "That's a moon joke."

The comment struck Hesp as more sad than funny. She kicked Santiago's shin lightly when he laughed too loud and long.

Hesperina and her husband paper-scissor-rocked for the bottom position after the dance. They both loved to stare at the Earth as they climaxed.

"You know the best thing about honeymooning on the moon?" Santiago said, afterward, as they burrowed deeper under the covers, chilling slightly from the sweat evaporating from their skin.

"The sex?"

"That too. For the rest of our lives, every time we see the moon in the sky, we'll remember this."

"What if we had some big fight before we leave? Then think what would be hanging over our heads every night for the rest of our lives."

"I didn't realize you were a glass-half-empty type of girl."

"I may see the glass as half empty, but at least I'm not too blind to see it at all."

Santiago bought them seats on the "Chase the Sunrise" tour the next day. Sarah was again their tour guide. The attendant had them suited up and strapped into the shuttle before she arrived.

Thirty minutes after departure, they spotted the line of demarcation between day and night, retreating slowly before them. The shuttle passed through the line, plunging them into darkness. Now, Hesp could look behind them and watch the light chasing them.

The shuttle slid down the trough to a stop at a platform in the middle of the wide plain of the Sinus Iridium. Sarah herded them out, lined them up on the ground parallel to the advancing line of sunshine. "One hour, people. We don't want to get too far from the shuttle. Wait for the sun to reach you, then walk with it. If you walk on the dark side of the line, your suit will have to work very hard to keep you warm. The moment when the sun hits the mountaintops ahead is my favorite sight on the moon; don't miss it."

The sun passed below the horizon. Hesp and Santiago let the line advance a couple of meters in front of them before beginning to walk. Sarah fell in beside Santiago.

Almost immediately, they saw moon glitter. Hesp watched the ground sparkle, small pinpoints of flare like fireflies in the June meadow back on the Pampas.

"Minerals in the soil phosphoresce," Sarah explained.

"Sometimes," Santiago said, "I'd rather not know why. I'd rather believe in magic."

"That's exactly what I said the first time I saw it," Sarah said. She reached down and picked up one of the flaring rocks and dropped it in his hand. "There's no law that says you can't take a little bit of magic home with you."

Hesp shook off the impression that Sarah's hand rested a moment too long on Santiago's, telling herself that everything on the moon seemed to transpire more slowly.

When they reached the shuttle for the return trip, Santiago handed the rock to Hesp, and said, "Make sure we pack this to take home."

The group arrived back at the hotel just as another tour was queuing up in the staging area.

"Where are they off to?" Hesp asked the attendant as she handed him her suit.

"The Schröter Valley," he said. "Every other day at 5:00 GMT."

"Not the youngest crowd I've seen," Santiago said as he shed his suit.

"It never is," Sarah said. She took his suit and carried it to the rental counter.

"There's Esther," Hesperina said, pulling Santiago's arm to draw her attention.

185

Esther was at the end of the line waiting to enter the shuttle. She was just sealing herself into a utilitarian white suit, like those of the workers they had seen through their room portals, working on the sculpture garden that surrounded the hotel. Hesp waited for Esther to make eye contact, but neither she nor any of the other seven oldsters on the tour looked their way as they filed one by one into the shuttle Hesp and Santiago had just exited. As the door slid shut, she caught a glimpse of Tariq through his faceplate.

They dined alone that dinner. Hesp found herself missing Tariq's company. She tried to recall if Santiago had always smacked his lips while he ate, or if it was a trait he'd acquired since they arrived on the moon.

"I gave them the go-ahead on the Buenos Aires apartment," he said, as the waiter delivered after-dinner French-press coffee and small glasses of Armangnac to the table.

"Was that decided? I thought we were going to discuss it."

"Dad said the landlord refused to hold the lease for us without a deposit."

"What about the house?"

"We can save up for a better house. The apartment is in the Puerto Madero. You'll love it; right on the water. I can walk to the office."

"What about my mother? It'll take her at least an hour on the bus."

"Now that we're married, I wouldn't expect her to stop by every day. By the way, I asked my mother to keep an eye out for a housekeeper for us."

"Why don't you let me handle that? It will be our home, after all."

"When we can pay for it ourselves, I'll consider it our home. Since my family has the money . . ."

"And my family has, what? The squalor?"

"OK. Sorry. Forget I mentioned money. Tonight's casino night. What do you say we play some blackjack?"

"You just said, forget the money. Then you want to play blackjack?" She tossed back her cognac, enjoying the slow burn down her throat as it flowed, one-sixth gravity, to her stomach.

"You're not in the slums anymore. This is how we live. Loosen up a little, for Christ's sake. "

That night, for the first time, she found herself noticing the ceiling surrounding the view port in their room, the places where a careless painter had dragged the color onto the edge of the clear window. As Santiago moved into her, she was conscious of dryness in the air. His skin had grown slightly abrasive, desert dry. She counted her heartbeats as she waited for him to finish.

They ended up at the same blackjack table as Tariq that evening. He was seated behind a small stack of chips and a half-empty tumbler of whiskey.

He acknowledged them with a nod, but Hesp knew enough about gambling protocol to not attempt a conversation. She watched over Santiago's shoulder as he played his usual illogical blackjack, sometimes asking for a card while holding sixteen, sometimes sticking at fourteen. She knew his stack wouldn't last long.

Tariq appeared to play a similar game. He tossed chips to the dealer with apparent disinterest. Win or lose, the worry lines above his eyes didn't change. The only time she saw emotion on his face was a smile when he threw in his final chips. He looked up and caught her watching. She smiled and nodded at him.

When he left the table, Hesp and Santiago joined him at the bar. Santiago ordered a bottle of vintage Chateau Petreus.

Tariq said, "Are you two happy? With one another, I mean?"

The question took them aback. "Of course. It is our honeymoon, after all," Santiago said.

"What do you mean by that?" Hesp said. "Like we shouldn't expect to be happy after the honeymoon is over?"

Tariq waved his hands. "I didn't intend to start an argument. It's just something we talk about a lot, up here. Since most of us have been married for a long time."

"Were you happy with your wife?" Hesp asked.

"I believe I was. The longer she's gone, the more convinced I am that we were happy."

"Do you miss her?" Hesp asked.

"The older I get, the more I miss every person I've ever lost. Every new person I meet resembles a bad copy of someone I've lost."

"I've never heard anyone say that before."

"We have a term for it, up here. We call it 'moonsick.'"

"What can you do about it?"

"We wait. Nothing lasts forever."

Hesp woke once in the night. Santiago's side of the bed was empty. She was accustomed to his insomnia, his habit of taking walks in the middle of the night, back home. She lay awake for a long time, wondering when he had gone, just as she did back home.

She woke to the smell of coffee. Santiago held a cup out to her.

"Got us two seats on the Schröter Valley this afternoon," he said. "Turns out the attendant likes blackjack night more than his budget does. One of the couples scheduled for today is as hard up as he is, so I bought their tickets from him. It must suck to be poor, but it sure makes life easy for us that aren't."

"I didn't know we wanted to go on that tour," she said. "Tariq didn't speak well of it."

He leaned over to kiss her. She tried to place the faint fragrance carried in his hair.

They arrived early for the tour. The old attendant gave them different suits. "These belong to the couple whose spots you're taking. We aren't supposed to allow substitutions, so sit in the front seats and pretend you're taking a nap until the shuttle is under way," he told them. "Most folks here take naps all the time anyway. Once you're away from the station, they won't turn around."

Hesp and Santiago climbed into the front two seats. With the hatch behind them, and the seat headrests beside them, no one could see their faces. Out of the corner of her eye, Hesp watched one of the passengers open the small luggage hatch next to them to store a small parcel, the size of a flight pillow.

Her frisson of fear evaporated as soon as they felt the first tug of acceleration. To her surprise, Hesp dozed off as they passed over the Mare Ilium.

She woke as they reached the Schröter Valley an hour later. At first sight, from her shuttle window, Hersperina was disappointed. She had expected something with the breadth of the Copper Canyon, but this reminded her more of the Black Canyon of the Gunnison; deep, but narrow.

First in, they were the last to exit the shuttle. Their guide waited for them to join the lineup. To her surprise, Hesp recognized Tariq behind the faceplate of the guide suit. At the same time, he recognized theirs.

"What do you think you're doing here?" Tariq said, hands on his hips.

"It's a public tour, right?" Santiago said. Hesp cringed at his callous tone.

Tariq frowned. "Let's go," he finally said and turned his attention to the others.

Hesp noted that they were the only young people on the tour. The others were closer to Tariq's age, with vintage suits showing wear spots, patches and personalization. The man next to her had a painted Ganesha's head on the tankpack of his suit.

Hesp and Santiago lined up for the tether, but to their surprise, the visitors shuffled off without it. Tariq brought up the rear.

"Don't tell the boss," Tariq said. "Nobody likes to be tied to another person when he's standing at the edge of a cliff."

The group worked its way up the switchbacks to the canyon lip. Tariq pointed out that the sun was to the south and the valley ran east to west. Consequently, only a hundred meters of the canyon wall was illuminated.

Hesp noticed an immediate difference between this tour and previous ones; a lack of chatter. The visitors weren't talking to one another, and Tariq wasn't providing guide narration.

"Isn't this beautiful?" Hesp said to Santiago, as they crested the rise and the sharp, ragged slice of the canyon appeared before them, trailing away toward both sides of the horizon.

"I've seen better," he replied. "Reminds me of the Royal Gorge. Without the souvenir stands."

"You can buy the t-shirt back at the hotel," Tariq said. "'My Parents visited the Schröter Valley and all I got was this crummy t-shirt.'"

The group moved cautiously onto the first viewing platform, little different from the surrounding cliff side except for a six-meter-high railing. Hesp took her place at the railing, leaning through the rails until she could look down. She was startled when an arc of light suddenly illuminated the canyon to a depth of she guessed at 500 meters or more. The canyon sparkled.

"The walls of the canyon are full of phosphorescent minerals. The bottom of the canyon never sees the light," Tariq explained, "so the company added some spot lights. To enhance your moon experience." He touched a pad on his forearm, and the wash of the lights began to cycle through colors; magenta, violet, sun yellow, grass green, Polynesian blue.

Hesp was so entranced by the light show she didn't notice at first when the others left the platform. Movement below and beside the platform caught her eye. She pulled Santiago's arm to gain his attention.

The other tour guests had circled around the fence to gather on the unprotected cliff edge in a semi-circle facing Tariq. One of them unrolled the small package that had been carried in the storage bin. Inside, Hesp could see roses, dried but still an almost hallucinogenic scarlet against the grey background. The flower bearer handed each in the group a flower.

"What are they doing?" Santiago said.

Hesp shook her head.

Tariq stepped back from the group to the lip of the canyon, two flowers in his hands. He looked up at Hesp and Santiago. "We have a little tradition up here. When you live on the moon, sometimes you can reach a point where your body doesn't know enough to die, but the rest of you doesn't have any reason to live. Moonsick. Like Esther.

"For me, the first one hundred and thirty years wasn't too bad. The one year without my wife? That was one year too many. You Earthies can have the rest of the moon, but the Schröter Valley belongs to the moonsick."

He fumbled with the latches on his helmet until it suddenly popped free, then he took another step back, into the space beyond the cliff's edge. As he slowly fell, through the blue light, yellow light, and red light, he placed a flower in his teeth. Then he was gone into the depths of the darkness. One by one, the others stepped to the edge of the cliff and dropped their flowers into the valley.

When Santiago did not move, as through transfixed, Hesp grabbed his arm and pulled it around her. She tried to bury her helmeted head in his chest. She ached for the feel of his skin under her cheek, but could feel nothing through the shell of her helmet and the fabric of his suit. Not even his heartbeat.

A Dream?
by F.V. "Ed" Edwards

The being felt a powerful expulsion and a dizzying sensation. A steady increase in temperature and wind velocity was ended by a jarring collision. That was followed by what seemed a long skid on a bumpy surface which made a horrific clattering sound. Movement stopped. There was silence and a dense fog-like darkness. The atmosphere grew frigid. Detached consciousness began shifting to terrified awareness. The being wanted to cry out for help but had no vocal system. There were no limbs to move, or muscles to flex. The clattering sounds had been heard. Wind and temperature changes were felt. That clearly meant there was sensory perception. Thoughts and emotions were present. An attempt to assess the situation caused it to think "Where the hell am I, and why?" accompanied by strong demanding emotions.

Jumbled images began spinning within the consciousness. As frustration and anger built, the maddening carousel gained speed until there was an incomprehensible blur. The being realized it was necessary to take a deep breath, relax and let the insane parade slow down. That thought brought the recognition there wasn't a breathing function through which to calm nonexistent muscular, tendon and nerve systems. A brief state of fury caused intense pain until the being created a mental image of taking a deep breath. The blur slowed enough to allow focus on finding some cohesive organization in the cognitive whirlpool.

Slowly a few matching pieces came together in kaleidoscopic form, only to stay briefly before another set of pieces matched. Wanting to stop the unending parade of scenes that moved the moment there was an inkling of recognition, the being strongly thought, "Slow down or stop."

The scope stopped and froze on a picture of streaking and fixed stars somewhere in an unknown universe.

An eerie voice said, "The scenes will come together so you may understand why you are here. Your ability to comprehend and maintain focus will determine the speed and content. You've already noted attitudes of frustration and anger cause the images to change at a nightmarish speed. The process will continue until daylight and begin again with darkness."

Pleased there would be light, the being thought, "Who the hell are you,

191

and how long do I have to stay here?"

"I know who I am. You are here to discover the truth of yourself. You will determine how many eons you stay. I suggest you observe your past in the dark, and use the periods of light in wise reflection. Learn why you are here and you will discover the way to leave."

The kaleidoscope started moving. A desire to scream sped it up.

Visualization of a deep breath brought scenes to a pause. When recognition was strong, one would linger longer. The memories of that period lasted until the being felt vindication regarding the portrayed actions. The process seemed impossible to stop. In about half of them the being was a male, in others female. The thought query "What am I now?" brought no response. If anything, movement from scene to scene seemed faster. Shuddering with the chilling temperature and the struggle to maintain thought control of itself, the being was sure one or two eons of terror must have passed.

A dim light was sensed, ending a fear of eternal darkness that had slowly evolved. Visual capability was welcomed and a sun was seen rising over some distant mountains. The immediate foreground was not clearly discernible. As the sun rose higher, the temperature climbed rapidly. The glare hurt vision and the being discovered there were no eyes to close. An unbelievable combination of unlimited peripheral sight allowed thoughts to change the view to another sector. The heat was intense, but at least vision was not blinded. Wishing the painful visual capacity to end didn't help. There were only desolate views of what appeared as an unending plain of small rocks in all directions except for the mountains seen before the sun cleared them. As the sun approached the zenith, a small trench leading up to the view point could be seen. "My God, how can I be a rock? Rocks don't have thoughts," the being would have screeched if it had vocal capability.

Heat from the sun was becoming unbearable and made it more difficult to maintain focus. The thoughts cascaded through millions of possibilities that eventually settled on two. Residing inside a rock in the middle of nowhere, blistered by a sun and frozen in the darkness, was either a nightmare or an unacceptable reality. The voice had said the nightmare would resume at sunset. If the voice was a part of the dream, then reality should return upon awakening. It made sense to flow through to the end of the dream without resistance. The mountains turned to a shade of reddishness as sunset approached. The sight brought the snide thought question, "Why am I not important enough to be a mountain?"

Eerie laughter was followed by the voice saying, "You are awake, and the sooner you accept your present reality, the quicker you will begin learning the truth of yourself. You've wasted this period of light."

"Who the hell do you think you are?" was the responsive thought.

"Mine to know and yours to discover." The voice was deep and authoritative. "You aren't residing in a rock. You *are* a large igneous rock, and you are here for a purpose. You have not practiced the underlying truths in recent forms, thus you're here to relearn the primary lessons of universal existence."

"If I'm a rock, what's my name?" the being asked, playing along with the dream wondering when the alarm would bring sleep and the nightmare to an end.

"If you wish to have a name, pick it. Think of yourself as that name if needed, knowing that in truth, beings have no name. Some creatures seem to need names to express individuality within an existence. Are you able to quote the name of the last fly you swatted?"

"Since when has a fly been a being?" was sent as a strong thought.

The eerie voice seemed to chuckle as it asked, "How many eons will you question the ways of the universe before you accept the truth? Your own choices led to becoming a rock on this desolate planet."

A dark fog ended visibility. The temperature plummeted. Sounds like a fire alarm bell rang. Kaleidoscopic images began clicking in and out of patterns. The being with no name tried to rouse its named self from the dream to no avail.

The Days After
by Jean-Michel Calvez

Lord wiped the back of his sleeve over the dusty cap of the large paint can. The lid had been frozen shut by time and a rim of rust encircling it. He pushed hard under the edge of the lid with the broken blade of his knife and finally pried it open.

The heavy consistency and creamy color of the paint half opened the door of fond childhood memories long concealed in dark corners of his mind. But the moist, acrid smell of solvent turned his stomach and drove away all other feelings.

He slowly stirred the mixture, as gummy and thick as tar. It had long since gone out of date. But if he could dilute it, it would serve his purpose: to lighten the dark green he had painted on the inner face of the plastic leaves intended for the Tree. The leaves were slowly drying in the humid air and lying side by side on a rough piece of canvas he had spread on the ground.

A coughing fit took him by surprise and almost made him drop the slimy wooden stick he was holding. He wiped the stick with a rag and then closed the lid on the can with a single blow of his fist. Anyway, the leaves were not ready yet. He would continue painting tomorrow, in the short hours when a fragile sun finally broke through the deep fog that always coated the evenings.

His aching eyes burned in the corrosive fog under the pale, feeble light, and they soon became exhausted as he went about his painstaking work. Cutting out the leaves one at a time with a knife on a flat stone required eye-straining concentration.

Lord stood up slowly, avoiding sudden exertion that might suffocate him in the rarefied atmosphere. The oxygen level must be very low, but he had no instruments to measure it precisely. He had also made a determined effort, some time ago, to stop building fires against the everlasting twilight—a pathetic and somewhat illogical attempt to save both breathable air and the remaining rotten wood.

Lord went out to the Tree. It had no leaves yet, but even so it was the only one that looked healthy in the dying forest. Most of the other tree trunks would not collapse right away; that is, as long as the wind didn't pick up again. They stood motionless, like wounded soldiers abandoned without hope or care on a battlefield. He would go up to them quietly, as though they were children stricken by fever. He scarcely dared brush his fingers against them for fear that the bark might break and fall off, making a disgusting display of the pulpy, almost spongy matter oozing out from irregular cracks in the wood.

Halfway up the slope, Lord stopped for a short rest. He was gasping for breath, exhausted simply from standing up. He had forced himself to take on the painful chore of carrying his few tools and, especially, the long, rusty metal rods that bit into his shoulders every time he stumbled. And then there were the dozens of buckets of water, sand, and concrete mix.

But he was determined to build the Tree—to make it grow, he liked to think—on a place in the landscape that was visible from afar. It didn't matter that it could only loosely be called a hill, strictly speaking; it was the only height he was still able to climb.

If they came back some day, it would be easier for them to find.

Lord leaned back against the solid tree trunk and gradually caught his breath. He tried to forget how icy the concrete felt against his shoulder blades. A drop of sweat trickled from his forehead down into a wrinkle on his hollow cheek. With only the scarce materials he had, he found it impossible to imitate the warmth and gentle roughness of living wood. Anybody can picture life, talk about it, sculpt it, copy its outward appearance, but nobody can create it with his hands. And yet he sometimes felt a certain rush of pride when he gazed fondly on the stark lines, curves, and elegant unevenness of the painted concrete.

He had taken bark fragments from trees sagging under their own weight and eaten through by disease, and he had moulded the pieces of bark into the still-fresh concrete. He was finishing the work by hand, adding lines of wood grain where they were missing between the patches of bark. He traced them with his blunted knife, as though he were filling in spaces in a jigsaw puzzle. He was sorry that he could not ward off the slow death of the last trees, but he could not bear to strip the last shield from those still standing. He knew that was all he could do for them anymore.

New shreds of grey mist kept rolling in from the eastern twilight like flocks without a shepherd. The surrounding forest changed into an ancient, ghostly nightmare reflected in infinite images like an optical illusion, one that Lord might have banished merely by shutting his eyes tightly or shaking his head forcefully to wash away the stench of rot.

Had not he, too, been afflicted with the disease? The fog was its only material form and the only—almost palpable—evidence of its existence. His skin was dry and his eyes burned; he suffered constant weakness, moved clumsily, and had trouble breathing the thin, oily air that seemed to have lost its substance. Were those not symptoms of an incurable illness like that of the trees, an evil that was dissolving his flesh under the bark of his pallid skin?

In the first days, Lord had searched for comrades in misfortune but found none. He then withdrew into himself like a suffocated plant. He gradually awoke and realized how important his mission was. He was alone. All alone. He alone was entrusted with the mission to deliver the message and perpetuate the images of a life that was gone and that he remembered.

At first he had dreamt too big and conceived a mad scheme to lay out winding brooks on the plain. The streams would carry messages or love notes to a distant observer. He imagined vast fields of flowers that he would paint one by one in bright colors and dispel the surrounding grayness. He also wanted to build—no, to plant!—an incorruptible forest in which he would hide a real waterfall, one that he would design and build with his own hands, one that would be as alive as an animal and as resounding as life itself.

But the evil, illness, and pain were in him, and their irritating, ever-present fatigue and lassitude wore down even his motions and, sometimes, his thoughts. Or was it only time marching faster and working insidiously to restrict a bit more, every day, the scope of the work that he could imagine undertaking? And yet one trace must remain: the Tree must survive upon the hill. At least that. At least one thing.

Suddenly Lord felt dizzy and almost fell. To keep from collapsing into the sterile, muddy soil, he desperately threw his arms around his unfinished Tree as though embracing a beloved woman who was indifferent. And very cold.

The unbreathable fog thickened around him. And Lord prayed, his lips pressed to the rough surface, that they would understand, or at least know what he had tried to do and what he might accomplish before they came back.

If they did come back . . .

Ozymandias Redux
by Skadi meic Beorh

On nights as this I see a bronze platoon
marching through this wasteland;
dreary, shifting sands.
A cohort hailing from forgotten land,
weaving its spell when looms Diana's moon.

Near a broken fane a wailing loon
feathers the cold as if sensing festoon
where pillars sink and rise like misused wands.

The troops present their arms to mute commands
and marshal near the ruin's clearest rune.

For some now unremembered fight they wait,
pining for validation in affray.

They drill and train here; rehearse, simulate
campaigns they trust will drive to disarray
an enemy whose swords have become rust;
whose wary eyes have long since turned to dust.

—after Michael Fantina

All Quiet on the Vega Front
by Chris Benton

Tam Heller was on day 176 of his one-year tour of duty aboard Vigilance Point 1771, the sole living occupant of the outpost. Desperate for something to do that didn't involve videos, books, or calisthenics, he busied himself polishing the viewport windows in Primary Control while Mozart's *Jupiter* Symphony blared from speakers placed high in the ceiling. It didn't matter that the windows didn't need polishing; Tam was grateful for the chore. He knew better than to think too hard about makework in a place like this. Some days, it was the only thing that kept him tethered.

The outpost had not been well-maintained over the years. The armistice with the Lyrans was now twenty-one years old, and the passage of time had taken its toll on both the station and the motivation behind establishing it in the first place. Political bickering amongst the clerics in the Centrum, budget cuts, and a growing belief that the Vigilance Points were a relic of a bygone age were all responsible for the deterioration. The outpost still functioned, but barely. Tam spent a good amount of time fixing minor problems that would never have appeared had anyone still cared enough to fully fund the place.

Examining his dim reflection in the sparkling glass-composite, Tam wondered if the other manned VPs had the same problems. Tam's Vigilance Point was the outermost in the entire shell of five thousand, near Vega, the brightest star in the constellation Lyra as seen from Earth. Only a fraction of the outposts were manned; the rest were automated. Tam's VP controlled several hundred of the automated ones, and it was sometimes a daily struggle to make sure that they were in communication with each other. As always, though, he stopped short of complaining about the outpost's shortcomings. Repairs gave him something to do.

Besides, he *wanted* to keep the outpost in peak condition. Tam took his job seriously. He had reason to. Unlike many who served aboard the Vigilance Points, he was a veteran of the Lyran Conflict, and he had seen first-hand what they were capable of doing. The thought that they could ever come back was a haunting one.

Satisfied, he climbed down the stepladder and took a few steps back. He nodded. Like new, in contrast with the rest of the room; which, like the entire outpost, was dingy, worn, and quite beyond the ministrations of a single man. The view of the Barstow Nebula, a seething mass of bright green, yellow, and white on the left side of the viewport, was spectacular. The nebula itself was a holdover from the Lyran Conflict, the star that spawned it the victim of a hideous superweapon mistakenly deployed. Tam scanned slowly to the right across the viewport with a contemplative expression, his eyes leaving the brilliant nebula and coming to rest on its polar opposite: the empty, inky blackness of space.

Tam knew he shouldn't look out the viewport for any long length of time. It was always a mistake. It caused him to focus on the wrong things. His predecessor had said something to the effect that leaving a man alone with his own thoughts for too long was dangerous. The tour of duty on a Vigilance Point was tough. He'd had no human contact apart from official dispatches for almost six months, and he had another six like that to look forward to. With no family, and with Darius out of the picture, he also had no one to communicate with back home, isolating him even more. This meant he had—and would have—an awful lot of time to think, and a man's thoughts in that type of isolation, with no outside voice to mediate them, could wander in shadowy directions.

Tam found that happening more often than made him comfortable. It was quite sobering to realize that, at that moment, he was the most far-flung human being in all of colonized space. Vigilance Point 1771 was perched at the very edge of human territory. Of the billions of citizens in the Communion, he was the most removed from anything resembling companionship. The thought often made him melancholy; sometimes it even scared him. He'd always thought of himself as a loner at heart, even when he was with Darius. Who did he really need other than himself? But out here, he realized that even loners needed the *option* of human interaction. Six months into his tour, and he was ready to trade his eye teeth just for the opportunity to overhear a whispered conversation, or to trade banal repartee with parishioners after Prayer, or to bump into someone on the street just so he could say, "Excuse me." Just laying eyes on a flesh-and-blood person would be enough right now.

As *Jupiter* came to a crescendo around him, Tam pinched his eyes shut and forced himself to turn away from the viewport. It was nearly 22:00, and the weekly dispatch had not arrived yet. Tam yawned. "Probably arguing over what to censor this week," he thought aloud, mainly to remind himself that he could still talk. Distractions, in the form of letters from home or certain types of news, were heavily regulated and only allowed at certain intervals. *Live* contact with the outside world was forbidden to him as an Operator, the idea being that slavish devotion to monitoring Lyran space would ensure that any attack would be detected in plenty of time. Tam had convinced himself that he was used to it. But sometimes, when the music was off, the videos were watched for the tenth time, and there was nothing but the whirr of the air recyclers for company, he doubted.

Just as *Jupiter* finished up with a majestic sweep, the communications console came to life, its annoying buzz indicating an incoming transmission. "Finally." Tam sat at the scratched and dented console and pressed the worn ACCEPT key. The image of a dour, middle-aged colonel appeared on a section of the viewport.

"Great," said Tam. "Braxton."

"This is dispatch #26 intended for Sergeant Tamerlane Heller, Communion Armed Forces—"

"Ceres Regiment, Seventh Division," muttered Tam along with the recording.

"Standard security will be observed. This message is intended for the recipient's eyes and ears only."

"So I should send my entourage home, then?" asked Tam.

"Updates from all Vigilance Points are being collated and processed for analysis. Preliminary analysis indicates that Lyran space is quiescent, with no activity, hostile or otherwise, detected."

Tam wasn't surprised. In the twenty-one years since the ceasefire was put in place, the Lyrans had neither been seen nor heard. No one knew what, if anything, they were up to, and no one dared cross the armistice line to find out. The ceasefire stipulations—hammered out in agonizing fashion by both parties, neither of whom could speak the other's language—were very clear about what would happen if anyone did.

"As your Vigilance Point is the closest one to the armistice line and, therefore, to Lyran space, it is vital that you maintain the same rigorous level of surveillance we have come to expect from 1771. You are the first alert in the event of an attack. I'm sure by now that you're probably weary of us reminding you, but when one is as isolated as you are, Sergeant, one can often be overwhelmed by the conditions under which he is expected to perform. You're doing a fine job, and we are confident that you will continue to do your duty admirably."

"Just keep sending me my filet mignon," murmured Tam as he rose from the chair and turned the volume up. He had, indeed, heard it all before. He set the apparatus on "broadcast" so that he could hear the transmission in any part of the outpost and stalked toward the kitchen. Colonel Braxton continued uninterrupted.

"Your six-month supply ship has launched and is en route. There was . . . some difficulty in getting it underway, but that has been resolved, and you should be receiving it in two days." Tam wondered about the pause in the general's voice. He was sure he was holding something back, but since his news was censored, he probably wouldn't know what it was until his tour was up. He grabbed a mineral water (alcohol was expressly forbidden aboard Vigilance Points) from the refrigerator and continued listening.

"I encourage you to review the protocols involved in the docking, unloading, and departure of your supply ship. The procedure is straightforward, since the supply ship's operations are largely automated, but they should be followed to the letter. I'm sure you were briefed on the mishap at VP 4023. We don't want a repeat of that, especially on an outpost as sensitive as yours."

"I remember, all right," said Tam with a small shudder. He leaned against the bulkhead and took a long pull from his bottle. The Operator of Vigilance Point 4023, some six light-years away, had failed to check for a hard seal at the airlock when his supply ship docked, and when he opened the outer door, the cargo bay immediately decompressed. There were rumors that it had actually been a suicide (not unheard of with this kind of duty), but the official report cited "Operator negligence" as the cause of the accident. Not the way Tam planned on leaving his own VP.

The rest of the dispatch was a laundry list of things Tam couldn't have cared less about. It amounted to a military gossip column. Finally, it came to an end.

"We're still working on getting you a permanent liaison. With the Centrum demanding more oversight of Vigilance Point activities, I'm afraid you're going to end up with someone of their choosing if we're not very careful. But before then, this is still a military operation, and we're doing everything in our power to get them to back off. That's all for now, Sergeant. This is Colonel Braxton, Communion Armed Forces, signing off. Until next week, alo vigilo."

The transmission ended with a beep, and Tam reentered Primary Control and shut the apparatus down. He yawned again. Sitting before the main console, he spun his chair around slowly. The ceiling whirled overhead, water-stained, half-lit in the glow from the nebula outside. Primary Control was about the size of a large living room; large enough to stave off claustrophobia, but not unwieldy or inefficient. Everything about a Vigilance Point was small and unobtrusive. And shabby. Tam brooded. He'd explored the entire outpost in about an hour and a half when he'd first arrived. It only took that long because he'd stretched it out as much as he could, figuring he'd kill the entire first day just poking around. But there were only three small decks, two of which were wholly devoted to sensor equipment, with the middle deck consisting of Primary Control, living quarters, and the cargo bay. He wished now that he hadn't been so glib with the man he replaced. When he first boarded the outpost, a year didn't seem like a long time. And the perks...

He'd met his predecessor only once, as he handed over the security codes and passkeys on his way to the airlock. They'd had roughly a half hour conversation. Tam now recalled his face: pale, haunted. The man was coherent, even friendly, but Tam could tell that this place had robbed him of something. "A year out here is like ten planetside," he'd said. "I don't know what you were told before you shipped out, but this ain't a picnic."

"But the food is good," quipped Tam. "Or so I was led to believe."

"Best in the Communion. Best of everything, in fact. Videos, games, meals, you name it. All part of your hardship pay. It makes the dirty bulkheads and scuffed furniture easier to take. But trust me on this, sergeant." The Operator drew close and spoke in a low, desperate voice. "Find something to keep your *mind* occupied, not just your senses. Believe me, it'll save your life."

Tam looked at the Operator, puzzled. As a recluse, he couldn't imagine a single year of isolation being all that bad. He smiled. "I've got a lot going on up here," he said, tapping his skull. "And lots of thinking to do. I don't think I'll have a problem."

The Operator gave him a look that might have been pity. "I hope you're right, Sergeant Heller. But be careful what you think *about*. This place..." He looked around and shook his head. "Loneliness does strange things to a man, even if he *likes* being alone." He dropped the passkeys into Tam's hand and, without another word, cycled the airlock. He was gone a few minutes later.

Tam finished his water. Loneliness. He thought it wouldn't get to him. *Couldn't* get to him. Not after...

"Not after Darius," he muttered. He shook his head and headed for his quarters, the previous operator's words on his mind.

"Be careful what you think *about*."

Tam dreamed.

Rather, Tam *remembered*. His sleep wasn't troubled by dreams, anymore. Instead, sleep was where the *memories* held sway. When he was awake, he could force them away with tasks, or reading, or other diversions. In the few hours of sleep per night that he could steal, though, he was defenseless against them. And as the days of his deployment played themselves out, the memories became more persistent, more demanding.

He remembered his forty-first birthday. It was the day before he left for his deployment to the Vigilance Point. He'd fought bitterly with Darius. Their relationship was coming to an end, anyway, but to Darius, Tam's volunteering for this duty was a final, unforgivable slap in the face.

"You'd run to the edge of the universe just to get away from me? Do you really hate me that much?"

"I've never hated you, Darius. I could *never* hate you. That's not what this is about!"

"No? Then why didn't you take the Centauri posting?"

"Look, this is an opportunity. A *good* one. There are only a few of these slots open, and few at my rank are ever chosen for them. It's a year. One year! I've done worse duty than that."

Darius shook his head, his face radiating the hate he felt for Tam at that moment. "You know, there's no reason in the world I should care what you do, anymore. But I can't help it. And God help me for that. Four damned years . . . "

"Darius—"

"Save it! We were done a long time ago. I guess I've been in denial all this time. But this is it, isn't it? This is really it."

Tam closed his eyes and nodded. He reopened them and looked at Darius sympathetically. "Yes, this is it. I'm sorry. I'm so sorry."

Darius sneered and turned away. "Don't bother. Just go. Go to your damned Vigilance Point. Go fight your damned war. It's not like you ever stopped."

"Darius, please don't—"

"Go!"

Tam opened his eyes. He was awake. The clock read 06:25. There was wetness on his face. He'd cried a little. Angrily wiping the tears away, he sat up in his rack and rubbed his forehead. The supply ship would be at the airlock in about an hour and a half. He'd better get ready for it.

Stumbling out of the rack, he wrinkled his nose. There was an odd smell in his quarters and the adjoining corridor, like sweat and mold blending together. *The air purifiers are acting up again,* he thought. A squeaky fan in one of the intake shafts had been keeping him up nights. He'd fixed it, but he wondered if the repair had made the situation worse. The entire system was in desperate need of an overhaul, but he didn't see parts for it listed on the incoming supply ship's manifest. *This whole place is held together with sticky tape and rubber bands,* he thought. *I'll rig something to fix it later.*

He thought about Darius as he made his way to the shower. He had done as Darius asked. He left. With no parting words, without even looking back, he left. After four years of ups and downs, fights and reconciliations, his last memory of Darius was of his face twisted in hate; hate for him, hate for the Service, hate for the knowledge that things had been coming to an end before Tam had even received his orders. Hate, and hurt. Terrible hurt.

"No. Not today," said Tam as he turned the water on. He willed himself to think about the task ahead: unloading the supply ship when it arrived. Nothing else mattered. Darius was ancient history by now. *All* of his old concerns were. There was nothing left but job and duty.

If only he had somebody to talk to!

The shower invigorated him, helped to clear his mind. He dried off and punched up a particularly bombastic symphony by Simcoe, who had been gaining some notoriety in the Communion with his bellicose offerings. For him, as for Tam, the Lyran threat wasn't over. Tam approved.

He ate a leisurely breakfast and reviewed the docking/unloading instructions for the supply ship as Braxton had suggested, more out of a desire for something to do than for reinforcement. He'd practically memorized the manuals for every procedure on the Vigilance Point. Checking his watch, he realized that it was due any minute. He'd eaten up enough time.

Simcoe's *Symphony Number 2: La Victoire* pounded through the speakers as Tam went to the airlock and activated the external viewer. There was a growing speck at the center of the viewable area: the nosecone of the supply ship. A helpful automatic voice informed him that it would dock in ten minutes, and then it began to recite a litany of instructions, the ones he had just read. "They *really* don't want another 4023, do they?" he asked.

The computer didn't respond.

As he gazed into the viewer, he could just make out his reflection in its glass-composite. He looked tired. That was nothing new. He barely slept anymore, and the drudgery of his duties was wearing him out. He hadn't shaved in two days, and his uniform was wrinkled. Command would have a fit if it knew what he looked like right now, but he never worried about that. His only visitor in the next six months would be his replacement, and Command would only ever see him if he had to transmit in person. It was as his predecessor had said: You either obsessed about the day-to-day formalities of hygiene as a way to stay focused, or you dropped them, one by one, as they ceased to matter. Tam was not happy to observe that he'd fallen into the latter camp. He resolved to tighten up. If nothing else, he'd be more particular about his uniform. Regardless of circumstances, he still honored the Service.

Ten minutes later, the small supply ship had come alongside the Vigilance Point and attached itself to the airlock. Tam double-checked for a hard seal. Satisfied, he cycled the lock. The cargo door on the supply ship hissed open automatically.

Tam went aboard the supply ship and made a cursory inventory of its contents. He then grabbed a maglev pallet and began to load containers onto it. He figured six round trips would take care of it.

Tam smiled a bit as he read the manifest. Part of the hardship pay awarded to Operators of Vigilance Points was top-quality food and virtually unlimited access to music, videos, and games. Filet mignon, veal cutlets, specially-prepared gourmet vegetarian dishes; it was better food than he'd ever eaten in his life, and yet another "wasteful extravagance" that the Centrum clerics demanded be brought to heel. Tam wished that each dissenting member of the Centrum could be compelled to do a single tour aboard a Vigilance Point. *Then* let them complain about a few creature comforts. But the irony of his situation did not escape him. He probably ate better than most anyone in the Communion, but there was no money to provide him with fresh air.

Simcoe was winding down his second movement as Tam finished unloading the supply ship. Gazing around, he inspected his handiwork. The cargo deck was a mess. In order to stretch out the job, he'd set the containers down haphazardly, figuring he could kill an hour or two putting them all where they belonged.

He was puzzled when the ship didn't decouple and leave after he'd sealed the airlock. The supply ship was fully automated and programmed to depart when the last items in its hold were removed and the airlock sealed. But it was still sitting there. Frowning, Tam re-cycled the lock.

He entered the ship and looked at the digital readout that showed the gross weight of the vessel. Even accounting for his own weight, it was off by about eighty-five kilograms. Tam looked around to make sure he hadn't forgotten to unload anything. The hold was empty.

Well what, then?

"Terrific." Tam passed through the airlock again and hunted around for his small toolkit, figuring the scales in the hold might need to be calibrated. He had only a vague idea of how to do that, but like anything else that occurred on the Vigilance Point that was out of the ordinary, he welcomed it as a diversion. He re-entered the ship and looked at the readout again. It was now jiggling up and down by five or six kilos. Frustrated, Tam jumped and slammed his feet to the deck.

The scale's display fluttered, settled down, and finally read correctly.

Tam rolled his eyes as he added this incident to the ever-growing list of grievances he had about this tour. Candidates for Vigilance Point duty underwent rigorous psychological testing before being accepted, but death by a thousand petty annoyances wasn't covered by any of the training he received. He actually felt himself becoming *angry* about it. Totally irrational, but he felt it brewing nevertheless. "One goddamned thing after another," he said as he leaned his head against the bulkhead of the ship. Big problems were rare and took care of themselves with only a little help from him. The *small* things, though; the dozens of minor, petty issues that cropped up on an almost daily basis, *those* were the ones that probably drove the Operator of 4023 crazy, and who knows how many others? He never realized just how *insidious* the small stuff was until he was forced to deal with it by himself. In the six months he'd been stationed on the VP, he'd come to appreciate the value of something he'd always taken for granted: a sounding board. Just five minutes with someone to whom he could vent . . .

He took a few deep breaths and felt his heart rate slow. He then thought about how easy it would be to sabotage the readout and make it appear that the ship was empty, then seal the airlock and fly away with the ship. He wondered why no one had thought of it before.

"Tempting," he said. He dismissed the thought almost as soon as it was formed. He'd never abandon his post. No matter how bad things were, or might be later, they could never be *that* bad. He'd fought the Lyrans hand-to-hand. A leaky pipe, or a faulty sensor reading, or a malfunctioning scale on a damned supply ship wasn't enough to push him over the edge.

He hoped.

As Simcoe's symphony continued to thunder, Tam exited the supply ship and sealed the airlock. In a few seconds, the ship decoupled from the airlock and was on its way. Tam watched it glide away until it became merely another pinpoint amongst the stars. He envied its freedom.

"There's always the escape vessel," he murmured, then chastised himself for thinking again about abandoning his post. His face grim, Tam set about straightening up the cargo hold.

A few hours later, he had showered again and was sitting in Primary Control, a chef's salad before him and *Sly Gypsy* on the viewscreen. It had to be one of the stupidest shows he'd ever seen, yet he found himself unwilling to turn it off in favor of something better. Outside, the Barstow Nebula roiled and cast the left side of his face in a green hue. Tam's left eye winced at the glare as he continued to watch what was now passing for comedy in the Communion.

From time to time, he looked away from the video and out at the blackness on the right side of the viewport, where he tried to visualize the armistice line between Lyran and human territory. In his head, he saw it as the meandering yellow streak on the map he occasionally called up on the Vigilance Point's computer. He shook his head slightly and sighed. What an absurd notion. Outer space was limitless. *Borderless.* The human need to quantify, to define boundaries, had been taken to the stars. Could no one see how illogical it was to try to carve up space into spheres of influence? Buoys marked the border between Lyran and human space, but what good was that, really? What was to stop them from simply enveloping the Communion, claiming all of the space around it as theirs? What was to stop some other race from doing the same to the Lyrans?

And what if, despite our best efforts, we never see them coming?

He'd just put a mouthful of the salad into his mouth when the communications console came to life. The buzz of an incoming transmission made him jump. This was highly irregular. There had been nothing but the standard weekly communiqués since he'd arrived. He leaned forward and dimmed the sound on his video, then tapped the ACCEPT key, wondering what was up.

"Urgent communiqué for Vigilance Point 1771, Operator Tamerlane Heller, sergeant, Communion Armed Forces. Complete analysis of reports from your sister Vigilance Points shows that there has been unusual activity in a particular sector of Lyran space in the past eighteen hours. Although the exact nature of the activity is not clear, and we are not, at this time, suspecting enemy movements, you are ordered to a state of high alert. The sector coordinates will follow this message. You are ordered to increase surveillance of this sector and report any unusual activity immediately. Elevated security protocols are now in place. Alo vigilo, sergeant. Message ends."

Tam felt another squirt of adrenaline. "Elevated security protocols" meant only one thing: He was now *truly* on his own. He would be under a total news and communication blackout. If the worst were to happen, his standing orders were to send as much telemetry to Command as possible; then, upon confirmation, scuttle his Vigilance Point. He made a mental note to check the condition of the escape vessel as soon as possible.

Eventually, he turned up the sound and finished watching *Sly Gypsy,* convincing himself that elevated security wouldn't be so bad. After all, it wasn't like he had much to miss. Braxton's grim mug certainly wasn't among the things he depended on way out here. When he felt himself nodding off in his chair, he rubbed his eyes and turned off the video. He fed the coordinates he was given by Command into the VP's surveillance system and set the sensors and scanners to their highest sensitivity. "Somebody saw a goddamn solar flare," he grumbled. Still, it was the most interesting thing that had happened since his arrival.

But he knew he would sleep unevenly that night, if at all.

He knew the scent. The last time he'd smelled it was over twenty years ago, on Bargeld, a humid world with dense, steaming jungles and a sickening, pinkish-red sky. It was the scent of a particular Lyran skin secretion, a waste product. Tam shuddered.

Memory took hold of him. He was back on Bargeld, in the waning days of the Conflict. He and his unit were deployed around a landing zone on the north continent, deep within enemy-held territory. Rather than try to roll the Lyrans up along a front, Command decided to drop large squads right into their lines, having learned early on that Lyrans preferred frontal assaults and were confused by guerilla tactics. Where the Communion was tactically weak in space, it had the upper hand in ground-based combat.

It was during this battle that Tam had his first face-to-face encounter with a Lyran. Until then, he'd only seen pictures and low-resolution videos of them. Nothing could have prepared him for what he saw with his own eyes, or for the ferocity with which they fought.

He saw the Lyran foot soldier before it saw him. Both had been separated from their units, and Tam was just about to barrel into a clearing when he glimpsed its profile. Skidding to a halt, he had just enough time to bring his weapon to bear before it turned around. At that point, he was a mere four meters away from it. What he saw would stay with him forever.

It stood a full twenty centimeters taller than him. Most of the Lyrans encountered by humans wore bulky suits that concealed what they looked like. This one, however, was clad only in what appeared to be a brown singlet with inscrutable insignia, its green-gray amphibian skin exposed and glistening with that odd-smelling secretion. In its oversized hands was a projectile weapon so alien in construction that Tam could never in a million years understand how it worked. There was nothing about the Lyran's face that could convey human emotion, yet he sensed the hate in it. It hissed at him violently; a high-pitched, wheezy sound that chilled his blood.

In that moment, Tam knew hell.

He shot at it, and it flailed its right arm as the shot impacted with its shoulder. It dropped its rifle and squawked hideously. Tam fired again, but he had run out of ammo. Running purely on adrenaline and instinct, he launched himself at it, knowing that either he or the Lyran alone would walk out of that clearing. It fought like hell, trying to stomp him with its feet, its huge hands slapping him from side to side as if he were a rag doll. Finally, it managed to get both of its hands around his neck. Rather than strangle him, it seemed to be trying to wrench his head clean off. With what was left of his strength, Tam plunged a knife into the Lyran's thorax. It went limp instantly, and with barely a whisper, it died.

He limped back to his unit with the smell of the dead Lyran all over him, its blood and that mucous-like secretion soaking into his uniform. He'd never forgotten that smell. Stale, antiseptic. There was no reason for him to be remembering it now, except for the fact that the new waste solution in the Vigilance Point's privy carried a vaguely similar smell.

"I can't even go to the bathroom in peace anymore," said Tam, holding his head in his hands. The memory of the Bargeld battle had jarred him, and he remained in the privy for several minutes, trying to regain his composure. He wanted to find the person who formulated the waste solution and strangle him, or put him in front of a live Lyran.

Eventually, he wandered back to Primary Control and resumed his usual duties. He had been under elevated security restrictions for four days, and the "unusual activity" in the sector he was ordered to monitor had failed to materialize again. In those four days, he actually slept through his entire allotted cycle, but unpleasant memories haunted him every time he closed his eyes. Even if he got a full eight hours, it sometimes felt as if he'd never slept at all. Some of the memories were vivid enough to resemble wakefulness.

He went over the readings one more time and, satisfied that nothing was going to launch itself at him within the next hour or so, he punched up an ancient, ponderous symphony by the genius Mahler and headed for his quarters. Spots swam in front of his eyes, and his gait was unsteady. *Need to feed myself,* he thought. He never thought he could get tired of the luxurious food he was provided, but even Kobe beef got boring after awhile. *Six months. How the hell did everyone else do this for a whole year?* Of course, he knew how. Most of them had probably either left nothing behind that they cared about, or they had nothing to leave behind to begin with. Tam wondered if a sociopathic streak was necessary for survival on a Vigilance Point. If a man wasn't a sociopath when he arrived here, Tam felt sure that he would be before he left.

"Learn not to care. About anything. That's the key," he said to himself. But he'd never been good at that. He'd never let the war go, for instance. He was very young when the Lyran Conflict had started, and though he'd been drafted, he'd served with distinction for a man of his age. But war is hardest on the young. The battles, the times when he'd emerged from combat when he should have been killed; all left an impression on his psyche that neither time nor his will could easily wipe away. It was the same with Darius. Survivor's guilt, in both cases.

He thought of Darius again, practically on the other side of the known universe; one of the few people in his life with whom he'd had any meaningful connection. And he'd let his demons win out over love. What was he doing right now? Who was he with? Did Tam even factor into his thinking anymore? For four years they'd tried to make a go of it, to have a relationship around Tam's military service, around his nightmares, his refusal to reenter counseling or to take the medicines that might have made his dark memories more manageable; more like afterthoughts instead of the living, breathing phantasms they were now. They'd even discussed marriage, to the point where Tam was ready to go to his priest to seek the blessing of the Church (mainly for Darius's benefit, as he was the true believer in their pairing). Instead, their long course had led, inexorably, to that ugly scene on Tam's birthday and their final sundering. And the worst part for Tam was that the love was still there. Love, coupled with a deep sense of remorse. What Tam would give to make everything right, to tell Darius that he'd see his counselor, to submit himself for medication, just for the *chance* of being with him again.

Dear God, I miss him so much. How did one learn not to care when the love remained behind and refused to be sent away?

When he reached his quarters, he felt under his rack for one of the few personal possessions he was allowed to bring with him: his mother's copy of the Novi-Catholic Bible. At the time, he didn't know why he'd brought it, other than the fact that it belonged to her, and she was the only relative for whom he'd ever felt affection. He'd been brought up in the Novi-Catholic faith, the officially sanctioned religion of the Communion, but had lapsed in the years between the war and his appointment to 1771. That was unpopular in a theocratic democracy, but the war, the aftermath, and the failure of the clerics to see God in the destruction had badly shaken his faith. He'd taken to keeping the Bible on him merely for display purposes, because a professed faith in God and appearance at Prayer were compulsory for military service. Tam only paid lip service to the faith in later years, but no one seemed to notice. He certainly wasn't the only veteran to do so.

He pulled out the Bible and held it in his hands as he sat on the edge of his rack. He ran his hand over the worn, pebbly cover and flipped it open to a section he had marked some time ago, figuring that meditation would help calm him, maybe banish some of the memories. It had been awhile since he'd attempted it, but he remembered it working when he was a youth. The Bible felt comfortable in his hands, as if it belonged there. He gazed at the words on the pages, only half-reading them, letting his mind wander freely. He felt himself begin to nod.

His head jerked up as he heard a sound in the corridor. Frowning, he put the Bible down and went to the door to his quarters. Out of the corner of his eye, he saw a blur of movement at the door to Primary Control. Someone had gone in!

He scrambled backward into his quarters and felt for his sidearm, never taking his eyes off the corridor. He managed to manhandle it out of the top drawer of his bureau. He held it in front of him, his hands shaking slightly, and crept slowly into the corridor.

How the hell did an intruder get in here? he thought. Why hadn't the breach alarms gone off?

He reached the doorway to Primary Control. Taking a deep, shaky breath, he spun quickly and filled the doorway, sidearm pointed directly in front of him. Aghast, he lowered it to his side and dropped it.

Darius was standing in the middle of the room. Tam shook his head as if to clear it and blinked several times. He was still there, looking at him with a pitiful expression. From somewhere, a peculiar, low keening had started. It wasn't loud, but it made Tam's teeth vibrate, and it was unpleasant to hear. From overhead, the Mahler symphony continued to thunder, adding to the cacophony.

"Darius . . . how . . . "

"Little late to be rediscovering the faith, isn't it?" asked Darius.

Tam shook his head slowly. "I don't understand. How are you . . . *why* are you here?"

Darius shrugged casually. "I'm here because you called me. Because you *keep* calling me. Why can't you let me go?"

Tam guessed at what was happening. "You're not really here," he said. "The Bible . . . "

"Maybe," said Darius, shrugging again. "Maybe you're having a Holy Vision, as outlined in the Scriptures. Or maybe I really *am* here. Or maybe you're just tired."

"I am tired, Darius. I've never been so tired in my life. And I miss you."

Darius nodded. "I know. I told you that you were taking on more than you could handle. You left so much behind, Tam. You're not one to just walk away from the things you care about. You know this deployment was a mistake."

Tam shook his head vigorously. "No, that's not true. I did this because it's an opportunity. Because it would've been good for *us*, eventually. A chance at career advancement—"

"You did it to run away from me," said Darius. "It was *never* about us. There was hardly any 'us' left by the time you got your orders. I made my peace with that. You wanted to serve. I made my peace with that, too. The Centauri posting was right there. But that was too close, Tam, wasn't it? Too close to the things you couldn't deal with. Too close to *me*. So you came here, the one place in the Communion where you thought I couldn't follow you. But here I am, anyway. And I'm only here because you won't let me go."

"No! I loved you, Darius. More than any human being alive. More than myself."

Darius smiled sadly. "But don't you see, Tam? That's the problem. You were never the independent soul you thought you were. You've *always* needed people. And you've always resented yourself for it. You loved me, but you resented me, too, because I represented your *need;* a need you hated. You had to prove that you could fend for yourself when things got bad between us, so you took this posting instead of the Centauri one. You had to prove that you could be alone. But now you're falling apart, and it's only been six months."

"You don't know what it's like out here," whispered Tam like a haunted man. "Why are you doing this?" He wanted to reach out to Darius, to embrace him, but he couldn't move. He didn't care if this was all in his head or if it was real. Darius was *here,* and he was *talking* to him! For the first time in six months, he was having a conversation. So what if it hurt?

"Because you have to let me go!" shouted Darius. "You have to let it *all* go! Me, the war, your mother, all of it! You won't survive out here unless you do! You only left us behind *physically.* You have to leave us behind in your *mind!*"

Tam was shocked. "I can't! I can't just forget you! I can't just turn you all off! Especially you! You're all I have out here!"

Darius's expression was pained. "If you don't, then you're doomed. Face the *real* reason you came out here, Tam. Admit it to yourself. Consult your Bible. Make your peace with your decision, as I did."

"Do you hate me?" asked Tam weakly.

"If I did, Tam, I would turn my back on you. I'd leave you alone with your memories, and your guilt, and let you suffer. But I still love you, God help me." He crossed himself. "And that's why I'm here, right now."

"You don't know what you're asking," said Tam, who finally let the tears come.

"Yes, I do," said Darius with sympathy. "Yes, I do. I'm asking of you what was required of me when you left me. You're strong, Tam. But you must be stronger. This is no place for a man to be on his own. But you chose it. And if you want to survive out here, you have to let go. Be alone without being *lonely*. The alternative is madness, or death. Remember 4023."

"I don't know how," pleaded Tam. "I don't know how to let you go."

Darius gestured toward Tam's quarters, his voice determined. "Find a way, Tam. Look as deep into yourself as you dare. Rediscover your faith, if that helps. You said it best yourself, didn't you? 'Learn not to care. About anything. That's the key.'"

"If I look away from everything that mattered to me, what will I have left?" asked Tam. He put his hands to his ears. The keening had grown louder during the course of their conversation. It was now filling the room.

"A clear conscience," said Darius. "The most important thing you can possess out here." He looked over at the viewport. The keening grew louder still. He looked back at Tam with urgency. "And you'll need all the clarity you can get. Time to wake up now."

"What do you mean?" asked Tam through clenched teeth. "I *am* awake." The keening was unbearable.

His head jerked again, and he was back in his quarters, still on the edge of his rack. He looked around as if he didn't know where he was. "Darius?" he called. He barely had time to ask himself whether it had all been a dream when the keening resolved itself into a klaxon; a shrill, staccato chirp that he hoped he'd never hear.

The proximity alarm. "God, no."

He catapulted himself off his rack and sprinted down the corridor to Primary Control. Skidding into the room, he halted abruptly when he saw what was waiting for him just beyond the viewport. A cry of anguish caught in his throat.

Outside was a massive fleet of ships, at least five thousand of them in his field of vision alone. Harshly outlined against the Barstow Nebula, they were vast, inhumanly strange, and deadly. They were slowly passing over, under, and around his Vigilance Point, in the direction of the Communion. The ships were utterly silent, sliding through space without the merest signal or transmission. It had been over twenty years, but there was no mistaking the origin of that fleet. After their long, watchful silence, the Lyrans were returning.

Tam swallowed hard and jumped into action. The proximity alarm had been going for several minutes before he noticed it, and he was afraid that a substantial part of that colossal fleet had slipped by before he started transmitting his telemetry to Command. "God, forgive me," he said under his breath as he desperately collated the flood of data coming in from the VP's sensors. The ships outside took no notice of him. That only made Tam more horrified. It meant that they didn't see him or the other Vigilance Points as threats. They were headed straight for higher-value targets, maybe even the Centrum citadel worlds themselves.

Tam's hands shook as they flew across the controls. For once, everything worked the way it was supposed to. He looked up, from time to time, at the viewport. The ships were still coming, veritable *clouds* of them; the Mahler symphony providing them with a martial beat. His sensors overloaded, and he dumped everything he had into a single large-burst packet and sent it ahead to Command, clearing his buffers. He sat back, exhausted beyond measure, and gazed at the spectacle outside.

The armistice with the Lyrans was over. They were again at war. But this time, the Lyrans were coming in incalculable numbers. Tam knew that the Communion had nothing that could withstand such a colossus. Political torpor and public indifference had taken their toll. He offered up a prayer as he waited for Command's final orders, realizing that he was likely at the forefront of the twilight of the human race.

Finally, he received feedback from Command. It came in the form of a single sentence: *You are hereby ordered to scuttle your Vigilance Point and seek escape in the vessel provided.* A burst of coded traffic indicated that coordinates were being sent to the escape vessel. Tam lurched forward and ran the routines necessary to detonate the one gigaton warhead at the heart of his VP. The terse order meant that Command was scrambling to mount a defense, and that there was nothing left for Tam to do but get out as fast as he could. To the right of his vision, at the very edge of the viewport, a tiny disk of light flared and slowly died. One of the other Operators had destroyed his Vigilance Point, hopefully taking some of the enemy with it.

Tam set the countdown for ninety seconds and hurried down to the lower deck, where the escape vessel was tethered. It was already starting up when he arrived. He strapped himself in and waited for the bay doors to open. A monitor inside the vessel showed the countdown to detonation.

He had no idea what he would face when he got home, or whether home would even exist. He only knew that he had to see Darius again, to tell him that he couldn't—*wouldn't*—let him go. He'd tried, and failed. Darius had been right about that. Even with the horror that was passing over his head, threatening to destroy everything he held dear, he felt calm and determined.

217

He'd pushed Darius away, but he couldn't be apart from him now, not when all was on the brink of annihilation.

"I'm not letting you go, Darius," he said as the bay doors opened beneath him. "And I'm coming home to tell you." The docking clamps gave way, and Tam felt the ship accelerate away from the Vigilance Point on its preprogrammed course. He didn't turn back to see the VP vaporize itself and whatever ships may have been in close proximity. None of that mattered to him right now. He only wanted to beat the Lyrans back to his home world. They could roll across the universe like a juggernaut, for all he cared. All that mattered to him was seeing Darius and being with him at the end. He would even shirk duty to make that happen.

Accumulated exhaustion had finally caught up to him, and Tam slept soundly as the escape vessel plunged toward the rendezvous point. For the first time in months, the memories were silent. On the cusp of oblivion, Tam Heller was at a peace he'd never known before.

Adrift
by Willis Couvillier

The plane of Saturn's rings was spectacular. At this angle the light from Sol hit the icy rocks perfectly to give the appearance of glittery dust, a staggered circle of brilliant diamonds framing the colorful surface of the planet. Slowly the view of the original ringed planet shifted and the edge of Titan crept into view from the opposite side. At this proximity the moon dominated the view, easing around to eclipse the planet. As more of the living surface of this dwarf-planet satellite came into view, only one thing entered Maarren's mind—

This was *not* the vision he'd thought he'd experience as he died.

What the hell was he doing out here?

And why? *Why?*

Liu Han Maarren felt like he was in a coffin, buried alive. The safesuit meant anything but safety to him as he drifted, a tiny mote being merely another particle of ring dust to the uncaring planet lurking behind its moon. It was a confining encumbrance that he loathed, hated with everything in him. He didn't care if it was all that kept him alive. The only thing he saw in that was the torture as it delayed the inevitable, while he thought about it, over and over and over.

God he hated it.

He suppressed the impulse to strike his faceplate. The feed of data from his medcites scrolled over the inside top left of his visor, a mocking countdown to his death. Oh, he knew that he was beginning to experience the signs of oxygen deprivation. It was not like he could escape the demonic red digits scrolling across his peripheral view, reminding him of it. No, striking the faceplate was out. Any movement was out. The exertion would use extra oxygen. And that would shave crucial seconds from his life. Movement was anti-life. He could die with just the stars as his companions, instead of his good friend Saturn and her little boy, Titan.

He closed his eyes. Being angry at the universe and fighting helplessness drained him, leeched away his already fading energy. He didn't know what he wanted. With one thought he longed to sleep away the few hours until his final sleep, so that the torture would pass quicker. With the next thought his mind was fiercely awake, riveted with the tension of the situation, frantically seeking solutions to survive. He realized that he couldn't relax, couldn't sleep. Over and over in his mind scenarios churned, many crazy, few realistic, and none practical or do-able.

Calm down, he told himself.

How! he answered.

At the lower left corner of his visor the data feed from his safesuit's systems diagnostic continued to pulse, bright. In the corner of his vision he saw a green indicator blink away then return, orange, leaving the one indicator continuing to blink green—the useless one. The one that let him know that the beacon was working fine—not that anyone would find a warm body to rescue if they could reach him any time soon. And then there was that orange light. He wanted to scream at it. He *knew* the suit's oxygen was low!

Titan slid from his view, being replaced with the panorama of the star field. Multi-colored and variously sized specks clustered, forming constellations, with slightly larger specks of galaxies dotting the mesh. It was an incredible sight, truly awe inspiring—the full Milky Way crisp and unfiltered by any atmosphere or man-made illumination. Maarren missed the twinkle, the glitter that an atmosphere gave to the stars. Without that, this grandeur was— passionless, cold.

Atmosphere or not, the view didn't do much for him, under the circumstances.

It would be a while until his rotation would bring Saturn's rings back into view. Until then he'd just have to settle with seeing spots, rather, small colorfully tinted dots swarming against lots of black empty. He could admire all this, and he had, when the circumstances had been different. Part of his drive to get out here had come from his admiration, his desire, to experience the grandness of this magnificent immensity. It lifted life's perception to a new level, this did, and gave a person a humbling respect for the sheer magnitude of everything. Each time he'd had to be suited up and out, he'd taken a moment to admire his universe, drinking in the ambiance. In these moments, it was his, all his. The universe was *his* baby . . .

God was a jealous god, however.

It was the only explanation.

He, Liu Han Maarren, had dared to claim all of this for his own, and had seriously pissed God off. And now he was experiencing the consequences of that. He couldn't classify the chain of coincidences that'd put him here any other way.

* * *

The reflexive explosion of the residual fluid from his lungs forced Maarren into awareness. He turned his head to the side to spit out the driblets of Cryo-Plus from his mouth, then, grimacing from the metallic mint aftertaste, turned back to review the data scrolling on the inside face of the cyro cylinder. He remained still for a moment to gather his thoughts, then, as soon as his head was clear, used the virtual glove controls to open the chamber. Since he'd been brought out of cryo, there had to be a problem.

Maarren realized what was wrong as soon as he left the cylinder. Pushing out, he floated directly up, hovering over the bank of passenger cylinders. There wasn't any direct thrust to generate a directional pull from the momentum. Since the computer deemed it necessary to wake him, the automated system must have failed to correct the problem with the drive.

"Date check, AI."

"It is currently 12:42 hours on Novenber 14th, 2182, Commander Maarren." The AI replied immediately with its default feminine voice, doubtless meant to be soothing. The original AI programmers had never been in space, obviously.

Just under 8 weeks until dock. "ETA and course update."

"We are 3.7 hours behind schedule. We are maintaining course, Commander."

Not too bad—yet. "What's wrong with the barge."

"The drive has malfunctioned."

Indeed. "Auto repair?"

"The automatic repair system does not respond to the activation command, Commander."

"Give me a systems review." Maarren pushed over to the console chair while the AI summarized the state of the ship's operations. It'd been a couple of centuries since that first ion drive had been tested, and they still couldn't get it right. On that historic run, the ionization grid had shorted out, shutting down the drive. The problem had cleared itself, amid speculation of stuck comet dust, but it wasn't until private industry jumped into the space race and took up the challenge of making space profitable that the earlier speculation was confirmed. Their engineers came up with a design that included a fairly effective self-cleaning repair function, which led up to the design of the first barge transports. Since those early days, ion propulsion barges had been found to be an ideal way to supply the outer science orbitals. With cryo for personnel and with most systems automated, regular shipment runs had been developed, providing an effective supply source to the stations. For decades the system had proven itself, since the first staggered runs to now, with only moderate changes to ship design being required. The barges pushed along smoothly—unless, however, the grid picked up dust that the automated repair systems couldn't completely clear.

Then a human had to be awakened, such as was the case now.

Maarren shook his head, giving the console screen a last glance. Pushing out of the chair, he set his motion toward the rear hatch. The longer that the drive was down the worse the situation could become. The barge was nearing the reversal point, and needed to have the main drive operational. It had to reverse for braking—the barge was already in Saturn space and approaching Ring Station 2, and although all of the positioning jets were fine it still required the main drive to slow the ship down to a safe docking speed.

Maarren finished sealing up the safesuit. Ready to exit to the hull, he said, "AI, communications open?"

"Yes, Commander. Your transmission is clear."

Everything checked okay—the results from the pre-exit diagnostic scrolled on the inside of the visor of the safesuit, updating him with the status. All the gasses were fully charged, the line connectors secure, the suit magnetics checked ok, the nanite repair system at ready, the medcites were logged in to the safesuit's computer system. Everything was a go.

"AI, evacuate the chamber." He could feel the air being withdrawn from the room more than anything else. The safesuit was a secure safety environment, and filtered out everything that couldn't be transmitted in. He could see tiny movements of dangling items as the air was sucked away, but not hear anything.

"Completed, Commander. The vacuum is established."

Maarren opened the outer hatch, slowly pulling himself out. At about the half-point, he reached over the lip and secured the physical line to the drag mount. Still holding onto the line, he adjusted his motion until he could snap down his feet and lock down the MagStrides. Once he was secure, he moved towards the rear engines, a figure advancing slowly, appearing not unlike a staggering robot as he walked on the hull.

"AI, try initializing the engine again."

Nothing. A moment later the AI's voice entered his helmet again. "There was no response, Commander. The diagnostic continues to indicate a grid short."

Damn. Of course this wasn't going to resolve easy.

"Initialize the rear engine manual repair console."

"Done, Commander."

Maarren took a moment and stood on the hull looking at Saturn. The barge passed close to Titan on this route, and this was one of the rare times a person could admire the incredible view that the proximity to the ringed giant and its satellite offered. At this moment, this was his, all his.

But he had a job to do. Sighing, he turned back to the task, sliding his tread, pulling the tether line along. He eyeballed one of the gas jet thrusters, but continued when everything he could see verified the earlier systems report. Soon he was at the rear, and there, turning off the boot magnetics, he swung around the tail cup in a controlled flip and float that landed his feet back on the metal, on the inside of the tail cup's rim. As he contacted the surface, he re-initialized the magnetics, re-securing himself. A couple steps in and he was at the control pad to the repair port.

Sliding open the locker-sized chamber, he pulled out The Brush. A running joke, it resembled nothing less than an archaic Earthside cleaning brush. Dust particles frequently accumulated in the grid. Automatic repair worked by rapid heating and cooling of the grid, with the result of the dust being dislodged by the expansion and contracting of the metal. Ideally this would be all that was needed, but occasionally dust wouldn't work itself free, maintaining the short. For these times there was The Brush—a tool with numerous nozzles and a pressurized hydrogen flow designed to blow dust free.

Maarren crept along the grid, carefully covering the surface with the gas. Then, a third of the way into the job, it happened.

The MagStrides failed.

The Brush blasted him directly into space, with force strong enough to snap him back when he reached the length of the tether. Dazed, he whipped back, striking the round of the barge's tail cup full on his side, jamming the tether joint hard into his ribcage. For a moment he blacked out, and then as consciousness returned he saw he was free-floating away from the barge. The impact had snapped the tether from its connection to the safesuit.

Still dazed, he threshed around, flailing like an infant tossing a tantrum. Closing his eyes, he breathed in twice, deeply; calm, relax, control the panic, use the training to clear the mind and assess the situation. Finally his thoughts settled down—when he faced the barge he set off a short gas burst to push him to his ship. Nothing happened. Trying again and getting the same result he began to feel the panic set in, then frantically worked the virtual control pad, trying to get the jets to work. As his drift slowly turned the view away from the rear of the barge, the chill of realization struck.

He was adrift in open space. And he was alone.

* * *

Maarren rotated to a position that brought the distant tiny circle of the rear of the barge into view. He had tried to contact the AI after he'd snapped loose, but hadn't received an answer. His gas gun dead, his transmission non-operational, the integrity of the nanite patch down to 89% and dropping, his hope for rescue dim—Maarren had little to keep his mood positive. Then he saw the clincher—the barge's ion drive momentarily flickered, and then the ion stream flared out as the drive fully came online.

Yep, God hated him. No doubt about it.

Times such as this definitely made it hard to keep the faith. Perhaps, though, a time like this was when you had to.

The close edge of the outermost of Saturn's rings came into view. In the distance—not that anything here was close—an elongated speck sat offside in the midst of a galaxy blob. He once knew the name of that comet. He didn't know where that knowledge was now, but it had been there once. Most that came to mind was that it was a number. There were a lot like that, this far away from home. There were so many objects out here, from the larger asteroids in the belt to the smaller moons around the giant planets to all the new finds being made out in the Kuiper Belt, all just numbered. So bold and magnificent, yet made so anonymous.

The status lights at the lower left of the visor display continued to blink, the orange one now red. The green beacon indicator remained unchanged . . .

Maarren's breath was hard and would probably mist the faceplate if the safesuit weren't designed against it. He didn't need the red blinking indictor to tell him that the air was critical. His own body told him that, more and more so each time he turned. His rotations were his count-down clock. He lost count long ago, so he could only figure the end was soon. He'd lost sight of the barge a few turns back, but by then it was only one bright ring spot amongst the vast myriad glitter of ring spots.

Maarren weakened. He felt it from the fatigue pushing in on him. He felt it from how his feelings changed, how he didn't have the hate any longer. His desire to fight was fading, and he realized that it wouldn't be long before his cognizance would follow. It wouldn't be long now before he would fall into a coma.

There was a ripple on the cloud-haze on Titan's surface that hadn't been there last time he tuned. Blinking the wet from his eyes, he looked for a moment, thinking God how he loved that fried shrimp po'boy he had the one time he visited Earth. They didn't have anything like that back home in Mars Polar.

His breath caught. He wasn't sure whether it was from the worsening air or a sob. He didn't care, not that much, anyway. He would take care of it. He would decide his death, not wait, not let it just happen.

They did wonderful things with frozen people, they did.

He just hoped his eyes wouldn't rupture from the decompression.

Mom, I hope I made you proud, he thought, blinking at the moisture again. *I'll see you soon, Mom.*

The indicator didn't blink now. It was a solid red bar.

Maarren reached up to his faceplate to release it. It wouldn't move, the seals seemed frozen and wouldn't take his command—was that *also* malfunctioning? He felt his arms at his sides, realized they hadn't moved . . .

For a moment it appeared that his mother saw him.

He knew that is wasn't real. She'd been on the machines for a month now. He couldn't remember if he'd even told her he loved her, before she fell into the coma. She was all the family he had, and he couldn't even remember if he'd told her he loved her. The last thing he remembered them talking about was how he thought about joining up, getting out to work the outer stations, maybe even working on the new science station that was going up in orbit around Uranus.

That was before their last fight, though.

Now she was dead. She was flesh, with machines and tubes and electricity keeping the flesh warm.

It didn't matter their differences. He loved her. He knew she loved him, too, even with their disagreements. They were all that each other had.

A couple meds and a nurse waited by the machines. "Mr. Maarren . . ." one of the Meds said.

He nodded. He couldn't say a thing, now. He watched, distant inside of himself with expressionless eyes.

One by one the Med who had spoken shut down the machines. The nurse removed the tube from her mouth. He turned away as she began to pull aside the covers to remove the other tubes.

His mother was dead.

He killed her. He hadn't even been able to tell her he loved her.

He could never let this happen to him again.

He came out of the hallucination, the memory, with damp eyes and an echo of the past pain heavy on him. The space agencies screened all applicants deeply, with long batteries of psychological sessions. An applicant had to be capable of dealing with solitude, and had to have minimal ties to any place they may call home. When he'd been accepted, it'd been the happiest moment of his life.

He wanted to go home.

"God," he thought, *"I'm sorry. Can I go home? I don't want to be here anymore, please . . . "*

Boy that had been one fantastic sandwich!

For a second he regained clarity, but it didn't last. His vision was becoming spotty now, with moments where it faded inward from the edges, then moments where bright haze blotches flared in to obstruct the view. He was about to die and all he could think of was food. No memories from Mars Polar, nothing from his childhood, just a sandwich he'd had once on a tour of Euro-Chin Space Agency from a stand that wasn't even on the same continent as Old New Orleans.

The haze from Titan stretched from the surface, grasping up, reaching into his safesuit. Even the non-stop data stream generated from his medcites to his faceplate monitor was swallowed into it as the haze thickened, as it brightened into an all encompassing living thing that took him up, and slowly faded him towards a deepening darkness.

Mom . . .

He was—aware.

He was being jostled around with enough force to pull him from the thick darkness. Slowly lucidity returned to his thoughts, and as he become aware of light on the inside of his eyes other things also began to register. Sounds of breathing other than his. Odors other than his sweat and breath and fear. Sounds and scents and the feel of life. He tried to say something, but nothing made it out. He couldn't even get his eyes open, and the strongest sensation he was aware of was the darkness attempting to re-take him. Relentless, it gently eased in seeking to reclaim him, then backed off only to push in again at the edges of his mind trying so hard to keep him in it. Again he tried to speak.

The voice was the sweetest thing he heard.

"Oi!" The gruff bark was familiar, the voice of Miles Hammond. One of the other station crewmen being transported back on the ion barge, he and Maarren often got together when Maarren was at station. "Mom! I ain't nobody's Mom, what!"

"Miles. He is delirious, we have to get him into the tube. We have to get the StemRegen treatment going," Grady Paine admonished, his voice serious, determined. Both of the rotation crew were out of cryo? They had to have been his rescuers. No one else could have been close enough to get to him in time.

Lady Saturn with her diamond tiara. What a sweet vision she is, he thought.

The jostling worsened. He had to tell them, had to let them know. He had to tell them how thankful he was. He croaked out a bit of noise, not knowing if anything intelligent made it out. Then, as he began to fall back to the darkness:

"Hurry!" Paine's voice came as the jostling grew stronger, more rhythmic.

"Going!" Then, "What the 'ell's a po'boy?"

A Requiem for the Sons of Kings
by Jennifer Crow

The knock startled Nicholas—he couldn't remember the last time he'd had a visitor. When he opened the door, there was a stranger, a woman, standing on the other side. She turned toward Nicholas, and he saw the dull, greenish glow of a molecular blade. He moved to shut the door, but she turned and stuck her boot in the way. Slender but not beautiful, she had the corded, pared look of someone who'd been hungry often and angry always.

"Please," she said, in a way that told him she didn't say that word often. "There's something out there."

The wind had picked up as the day drew to a close. It howled along the eaves of Nicholas' hut, and through the branches of half-dead trees at the brink of the escarpment. Rithel's sun had set, leaving streaks of rose and gold along the horizon.

He gestured at the knife. "You won't need that inside." Once she'd thumbed off the power, he stood aside and let her enter. "What brings you here?"

"Family."

He shuttered the windows against the darkness. "No one has family here anymore. And this is forbidden territory."

"I have a pass from Kundagar, from the governor of the sector. She sent you this." She held out a metallic wedge about the size of Nicholas' thumb, its surface clouded with an iridescent sheen.

Nicholas took it reluctantly and turned it over in his fingers.

"Aren't you going to watch it?" she asked.

"Watch it? I don't think that's necessary." He weighed it in his hand. "I know it's a counterfeit." When she opened her mouth to protest, he added, "I know how the government operates."

"You've been here a long time. Things have changed."

"Not that much." He pocketed the chip. "I'll give you a little something to eat before you go back."

"Back where? They didn't even give me a manned escort—just dropped me off in one of their probes. I'm supposed to call when I'm finished. Though it was clear they weren't expecting to rush back."

229

"It's getting dark." When he lit the lamp, she gasped.

"You're—you're *him*. The one they call the Apostate."

Nicholas nodded, wary. The past clenched its fist around his neck. To ease it, he went into the kitchen and began setting out supplies for his evening meal. Dried foods, mostly, hermetically sealed, without much texture or flavor.

"Some people say you're to blame."

Nicholas dropped a foil packet of dehydrated meat on the floor. "I *survived* the first attack of the mutagen on Jura. The investigators cleared me of any blame."

"I see they didn't let you leave Rithel, though."

Nicholas sighed and ran his hands through his hair. "Sit? No? Well, I will. I stay because I choose to stay." He'd had this conversation before. Angry relatives, friends, lovers, they came to Rithel because they needed something. Needed someone to blame.

"So you feel guilty." Her voice held a note of triumph.

"I feel *responsible*," he corrected. "Those who ... suffered ... their friends, their families abandoned them. Even their gods. Someone had to stay and listen. And I had nowhere else to go."

She shifted, not meeting his gaze.

"Do *you* feel guilty? You won't find absolution here. You might as well go home." When she shook her head, he shrugged. "Fine. I'll take you down to the edge of the city in the morning. You can see for yourself."

"Now. Tonight."

"There are things out there that like the darkness." He pulled two cups and two plates from the cupboard.

She slapped something on the table, too, so hard that the rims of the cups chimed. "You knew him. My brother."

When she moved her hand aside, she revealed a picture of a much-younger Nicholas with his arm draped over the shoulder of another young man. Behind them, a wall of dark trees guarded distant towers. "I remember that day. His father took the pictures. We drove out of the city together—'just the men,' he said. He wanted to tell Etan about the bride they'd found for him. About her family, her beauty, her dreams."

"I don't need your memories."

"We were kings then," Nicholas murmured, as though she hadn't spoken. "And the sons of kings." For the length of that bright summer, he had let himself believe the worst was over.

At last the silence grew too heavy, even for Nicholas. "Who are you?"

"Jorra Estes. Etan was my brother."

"He didn't have a sister."

"I was born after."

"After your parents ran away. Abandoned him."

"They did what they had to, to save the family. They told me that. Told me you—" She reached across the table and slapped him. Nicholas bit the inside of his lip, filling his mouth with the hot, metallic taste of blood.

"Get out. Go back to whatever safe little hole your family crawled off to."

"Not until I see his grave."

"You don't deserve it."

"Fine. I don't deserve it. I don't understand what you've suffered. But I will sit here until you *make* me understand. And when I run out of patience, I will call one of the powerful people who helped me get here, and they will have you dragged off to a far corner of the galaxy and put on trial for this." Her sweeping gesture encompassed the planet Rithel and its tragic history.

"You can't!"

"Does that frighten you? Good. Give me what I want, and I'll leave you in peace. If you can find peace."

Peace. He could have laughed out loud at the irony. "Very well. I'll need to get a few things together. If it's the only way to get rid of you, then I'll take you down there." But for a long moment, he studied the picture. Printed on a sheet of tough, lightweight nanopolymer, it was designed to survive almost anything. Someone had tried to destroy it, though—the edges were ragged, and one corner bore singe marks.

"It's not far," Nicholas told her as he readied a pack with food and drinking water. "We can go and return before night falls again."

"If I finish what I need to finish," she said. And they set out for the city.

An hour or so later, Jorra stopped at the top of the road that led down to the city. The light of a faint, reddish moon glinted on toppled walls and algae-stained water. The light of their headlamps only cut so far into the darkness, leaving the burned shells of buildings in shadow. Jorra studied it all with her arms folded and her shoulders up around her ears. Nicholas hoped she was in the process of changing her mind.

"This is . . . where it happened?"

He cleared his throat. "Yes. It was busy once. Growing. And then . . . " Something moved, a pale, low-slung shadow slipping across a dark stain between two broken buildings.

"How can you stay here?"

"Where else would I go?"

"You mean, who would have you?" She started down the road again. Her toe caught a loose piece of paving and sent it skittering. The sudden clatter startled a flock of gray viprangs, which took to the air with vehement screeches and the flap of leathery wings when the headlamps illuminated them. "Horrid."

"We should turn back," Nicholas said. "A few viprangs will hardly be the worst of what we see down there."

"I'm not afraid of them." A whip-crack of contempt edged her voice. "Let's go."

Nicholas, stifling a sigh, trailed after. The viprangs settled again, though he could feel their reddish eyes on him as he passed. Long ago he'd been told they were stupid creatures, but the plague had changed many things, and a new order had taken shape in the aftermath. Their attention made him uneasy.

He and Jorra stopped halfway down the escarpment to drink from their supply of water. "Save some for later," he warned Jorra. "There's nothing fit to drink down there."

"How do you live?"

"Supply ships from the regional government—they drop a drone when they're in the sector." He noticed she was staring at him, and realized she meant something else. "I like being alone."

"Enough to kill for the privilege?"

The damp air weighed on him. Sweat trickled down his spine. "Don't be ridiculous."

"Am I? Being ridiculous?" She reached into her pocket and waved the picture at him, the old portrait of him and her brother. "You're a liar."

"I never said I wasn't." Nicholas took one last sip of water and put the bottle away. She still held the picture in front of him, so he snatched it from her and stashed it in his pack as well. "You wouldn't like the truth. And you have no right to it. You weren't here."

"I was in my mother's womb," she said.

"That means nothing. You didn't see—"

"I saw what it did to my parents. His death. *This*." Her gesture encompassed the broken city. "I'll make it right if I can."

"There is no right anymore." Fear sank its teeth into Nicholas' heart. In a sense, it came as a relief, that he could still feel it and recognize it. "You could kill me, but it wouldn't change anything. Wouldn't bring him back." He passed her, striding ahead for the first time on their journey. Ahead stretched a barrier, razor wire hung with biohazard symbols. A gate with a locking mechanism cut off the road, but Nicholas pried it open and swung the gate wide.

"Not much in the way of security."

"What for? No one's come here in a long time. And *they* don't have much of an urge to leave. I used to round up the escapees, but I learned to leave them alone, and they avoid me."

She ran her finger along the wire, gasped, and pulled back. Blood welled up and trickled down to her wrist. As he sprayed the wound with liquid field dressing, she bit back a laugh. "You're not much of a man. Living here alone, after all you've seen and done."

Nicholas carefully closed the gate. He let her take the lead so she couldn't see his face and read too much there. After so long alone, he was surprised to discover there were things he wanted to say—that it was her brother who'd insisted on the tests, drawn him out, ended his self-imposed isolation the first time. But what did words matter?

He caught up with her where the first of the broken walls marked the outer ring of the city like the points of a shattered crown. "I lived near here," he said, mostly to break the silence.

"I don't want to talk."

"Kick rocks, then." When she glanced at him, he added, "Some of the things here are afraid of noise."

If anything, her steps grew more quiet and hesitant. It had been only a few weeks since Nicholas had walked down to the city, but already it showed signs of further decay. Purplish fungal growths spread over the stones, and something brittle and ivory-colored crunched under foot. Bones.

He shuddered and looked for a clear place to step. Something had gathered them, or used this plaza as a dumping ground when it cleaned its burrow. Jorra saw what was beneath their feet, and started. "It wasn't like this even a month ago," he told her. "But it's changing—something here doesn't like the dead. Or the living."

"It doesn't change my mind." She kicked aside a fragment of skull. It came to rest with one empty eye socket watching them, its rim festooned with dried algae.

"What good will it do for you to find him like that—or worse?"

"What's worse?"

He heard a scurrying sound in the thick plants that overhung the path and raised his hand to stop her. As if on cue, the rustling reached a crescendo, and something sleek and pale darted into the middle of the road. It was about the height of a three-year-old child, but slender and narrow-skulled, and it held something dripping and red in its hands. The long fingers twitched convulsively, and it screamed a challenge at them. When it darted toward them,

Jorra screamed as well, and Nicholas moved between them, waving his hands and stamping his feet. The creature froze, studied him a moment with huge, dark eyes, and then fled back into the bushes.

"What—"

"A survivor. One of them, anyway." Nicholas took her arm. "If you want to turn back, say the word. But I remember where your family lived. If you want to . . . see for yourself."

She swallowed. "I want that."

Nicholas tightened his grip. "You see why the place is forbidden. Why no word has gotten out. If you tell—"

"I won't."

"Not even your parents."

"As if this would bring them peace of mind." She shook off his hand, bent for a stone, threw it into the bushes. "But I'm not afraid of them."

"They're more pitiful than anything else." Nicholas set out toward the city center. He didn't want to talk anymore. Talk dredged up memories of the days when the infection first struck—the deaths, and later the feeling that death was preferable to survival. Those who resisted the pathogen fled—all but the few who felt a need to protect this unholy birthplace. One by one the others—the apostates—had succumbed to disease or madness, leaving only him. He had never spoken of it—the confusion, the pain, the violence. The dread as he watched old friends change into something he did not recognize, who in turn failed to recognize him.

"This way," he said, and turned down what had once been a wide avenue, but which had disintegrated to a field of rubble. "That—" he pointed to a broken spear jutting on the horizon "—was the city center. Your family hoped that it might one day rival Kundagar in power. But . . . "

"You think Kundagar unleashed the pathogen?"

He stared at the broken building, though he'd never found an answer in its cracked façade. "I'd like to think no one is that reckless. That *stupid*. But who really knows? It didn't originate in Kundagar. That much I do know."

"No." She turned over a flat sheet of white stone and scraped at the purple fungus on its undersurface. Something yellowish and slimy skittered away from the light. "It started on your home world."

"I told you—"

"They ruled it wasn't you. I heard."

A knot tightened in his chest. Of course she didn't believe him. He didn't believe himself, not in the dark reaches of the night, listening to the changed world creep around him. He made himself walk on in the direction he'd pointed. She followed, her boots crunching an echo to each step he took.

And then he noticed another sound, almost masked by their footsteps. "Hold." When he raised his hand, she stopped at his shoulder.

"What?"

He cocked his head, listening. Whatever it was—if it wasn't simply his imagination—knew enough to stop when they did. "Keep your eyes open," he told Jorra.

"What is it?"

"Maybe nothing. Maybe...not."

"You can stop trying to scare me." She strode ahead, but he waited, listening again. "It won't do any good."

Nicholas, watching her retreating back, thought, *Nothing I do is enough. Even my death wouldn't give her satisfaction. Not that I feel like being so accommodating.* It occurred to him to wonder what he'd do if she meant to kill him. *Defend myself? Or accept fate?*

"'And enter, here, the halls of shadowed fate,'" she quoted, as if reading his mind. It was one of her brother's favorites, he recalled, a line from an obscure local poet. She might not have languished in obscurity had she survived, but the plague cut short her life and her prospects. "Which shadowed halls belonged to my family?"

He scanned the street, and pointed out a wreck with a verdigris roof. "That one." He led the way to a building where broad front steps led to nothing—a caved-in wall and a floor that showed the basement beneath. Nicholas didn't bother telling her to take care—she had to have both recklessness and caution to have come so far alone, and she knew on which quality to draw. They stepped carefully, balancing on thick beams that had once lain under the flooring.

Dampness suffused the air and rotted what had once been rich paneling on the walls. The stairs leading to the upper floors had no banister, and some of the treads tilted at odd angles. Jorra tried one, but it gave a mighty groan when she rested her weight on it. "How can we see anything if it's all like this?"

"If it's truth you want, we can't go up, anyway. We have to go down." Nicholas aimed his headlamp. The beam jabbed toward the back of the house, and dark moths, startled, fluttered about. Jorra shuddered and waved them away.

"The stairs are this way." He led them further into the house, past pictures so badly stained that he could make out nothing of what they'd once shown. Here the floor was more stable, so tatters of rugs curled up under his feet and small, discarded objects formed metal-and-plastic drifts in the corners of the room. It was like that in any house in the city—ruined and abandoned. Abandoned, at least, by anything human.

At the back of the house stairs led down into the cellar. Some attempt had been made to keep the steps in repair; their headlamps revealed broken boards stretched over the gaps. And something else—a wire hovered a hands-breadth above the top step, so thin the light barely caught it.

"A trap?" Jorra whispered.

Nicholas nodded. "They know it's not safe."

"They—more Survivors?"

"In a manner of speaking." He didn't try to detach the wire; just took a wide step over it and balanced on a creaking step as he helped Jorra over in turn. Only when they'd crossed did he show her the rough sheet of metal suspended in the darkness above them, one edge polished to a gleam.

Nicholas laid his finger on his lips and beckoned her to follow into the subterranean chamber. They rounded a corner and found a wide room with a blackened fire pit at one end. It wasn't that that caught Jorra's eye, Nicholas noted. He stepped aside as she went to an overturned crate covered by a moth-eaten and mold-stained tapestry. On it, someone had arranged a clutter of objects—a broken glass, a child's painting, the cover of a book. "It's like an altar. But a mad one." She turned over a flat piece of paper and gasped. "This . . . these are my parents."

Nicholas sighed. "He hasn't forgotten entirely. Something in their faces calls to him."

"Who?"

In answer, he went to the corner and made gentle motions with his hands. A bent figure eased into the light, a shadow-gray form with lank dark hair spilling across its forehead to obscure lumpish features. "Your brother."

"That thing? That is *not* my brother."

"Are you sure?"

She shook her head. "My brother is dead. My parents told me so."

"They wanted to believe it, I'm sure. Maybe they believe they buried him, too. It was only after the evacuation that the truth became apparent to those of us who stayed. The pathogen sends its victims into a sort of catatonia, so deep that it seems all life functions have ended, while the changes take place. At the height of the terror, many people didn't wait to be sure of their loved ones' demise—"

"No. *No.*"

"I do not accuse them. The first time, I ran. And just in time—the regional government fire-bombed my home world to ashes. This time, I determined to stay. To see what the world would become. To convince the government . . . " He shrugged. In truth, he couldn't say what he meant to convince them of—the sentience of the changed Survivors? No one could call these remnants of humanity an improvement. Etan hung limp in Nicholas' grip, cowering before the woman he couldn't recognize as his sister.

Jorra paced around them with the restless, snarling gait of a predator denied its prey. "How could you keep this a secret?"

"What would it do to your parents to know the truth?"

She paused and turned away, scanning the walls and floor. "What's this?" Her examination turned up a pouch, its crevices dark with some dried substance. When she turned it right side out, it revealed the Kundagar government's insignia and the words: Emergency rations—rice and beans. "Your rations."

"They don't belong to—"

"They were sent for you. And you brought them here instead. For the others." Jorra shook her head. "I ought to call you a fool."

"I've been called worse."

"And deserved it, no doubt."

He shrugged. When he went to let go of Etan, the broken man keened briefly and clutched at him. For a moment, arms around each other, they formed a parody of the picture Jorra had brought. Nicholas tightened his grip briefly and let go, easing the other man away. "It's best if you don't get too used to me holding you up, old friend."

Jorra went to the foot of the stairway and sat, her hands on her knees, staring into the darkness overhead. "We can't stay much longer," Nicholas told her.

"A moment more." She began to sing, soft notes that filled the cavernous basement with a sound deeper than silence. Etan bolted for the shadows, paused, and inched back until he crouched at Jorra's feet. For a long moment, as the last notes died, their eyes met. She reached out and brushed away a lock of hair where it had fallen across her brother's cheek. "Be at peace, brother."

In her other hand, the molecular blade blossomed, its power source giving off a greenish glow and a high-pitched hum. She swung, but clumsily. Blood spurted from Etan's neck and he howled and scrambled backward.

"No!" Nicholas threw himself between them and felt the blade bite into his pack. It severed a strap, leaving the scent of burning leather in the air. The heavy pack sagged unevenly, upsetting Nicholas' balance as he fought to separate Jorra and her brother. "Leave him alone!"

"I can't." Jorra panted as she tried to lunge past him. Etan hid in a corner, keening. "No one can know of this. My father—"

"Your father already killed him once by leaving him here. He has no right—"

"You don't understand. He's trying to unseat the governor. You don't know the corruption that's grown up in the past few years. People are afraid of this pathogen, and they'll do anything to protect themselves. If they knew my parents had been exposed—that they'd lost their son to it—"

"So you came here to make him disappear?" Nicholas all but spat at her. "Get out."

"Not until I finish." She held the blade between them, its green fire twitching, tempting. "My parents always said death was too good for you. But I'm willing to do it, for the greater good."

Nicholas heard something skitter overhead and looked up. "There's a—"

"Don't bother trying to distract me," she said. "For all the rumors and phobias, the pathogen didn't make monsters—only freaks."

Nicholas took a step back, careful to keep himself between Jorra and her brother. As he took another step, she feinted again, trying to draw him off-balance. But before she could follow through, the ceiling splintered, showering them with shards of rotten wood and chunks of plaster. Something ash-gray and hairless landed on Jorra with a grunt. It backhanded the blade out of her grip.

She screamed and ducked back, just as it tried to take a chunk out of her face with its thick, yellowish teeth. Nicholas blinked dust out of his eyes and tried to free his own knife from its scabbard on his belt. Jorra was pressed to the wall by the beast's onslaught. And though she jabbed her thumbs in its eyes, it didn't retreat.

Something brushed past Nicholas—Etan, he realized, the molecular blade awkward in hands that no longer bent the way they once had. Still, he advanced on the beast, slicing its back, its legs. Only when it turned to face him did Etan go in for the killing blow. The blade's whine deepened in tone as it darted into the creature's chest and out again.

The beast collapsed with a last, quiet exhalation. In the aftermath, the three survivors stood watching its blood pool on the floor. Then Etan turned off the molecular blade and set it down on the floor, gently, as though it might break, and curled up on the floor, not far from the dead creature.

"You asked why I didn't tell your parents he'd survived? I didn't trust them. They couldn't accept he . . . cared for me. How could they accept what he'd become?" Nicholas bent and pocketed the blade, pausing only to lay a hand on Etan's back. Etan flinched away with a whimper.

"Why did he save me?"

"Maybe he didn't want to see it turn on me next." Nicholas glared up at her. "Don't flatter yourself that he was trying to protect *you*. He knows enough to understand what you meant to do. He's still better than all the rest of his kin combined. Now, go."

"I'll tell them I saw his grave, or his body. Something." She shrugged the weight of her pack into a more comfortable position. "You don't have to worry."

"To love someone is to worry."

Jorra's shadow swept over them. Nicholas folded himself over Etan's unconscious form. But she passed on without another word; heading back, he supposed, to the launch she'd flown down to the planet.

Nicholas wet the corner of his shirt with the last water from his canteen, and used it to wash away some of the blood caked to Etan's neck. Then he took the picture from his pack and folded Etan's hands around it, so he'd see it at once when he awakened. "We were kings once, and the sons of kings," he whispered. And then he stood and slung the remaining strap of his pack over his shoulder, and returned to his post at the edge of Etan's world.

End of Time
by Mari Ness

W hen they reached the End of Time Monica demanded a picnic.

"A picnic," said Alan.

"A picnic," repeated Monica.

"With what food?"

She rummaged in her bag. "Two chocolate bars, and a single serving box of cornflakes."

"That isn't a picnic," said Alan, suddenly shivering, but not from cold.

The End of Time was an utterly barren place, not cold, not hot, not moist, not dry, just, just—empty, was the only word that came to Alan's mind. It stretched around them, for endless empty kilometers, light brown sand dunes and deadened grass, with only a tall iron gate in the center of this nothingness to mark the end. It was, in his opinion, a terrible place for a picnic.

"It's all in the arrangements," Monica said, and knelt. From her bag, she drew out an old towel, and spread it in front of her knees, and then carefully placed the box of cornflakes in front of her, placing one chocolate bar on each side of the box at an exact equal distance. "Come on. Picnic."

"Or we could just go in."

"Picnic first," Monica announced.

The gate should have had an aura of dread, of power, or of happiness, or light, or—it should have had an aura. In all the stories, all the movies, all the books he had seen or read, final gates had a—*something*—about them. This gate was just—tall. And it was a gate, most certainly: two dark grey pillars stretching up endlessly before them, joined by wrought iron gates, closed against visitors. The gates were utterly plain, barren of any decorative pattern that he could see; the pillars, at a distance, had seemed to have lines and patterns to them, but when he walked up to look at them closely, he could see that they were utterly unmarked, utterly ordinary, utterly plain. Except that this was the End of Time. And except—caught by something, he looked closer.

He could not tell if the pillars were made of stone, or wood, or plastic, or some other substance. He reached out a hand towards them. Almost, he sensed, he could feel a buzzing sensation, as if he were touching something filled with static electricity. He hesitated, and then suddenly touched the pillars. Nothing. Only a slick surface, as smooth as highly polished rock, although warmer and slightly softer than rock. Petrified wood, perhaps, although as soon as he thought that, he knew he was wrong. His fingers glided over the surface. Some ordinary extraordinary substance. He looked at the gates between the pillars. Those, he sensed, were pure cold iron. He found himself shivering again. He could not tell what had caught his eye, but despite the utter plainness of the gates and the columns, he thought something seemed wrong with them.

"Picnic," repeated Monica.

"I can't believe that we've reached here, and your main thought is to eat."

She looked at the gates. "I can't believe that we should go through them without eating."

"Is that what we're going to be doing? Going through them?"

"Why else are we here?" she asked. She opened the box of cornflakes. "Come on. Eat."

He stepped away from the gates and sat down across from her, staring at the cornflakes and the chocolate bar. "Why are we here?" he asked.

She took a bite of chocolate. "Go on, eat," she urged. When he did not reach for the food, she sighed. "You might as well ask how we got here."

He opened his mouth to ask that, and found his mind flinching away from the question and its answer. They had walked to the End of Time, he knew—he remembered that; but he could not remember why, or how they had started the trip, only that it had been a long, rocky path.

"Is it what you expected, at the end?"

Monica stared at the gate. "The difference between us," she said, finally, "is that I never really expected anything. Anything at all. Not—not back there, not on the way, not here."

"I expected—"

"Meaning. It's what you always expected. No, not expected. *Wanted.*"

"And you didn't?"

"I don't think so," she said. "Although here, at the end—I can't be sure."

He finally reached down and opened the chocolate bar, taking a bite. "I don't think I expected meaning," he said, while the chocolate was still melting in his mouth. "I think I expected an utter end. And not a beginning."

Monica looked at the gate. "That might be what this is, you know. An utter end."

"Then why does it have an entrance?"

They both stared at the pillars and the gate between them. Monica reached out a hand and touched the gate, and snatched her hand back quickly.

"Ouch," she cried out. "It *burns*."

"It's hot?" asked Alan, surprised.

"No," she said, clutching her hand to her chest. "No. It's so cold that it burns." She pushed her hand out briefly to show him, and he saw the brilliant red markings crossing her palm. He remembered, not entirely irrelevantly, that they had no medical supplies at hand.

"That should go away in time," he said.

She looked at him. "In time," she repeated.

"Yes." A memory came back to him. "Like the time I burned my foot when the water in the bathtub was too hot, remember? It seemed to take forever, but it just took time."

"But we don't have any time," she said. "This is the end."

They both turned and stared at the gate.

"In which case we don't have any time for a picnic," he said.

"Or we have endless time for a picnic," she answered.

"This is how you want to spend the end of time?" he asked. "On cornflakes and chocolate and not healing?"

"It's what we have," she said. "I won't have time to heal. I wouldn't even at the other side of this, the beginning."

"Picnic," he said.

"Picnic," she agreed.

So they sat down again by the cloth again and ate the cornflakes and the chocolate bars, slowly, lingering, although Monica's face flinched every time her burns touched the food, or indeed anything else.

"We're ready, I think," Alan said.

"Any time," Monica said.

"Well, this is any time."

"And ending time."

"We've said that."

They stared at the pillars and the iron gates hanging between them.

"We could walk around them," said Alan.

"And waste the picnic?" asked Monica.

"Point," said Alan.

He took a step towards the gates.

"Anything else that you want to do?" he asked.

Monica thought. "Maybe," she said. "Maybe not."

"Anything else that you wish you'd done?" he asked.

Her eyes in the endless light were luminous and utterly unreadable. "I've reached the End of Time," she said. "What more could I wish to have done?"

"I don't know," he said.

He tried, for a moment, to think of his own life, of the twisted path that had led him to these gates, of the things he had done and not done. But the barren landscape around him washed out those thoughts, washed out his mind, and he found he could think of nothing but Time.

"Right," he said, and reached out to take her hand. She flinched as he grabbed it. They stepped forward, staring at the iron gates. He breathed deeply. "We're ready," he said, and placed his other hand on the gates.

The pain shocked him, but he pressed forward, only half noticing that Monica, too, was pushing the gates with her free hand, gritting her teeth against the pain. With both their hands against the iron, the gates gave a horrible creaking sound that echoed through the barrenness. And then they were open, and they could not see the other side.

"Really ready?" he said.

"Yes," she said.

And with that, they stepped through, leaving time behind them.

Enlightenment
by Douglas Smith

They're dead now, the Be'nans. Ta'klu was the last to die. Her body hangs in my arms, as heavy as my guilt, as my footsteps echo in these empty alien streets. And soon we'll be gone from this world, too. I'm the last human in this bizarre, beautiful city. Fan is still here with me—but she's already dead.

The High Places rise above me: two bone-white curves sweeping hundreds of feet into a morning sky from opposite ends of the city, bending inwards like two impossible fingers yearning to touch. Built by generations of Be'nans and now only a body length apart at their lofty tips, the High Places reach for each other. But they don't meet, don't connect. Not yet.

I'll go to them soon, to try to keep a promise. If I fail, and if Ta'klu was right, then what happened here will happen on another world. And another.

But first I must prepare Ta'klu in the manner of her people. She used to laugh when I called her Ta'klu, a name never meant for a human throat. Little here was meant for humans. We aren't capable of understanding. Beside me, Fan nods in agreement.

My first view of the planet Be'na came just before our attack: from orbit, on the darkened observation deck of the *MCES Anvil*, a Merged Corporate Entity ship, manned by RIP Force soldiers of which I was one. I stood with Colonel Keys, staring at the white-green swirl of the planet on the viewplate that covered the bulkhead wall. Fan sat at my feet, unseen by Keys.

Unseen, for Fan was a ghost. I thought of her as a ghost, anyway. One that only I could see. *My* ghost. My guilt ghost. The alternative was that I was insane, and she existed only in my mind. I had not entirely ruled out that possibility.

The screen lit Keys's profile in hard, cold lines. "Did you know, Captain, that these *ips* once had interstellar capability? Gave it all up over five hundred Earth years ago," he said.

Ips: I.P.'s, Indigenous Peoples. A Ripper slur for aliens. RIP: Relocation of IPs, wherever they interfered with planned Entity operations, in this case mining. Survey teams had pegged Be'na as rich in an isotope of berkelium, a rare trans-uranium element and a key material in the shielding for Ullman-Gilmour interstellar drives. But I'd been with the Force long enough to know that RIP held more truth as a word than as initials. "Relocate" was open to interpretation. Fan's people had been relocated. Fan began appearing to me shortly after that.

I'd heard about Be'nan technology. "Do we know why, sir?"

He shrugged. "Dunno. They've reverted to a very simple life style. But from the terraforming and climate control we've seen, they still have technology available somewhere." Another shrug. "Doesn't matter. They've no military capability."

No way to protect themselves from us, I knew he meant. Just like Fan's people. I called her Fan. I didn't know her name. Her people had lived on Fandor IV. They were dead now. Fan was humanoid, but her red fur and the pointed snout and ears gave her a feral look. She was young, maybe four or five, about three feet tall, and reminded me of a stuffed puppy I had as a kid.

The screen switched to an image of an adult Be'nan of unknown gender. Thin, stick-like. Bony face, lots of angles. No hair. Wide eyes, black on silver. Nostril holes over thin lips. Long purple gown, unadorned, straight lines, silky sheen.

Keys snorted. "Not much to look at. At least they're tall. Big buildings, high ceilings." High enough for reuse by us. And empty after we did what RIP did, so we wouldn't waste time and money making our own shelters. The Entity expected a high return from a project world. "Landing fleet ready?" Keys asked.

Fan's earflaps opened wide. I avoided her eyes. "Yes, sir. You still need to set their dosage levels for Scream, sir."

"Level two for pilots, five for the surface teams," he said.

Level five—full combat hits. I pitied any Be'nan that resisted. I saluted and headed off to CommCon to release the dosages, hoping Fan would stay behind. No such luck. The elevator shushed open, and she stood staring at me, tears running from those big brown eyes. She remembered what RIP did to her people. What Scream *made* them do. Made *me* do.

Think of human emotions as a sine wave function: valleys of pain, peaks of pleasure. The greater your joy, the higher the peak; the greater your pain, the deeper the valley. Scream took valleys and flipped them, made them peaks too. Screamers reacted to events based solely on the *intensity* of the resulting emotion. Pain brought pleasure, grief gave joy, horror rendered ecstasy.

On Scream, killing was an emotional orgasm. Some nasty side effects, such as a lack of concern about exactly who you killed, meant we weren't given

Scream until after military discipline programming in boot camp. RIP kept senior officers clean, but every Ripper below Major was addicted. Withdrawal was long and painful—and fatal. RIP was our only source, keeping us loyal and obedient.

Screamers burnt out fast on RIP work, so they rotated us off every six months. Or sooner, if we showed unusual stress symptoms—like trying to kill yourself on Fandor IV. In my rehab role as Security Officer, my dosage was just enough to avoid withdrawal, but not enough to let me enjoy my depression.

The elevator opened on CommCon. Returning salutes, I walked to the control board. Fan's eyes burned into me as I punched the commands to administer Scream to the landing fleet via the life support systems in their field suits. I informed Keys, and a moment later he barked the landing order over the intercom.

With Fan sobbing silently beside me, I watched in the viewplate as our ships swarmed from the main bay, descending on Be'na like a plague of black shining locusts.

I enter the Place of Judgement, the *be'tig'lacht*, the sole Be'nan structure I've found without windows. Only the Be'nan judges, the *be'ti*, saw what was done here. The single vaulted chamber, tall even by Be'nan standards, is thick with the smoke of torches and the sweet fumes of the *do'aran'qua* bubbling in a vat beneath the blackened floor boards. Fan peeks from behind my legs, not wanting but wanting to be in this place.

Ta'klu taught me what was done here. I lay her in the Frame of Judging, the *tig'thar*. I'm not worthy to judge any Be'nan, let alone Ta'klu, but I owe her this. The *ba'aran*, the Book of Forms, lies on a stone table. From it, I choose a *do'aran*, a pose, for her upper body. Her cold flesh makes my hands tremble as I position her arms in the High Form—raised above her in two curves, hands just touching at the fingertips. It represents the completion of the High Places: the form reserved for the most holy. Ta'klu wouldn't approve, but Fan nods her agreement.

I plan to arrange Ta'klu's spindly legs, not in accordance with any form in the Book, but rather to fit her final resting place, her *do'lach*. To the Be'nans, the place and the pose became one, together forming the final judgment of a Be'nan.

Yesterday, in Be'nan tradition, I climbed to the place I've chosen, to make an exact cast of where she'll rest. My clothes are torn from that climb, blood crusting on my knees and arms. I washed the cuts on my hands, but they burn and bleed whenever I use them. Staring at the wounds, I think of crucifixion.

I carry the mould I made from the cast to the frame of judging where Ta'klu hangs. Fan urges me on, but the Be'nan sun climbs halfway up the High Places before I've attached the mould to the frame and positioned Ta'klu's legs properly within it.

I step back, judging how I've judged her. I'm not pleased, for there's no pleasure in this duty, but I'm satisfied that I've met my intent. I remove the mould from the frame, and crank open the vat of the *do'aran'qua*, the milky liquid used in this ceremony. As I wind the winch that lowers Ta'klu into the vat, her position on the frame reminds me again of crucifixion, of her, of an entire race—with us placed beside and below them as thieves. Fan bows her head in a final good-bye to Ta'klu.

Keys chose the city nearest to the berkelium deposits as our base of operations. As it turned out, that was the main city of the Be'nans—*lach'ma'pen'lache*, the Place of the High Places.

Dropping forces outside the city, we secured the perimeter before landing in the main square. Twenty LAShers—Low-altitude attack ships—hovered above for emphasis. Unnecessary emphasis. To say that the Be'nans offered no resistance would be misleading. They seemed completely indifferent to our presence—just as well for them, with every Ripper on full combat dosage.

We moved troops into the buildings forming the main square. I didn't ask Keys what he had done with the original Be'nan occupants. I knew. Fan knew too. Her eyes accused, condemned.

The next morning, I walked with Keys through the city. Fan stayed well back—she didn't like being close to Keys. Be'nan architecture, at least in this city, had an air of delicacy and openness. Most buildings were two or three stories, often with no walls, simply a domed roof resting on tapering pillars or thin arching supports. Where walls were used, they consisted more of window than wall, in a variety of locations and geometric shapes. The predominant color was white, accented by purple cone flowers and the blue-green of a vine that seemed to grow as it wished. The air was heavy with the musky fragrance of the flowers.

Above the city, large gray balloon-shaped creatures drifted. The project file identified them as mammalian, levitating by abdominal gas sacks. Other Rippers shot down several before the herd floated out of range. Fan cried at each corpse we passed.

But the dominant feature of the city were the statues: life-size Be'nan figures in an endless variety of poses and locations, carved from some smooth, milky material. "Their sculpture arts seem rather limited," I said. Oblivious to us, two tall Be'nans, some of the few remaining in the city, paused before a statue and bent forward to touch their foreheads to it. Looking for Fan, I was surprised to find her crouched before a statue, head bowed.

Keys grunted, then nodded his head at the two huge white arches that loomed over the city. "Had a squad check those out. You know what they're made of?" Not waiting for any guess on my part, he jerked a thumb at a statue. "Those things. Can you believe it? They've built those damn arches from statues. One by one, fit together like a giant jigsaw puzzle." He moved on.

I stared up at the High Places, trying to fathom how many statues would have been needed to build the looming fingers. Hundreds of thousands, maybe millions, each carved to fit with those placed before, slowly rising to the sky, reaching to touch each other. How many generations ago had it begun? And *why*?

Suddenly, that question was important, as if an answer would explain why I felt so apart from RIP, so disconnected. As if the space between those tips was the distance between myself and the world around me. Just then, the sun peeked over the High Places, melting the shadow where I stood. Beside me, Fan stared at the arches, her face as sad as ever, and yet peaceful. She nodded.

Removed from the vat, Ta'klu has hardened in the pose I gave her. The liquid has saturated her body, mummifying and encasing her corpse in a super-hard, super-light shell. She stands before me again, but now as a *be'nan'ti*, a Judged One. I polish her white surface with ceremonial rubbing creams until she gleams. Her face is turned to the heavens, eyes hidden behind this shell. Fan backs away. Yes, Fan, now we've truly lost her. Somehow, while her body appeared as in life, she was still here with us. Now, she's become a thing. Only my duty to her remains.

I prepare to transport her to her final resting-place. Although she stood a head above me in life, in this pose she's below me in stature, so that I'll be able to carry her. I smile. Below me in stature? In physical stature only.

After attaching straps to her arms, I turn and reach back to grasp the straps. Hunching forward, I pull on the straps to lift her onto my back. She's heavy. I shrug her weight further up until her feet clear the ground enough to let me walk nearly upright. Moving to the door, bearing her like my cross, I step onto the silent streets where Fan already waits.

Keys and I explored much of the Be'nan city that first day. Fan tagged along behind, keeping her distance from Keys. He was mostly silent. I knew that the Be'nans reaction to our presence, or rather lack of reaction, had unnerved him. He scanned each alcove we passed, as if expecting a belated uprising to begin here. We turned a corner onto a side street.

And stopped.

On this street, sculpted arms rose from the pavement itself, twisting and writhing upwards like frozen serpents. Hands clutched, fingers clawed, as if grasping at something, anything, to tear themselves free of some hidden hell. Upright statues lined this street as we had seen throughout the city, but with their backs turned to this display of pleading arms. Behind us, not daring to enter the street, Fan peeked around a pillar.

Keys and I walked slowly along that strange avenue, weaving a path among the arms. Between each pair, rising just enough out of the pavement to be discernible, lay an upturned sculpted face.

Perhaps it was the silence of that street or the Be'nans indifference to our power—or the expressions on those faces. Whatever the reason, Keys kicked suddenly at an arm. Despite the sculpture's delicate appearance, his attack had no effect, beyond generating a pained look on his face and a mournful bell tone that echoed down the narrow lane. He stood there in silence, his hands clenching and unclenching. Then he drew his Tanzer and fired a thin beam at the arm. The arm glowed blue as I felt the radiated heat. Keys holstered his gun and kicked the arm again.

This time, it broke off with a snap. He picked it up, staring at the broken end. I heard him mutter "My God." Then he waved me over. "Captain, look at this."

He handed me the arm, and I examined the end. Instead of the solid substance I expected, the outer whiteness of the arm appeared to be merely a shell. I stared at the contents inside. Although Be'nan physiology differed from ours in many respects, I'd seen enough dismembered corpses in RIP to know that I was looking at bone and mummified flesh.

I've carried Ta'klu only a small way through the empty city and already I'm tiring. Lowering her to the pavement, I slump against her, resting a moment between the twisted upraised arms here on one of the *mephi'cou*, a Street of the Low Ones. Fan huddles close to me, sensing the evil in this place.

Elsewhere in the city, Judged Ones appear in a *li'do'aran*, a pose of purity, placed so that passersby must look up to them. Those are the majority—not saints, not devils—just good people. Could humans say that of our own race? Fan shakes her head.

But the Streets of the Low Ones interred those judged to be impure, to have regressed from birth on a path to Enlightenment. They were placed beneath the feet of the people, most of their encased bodies hidden, imbedded into the actual roadway.

Such a judgement was never given lightly. Any Be'nan that gave it would rest here as well after death, lining this street, their back turned to the display, a symbol that the Be'nan people rejected the lives of those interred here.

I know each face, each story. Here lies Ves'wa, who opened the way for the Ones Who Watch, from where Ta'klu's ancestors had banished them eons ago—and to where they were returned after the Battle of the Terrible Silence. There I can see the twisted beauty of Ne'sto, whose passion for lovers was equaled solely by her passion for adornments made from those lovers. Beside her lies Ke'bi, who danced with the Dead Things in the City With No Name.

And there, in a darkened alcove, segregated even from these, is Det'syek, a judge himself, who let a desire for artistic impression override objectivity in the poses he gave.

Fan pleads with me to leave here. Sighing, I rise and take up my burden again. For there's another class of Judged Ones: the Be'nan equivalent of saints or buddhas, those who achieved Enlightenment. The Be'nans reserved a special location for the Enlightened. I raise my eyes to the High Places.

The next day, to the surprise of all, Keys halted the removal of the Be'nans from the city. He called me to the house that we'd appropriated for RIP HQ. News of the true nature of the statues had spread quickly among the Rippers. A wariness now replaced their arrogance, an unease amplified by the ubiquity of its source: the statuary literally surrounded us at every turn. Walking from the officers' quarters, I passed several toppled and smashed statues. Fan paused at each one, touching it, head down.

I found Keys in the Ops room, a central airy dome supported by arching buttresses and speckled with high windows. He paced beside a stone slab that now served as a map table. I noted that someone had removed the two statues that had stood on the slab.

"You stopped the relo," I said, feeling Fan's eyes burn into me. Relocation. Even after all the RIP missions I'd been on, all I had seen and done, I still couldn't call it what it was.

Keys stopped pacing and pinned me with a stare. "I've been talking to a head honcho ip. Some sort of priest caste."

"Talking, sir?" I asked. Fan grew suddenly still beside me.

"Talking. As in what we are doing right now."

I was shocked. With no earlier direct contact with this culture, we had estimated a year to figure out their language. "CommOps has made remarkable progress."

Keys snorted. "Those cretins? They'd still be pointing to holos and building goddam syntax charts." He shook his head. "The ips did it. Yesterday, this Tatoo or Takoo or something, she walks in here—at least I think she's a she—and just starts yapping. Perfect Entity Standard English." He plopped into a chair beside the map table and motioned me to another.

I sat, and Fan curled on the floor. "What did she want?"

"After yesterday, the men started breaking those . . . *things*," he said. I knew he meant the statues. "She wanted us to stop."

"That's their first reaction to anything we've done. What did you tell her, sir?"

"I agreed. I ordered the men to cease and desist."

RIP Colonels neither sought nor took counsel from ips. My face must have shown my surprise. Keys leaned forward. "She doesn't just know our language, Captain—she even knew our slang. Called us Rippers, talked about ips, Tanzers, LAShers."

I hesitated. "That could be a result of how they learned our language. They must be recording our conversations, then applying sophisticated pattern recognition and context AI."

"She knew that we're here for the berkelium."

"The men might have talked about that."

"She used our MCE project code. Only you and I know that."

That stopped me. "Maybe they hacked into our ship systems?"

"There's more. She knew stuff about me that isn't on our systems. Stuff from my childhood. Little things, trivial, not something I likely ever told anybody in RIP."

Again I felt the isolation and loneliness that had flooded me on first seeing the High Places. I felt suddenly naked, exposed to the alienness of this world. "Telepathy, perhaps?"

He shook his head. "I didn't even remember this stuff until she said it. So I thought it best to agree to her request, until we know more." He looked at me. "Which is where you come in."

"Me, sir?" I replied, as Fan's ears snapped up.

"I want you to be our liaison with these ips, through this one. Find out what you can about them, what else they know about us. And, goddamn it, *how* they know it."

"Why me, sir?"

Keys frowned. "You're my 2IC, and our security officer."

Fan shook her head. He was hiding something. I swallowed. "If I'm to succeed, sir, I need to know everything about this."

Keys glared at me, clenching and unclenching his hands, just like he had done before he shot the arm on that street the day before. "All right, Captain. She asked for you. By name."

The vines now cover these silent streets. They part before us as we walk, showing me the way though my goal hangs clear and bright above me. They know who I carry.

We pass many Judged Ones, toppled by Rippers. They stand once more, resurrected, raised up by the vines, broken limbs held in place by blue-green coils, cracked wounds concealed behind leafy veils. Fan tilts her head as the wind mutters in the rustle of the vines, giving voice to dead Be'nans. I know the words they whisper. All life here knows the deed that was done.

And the price the Be'nans chose to pay, in vain, for us.

Keys led me from the Ops room to a garden inside the HQ house. I was surprised to find the garden, untended for only two days since our occupation, already overgrown. Vines choked the paths, and a pungent scent of flowers hung like an unseen curtain. A tall Be'nan stood between two arching fountains.

A vision of the High Places came unbidden to me. In it, this Be'nan hovered suspended between them, as if those strange great fingers were pointing at her, indicating her. Then she stretched out long thin arms to touch both tips, bridging the narrow gap, finally completing the High Places. Or did she hang crucified on them?

The vision vanished. I turned to ask Keys a question but found him gone. Turning back, I jumped, startled to find the Be'nan now standing beside me.

She touched the fingertips of both her hands together in an arch before her, the Be'nan greeting, then repeated the gesture but facing slightly to my left. I turned. Fan stood there, staring up at the Be'nan, lips pulled back in the smile of her people. I'd never seen Fan smile. This so struck me that it was several seconds before I realized the implication of what just happened. I turned to the Be'nan. "You . . . you can see her?" The Be'nan just smiled a very human smile. I cleared my throat. "My name is Jarrod," I said, not knowing what else to say.

She spoke a sound, her name I supposed. Clicks and bird songs to me. "Ta'klu?" I offered, like a child before a teacher.

She smiled again. "That will do."

So began our friendship. And the end of a world.

*   *   *

My muscles burn and scream, but I refuse to rest here. Fan runs ahead, anxious to leave this place behind. Even the vines avoid this street. Here the killing started. Here the Ta'lonae, the huge gas-bag creatures, were slaughtered. Their corpses drape statues and buildings, and cover the street.

Their flesh doesn't rot in the normal way. It liquefies into a thick grease that drips around me and on me, making the street slick and treacherous with the load I carry. The stench, sickly sweet like some strange spice, is overpowering.

As are my memories. I struggle on to where Fan waits.

I lived with Ta'klu from the day we met, spending all my time with her. I don't know if that had been Keys' expectation, but once we met, it never occurred to me to do otherwise.

Ta'klu never explained why she had asked for me, nor why she gave me what she did—more than just all of her time, I received her complete attention, her focus. She took me everywhere in the city, taught me of their culture, their history, their beliefs.

And of a thing called Enlightenment.

"What is it?" I asked Ta'klu one day as we walked in the city, Fan scampering around each vine-covered pillar we passed.

"Your people will call it omniscience, but it is less than that—and more. It is connecting as one with life around you."

"On Be'na?" I asked, touching a statue as we passed.

"And beyond." She raised a long thin hand as I opened my mouth to protest. "More I cannot tell you, Jarrod. Not yet."

"Is it something that humans can aspire to?"

"Your people will desire it."

"But can we achieve it?"

She looked at me for several breaths. "We do not yet know."

"Then can you give it to us?"

"We can open a way," she said, smiling down at Fan.

"Keys will want it," I said. Fan stopped, suddenly solemn.

"Yes," Ta'klu replied.

"Will you give it to him?"

"Can a broken cup hold an ocean?"

I took that as a "no." But I knew RIP and the lengths to which Keys would go. Fan looked up at me. I thought of her people, wiped out by RIP, and my role in that. And I decided. I resolved to withhold all that I learned of Enlightenment from Keys, though I knew that if he discovered this, I'd be court-martialed. Fan smiled. She smiled a lot lately. I liked it.

In those early weeks, Ta'klu showed me what it meant to be Be'nan. Then Keys showed us what it meant to be human.

I awoke one morning to the sizzle of Tanzer fire. Fan stood at an arched window in the room in Ta'klu's house where I slept, gesturing to me. I rose and walked over. A swarm of Ta'lonae hovered above a nearby street, circled by a ring of LAShers. The shimmering around each ship told me that they had their shields set at a wide dispersal: they were herding the Ta'lonae.

For the slaughter.

Houses blocked my view of the next street, but Tanzer beams flamed upwards. No pattern, just Rippers firing at will. When hit, most Ta'lonae would rupture and float down like a huge leaf. But every so often, one exploded loudly in flames, to a chorus of cheers, as the gas inside the creature's sac ignited. Fan jumped at each explosion, and the herd screeched in mournful whistles.

I felt Ta'klu beside me. "So it begins," she said.

"You expected this?"

Her eyes lifted skyward, the Be'nan equivalent of a nod.

"But why? Keys stopped them doing this before."

"He has learned of Enlightenment."

I swallowed. "Ta'klu, I've told him nothing."

Smiling, she laid a spidery hand on my shoulder. "I know."

I considered that as I watched the killing continue. "How do you know?" I asked. When no answer came, I turned and found myself alone. Below me, Ta'klu and Fan emerged onto the street and headed in the direction of RIP HQ. I rushed to follow them.

Keys stood in the Ops room with three Rippers—two sergeants and a lieutenant—facing Ta'klu. Keys fixed me with a look I didn't much like, then returned my salute. The others saluted me only after glancing to Keys. He pointed me to a chair. The other Rippers remained standing, and I knew he'd discovered my duplicity, my failure to inform him of all that I'd learned. I was through. Fan came to stand beside me, as if in support.

Keys turned back to Ta'klu. Even on relo work, I'd never seen his eyes that hungry. "They tell me you're the head ip."

"They?" I asked.

Keys glared at me. "They. All of them. Any of them. You didn't discover that too? They *all* talk our language now. And every one I ask says the same thing—Ta'klu speaks for Be'na."

Ta'klu bowed. "I have been given this honor."

"Then you have the honor of explaining to me." Keys strode over to her. I think he regretted the move. She overreached him by a good foot, forcing him to look up to her. "Tell me how you manage food production, terraforming, weather control—entire planetary environmental management—all with zero technology."

She did not reply. Fan crept closer to me.

"Or how you can give us exact locations of berkelium, more precisely than we can manage with our instruments—drill depths, yield percentages—again without the use of any technology?"

No reply. Fan looked up at me, as if urging me to act.

"Or how you know as much about Earth and Earth history as we do? Or how you can be in one location, then be reported in another spot, hundreds of kilometers away, only minutes later?"

I felt that I had to do something, that it was my duty to protect her as hopeless as it was. "You said yourself that they look the same. And their technology could be hidden—"

"Jarrod." It was Ta'klu. She shook her head, and I stopped. She turned to Keys. "It is called Enlightenment."

Keys smiled, no doubt thinking he had won. "What is it?"

"You will call it omniscience. It is not."

Keys' smile broadened. "Whatever. I want it."

"No," she replied, like a parent to a petulant child.

Keys walked back to the Ops table and sat on the edge. "Oh, I don't think you want to tell me that." He fingered the StAB rod at his belt. Fan hid behind me.

Ta'klu ignored him. "I believe your people have a saying—"

"We have lots," he snapped. "Like 'Don't piss into the wind.' We're the wind, ip, and we'll goddam blow you away."

"I was thinking, 'Beware what you wish for—it may come true.'"

Keys snorted. "Are you saying your knowledge is dangerous? That we couldn't handle it?" Snickers ran through the Rippers in the room. "Well, sister, knowledge is power, and we deal with power every day. We carry it with us. We hold it in our hands, and we wield it as a terrible swift sword. You can't scare us."

"Some knowledge can kill," she said, a chill in her words.

Keys stood again. His hands were making and unmaking fists at his sides. "So can I, ip." His voice was low, calm and cold. "You'll give me the secret . . . or I'll kill every last one of you."

A terrible silence descended on that room, like a beast waiting to devour the next sound. Ta'klu stood in that silence, her head down. I wanted to scream at her. *Tell him! You don't know what they are capable of.*

She looked down at Keys. "No," she said.

I bowed my head. Fan stared at me, her face unreadable.

Of all the places in this tomb of a city, I didn't expect to rest here—an open-air amphitheater sunk below the ground, terraced rows sloping down to a round pool. But the bodies of the Be'nans that had filled this huge bowl are gone now, removed by the vines. Water shimmers again below as the vines refill the pool. Fan leans over the water, staring at her reflection.

I look up to the white arches that dominate this alien sky. Ta'klu's people believed that when the High Places finally met, all of Be'na would achieve Enlightenment. Would that such a gift had never been granted to the humans here.

I was court-martialed. Keys could have killed me but that would have been too kind. He had a couple of Rippers beat me up while he watched. They dumped me on the street, and he knelt down beside me grinning, while I spat out teeth and Fan cried.

"Maybe the ips won't talk, but you, Jarrod, you're going to need a hit soon. Then you'll tell me what you know." He kicked me, then walked away laughing.

Panic seized me. RIP was my only source of Scream. Withdrawal meant weeks of agony, without the filter of Scream, then death. Fan shook her head as if to say "No, don't worry." Fine for you, little one, I thought. You're already dead.

In the first week after his ultimatum, Keys killed one hundred Be'nans. Chosen at random, each was taken to stand in front of Ta'klu's house. Shot with Tanzer, touched by StAB rod, knifed, hung, bludgeoned, burnt alive— Keys told his men to use a variety of methods to see if one particularly unnerved the "ips."

Ta'klu simply stood at her window and bowed to each victim, making the sign of the High Places with her hands. They would return the bow. Then they would die, some quickly, some slowly. Fan stood quietly beside her each time, strangely calm.

I pleaded with Ta'klu. "Why do you let them die? Why don't they resist? Why doesn't someone give in, tell the secret?"

"Some do not know and so have nothing to give. Those of us who do know, know also that the secret would kill your people."

The implication of her words hit me like a charged StAB rod. "You die to protect us? Your killers?"

She smiled. "One day, Jarrod, perhaps you will understand."

That was not my only surprise in that first week. I experienced no withdrawal symptoms from Scream. When I mentioned this to Ta'klu, she just smiled. "A gift to my student," she replied. Fan bared her teeth at me in an I-told-you-so grin.

Keys killed a thousand the second week. Still they bowed and died. Stranger still, I perceived no change in the attitude of those Be'nans that I passed in the ever more empty streets. No panic ensued, no resistance, no flight.

By the third week, the RIP bio-weapons team had engineered a Be'nan plague virus with a short air-borne vector. Keys must have been desperate. RIP used bio-weapons sparingly. You could never be sure of the propagation rate. Too high a rate, and bodies piled up faster than you could get rid of them. Plus they raised the risk of impact on humans and the rest of the planetary ecosystem. I explained all this to Ta'klu as Fan cried.

Keys threatened its release. Ta'klu still refused him the secret. Keys ordered it dropped on a city on the far side of the planet. A week later, a survey team to the city reported one hundred per cent kill rate. The Entity had added another nasty little bug to its product list. And Keys added a second city the next week and a third the week after that.

Still Ta'klu refused to cooperate. Still the Be'nans appeared indifferent to their own slaughter.

Then Keys must have recalled our sole earlier act that had finally prompted a reaction by the Be'nans to our presence: the destruction of the statues. But he was smart enough not to waste time toppling figures around the city.

I was awakened one morning by Ta'klu, her usual air of tranquility gone. Her head moved from side to side, a sign of agitation. "He will destroy the ma'pen'lache, the High Places," she said. Fan scurried about her in frantic circles.

I struggled to wake. "Keys? What . . . how do you know this?"

"He is attaching mechanisms to the base of each. Explosive devices that can be detonated remotely." Ta'klu bowed her head. "He has won." Fan stared at me, as if willing me to some action.

I shook my head. "He slaughters your living, and you do nothing. He threatens a monument to your dead, and you cave in."

"They are more than that, Jarrod." She turned and left.

"Ta'klu, wait," I called after her. Rising, I went to the window as she stepped onto the street, Fan running behind her. "What *are* the High Places?" I called, but Ta'klu kept walking. "Why do you protect them but not your people?" No reply.

Again I followed her to RIP HQ. Again I found her and Fan facing Keys and his officers. Keys wore a grin that I wanted to wipe away with a Tanzer. He looked startled to see me, but then the grin returned, and he turned to Ta'klu. "Got your attention, I see," he said. "Your call, ip. What's the decision?"

"You are making a terrible mistake. You—" Ta'klu began.

Keys swore. "Captain, radio your men to stand by to detonate." The Captain saluted and spoke into his PerComm.

"You will die. You will all die," Ta'klu said.

Silence choked the room. The Rippers looked at each other, but Keys laughed. "If you had any power, you'd have used it."

"We are protecting you."

Keys laughed even harder, but few Rippers joined in. This planet, this city, the indifference of the Be'nans to their own genocide—all had taken their toll. "Protecting us! How kind." His smile died. "Last chance, ip." He nodded to the captain who raised his PerComm again, but Ta'klu froze him with a look.

"Very well," she said. "I warned you. Remember that." She looked at me, and suddenly her voice whispered inside my head. I had never experienced that before. *You, Jarrod, I will shield. A role remains for you. To you, I grant the boon of ignorance.*

Raising her hands, she touched them together over her head. Like the High Places, I thought, as Fan hid behind me. Every object, every person in the room began to brighten, to glow as with some inner light. "I grant you . . . ," Ta'klu cried, " . . . *Enlightenment!*"

We turn onto another Street of the Low Ones—and he's there.

Keys. He lies among the twisted arms and grasping hands, face up, his own arms outspread. He has crucified himself, driving a spike through each of his feet and through his left hand into the ground. A mallet lies beside his right hand. He mutilated himself first, his crotch a bloody mess, and gouged out his eyes.

Fan looks away while I pause long enough to urinate on him.

A while later, we reach the nearer of the High Places.

One month after the plague release and a mere week after the "gifting" of Enlightenment, I walked an empty city searching for food, Fan beside me. The only Terrans we found were corpses, all obvious suicides—hanging from archways by ropes or vines about their necks, lying headless with Tanzers in hand, impaled on the broken arms of statues. Fan wouldn't look at them. I hadn't found Keys yet and wondered if he too numbered among the dead.

That night, I sat beside Ta'klu as she lay dying. She hadn't eaten since her gifting to the Rippers, and the plague had finally touched her. Fan stood, head bowed, on her other side.

The east wall of Ta'klu's room was just a series of pillars, through which a cold wind now blew. In that direction, you could see the High Places reaching for each other against a starry sky. With an effort that was painful to watch, she turned to gaze at them. "I die, my people die, with our great work unfinished."

"What *are* the High Places?" I asked. "What is their power?"

Her gaze never left those great arches, but she smiled. "No power beyond what a symbol can hold. You know the power of a symbol, don't you, Jarrod?"

Fan made the sign of the cross, and I nodded.

"The ma'pen'lache represent an entire race and its resolve," Ta'klu whispered. "A people complete, connected in a belief, in a noble goal: to regain awareness of the universal life force, an awareness we hold at birth, but soon forget. In one moment, to be part of all life in all places. To be one with the creator."

"Is that Enlightenment?"

"That is what it would be, once all life has achieved it. What some of us achieved is only what an individual may aspire to, but less than an entire race, and much less than what all of life could do. And as each who had reached Enlightenment died, the ma'pen'lache grew."

"What did you give to Keys and his men?"

"What was mine to give. A universal body exists: a web connecting all living things, across time, across space. Life is not the sum of those living things, but the web itself. We cannot know life until we can see the web, feel the strands that join us to each other, to everything. That is Enlightenment."

I swallowed. "You let them touch the web."

She turned to me then. "Yes."

"And they were given knowledge of the life around them."

"And their place in that web of life, and the knowledge that life had of them," she finished.

I began to say that I didn't understand, then her words connected with a part of me that seemed to be born in that moment. *The knowledge that life had of them.*

She knew my thoughts. "Yes, Jarrod. The most dangerous encounter is with a perfect mirror. A mirror that shows us as the universe sees us. As we truly are."

She collapsed further into the pillows. "Your people saw the place that they had chosen in the web. Saw each life they took, each strand they broke. They saw how life regarded them: a thing apart, disconnected from the universal body, an invading disease." She closed her eyes. "And they saw the cure."

"Why did you protect me?"

A smile lived briefly on her lips. "I know *your* place in the web." Beside her, Fan nodded and looked at me, smiling.

"What do you mean?"

"A task remains. You remain. *The two become one.*"

"Ta'klu, no more riddles. Tell me what to do," I pleaded.

"I cannot. You must find the way. It is part of the task."

"But I'm no less a murderer than the others who were here."

"Who better to lead the way through darkness than one who has lived in the night?"

"I don't have the strength."

Her eyes opened for what was to be the last time, to look at me. "You have more than you know. Promise me you will try."

I swallowed, barely able to speak, feeling Fan's eyes burn into me, waiting for my reply. "I promise," I said to Ta'klu.

She smiled, perhaps recalling when we met. "That will do."

She died with the light of day, never speaking another word. Laying her hands on her chest, I looked up. Fan stood at a pillar, staring at the morning sun rising beneath where the High Places strained to touch, to become one. Become one.

The two become one, Ta'klu had said. I looked down at her body, knowing then what I must do.

My climb with Ta'klu up the High Places has taken hours. The Be'nans bore their honored Judged Ones by this path for centuries, adding to the structure death by death, but none would have come alone as I have. The initial climb was almost vertical, up steps meant for longer Be'nan legs. I'm cold and exhausted, but each time I stop to rest and drink from my flask, Fan urges me forward again, jumping up and down, pointing ahead.

Now at last I near the tip of this finger. The rise has leveled off, but this final part of my journey is the most dangerous. More than three hundred meters above the ground, the finger narrows and slopes to each side. The light is failing, and my footing is unclear. A rising wind sways the High Places, threatening to rip me from my perch. It moans between the dead beneath me, each moan the voice of a ghost, accusing, condemning.

Another twenty meters remain. The wind's too strong. I set Ta'klu down and crawl forward, pulling her behind me. Ten meters to go. She catches in the spaces and on other statues, and I must go back again and again to free her. Five meters. Three. I can see her resting-place. I move behind to push her the final couple of meters.

We reach the tip. Now I must stand again, lifting her by the straps, to position her feet above the exact spot, her arms reaching out towards the other side. Fighting against each gust of wind, I lower her centimeter by centimeter toward her do'lach. I strain to see past her, to see if her outstretched hands will bridge the gap. She settles into place, her legs melding exactly with the limbs and torsos of those who went before, entwined like lovers. And her arms reach for the other side as if in prayer.

But they don't touch. The High Places don't meet, don't become one. They stay disconnected. And somehow, so do I.

I sink to my knees. The wind carries my cries away, making my grief as impotent as my effort to complete the High Places. But in the wind I hear words, a voice, Ta'klu's voice. I look up. Fan stands at the tip of the other finger, arms stretched towards me. I consider the distance across the span. No more than an arm's length. Could I touch the other side? If I crawl out, balancing on Ta'klu's arms. If I don't fall. If the wind doesn't pluck me off. If Ta'klu will support me in her arms.

Despite my grief and pain, I smile at this last thought and decide. She wouldn't let me fall. I'll try.

Crawling on my belly, my legs gripping each side of the tip, I begin to inch my way out to the end. I can't say why I'm doing this. It just seems right. A way of bringing closure before . . .

Before what?

Before I leave. I realize then that I'd climbed here not just to lay Ta'klu to rest, but to kill myself. I intended to throw myself from this height, final payment for the crime that we've done here. But somehow I know that my death wouldn't be repayment: it would be an escape—from a debt, a duty. I know now what I must do: return to Earth and make my people aware of what has been done here. Of what is being done on other worlds.

I stretch across the gap. Almost. A little more. The tip sways and lurches. The wind claws at me. And on the wind ride phantom sounds and spectral voices. I hear the crash of statues and the screams of Be'nans. I hear Keys laughing.

But above it, yet softer somehow, I hear Ta'klu. *Try*, she says, and I remember my promise.

I edge farther out still until my waist extends past her fingers, and I must grip her body with my feet. On the far tip, Fan gestures me on, pleading with her eyes. I reach again.

And touch the far side.

Electricity, energy, power, a force I can't describe thrills down my arm as my fingers brush the other tip. A chorus of a million Be'nans deafens me. Visions of generations of Be'nan lives burn my sight from me. Fragrances of a world of flowers and the stench of a mountain of corpses choke the breath from me.

And I fall from heaven.

I slip from Ta'klu's dead, hard, cold hands and from the High Places. I scream as I fall, and the world rushes towards me and I scream again. Then I am silent. For the world has slowed, and I watch my body fall away from me, falling slowly like a feather sinking in amber.

Ta'klu is suddenly beside me, holding Fan by the hand. Other Be'nans hover with us above the High Places, spread across the heavens in an arc, ephemeral hands linked in the web. Ta'klu reaches out to me, and I to her. We touch.

And I am Enlightened.

I look down. Somewhere below me, directly under the High Places, my body now lies. That seems both strange and correct.

I sense Ta'klu with me, clear to me even among the seemingly infinite lives of which I am now aware. I hear the question that she asks me: *Now do you know your role?*

My people must learn, I reply. *But I've no body.*

A human awaits your coming, waits for you to speak through him. When they strike him down, another will accept you. And each time they strike you down, you will rise again, stronger, carrying more of your people with you. You are the prophet.

I remain silent.

Do you accept your place in the web? she asks.

Suddenly we are in the garden again where we first met, and I smell the flowers and hear the fountain. Vines curl around my feet, and through them I sense the infinite web of life of which I am now part. The vision fades, but I know my answer. *I'll try.*

I feel her smile. *That will do,* she says.

I span star systems in a mind-blink to hover above a blue-brown orb layered in swirls of white. I feel Fan now as part of me, as she always was. I plunge through the white until blue resolves to seas, and brown to endless cities, and I sense the billions that dwell in those cities and under those seas.

I know them all, and soon they will know me. I fly eastwards, towards a coming sunrise, to the one who awaits me.

And I think of resurrection.

Husk
by Meghan Jurado

The cicadas are back.

Every year I come out here to spend a few days on what used to be my grandparents' farm. Every year I lay in bed at night, sweat running from my temples, listening to the swell and recede of the insect chorus. They, like me, return to this place because it has memories for them. It is where they know to go.

At first, I returned here to remember my parents. They vanished here, leaving me behind. I woke in the morning and I was alone; I could not find them or anyone, though I have searched high and low in the heat-dead fields. I came back for memories, but have found much more. Things are not right here.

There are sounds, things that call out in the night to be silenced. They live at the edges of my vision, never daring to dart into my direct sight. I could put them to rest if they would come to me, but they will not.

I rise early at the farm, waking just as the sun peeks over the horizon, searing the parched ground. There is a brief moment of silence as I step out of the door, but the wind stirs and the cacophonous wail of the cicadas returns. I walk out into the field, as I do every morning, and watch the sun rise. It warms my blood.

In this field, nothing grows. The grass is yellowed and the soil is dry, it crumbles under my feet and is like walking on the sands of a dead world. When I do see an animal, it is dead. The corpses have been torn apart, split down the back as if the inside wanted to get out. Nothing can live under the yellow sky. Why have I come here again? I torture myself with these remains of life; cradle the corpses to see if a heart still beats. There is silence.

The cicadas follow me through the day, my only living companions, my Greek chorus. At first, the sight of the swarm taking flight unsettled me greatly, but I do not think they wish me any real harm. They rest where I rest, and continue their symphony. They leave skins to be crushed into powder underfoot, brown husks in their exact shape. They escape their clawed confines, the only sight of growth in this deserted place. They leave their bodies for the release of flight. I cannot. I live on in the face of death, never changing, never seeming to grow.

I spend time out by the oil well, that pumped the lifeblood of commerce, trying to connect with the busy world that I have left behind. Leaning against the rusted pump and burning against the hot metal, the flesh on my back sears. I have no doubts the pump is dry, dead like the air, dead like the earth, but it continues to work, mechanical, unending. I sit at its base and stare across the land. I see things beckoning me far away, and I run to them, choking on the dirt and heat, but when I get there, there is nothing. Only wind. Only dust. I grow tired of hot wind. I choke on the dust.

When night comes, I am waiting for it. I sit on the rusted cellar doors, watching the sun go down, and the heat should cease, but it only stagnates, stale and murky like a half-dried puddle. If there was such a puddle, I would lay my face in it and soak up the moisture through my skin like an amphibian. There is no water, no way to slake my thirst—how can I go on?

Night is where the sounds are the strongest. I cock my head to the side and listen, but I never get a clear sense of direction. They are lost, I am lost, but we both are here. Existing on nothing, both very real.

Tonight the calling is very loud indeed. I hear it vibrating through me, twisting itself around my brain, squeezing what few fool thoughts have survived in a cruel vise. It ebbs and flows with the sounds of the cicadas. My sweat turns cold. The metal doors where I sit seem to vibrate. It is then that I understand why the sounds have not escaped. They are below me.

I lift the doors, straining my arms and back with the effort, my muscles dry, creaking, my skin ripping like ancient parchment. My brain itself is buzzing, trapped like a fly in a gourd, small and shriveled like fruit rotting in the sun. The buzzing grows stronger, then recedes, never releasing its grip. A line of blood runs from my eye and turns to rust powder in the wind; my thoughts seek escape through my aching skull.

The door opens, a gaping maw into the cool earth, a place where the heat does not touch, where the blight has not spread. I feel vibrations strongly here; my teeth rattle and hum, dead in my gums like dry stalks of corn. My hands are stained red with rust; I am marked. I start down the stairs. It is dark. I have only matches. I dare not light them too soon for the fear of combusting.

I reach the last stair. I cannot see in front of me, but there is a smell down here, a dry smell, cellar dirt and other things, dead things. I hear things, stealthy things, and I would gladly find a horror instead of the nothing that has embraced me for so long.

I light a match between my flammable fingers. My other hand goes to my parched, cracked mouth; I cannot believe family has been so close the whole time. Their spirit is not here, but they have left behind their shells, abandoned their hollow skin. Split down the back, they have escaped their mortal holds and have taken flight. My parents, flown away, have left me behind.

The match burns out yet my fingertips stay alight, so I do not strike another. Their bodies lay, insubstantial as paper, on the cool ground. I can see their faces: collapsed masks. I blow out my burning flesh so I need not see more.

I leave the dark hole and stand in the moonlight. The cicadas buzz overheard, lined up on the roof above. I stand and listen for a moment, head down, then raise my arms, a humble, broken creature. They swarm down on me, covering me with their prickly insect legs, beating at me with wings like parchment. The sound is overwhelming, invasive. As they cover me my skin begins to feel too tight, constraining. An insect thrums against my eardrum. Spindly legs explore my wizened tongue.

Suddenly, they are gone, leaving me a new escape. I begin to work my way out of my skin, starting with the split down the back. It tears away with no pain. I feel bigger than I was before.

Then, as the cicadas start their ancient song, I step out of my old husk and become a ghost myself, more than what I was. I have given up my earthbound remains. I have taken flight.

The Last
by Cavan Scott

Parkhouse stumbled for a second, throwing his hand out to grasp the twisted metal of the spire. That was a close one. One gust of wind this high and he'd be finished, splattered over the rocks far below.

A nervous giggle slipped past his lips. What the hell did he care anyway? He'd come up here to throw himself to oblivion. What did it matter if the wind blew him over the ledge or he screwed up his eyes and took one giant leap for man himself? The result would be the same; one ex-trooper spread like strawberry jam across an alien shore. No one left to shed one bloody tear. No one left to do anything at all. He was the last and he'd had his fill of surviving. Even if there was someone left, they couldn't blame him. If he'd been the one burnt to a crisp in the crash he'd bet that Will and Trent would be taking the same course of action—ready to meet their maker and tell him, her or it exactly what they thought of this bloody universe.

OK, maybe this wouldn't be the way Trent would have chosen. The stupid wuss had been scared of heights. No, Trent would have blasted his brains out or chucked himself into the warp generator. Not so scary but just as effective.

Thankfully Parkhouse had no such phobias. And besides after it had taken him all day to climb up here there was no way he was going to wimp out now. He didn't want to go down in history as the man who couldn't finish a job. All he had to do was lean forward and . . .

What was that? Something bleeping at the back of his skull. He used to know what it was, but now . . . well, there was one explanation but surely not. Not after all this time. No one had activated his communicator for months. No need. Everyone was dead and the recently deceased don't tend to get in touch. Not unless it was a . . .

No, that was idiotic.

There hadn't been a rescue mission in a year. Why would there be one now? How ironic would that be? The day Trooper M. Parkhouse, serial number 442244/2173 decided to flick the birdie at all creation and take his life, the cavalry arrives. Happy endings like that don't happen, unless you're stuck in the middle of a god-awful true-life holo-flick on the Hallmark channel. No, it'll probably just be a bit of interplanetary chatter-spam. A bot asking him if he'd be interested in looking at pictures of Martians taking it up the wrong 'un or whether he'd ever considered fitting a cybernetic todger.

But there was no point in just ignoring the call. Even if the last thing he ever heard was junk mail, it might at least be a human voice. Still clinging to the metal for not-so-dear life Parkhouse felt behind his ear for the communicator toggle buried deep within his flesh and couldn't help but offer a prayer to any deity that happened to be passing that salvation was on its way.

Click. Channel open, Captain.

"H-hello."

"Sir, sir is that you?"

Of all the voices in all the galaxies, it had to be that one.

"Sir, this is . . ."

"I know who you are, NUJ-911186. Now's not convenient."

The mechanical voice quavered at the other end of the line.

"Sir, where are you? We've been worried. UX-774170 has been running you a nice, warm bath and . . ."

"That won't be necessary 911186. I've just decided to step out for a while. Get a breath of fresh air."

"You've been gone all day and System shows that your vital signs are racing. Your adrenalin levels . . ."

" . . . are just right for a man about to jump off a thirty-story-high solar spire."

"Jump off! Sir, you're joking. You wouldn't . . ."

"911186, I forgot how to joke a long time ago. See you at the bottom. I'll be the liquidized corpse. Don't worry. I'll wear a carnation so you recognize me."

"Sir, I . . ."

"Parkhouse out!"

With a flick of his finger, Parkhouse cut the link dead. He could just imagine the panic. 911186 and his little band of droids running around like headless Slarvian-herders, fresh with the news that the last survivor of the Titan 53 Star Cruiser was about to take his own life in a—if he could say so himself—rather spectacular fashion.

Well, there's no time like the present. Best not to keep hell waiting.

Parkhouse let go of the spire and began the plummet to his unavoidable death.

The hulk-class Star Cruiser Titan 53 had entered the atmosphere of Planetoid 2311KH/X0 on 27/05/2338 old calendar. Immediately after the captain had given the order to abandon ship, the bridge had been consumed by the rupture of the port power-coupling. Trooper M. Parkhouse jettisoned his escape capsule exactly 24 seconds later and watched in horror as the Titan continued its death-slide to the planet below. But they were away and the capsule would guide them gently to the surface. Well, that was the theory anyway. Instead, the minute lifeboat careened into the side of a mountain, disintegrating on impact. Parkhouse had been thrown free and came to rest in the scarlet dust meters away from where his fellow troopers were instantly atomized. There he lay, life eking away with every moment until the rescue droids found him and transported his broken form to the wreckage of the Titan. The mechanoids somehow managed to save him and brought him back from the brink of death. Sure, three of his limbs had to be replaced but an amazing 34 per cent of his skin was still his own. The miracle of twenty-fourth century medical science had done the rest. Of course, the realization that his future consisted of continued treatment in the graveyard of a crashed ship by the remaining fourteen robots meant that he'd regularly cursed his good luck that there had been no brain damage. If he were a vegetable the mindless wait for a non-existent rescue mission would have been easier to bear. Of course, that didn't matter now. He had committed suicide and so was at rest. The sun had finally set on this squalid corner of the cosmos once and for all.

Parkhouse groaned. Just his luck. It appeared that the afterlife consisted of an exact replica of the Titan 53's shattered medibay. The nauseating, sterile smell was the same. The whine of the emergency generators was the same. The chatter of the droid was the same. Obviously, any sane man would immediately conclude that the fall from the solar spire hadn't finished him off and he was still firmly in the land of the living. But that just wasn't possible, was it? No divine joke was that cruel.

"We noticed you as you bounced off the first of the particle collection spikes," NUJ-911186 continued. "Thankfully the damage, while serious, was nothing that we could not repair. MW-87367 was able to prime the tractor beam and provide a sonic field that cushioned your fall."

No, this wasn't possible at all.

"Sir, are you listening?"

911186 leant into the bed, beady cameras whirring as they zoomed into Parkhouse's face.

"774170, are you sure there had been no trauma to Trooper Parkhouse's aural passages? I am not convinced that he can hear me."

"Of course I can hear you, 911186," Parkhouse rasped. Was that really his voice? It didn't sound like him at all. "You saved me then?"

"Ah, sir. How excellent to hear you speak. I am afraid you ruptured your vocal cords but 774170 has done a marvelous job replicating a new set."

"Just answer me one thing, 911186." Parkhouse asked, allowing his eyes to close in a renewed ocean of despair. 911186 looked up from its datapad, a look of what could only be a robot's version of confusion crossing its metallic face.

"Of course, sir. Anything at all."

"Why?"

"Sir?"

"Why do you keep doing it?"

"I am not sure I understand the query sir."

Bloody machine. Of course you don't. If you did, you would've been up there with me, ready to scatter yourself over the floor as well. Parkhouse took a deep breath, wincing as the air rushed over the fresh grafts on his windpipe.

"Over the last month, I've attempted to take my life seven times. And seven times you've caught me, wrapped me up and repaired my poor, little broken body."

911186 let the statement sink in for a minute and then, when it realized there was no more to come replied with a single, "Yes."

"Why, 911186? Why do you keep bothering to patch me back together when it should be plain to see that I want to die?"

If 911186 had been human, the rising pitch of Parkhouse's voice would have been enough for it to realize that its patient was a tad annoyed. But as 911186 was merely the chief robotic service assistant of the late Titan 53 such an observation was impossible.

"Sir, need I remind you," 911186 started, in a tone that indicated that he was about to anyway, "that you are the last surviving officer of this craft. Our programming is such that we are charged with keeping you alive, no matter what the situation. We will take all necessary measures to assure your survival."

"You don't get it do you, you infuriating bag of bolts," Parkhouse yelled as loud as his artificial voice-box would allow him, "I don't want to be the last surviving officer sharing my last remaining days with the likes of you. I don't want to grow old on this dust-ball. I want out. Do you hear me, 911186? I want out, now!"

The sudden silence in the medibay was as startling as Parkhouse's outburst. Calmly 911186 stowed his datapad.

"To be brutally frank, sir, your wishes are a moot point. Our mission is to sustain you until you die of natural causes. If you tried to slit your throat with a lazer-scapel now I would happily repair you. Besides, what with the rescue-craft entering the system earlier today, I find it hard to . . . "

It was at this point that Parkhouse knew he was dreaming.

"What did you say, droid? Rescue-ship? What rescue-ship?"

911186 looked quizzically at the trooper.

"The rescue-ship *Spearhead* entered this system at 1143 hours this morning. They intercepted your distress call and changed course to investigate. According to the message we received from Captain Jacques . . . "

"Captain Jacques?"

"The commander of the vessel sir. According to her message they should be coming into orbit within the next hour or so. I thought you had been informed, sir." 911186 continued to prattle before turning angrily—or at least as angrily as a construct with no human emotions could manage—to his robotic companion.

"774170," it snapped, "you did inform Trooper Parkhouse didn't you?"

But Parkhouse didn't care anymore. Suddenly someone had remembered to switch on the light at the end of the tunnel. He was going home.

The Star Corps records chattered and clicked as Jenny Jacques sipped her tea.

Trooper M. Parkhouse, it appeared, hadn't enjoyed the most successful of careers. It wasn't that he was necessarily sub-standard but his record was merely adequate. He did his duty but had never been in a situation that had pushed him to the limit. The corps was full to the brim with such types, enlisted young and shoved from one commission to the next, never achieving anything more than mediocrity. It wasn't their fault. Most of the time they'd not been expected to show initiative, but merely follow orders. A blunt tool, her father had described them. Necessary but without merit. He wasn't being cruel, just realistic. These were the cogs in the machine, essential for the Corps's continued development but never to rise to the top.

Not so for Jenny. She'd never been allowed to stay treading water. That's what came of being the only child of one of the shining lights of the galaxy. Admiral Richard Jacques had initiated more first contacts than any other Corps officer, had overseen more border disputes and, if you scratched slightly beneath the legend, bedded more alien princesses. He had been a rogue and an adventurer but had personified the romanticism of the great push out into the outer regions of galaxy.

And as his daughter she'd been expected to do the same. Well, not the princess part but she'd had a good go at the male contingents of certain royal houses. For a second she let her mind wander, absently running her finger around the rim of the cup. She really should look up Z'ginder of the Plastat. Now there was a specimen and a half. She'd enjoyed initiating first, second and

273

third contact with that one.

Anyway, she thought, snapping back to the job at hand and sweeping her mind from the gutter, there's a rescue mission to be had. What better way to finish the shakedown cruise of the Elite Class *Spearhead* than to save a poor trooper trapped on a dead world and be back to pick up the medals and glory before the ship's regular crew were even on board?

Time to be the courageous captain.

The doors of the bridge swished open as Captain Jacques entered. Exec Officer Hulban glanced up from his console and watched the sway of his commander's hips as she slinked over to her position. By the maker, he knew that cross-species pollination was forbidden by his race's decrees but even this devout Malarvian would risk censure to see what was under her uniform. Thankfully the shakedown cruise was almost complete and with it, his tour of duty on the *Spearhead*. In a few short days he would be whisked across the quadrant to his new appointment on Starstation Alpha-77. The *Spearhead* was crammed with state of the art equipment and more luxurious than any craft he'd ever served on but three month checking systems with only five crew onboard had caused all manner of tensions. It didn't help that Dr. Leudstret, the chief science officer was a member of the Eclit, a race that exuded powerful pheromones that would cause sexual stirrings in an eunuch. So far everyone had been far too professional to indulge in the stirrings that Leudstret caused but the atmosphere was reaching boiling point.

Of course, it could be that Jacques wasn't attracted to a seven-foot tall, purple skinned alien with a face full of tentacles. Her loss. At least the third eye in the back of his head meant that he could watch her adjust her top as she sank into her command post. Exquisite.

"Report Mr. Hulban," Jacques barked, Hulban swung to face her, trying his hardest not to focus on her ample chest.

"We're within three clicks of Planetoid 2311KH/X0, Ma'am"

"Excellent." Jacques absently tapping at her console. "Let's go find our little lost lamb."

The whine of the shuttle's door broke through the stale air of the planetoid. Jacques shivered as the biting wind swept into the airlock, cutting through her environment suit. It was bad enough that shuttle flight always caused her stomach to flip, but the sight of the landscape that stretched in front of her, made her skin crawl.

It was just so . . . dead. Cracked earth the color of mold stretched out as far as the eye could see, dust and debris whipped up by the sharp breeze. Above them the distant sun hung in the bleak sky, an impotent ball of fire that failed to heat this insignificant rock. The atmosphere was thin, but breathable. Jacques just hoped she didn't have to breathe it too long. It was time to get things moving.

Marching purposely down the ramp, Jacques barked an order at the exec. "Life forms?"

Hulban cleared his throat, an offensive wet sound that caused the captain's stomach to lurch anew. If she caught his piggy little eyes undressing her one more time, the disgusting, slime-infested squid would receive a sharp kick to his privates or at least a day scrubbing out the hyperspace generators with a toothbrush. The former would probably have her court-martialed but it would be far more satisfying than the latter.

"Trooper Parkhouse's signal is emanating from the wreckage straight ahead, Captain."

She couldn't be sure if the vile Malarvian sneered as he reported this— who could with all those tentacles twitching like a nest of eels—but one cold slap would wipe the smirk off his face. God, she hadn't realized how much she was counting the days until he was shipped to his new appointment.

"Well, there's no point hanging around admiring the view. Let's go get our man."

Jacques let Security Chief Carter take the first step towards the wreckage stretching ahead of them. It was a well-known fact in space faring that there was no point having a security officer and getting mauled by a nine-foot-tall beastie yourself. That was what security personnel were there for after all. And besides Carter was the quickest draw she'd ever seen. If there was something lurking in the shattered remains of the Titan there was every chance that he'd be able to gun it down before it could attack. He was the best guard dog she'd ever served with. There was every chance she'd ask to have the tall Texan transferred to her next command.

Whatever happened she hoped that one of her ships never ended like this. While it was a tribute to the engineers that had built the Titan 53 that so much of the craft had survived such a crash, let alone that some modules were still able to sustain life, the wreckage was horrific. Torn metal jutted out of the scorched earth like mammoth talons and the ground was scattered with broken personal effects. Everyone knew that Jacques was a hard-hearted bitch—she'd spent years creating the persona after all—but the sight of someone's favorite sweater, blackened by fire and dumped millions of light-years from home, caused water to gather at the corner of her eyes. So many people lost. And to think she had thought about this being a glory mission. Forget the medals Jenny, Jacques scolded herself. You've been holed up testing the *Spearhead* for too long. You've forgotten that this is all about people, not commendations. Look after the people and the commendations will look after themselves. She even guiltily shot a glance at Carter. Minutes before she'd been glibly dismissing him as just another security shirt. Of course she wouldn't be so flippant if something happened to him. She'd had to write letters of consolation to grieving parents, fiancés or siblings before; 'Dear so-and-so, I am sorry to inform you that Lieutenant what's-his-name lost his life during our recent mission to here or there. May I offer you the Corps's deepest sympathies for your loss and assure you that your son / husband / fiancé / lover died serving his people, yadda-yadda-yadda, blah-blah-blah.' They were horrible, impersonal things and she didn't want to have to sign another, even if it was Hulban who met his maker. Funny that it took something this extreme to bring everything back into focus.

"Captain?"

Jacques snapped back into focus. She hadn't even realized how her mind had wandered until Carter had spoken.

"Sorry, Chief. What was that?"

"You ok, Ma'am?" the Texan said looking at her, his face full of concern.

"Of course, Mr. Carter. It's just that a disaster at such a scale as this causes you to lose track sometimes. My apologies."

"Don't apologize, Captain. I know what you mean. This place sure is creepy. Like walking over open graves."

"Well, thank you, Chief," piped up Hulban, glancing from his scanner, "A wonderful image to put our minds at rest. You should become a counselor."

Jacques couldn't resist rolling her eyes at Carter who returned the look with good grace. The entire crew was used to Hulban's sarcasm by now and had learnt not to rise to the bait.

"Anyway," she continued before the Malarvian could quip further, "you were saying, Mr. Carter."

"Yes, Captain. I believe this is the quickest route. It will save traversing this corner of the hull."

The captain looked up at the scored wall of metal before them and nodded in agreement. She wanted to get this over and done with as soon as possible. Let's get the trooper out and leave the wreck to rust in peace before any ghosts were disturbed.

"Good work, Chief. Lead the way."

* * *

Parkhouse straightened himself on the medibed as he heard voices in the corridor outside the infirmary. For a moment he sat back and let the glorious sound wash over him. Real human voices. Not synthetic approximations but the sound created from living, breathing vocal cords. He had almost forgotten how wonderful they sounded, but he'd never take it for granted again. As soon as he got off this rock, he'd savor every experience. He'd been given a second chance.

The door before him tried to swish open as the newcomers approached but, with a screech of white noise, jammed halfway across the threshold. The 53 was slowly shuddering to a halt system by system but soon he wouldn't care anymore. Soon he would be safe on the *Spearhead*, zooming to the nearest base to be greeted by welcoming and concerned faces.

From around the door a massive purple hand appeared and roughly slid the door along its track, ignoring the mechanism's shrill complaint at being forced. The bruised skin around Parkhouse's eyes smarted as they widened at the sight of the hulking, tentacled creature that stooped to stalk into the bay. What the crap was that? It was moments like this that Parkhouse had wished he'd paid more attention in Xenobiology class at school. But whatever the monstrosity was, he—at least he assumed it was a he—was wearing a Corps environment suit. Shipwrecked beggars couldn't be choosers when it came to being rescued and besides the next figure was far easier on the eye.

"Trooper Parkhouse," 911186 chirped, "it's my pleasure to introduce Captain Jenny Jacques of the *Spearhead*."

The woman flashed a perfect set of teeth at Parkhouse as she nodded in acknowledgement. Even if Parkhouse had seen a real, here-in-the-flesh woman recently he would have still been stunned. Jacques was a honey. If only you didn't look like one of Frankenstein's rejects eh, Parkhouse thought sadly.

"Trooper, this is Security Chief Carter and Executive Officer Hulban," the captain said, waving her hand towards the man and, well, thing beside her, before walking towards the stool beside Parkhouse's bed. Adjusting her tunic, she sat in one swift motion and moved to touch his hand. She was good. She didn't even flinch when she brushed against the scars on his arm.

"From what 911186 tells me you're lucky to be alive. To survive something like this is a credit to you and your training."

Parkhouse shrugged guiltily, silently thanking 911186 that the droid hadn't obviously mentioned the numerous suicide attempts. Either that or she was a brilliant actress. Most captains were, he guessed.

"Well, I didn't have anything to do with it really," he commented. "The Titan's emergency procedures sort of took over when we crashed. I've just been trying to get stronger, you know?"

Jacques nodded.

"Of course. Well, it's time for us to take over from them now and get you out of here."

The tears began to flow and he felt his throat tighten with emotion. The captain merely squeezed his hand as if she knew exactly what he felt. He was hardly aware of the purple creature quizzing 911186 about Parkhouse's condition.

"So, it's still not safe to move him?" Hulban had asked. For a second, Parkhouse could have been forgiven for thinking that 911186 looked flustered. The droid whirred and clicked, picking up a medipad and repeatedly checking the results that flashed before its optical receptors. What an old mother hen. Finally, however, the tinny voice replied.

"I'm afraid we won't be able to transport Trooper Parkhouse for a couple of days, until his bio-grafts have stabilized."

Jacques's attractive face crumpled at the news.

"A couple of days?" she repeated, a hint of annoyance creeping into her voice. "Perhaps if my own doctor transported down here he could offer a second opinion?"

"I'm sure he could," the robot replied, "but may I remind the captain that regulation 3982/8 on the use of shuttle craft states that no one who has recently undergone surgery on more than 66 per cent of their person may be submitted to shuttle craft travel. The dangers of vibrations and gravitational stresses damaging the new tissue are just too great."

Jacques mood was obviously darkening by the second. No wonder, Parkhouse reasoned. She obviously wanted to get out of here as soon as possible.

"I can assure you, NUJ-9111 ... 9111 ... "

"911186," Prompted Hulban.

"Thank you, Exec." Jacques shot tartly. She obviously didn't like the squid-faced alien. "I can assure you, NUJ-911186, that Dr. Leudstret is at the top of his profession."

Her hand slipped away from Parkhouse's arm as her annoyance grew, the sheen of diplomacy falling by the second. 911186 calmly slotted the pad back into his dock on the bedside.

"I am sure he is, Captain, and may I offer a compromise. If we could have just a few short hours to complete our work here, why don't you and the rest of your crew, including Dr. Leudstret transport down at 2000 hours. The robotic staff of this craft will prepare a celebration banquet to toast the rescue of Trooper Parkhouse and to remember those poor crewmen and women who lost their lives. Then, your doctor can examine the trooper and if he believes that movement can be made you can send for one of your shuttle craft. Is this an agreeable arrangement?"

Jacques paused, taking this in before nodding, the diplomat in her returning.

"My officers and I would be delighted to join you for your banquet." She announced, ignoring the look of horror that Hulban obviously couldn't disguise. "And then we shall review Trooper Parkhouse's condition."

Jacques flashed Parkhouse a brilliant smile, leaving Parkhouse almost giddy with renewed hope.

"I'm afraid our stocks are low." Parkhouse joked: "All we have are a few dried supplies." Jacques's reply was another wonderful squeeze of his arm.

"Don't worry Trooper. I'm sure we won't come empty-handed to your feast table. There must be something the *Spearhead* can provide to honor those who served onboard this majestic vessel."

"And why do we have to eat with a cripple and a bunch of robots, Captain?" Hulban moaned as soon as the shuttle began its return journey to the *Spearhead*. Jacques sighed. Today was getting longer by the second.

"Because it's good PR, Exec. We get some footage of us sharing a meal to remember those who died, plus I'm guessing that the trooper himself will want to raise a glass to his ship-mates."

"You reckon?" added the usually quiet Carter. "Did you see the way his face fell when that droid suggested the meal. That's one guy who can't wait to get back to civilization."

What was this? Mutiny?

"Well, gentleman," Jacques commented sharply before making her exit, "I've made my decision. The entire crew shall transport down at 2000 hours and enjoy a meal with the last survivor of the Titan 53. We will smile, laugh, swap stories and appear that we enjoy each other's company. That's not going to hurt us, is it?"

Parkhouse's mobile medibed rolled into the hanger bay that was doubling as the mess hall. The stabilizers whined as it rumbled across the uneven floor. Parkhouse shifted uneasily in the dress uniform that 911186 had squeezed him into. Still at least he wouldn't have to put up with that mechanical moron much longer. Soon he'd be on the way home.

"Ah, Trooper Parkhouse. How smart you look sir," 911186 fussed. "Apologies that we are late—Captain Jacques and her crew will be along shortly. Here, this is your place."

As the bed slid underneath the table, its back automatically rising to seat him upright, Parkhouse couldn't help but be amazed at the sight that greeted him. When 911186 mentioned a feast, Parkhouse hadn't believe him, but before him was a spread of appetizing dishes. Piping hot meat-platters steamed in the chill of the bay and to his right a bowl of dark soup was providing an aroma so good that his mouth watered. Taking the look of wonder on the trooper's face as his cue, 911186 leant forward and ladled a portion of the soup into his bowl.

"Shouldn't I wait for Captain Jacques?" Parkhouse asked confused.

"Just a quick taste, sir. To see if all is well. I regret that as a mechanism I cannot test if the flavor is agreeable."

Well, at least that made sense. Wincing at the pain, Parkhouse reached for the spoon and swept up a sample of the broth, slopping it clumsily as it reached his mouth. My god, he thought as the soup washed over his taste-buds, that's fantastic. Hungrily he took another mouthful. Delicious. This must have come down from the *Spearhead*. There was no way that 911186 had been hiding something this good in the larders.

911186 looked on in anticipation.

"Does sir approve?"

Parkhouse smacked his lips.

"Yeah, 911186. That's fantastic. I'm really surprised. I never knew you had it in you."

"Marvelous. I must admit I was concerned over the consistency."

"Well, you needn't have been. My compliments to the chef," Parkhouse chuckled. "But tell me, where are my guests?"

"Your guests, sir?"

Parkhouse's eyes narrowed. Had 911186 finally blown a gasket?

"Yes, 911186. The crew of the *Spearhead*. Remember?"

"I'm not sure I understand, sir. The crew are here."

Parkhouse looked around the bay, but it was as empty as the moment he'd come in. What on Mars was 911186 talking about?

"You mean they're on the Titan?" he asked, trying to piece together what was going on. In reply 911186 clucked happily, obviously amused.

"No, no, no, sir. You misunderstand me. This is Captain Jacques, here."

Parkhouse's stomach reeled as the meaning of 911186 finally sank in. The droid's arm was pointing across the table directly at the soup bowl.

"And here is Exec Officer Hulban."

The pink flesh of the meat plate continued to steam in the fresh air.

"The remaining crew's bodies have been put in cold storage."

"911186," Parkhouse wheezed in horror. "What the hell have you done?"

"Sir," 911186 replied calmly as the bile rose in Parkhouse's throat, "you are aware that we are reaching the end of our dried supplies. The carcasses of the rescue party from the *Spearhead* have provided you with additional sustenance to keep you alive for at least two more months. Remember sir, our programming is such that we are charged with keeping you alive, no matter the situation."

Parkhouse whimpered as the droid's chrome face pressed close to his own.

"We will take all necessary measures to assure your survival."

The wreckage of the Titan 53 echoed with Trooper Parkhouse's screams.

Blown to Dust
by Stephen D. Rogers

The thin gray dust that appeared to cover the countryside now clung to my boots and pants, rising in a cloud every time I set foot onto this dirt road. While I could no longer see the Panzerkampwagon Mark IV F2 by simply glancing over my shoulder, I wouldn't have been a bit surprised to find my tank buried in ash if I could.

There were no tracks visible in the dust ahead, no footprints except for those stalking me from behind. We'd been lost in this God-forsaken Soviet wasteland when the aircraft attacked, disabling the tank and killing all of the crew but me.

We are born and we die alone but a tanker is nothing without the men he lives with day and night. When I'd gone back to Berlin on leave, I'd been unable to sleep from my nose twitching for the familiar smell of flesh and sweat and fear.

I walked because I didn't know what else to do and had no one to tell me otherwise. I certainly wasn't going to wait by the tank until I was spotted by a friendly patrol. The odds were too great that the enemy would find me first.

Besides, walking at least offered the slightest sense of a breeze. This insufferable country. If the Soviet Union itself wasn't trying to freeze us solid all winter long, it was trying to roast us alive during the summer.

I was moving through a heat so dry that I could feel the saliva evaporating off my tongue. I could smell the hairs in my nostrils burning. I could hear my skin harden and crack.

My eyes stung.

The lids scraped against my eyeballs whenever I blinked.

I pretended that everyone I loved back at home was long dead and buried, hoping to generate a few soothing tears, but the damnable heat sucked my ducts dry.

For that matter, maybe my wife and family were actually dead. I couldn't seem to remember, to think straight, my thoughts shimmering like the air above the road, shimmering and out of focus.

Maybe the war had killed them. Maybe they'd never existed.

Names floated before me and then dispersed before I could read them aloud. I recalled a lifetime of faces but couldn't put a name to a single one.

What was my name?

What was my rank?

My steps, maker of dust poofs, became shuffles. I generated a wake, signaled my approach, blazed a trail.

What did Hitler see in this cursed place that justified forcing me to stagger through this soot?

I would walk for as long as I could.

The tank too, had been in perfect working condition until it wasn't, the pride of German engineering reduced to a twisted hulk of blasted metal and now probably buried by this fine powder.

What I would give for a cool drink.

Was it I who was seventy percent water or was that the earth's surface? Or was that the portion of an iceberg that hid beneath water? Or something tied to the "Master" Race?

I dropped to my knees.

The dust billowed up, blinded me, slowly settled.

A name floated tantalizingly close. Gretel. Was that my wife? Mother? Sister? Daughter? The name of the tank I'd left behind?

I leaned forward, splayed my fingers, and placed my hands flat. Another cloud rose, coating the walls of my open mouth, bathing me with ash.

My fingers scissored to create a multitude of snow angels. The dust was hot to the touch, soft yet gritty, cooler somehow than the air I'd been breathing. That made sense even if nothing else did. Heat rises.

I lay down.

With one ear blocked, I was finally free to hear the heat murmuring to me, whispering its secrets, promising relief.

I watched a finger, lately so active, fall off my hand.

Crumble to a thin gray dust.

This was a God-less land inhabited by barbarians.

Cursed.

My right sleeve collapsed.

A quick cloud managed to squeeze through the cuff before it closed.

I knew that I would not be so lucky.

What was left of my body shifted as my legs crumpled.

Where was German supremacy now?

Examine the granularity of this good German dust.

No sub-humans here.

My eyelids fell away and I could no longer hide from the truth.

I would not be returning home.
Correction.
I was home.
This land was now mine.
And I, its.
A hot wind blew and scattered.

A Poor, Desert Planet
by Sue Burke

Elio grunted. "Move quick or I drop!" he lied. He had the strength to hold his end of the chest of drawers that he and Lincon were hauling up some steps, but to hide his origin, a planet whose strong gravity created strong backs, he had to lie.

And every time he lied, he thought about Orion, sometimes about its green and moist hills, often about his family, and always about how troubled it was.

His partner moved his grip to the lower edge of the chest wrapped in thick pads. The door to the apartment at the top of the steps was open, and a hot wind blew through it. Lincon was sweating and breathing hard. Elio tried to imitate him.

"Concluding step," Lincon said, and they were in the apartment, already crammed with boxes and furniture. Why would anyone rich come to Fuicas, a desert planet with a single poor settlement? Lincon set down the chest with a flourish that made a pad slip, revealing glittering Orion-style inlaid glass. Elio gasped, then tried to turn his gasp into a pant.

Lincon said something about the furniture being ugly.

"Especial ugly," Elio said. It was beautiful. Orion was beautiful.

"Plus heavy," Lincon said, "yet emprogression, agreed?" He grunted and clowned a muscle-man pose.

Elio didn't always understand Fuicasi, a patois of a dozen languages, but he nodded. "Where comes this owner?" He tried to sound casual.

Lincon shrugged and handed him a tag from a box. He couldn't read, but Elio could. The owner was Arthur Zogue from Mercury Crest Planet, where a lot of Orion refugees went. Maybe he was from Orion, too, and that posed a problem.

He followed Lincon down the stairs for another load. Fuicas had been good to him, despite the climate and poverty. The natives accepted strangers who adopted local ways. There was room for newcomers in its circles of drab buildings made of stone, adobe, and scrap metal, everything gritty with sand. For all that he thought about Orion, he had vowed to lead an apolitical life and avoid other refugees, had there been any on Fuicas. But he was lonely, and maybe a little companionship wouldn't upset anything.

Even before Elio left the building, he heard his boss's voice, Loli, each word slow and harsh.

"We champion all work, Mr. Zogue," she said, "if occasioned it, but we never. My men neverly unhold. And neverly slow." As he entered the glare of the sun, he spotted his boss, with her dyed-gold hair twisted into a fashionable crown. She was talking to the last person he had seen on Orion, Robert Peyton, the commander of Greenbriar Prison.

Elio stopped dead, and Peyton looked right at him, his furious eyes showing no interest or recognition—impossible, he had to remember—and turned back to Loli. He was a bull of a man among the scrawny Fuicasi, holding an ineffective translator like a weapon.

"You go about good, agreed?" Lincon asked, laying a hand on Elio's shoulder.

Elio jumped, for a moment remembering a prison guard's shove.

"I see," Lincon said. "No. To make rancid this expletive . . . . "

Elio turned, edged out of the ring of buildings, and ran down sandy streets. Then he stopped, out of breath. He had nowhere to go. He put a hand against the outer wall of a ring of buildings, the stone hot from sunshine. The next ship would take off in three months. He kept close track of the schedule, wondering with each departure if he should leave. A ship had come and gone the day before, and now he knew he should have been on it.

Peyton commanded the prison from which Elio had escaped. Many Orion refugees shared their horror stories with the galaxy, and Elio had learned from their accounts that Greenbriar was not the most famous prison of Orion, but it was as bad as any. The rest of the galaxy knew more about Orion than the planet's own citizens did.

Peyton must have come hunting for Elio, and Elio had fallen into the trap. In the building, he had left a mountain of DNA in the flakes of skin in sweat that had fallen on the floor as he hauled in furniture. A simple detector sweep would find enough to damn him a thousand times.

Elio was as good as dead. His old self, Carl Butterfeld, had "died" two and a half years ago, killed at Greenbriar Prison, and his death had been duly reported by Commander Peyton. His DNA would prove he still lived. If he didn't surrender, his wife and sons back home might pay. His escape had already impoverished them, and for what? So he could hide on Fuicas?

The circular wall he leaned on marked the place where a ship had launched centuries ago, back when ships used rocket fuel. Its engine had blasted out a crater and fused the desert sand into stone. The ship had taken off when

Fuicas was known as Ophicus Iota Two, and its lone oasis served as a stopover. Ships resupplied their air and dumped their waste. An outpost rose to service the ships, led by women whose elaborate hairstyles identified their old profession.

When the ships had stopped coming, the unlucky souls forgotten on the planet had to create a self-sufficient town. They scoured the launch complex for technology. They adapted the launch craters as foundations for rings of buildings that faced inner courtyards, protected from sandstorms. Barely, chaotically, Fuicas survived until ships came again.

In contrast, Orion had been a green jewel, with fertile valleys and natural wealth waiting to welcome humanity. Every Orion child learned its history: The first colonists planned a paradise and created it, each person with a place and a purpose, a government of the best for the best, a planet so blessed that eventually its king became a living god. A strong military protected it from jealous neighbors. Orion enjoyed happiness, beauty, harmony, morality, order, and plenty. Everyone said so. Elio still believed some of it.

He couldn't escape Orion justice, if it could be called that.

He stood up straight next to the old wall. He walked past men and women, heads bent to the wind stirring sand in the streets, past children squawking over toys, back to his fate, hoping that innocents like Lincon and chief Loli would not be injured when Peyton killed him.

But Peyton was gone. The truck with the furniture waited, as did Lincon. Loli, sitting in the shade of a feathery tree growing in the ring's center, arched a gold-dyed eyebrow at Elio, but said nothing.

They finished unloading the truck. He and Lincon crammed more furniture and boxes into the apartment, all of it the finest money could buy on Orion. Even as a prisoner, Elio had recognized the commander's exquisite taste. He remembered Peyton's greedy smile the day he set the bribe on the corner of his desk. Maybe the bribe had paid for some of this finery.

Halfway home after the job was done, he realized the obvious truth: Peyton had been found out. He had escaped or been exiled. But he could prove that Elio lived. If Elio had realized that only a half-hour earlier, he could have snatched something from the apartment with Peyton's DNA and evened their bargaining positions.

But what would he bargain for?

He wanted to know if his wife still loved him and to tell her that he understood if she didn't. She had been the only person on Orion he could talk freely to, something so extraordinary that he had recognized it too late. She wanted him to live, so he ought to bargain for his life.

He turned around. The blazing yellow sun was setting. Lights came on—electric lamps, storage crystals, candles, and ion fields: the mixed technology of Fuicas. Traffic among the buildings picked up as the wind cooled. Elio edged into the ring to look at Peyton's windows. They were lit. Peyton was home, but he would leave sometime. If Elio followed him, he could gather some DNA somehow.

He waited behind the fronds of a tree-fern growing in a crack at the base of a wall. Children screeched past, ignoring him. Stars came out. Finally Peyton appeared, dressed in an Orion tunic that did not hide his cool-suit, an extravagance on Fuicas. He paused at the ring's entrance, looking around as if he expected something unpleasant, then turned in the opposite direction from Elio. Too frightened to breathe deeply, Elio followed. Peyton stopped frequently, peering into other rings.

He spotted at a sign on a building: a plate and fork, a restaurant. He headed in, and Elio waited. Utensils would carry some DNA. But soon Peyton scurried out, a woman in the doorway cursing while a man's voice inside joined hers like a duet. They mentioned "deportment" repeatedly.

Peyton yelled back, "I could kill you for that!" Something green and greasy had stained his sleeve. "Idiots, all of you. How the hell do you eat around here?"

Elio knew: you pay first, then they bring you food, while on Orion, you help yourself to what you want and pay later.

Peyton left the ring, striding fast, and spotted a man pushing an apple cart, crying, "Fresh shipment! Sweet sweet sweet!" Peyton elbowed past a boy and an old woman, and grabbed two apples—bad deportment. He should have asked the vendor to select them. He held out a handful of coins like a child who hadn't yet learned to count money. The peddler sighed and selected the right coins.

Peyton took a huge bite from one of the apples, chewed quickly, swallowed, and gobbled another bite as he walked off. Elio followed. An apple core would have DNA on it. Peyton paused beside a blind man seated on the ground near a wall, his vision glasses turned off to preserve power. He was selling tiny paper napkins. Peyton took one, wiped his face and hands, and dropped it, with the apple core, into the basket set out for payment.

As Peyton walked away, Elio rushed up. People were watching Peyton, their faces split between shock and anger. Elio scooped out the used napkin and apple core and dropped in more than enough coins to pay for Peyton's theft. From down the street he heard a thud, and looked up to see the splatter from a clod of wet sand on Peyton's back. Peyton whirled around, looking for the person who threw it. A dozen impassive faces looked back at him. Elio turned to hide his own grinning face.

At that moment, he loved Fuicas.

Back in his little room, he rehearsed, pacing and staring out the window at the rusty walls across the courtyard. "We're both alive," he would say, "and we both want to stay that way. We can live in peace." He wished he could bargain as an equal, but their relationship had been established at Greenbriar, where Elio was a shivering, naked prisoner with fresh scars and Peyton had heat and clothes and food.

Elio had been a mere kitchen appliance repairman, and one day he refused to bow before a picture of the king. "It's just a picture," he said. He didn't know what had moved him, and by the time he did, he was in prison, hearing fellow prisoners whisper the same idea and even doubts about the existence of God.

Heresy on Orion, but not on Fuicas, where no one cared what anyone else said as long as they deported themselves politely.

The evening after he had acquired the apple core, he set out in search of Peyton. "Arthur Zogue," he planned to say, "I'm Elio Kaprelli now. I'm here with a proposal . . . . " With his lips moving, he walked through the sandy paths toward Peyton's building. And almost walked right into him.

"Commander Peyton," he said in shock.

Peyton searched his face, then looked around. He smiled. "Finally. I've been waiting. Every day this place gets worse. What do they call you around here?"

"Elio."

"Rank?"

Elio didn't have a clue.

"Never mind. At your service, Mr. Elio."

"I should have called you Arthur Zogue."

"From Mercury Crest, right. I should have gone there instead of here. Stinking dump. So, how about I buy you dinner and you can fill me in. Do I know you from Officer's School? Damn! I know. You're Gregory McKee, a year behind me. Right? You dog. I wondered what happened to you. So, how about dinner?"

Elio couldn't think fast enough to respond.

"They have meat on this planet, they have to," Peyton said. "The concierge at the building ring brings me nothing but tough soy. Cold. I don't think the bitch likes me. The coup is soon, I hope. The nearest restaurant will be fine. Just lead the way."

Elio was too confused, too cowed, to say no. He found himself sitting down to eat with Peyton, moving like a puppet. It had been rumored in prison that the working class was genetically tweaked for docility. Perhaps, horribly, it was true.

"Milk soup? Well, at least it's chilled. Needs salt. Are they short of that here, too? I can do a lot for you. I know who's loyal and who's weak. I can run far more than a minor prison. I knew there had to be a coup cell here, but how do you find anything here?"

Food at Greenbriar had been viciously oversalted. Elio picked out a line from his script. "Neither one of us wants to be discovered."

"Of course. And you'll have to check with your boss—unless you're the cell leader."

Elio remembered Peyton's prison office: art, a lovely caged bird, a dish of candy out of reach, music, brocade mats on the floor. Peyton, a bit plump, sat disdainfully upright behind a gilt desk. The room was warm, warm. He said, "What's your life worth? I don't care if you live or die. I care about me. I care about money, Carl. What does that mean to you?"

Now, too frightened to eat, Elio remembered thanking him for a letting him escape, and despising him for more just than his greed.

Peyton hadn't noticed his lack of appetite. They left the restaurant. "I'll be waiting for your next contact. I assume you know how to get in touch with me."

Peyton sauntered out of the ring. Was there a coup cell on Fuicas? How would a coup cell work? Was Elio truly docile?

That night, in his dreams, chirps of bugs became confounded with the chirps of prison door locks, startling him awake. A couple of days after he gave Peyton the bribe, his cell doors had opened and robot guards led him out of the prison and into the night. Six months in jail had taught him more about Orion than the previous three decades.

On Fuicas the next morning, Elio and Lincon hauled stone for a new building as Loli complained that Zogue hadn't paid his bill. Elio decided to deliver a message to Peyton: The coup cell wanted him to lay low for several months. It . . . feared assassins, yes, assassins. Peyton had to have more enemies than Elio could imagine. Peyton should lie low for a few months, and by then the next passenger ship would have come and gone, and Elio would be on it.

He left a note at Peyton's door asking him to meet him at the mission control ruins three kilometers southeast of town at sunset. He didn't want to be seen in public with Peyton.

Elio arrived as the sun touched the distant mountains. The ruins glowed like embers in the red sunset. They had never been much, just a cluster of quickfoam sheds for equipment and a skeleton crew, located on a rocky plain too far from water to be of interest after the ships stopped coming and the equipment was looted. The walls had been smashed to reclaim iron supports and eroded by sandstorms into eerie curves.

Peyton had seen Elio approach and walked out to meet him. He was furious about something. "What about Ruttershina?"

Was that a place, a person . . . ?

"You know him—remember the speech he gave at the graduation exercises? Is he with us or against us?"

"I don't know."

"You're not going to tell me, right? I'm tired of games! What happened to Shina? Don't lie."

Elio couldn't think fast enough to lie. He backed away.

"If you won't tell me," Peyton said, "I can't be sure about you."

"Then, we might be through." Elio hoped so.

But Peyton laughed. "I killed him, all hush-hush. Pity. He would have been with us. There are a lot of people who know the difference between a god and a king. It would be nice to have either one."

On Orion, a person could be killed for saying that.

"We have a concern," Elio said.

"There are things worth having. Power is the means to have things, and things prove you have power. Fuicas wouldn't be worth the warhead to destroy it." The sunset made his face grotesquely flushed and shadowed. "That's what I want to do, wipe this place out. Look what the laundry did to this cuff. The stain is still there, but the color got washed out. I can hardly buy enough water to bathe. You wouldn't miss this place, would you?"

"We have a concern."

Peyton waved his arms, fists clenched. "You judge things objectively by the quality of their belongings. I know you're trying to be incognito here, but doesn't it make you feel small to dress like that? Holes in your shoes! I can't stand this place. It's killing me." He kicked bit of broken quickfoam until it was dust. "The strong prevail. I'm better than this place will ever be."

"We have a concern," Elio mumbled. He remembered Peyton as cruel but in control. Maybe bad news would calm him down. Fear was having a sobering effect on Elio. "We think you might be targeted. I mean here, someone wants to kill you. You have enemies."

"You're not worth much if someone doesn't what you dead. Who?"

"A relative of a prisoner from Greenbriar." Elio wished he could remember someone threatening, someone in the government.

Peyton laughed—but too much, too hard. "Greenbriar never had a prisoner worth spit. Pitiful people, every one of them. Look at this." He took a small gun from his pocket, a black cylinder shaped for a robot clamp rather than a human hand, but Peyton held it effectively enough. Elio recognized it from Greenbriar. Set high, it could char. Set low, it merely singed. The robot guards had used them with machine precision. Prisoners went naked to be better targets.

"I don't know if that's wise."

Peyton waved the gun skyward. "Am I that important?"

"Yes. We have plans."

"Plans. What prisoner?"

Elio named the first prisoner he could think of. "Jenni Jorden." An elderly woman, a poet.

"That hag. I read her death certificate to her and she laughed at me. I had her frozen to death. Slowly. I'll kill anyone who even looks like they were related to her." He fired the gun in the air, laughing. "Greenbriar stank. The prisoners died like mice. Gods kill, that's what makes them gods. A god of mice, that's all I was. And they're not all dead. Some got away. I'd kill them now, on sight, the way I should have, or I wouldn't be here."

Elio realized with terror, a familiar feeling, that he was a long way from town with a raving torturer who might, in a lucid moment, kill him.

Two and a half years ago, guarded by robots, naked, he had walked down a wooded road away from Greenbriar as cold night became dawn. He wondered if Peyton would keep his end of the bribe and realized that he had no cause to. Peyton had his money and wouldn't want someone who could testify to the bribe. Elio would die soon. What a fool, wasting his family's money, and for what? For a naïve dream that he could sneak off to the wilds of Orion.

Finally, ahead, a young man waited in the road next to an anti-gravity pod. He smiled in a discomforting way and handed him a pair of coveralls. "I am Captain Mondez," he said in a thick accent, "and I own you. Get in." He locked Elio into a flight berth.

The pod rose past clouds into dark space. Elio had never left the planet before. If he had eaten, weightlessness or fear would have made him throw up. Eventually they arrived at a sleek ship.

For the next week, under Mondez's direction, he fixed aging environmental equipment, something he hadn't been trained for, but he made major improvements. Sometime during that week the ship left orbit. The crew consisted of two or three dozen loud young people who had no interest in him and who spoke a foreign language. They seemed to be permanently partying. But they treated him without rancor and let him eat all he wanted, and Elio went numb with relief. When his work was done, a woman casually shut him into a hibernation compartment and turned it on.

Periodically they woke him to fix things. He never knew who they were or what the ship was, though the party never seemed to end. The gauges on the equipment told him two months, eight months, a year, fifteen months had passed. At fifteen months, the crew gathered to pay him a drunken toast goodbye, and Mondez took him to the surface of a planet that turned out to be Fuicas. He left him at the edge of town with nothing but the clothes he wore and a bottle of vodka, which turned out to have a excellent resale value.

The desert, the harsh shadows, and the grit had become a comfort, even the people, stoic and simple. He would never see Orion again, and his wife and sons were reduced to memories. He had resolved to live according to the official virtues of Orion—humility, hard work, and discipline—for if they were truly obeyed, Orion would be a paradise, and he still believed in Orion. On Fuicas, he learned a new, mysterious virtue: equality. He spent many hours pondering this strange world, where everyone was her own queen or his own king.

But that peace had ended when Peyton arrived, and now he was out in the desert with a madman. "It's time to go back," Elio said, and Peyton too eagerly agreed.

As they walked, he called out "Jorden!" and aimed his gun at rocks.

"I should have been in Congress," he said. "I thought a lot about it. I had too much time to think at Greenbriar. I excelled in oration in school. I wrote most of Ruttershina's speech. I could have justified the edicts—we'd have fewer malcontents. That's what I can do in the new government." He aimed his gun at the water unit of a hydroponics crater.

Elio put his hand against the gun barrel to push it out of the way—and snatched his hand back. The gun was hot. Robot clamps needed no protection, but a man's hand did. And yet Peyton continued to grip the gun.

"We don't want to draw attention to ourselves."

"You're right. I'll have less to destroy when I come back with bombs."

They were at the town's edge. "Let's split up," Elio said.

"I'll keep an eye out for any Jorden toads and keep you posted. You can count on me."

Elio walked directly to the police. Peyton might kill someone. Elio was in sight of the chief, but he couldn't talk to her, despite the traditional ruffles and lace and cleavage of a Fuicas official. What would he say? He went home, lay on his bed, and stared at the ceiling in the dark.

At Greenbriar, Peyton had had fine possessions but little human contact. He had been the only human staff member. The rest was done by robots. Every prisoner knew that too much time in solitary confinement drove anyone mad.

Greenbriar must have made Peyton crazy, and Fuicas must be even more lonely than Greenbriar. Elio had co-workers, and he spoke the language a little. He could get along. He was, in a way, luckier—better—than Peyton.

Lincon had a lot to say at work the next morning. "You cannot forget the gilipoli from Mercury Crest, agreed? Who—"

"Who remains unpaid," Loli called from her desk.

"Expectably, I say," Lincon said. "Offworld clothes, offworld weirdo. At the Crater of Nine, I saw anight at the restaurant he ate uncompared food, then spit a last taste as if he put poisoned and left. Without payment, just as ladenous, chief."

"I will never achieve payment."

"And then sat in street, grumbling. We friends strolled dissembled of idleness to something. Elio, you speak offworld."

"Not Mercurian."

Peyton hadn't shot anyone, at least.

Lincon tried to repeat what Peyton had said. Elio recognized the word "god."

"These words stand unknown to me."

He avoided Peyton for almost a week, although Lincon reported his activities daily, always more of the same, sometimes with police intervention. Elio stayed in his room at night studying a book of philosophy that confused him—do you repay good with good and evil with evil, or evil with good? In either case, what do you do about an ongoing evil? But eventually Peyton found Elio, ran up to him between some buildings, looking thin and bright-eyed.

"How about some drinks?" He needed a bath.

Elio noticed people staring. He didn't want to be associated with Peyton.

"I hate this place, Elio. I hate these people. And I hate God, that fool we call God because no one has the guts to kill him. I want to rip his entrails out alive—no, too fast—to take him apart cell by cell, leaving the nerves." He continued graphically.

"Let's go." Everyone had seen them. He led Peyton to a bar in the courtyard of an unpopular crater and deposited him at a table partially obscured by a shrub.

"The strongest, that's what I want," Peyton said, expecting Elio to buy. He got them a bottle of fruit liquor. The frowning bar owner gave him two battered metal glasses.

Elio returned to find Peyton muttering at the sky. He snatched the bottle and poured himself a full glass.

"God—without God, what is there? And the mice. Does Fuicas have mice?"

Elio hoped Peyton would drink himself into a stupor quickly.

"In honor of my service to God, they allowed me to sneak away to the armpit of the galaxy and watch my money disappear. How did you get here, McKee? How did you earn the wrath of God? I would have killed you. I allowed mice to live. I sold the galaxy vermin. What more did they want from me?"

He had finished his first glass and poured himself another.

"But there were too many. God likes to make his people suffer. That's how I know that God still lives, because I am suffering. I was God for a while. I caused suffering for suffering's sake. But beauty. I have it." He described each piece of furniture and art in his apartment in detail, tediously, and he became more enthused with each one.

"Beauty. It's the only escape we have. Escape from what? From a universe that hates us."

Sitting in silence, Elio thought. The question wasn't good and evil, or how to repay Peyton, or anything about the past. Only the future mattered, and he had a duty, which was to survive, and an immediate danger, which was Peyton. Even a meek man had to solve his problems.

"I have to go."

"What will you accomplish with your coup?"

"We'll change everything," Elio blurted out, the first thing that came to mind, but now that he had said it, he harbored no more doubts.

Lincon was waiting at work the next morning. "What rockets you drank with that good-for-snot thief? You off-worlders parley, I say."

"I parleyed to uncover aptness to pay. He can neverly. I think not he has money, and he will neverly work. But we saw of his furniture." Elio's voice almost choked, anticipating his next words: "I say, we have police take to sell. And then, chief, you achieve payment."

"Water!" Lincon said. He approved. So did Loli.

Peyton, the day after losing his precious furniture, killed himself. Elio left Fuicas on the next ship out. Peyton might have eventually killed himself anyway, Elio realized. It didn't matter. Elio had done what he could to hasten and ensure it. He wished he hated himself, but instead he felt like a failure.

It had been easy. It didn't take a god. There was something that was hard to do in the universe, something that was the opposite of killing. He had glimpsed it on Orion and Fuicas, something infinitely better, and he would learn what it was and how to do it, and then he would go to Mercury Crest. Elio hoped a coup cell existed there and that it wasn't filled with people like Peyton. Finding it would be first step toward home.

Someone is Dying
by James Hartley

Someone is dying. I can't remember who.

The desert here is beautiful. In a stark, spare way of course. Rocks and sand, mostly, once in a while a tiny patch of lichen that manages to survive in the dry thin atmosphere. Nothing man-made anywhere in sight, unless you count my footprints, a trail leading back across the dunes to the camp and the Mars lander.

I'd better get moving again, got to take care of that errand. I wish I could remember exactly what it was. Something to do with death, someone is dying, but I can't remember who. I'll remember when I get there—if I get there—if I just keep walking.

Death entered Kurt Behrman's life early. Kurt was only three when they met.

"Mommy, what's the matter?"

His mother had just gotten a phone call, and now she was sitting on the couch crying. Kurt climbed up next to her and tugged at her sleeve. "Mommy, why are you crying? Huh, Mommy?"

She put an arm around him and for a while they just sat. Finally she said, "It's your Daddy. He's been killed in a plane crash. They say he died a hero, staying at the controls and fighting the plane down. The cockpit was totally destroyed, but he saved most of the passengers."

Kurt pulled away from her, fighting back tears, and walked in slow circles around the room, trying to understand. Finally he went back over to her. "Daddy's not coming home anymore, is he, Mommy?"

"No, he's not, Honey." She hugged him with one arm, while her other hand rubbed the bulging belly that was soon to become Kurt's sister, a daughter who would never know her father.

Later on when Kurt was older he understood what had happened to his father, and Captain Behrman's final heroic act shaped Kurt's life.

Footprints! How in the world can there be footprints out here? I'm the first one to come this far from camp. They look a lot like my footprints. Damn!

They *are* my footprints. I must have walked in a circle. Yeah, there's that little hillock, and the camp is just on the other side of it. Funny, I can't see the tip of the lander above the top of the hill, I should be able to, shouldn't I? Must be an optical illusion, things all look funny on this small planet, with the horizon so close. Doesn't really matter.

What matters is the mission. Someone is dying and I have to hurry. Got to get going. This time I'll steer a course by the sun, no more walking in circles.

Kurt was eight when his best friend Billy was killed. They were riding their bikes, racing down the big hill near Kurt's house, when Billy somehow lost control of his bike and ran into a phone pole. He was thrown forward, and the end of the handlebar was rammed into his stomach. When Kurt came back to him, Billy was just lying on the ground. There was no blood.

"Billy, get up, let's go." He mounted his bike and started to ride off, then noticed Billy wasn't following. He circled back, stopped next to Billy, and repeated, "Get up. Let's go." Once again he pedaled off, then returned.

This time he noticed Billy wasn't breathing. He jumped off his bike and ran for the nearest house and started pounding on the door. When it opened, he started screaming, "Billy's dead! Billy's dead! Call an ambulance!" over and over again.

Later he asked his mother, "Why is Billy dead? He wasn't hurt, he wasn't even bleeding."

"Billy died because he was bleeding inside. The blood ran out of his heart and he died."

"It was my fault Billy died, wasn't it? I didn't call the ambulance soon enough."

"No, Kurt, it wasn't your fault. I talked to Billy's mother. The doctor said it was so bad, even if the ambulance had been right there waiting for Billy they couldn't have saved him. Don't blame yourself."

But Kurt could never completely lose the feeling that he should have been able to do something about Billy, about Billy's death.

Where did this damn canyon come from? This isn't on the survey map, the only canyon is west of the camp and I'm going north . . . no, wait a minute, the sun's in front of me, I must have turned west. My pressure suit has a compass, why do I keep going off course? Let's just take a compass reading . . . that's funny, the compass clip is empty. How'd I lose my compass?

Well, that's not important, what's important is the mission. Someone is dying, got to take care of it. North along the canyon, that'll keep me on a line, keep me from going in circles. Time to get moving, someone is dying.

The death of Kurt's father came back when he was finishing high school, this time to help him. Kurt knew money was getting short, especially since he had turned sixteen and lost the Social Security benefits.

All the teachers in Kurt's school said he ought to go to college. The guidance counselor kept after him. "Behrman, why haven't you sent off any applications yet? You have to get them in early to get the best choice of schools."

"We don't have the money for me to go to college, Mr. Harwich. Sending applications is a waste of time."

"Nonsense. There are scholarships, co-op programs, student loans, all sorts of aid. All the more reason to apply early."

"OK, Mr. Harwich. I'll get to it right away." But he knew he wouldn't. He knew he would graduate from high school and get a job to help support his mother and his sister Cheryl. Especially since his mother had been getting sick a lot and couldn't work much. He knew what was best for him, and was determined to do it his way.

Then he got the letter from Senator Riggs. It said that the 15th anniversary of Captain Behrman's death would come during Kurt's first year in college. It said that Captain Behrman had been a hero, and that the country hadn't done enough for his family. It said that the senator had decided to give Kurt an appointment to the Air Force Academy.

What it didn't say was that the senator had a tough fight for re-election coming up. It didn't say that Kurt lived in a swing district that could win or lose the election, or that the senator planned to play up this appointment to the hilt. Kurt accepted the appointment, although he might have been stubborn enough to refuse had he known. Quitting when he found out several years later seemed far different from never accepting, and he stuck it out.

He did, however, worry about his mother and sister. "Mom, how are you and Cheryl going to get along without me getting a job?"

"Don't worry about it, Kurt. We'll manage. And besides, with . . . " She was interrupted by a fit of coughing from her self-diagnosed bronchitis. Finally the coughing subsided and she continued, "With you off to college, there's one less to feed, so the money will stretch farther. You go ahead. This is a great honor, you can't turn it down."

Where am I now? I don't see that canyon anymore, how can it vanish while I'm following it? Let me just check my compass . . . oh, that's right, the compass is gone. But the sun is over there, right over that little hillock. Damn!

That's the same hill, I still got turned around. Why is it so hard to walk away from the camp? I really better get moving, someone is dying, I have to hurry.

Kurt was a good student at the Academy, and ended up in the top twenty in his class. During the final year, most of the bull sessions were about the assignments they'd get after graduation, and Kurt was just as worried as any of the others. Finally, a month before graduation, he got a call to see the guidance officer.

"Cadet Behrman, reporting to see Major Prysock as ordered, sir."

"At ease, Behrman. In fact, have a seat. I want to talk to you about your post-graduation tour of duty. No doubt you've been wondering about that?"

"Yes, sir."

"I have something special in mind for you. Behrman, you're a good student, and I think you'd make a good officer. A good one, but not a great one. You have a bit too much independence, an ornery streak. Not enough for us to disqualify you, but someday, in a military situation, it could get you in hot water. So I'm recommending you for detached duty with NASA."

"NASA?" Kurt was so surprised he forgot the "Sir."

"NASA. They want younger men and women, even new graduates, rather than seasoned officers, to train for a special flight, the Mars Mission."

Kurt's jaw dropped. "Mars?"

"Yes. They've been doing preliminary work for over twenty years, ever since the first President Bush proposed it back in 1990. Now they're getting ready to really staff up. So, Behrman, do you want it?"

"Yes, *sir!*"

Kurt fit right into the work at Canaveral, and he loved it. But even here he wasn't immune from the effects of death. He was on the second day of a week-long orbital training mission when he got word of his mother's death, and he couldn't get back down until after the funeral.

When he finally did land, he requested and got leave, and bummed a ride on an Air Force plane back to his home. He managed to phone his sister to tell her when he would arrive, and she met him at the airport.

"Cheryl, I'm sorry, there was just no way down. It happened so suddenly, I never even knew what killed her."

"Pneumonia. That 'bronchitis' of hers, she would never see a doctor about it. Somewhere along the line it turned into pneumonia, but it was three or four days before I realized it was something worse than usual and dragged her to the emergency room. By then it was too late. It killed her."

Kurt stayed with his sister as long as his leave allowed, then went back to his training. He worked hard, and it paid off. He was selected for the Mars flight.

Why does this hillock look familiar? It can't be the one near camp, I would be able to see the tip of the lander over it. Someone is dying, I have to get busy and do something about it. I wish I could remember. I keep coming back to this hill, maybe I should climb up and look? Somehow, I'm afraid to . . .

The Mars expedition was a great success. The six-man lander came down perfectly. The men got out in their pressure suits and set up the ring of bubble tents that would let them live for a while outside the cramped confines of the ship. Kurt and the captain did most of this work, because the four scientists were already off on cloud nine performing experiments and making theories.

When all the setting up was finished, the captain sent Kurt out to check the area around the camp. He had been out a half hour or so and was checking out the area behind a small hillock when he felt the quake. In the low gravity it was easy to run up the hill to see if the camp had suffered any damage.

When he came in sight of the camp he stopped, aghast. The "quake" had been the explosion of the lander. The middle section was simply gone, and the tip was lying across one of the bubble tents. The bottom section was almost intact, just a few dents in the metal, but there wasn't enough left to lift off.

The other bubble tents were all collapsed, punctured by flying shrapnel. He couldn't tell where the men were, except for one pressure-suited figure lying near the lander. He was starting down the hill to see if anyone was alive when a ticking noise forced its way into his consciousness. He paused at the unfamiliar sound, then realized it was the Geiger counter. He grabbed it, not noticing that he knocked the compass loose from the adjacent clip as he did so, and looked at it. The meter was way up in the red.

My God, he thought, the reactor blew up. He looked at the Geiger again and decided that everyone down in the camp was dead anyway. He beat a hasty retreat over the brow of the hill, then looked at his suit readouts. Not more than an hour of oxygen left, and all the supplies down in that radioactive hell around the ship. If, indeed, there were any intact supplies. No real choice, oxygen starvation or radiation poisoning. He would be dead soon either way. No choice, but he decided he wanted to die somewhere alone, away from the ruins of the camp. He turned his back on the camp and started walking.

Someone is dying. I wish I could remember who, or why. Perhaps if I climb up on this little hill and look? Somehow, I want to and I don't want to. I

303

guess I'd better . . .   Oh, my God! Now I remember! The camp, the explosion, everyone else dead. Nothing I can do for them, why do I keep worrying that someone is dying?

It's awfully quiet here, I don't hear anything, not even the hiss of the oxygen. Why don't I hear that? That never stops. Oh. The tank's empty, I'm out of oxygen. May as well just sit down here and wait, it won't be too long, the air is already getting stuffy. But I was right. Someone is dying.

Gifts of Bone
by C. A. Manestar

The cymbals clashed and a blare from the trumpets tore through the noises of the crowd. All the laughing children fell quiet. Down the street the Altered started to sing, throwing their voices up into the clear sky like angels released. Their sparkling glitter-robes cast rainbows so bright they hurt my eyes.

"Death, the Glory!"

I strained to see my contribution: the little floating hover-mechs scattered pale blossoms through the air. I always loved this part of the funeral, more than the music, the floats and the candy. Those soft petals falling through the air were little symbols of rebirth.

"Death, the Beauty!"

The priests followed, whirling their incense burners, their painted bodies nothing more than dancing smears of color. Finally, the bier arrived, carried by the six plodding mechs. Their tread was so heavy I could hear the noise of their feet on the cobblestone path leading up to The Wall. The crowd rushed in when the final hovering mech scattered coins and candies.

"Heaven Beyond!"

As I moved to grab my share my pager alarmed.

Alpha Priority—immediate response—triple rate for first acceptance.

Nothing like work to spoil a good Tombing.

There's a shortcut across the city most people won't take. No one goes within twenty meters the Wall, which leaves a path all the way around the Dome. There were tales about monsters that crept from the Wall, snatched the living and stripped their souls away. When I was a child I had nightmares of the Dome, but I'd outgrown those superstitious fears.

I took the route at a fast jog. There were two more funerals on the East side but they were small affairs. Still the families were dressed in formal clothes and sang with a happiness that couldn't be faked. Some of the youngest children looked sad and scared.

I remembered that same excruciating feeling. It was difficult to be happy for the soul of someone you loved when you knew they were gone forever.

I put the Dome behind me and dashed for the green brick Guild Hall. I took the long flat stairs of the side entrance and patted the sweat off my face before I went inside.

The Guild chambers smelled like new paint and roses. Plum fleck paint covered the walls and all the trim was black wood and gold foil.

An Assistant sat touching the screens of her desk, her arms bare and patterned in the colors of the room. She had enough status to paint one cheek with a gaudy floral swirl. She didn't look up as I coughed.

"I'm here for the Alpha-call," I said. I handed her my pager and identification. "Has anyone else arrived?"

She blinked, showing off her powdered orange and malachite green eyelids. "You're the first, Karom. Guildmaster Saffique is waiting."

"A Guildmaster?" Damn. What under the Dome could that mean? "Do you know what the assignment is?"

"It's not for me to discuss," she said. "Come with me."

I followed behind her watching her silly fashionable slippers flopping with each step.

Vra Saffique waited in her private office. She stood by the windows overlooking the tree gardens. We were high enough to see the blue edge of the ocean and the sweeping structures of the harbor.

"Tech Karom Etarian, Vra Saffique." The Assistant handed over a tablet with my identification loaded in display.

I made the correct bow and hoped I didn't fumble the hand gesture. The last time I'd used it was at graduation and never in a personal situation. The Vra didn't notice. She spent a few seconds reviewing my record while I tried not to stare at her decorated legs. Even her knobby, ancient feet were decorated like a priest's.

"A good choice, Jilia." The Vra looked at me. Her eyes were as brown as the bit of skin showing around her hairline. Her makeup had folded into the skin around her eyes and formed deep grooves. "Karom, we need you to go inside there. We've had an alarm."

She tapped the glass window with one finger.

"Into the garden, Vra?"

"No. There."

I looked and still didn't see what she meant. The harbor towers weren't part of our jurisdiction.

"There, child." She didn't sound angry or mean but old. "We need you to go into the Dome. One of the mechs needs attention."

"Me?" I squeaked the word out. "I've never heard of mechs inside the

Dome. What kind of mechs? What do they do?"

Vra Saffique frowned. "We don't really know. The Wall and the Dome were constructed during the Golden Era. The details are vague."

A mad thought came to my mind. They were sending me to my doom. But how could I refuse an assignment from a Guildmaster? I'd never work again.

Everyone goes to the Wall eventually. Rich, poor, children and queens. Family. Friends. The Wall was supposed to be the great equalizer. The souls the dwelt under the Dome lived in glory. That wasn't much comfort.

Everyone went inside but no one came back out. I'd heard there were some technicians who repaired the Tombing doors but they didn't enter. All that was needed was some talent with a wrench. Any mechanic could fix a door. But no one living went through the Wall. No one went under the Dome.

"You were one of the top selected candidates," The Assistant said. "Don't worry. You'll have the best tools and all the information we can provide."

I stood at the door with a data sheet and a beautiful new tool belt and pack. These were the kind of tools a repair tech dreamed of owning: brushed titanium jigs, molecular steel saws, tiny finger lasers and diamond grit snips. No expense spared. Part of me wondered if they were going to write off the expense.

The Assistant presented them to me and said, "These are yours to keep."

"I can get a lot of use out of these if I come out."

She made an attempt at a smile but it failed. She'd dressed to match Vra Saffique in somber colors, dark maroons and blacks. They'd also removed any silver trim and pale shades: any color that could suggest mourning whites.

"Is there anything you think you'll need, Tech Etarian?" asked Vra Saffique.

I looked down at the data sheet. No one in living memory had been where I was going. All the childhood stories came back of what might happen to anyone who tried to break inside.

Stop it, Karom. You're a technician.

The alarming mech was sending out strings of code that matched nothing in our databases. Golden Era mechs just didn't break down, didn't alert, didn't need repairs. All the detailed information we had on the Wall filled a quarter of the page.

My job sucked gutter flop.

"No, I think I've got everything," I said.

I closed the door on their faces, balled up the paper and dropped it. The next person through could pick it up.

The tunnels beneath the city were clean and cool. Every few years they were painted with lines of color that directed techs to sections of the city. Orange stripes led to the train systems, tree-green to the parks and bruise-blue towards the medical facilities. I followed the white line, as thin as a wire, low near the floor until I reached the passages surrounding the Wall.

It took almost an hour. Up stairs, down stairs and through doors that seemed to appear at random. The walls transitioned into a light gray and even the floor became an unremarkable yellow. The monotony of the journey gave me too much time to think.

Vra Saffique had promised an elaborate funeral if I didn't come back. Cold damn comfort. Who wanted to attend a Tombing if there wasn't some naked, stripped down body, being placed into the Wall?

What was beyond the Wall? Maybe there were only tombs, small coffins for all the bodies. I could handle a mech that was built to stack coffins.

By the time I reached the Wall I'd convinced myself nothing would happen. Any step now my pager would go off and I'd be told to return. Ha-ha, just a joke. Or maybe I'd reach a blind end and have to return, job incomplete. Then I could look at the Guildmaster and quit.

I walked into the last room before I'd even realized it. The door slipped closed behind me.

It was a white room: the color of death. There were no sounds or smells. There were no grates or vents, no seams or buttons to open the door again. I was in a void where all the ceaseless noises of the living were sealed away.

"Don't panic now, Karom," I said. My voice sounded odd. I couldn't remember being any place this silent. "Something will happen."

You're going to die. Any moment now the door would open and some horrible mech would remove my screaming spirit from my body.

"Shut up," I said.

The thoughts kept piling up and colliding. What if the priests were right? What if it was Heaven? A beautiful place where all the souls lived in glory. Where exactly would I, a living person, fit? Would the mere act of crossing through the Wall sever my soul from my body?

I paced. Then fidgeted. Finally, I picked out the finger lasers from the pack and slipped one onto the second knuckle of my index finger and played with the settings. Keen. The second one fit my middle finger like it was a custom design. The settings could cut, solder, slice and drill.

There wasn't enough power though to cut through all the doors or the Wall if nothing happened, if something had malfunctioned and I was trapped inside.

"It will open or they'll send someone to find me."

I swallowed several times and then realized what was happening. The room was being pressurized. My ears popped. There was a sampling meter in the pack. I started to dig for it when I realized something had changed.

A mech stood in front of me.

The wall had opened on a silent, smooth track. The inside of the Dome was the same color as the room and just as featureless.

I hadn't noticed the mech until it moved. Everything was devoid of shape, flat. My eyes jittered. I could feel them moving, shaking.

Shades of gray, the palest yellows and bleached ochre emerged, just tiny variations. I squinted, caught the outline of the mech and looked beyond it.

For a moment I thought I saw buildings or trees, strange shapes, before my perception shifted again and it all disappeared. It kept flipping between one view and another, like an optical illusion that caused my head to swim.

Suddenly, with a lurching orientation everything snapped into focus. Nausea hit and I swallowed in reflex.

I was standing at the border of a city of bone.

I stood there for a long time, refusing to understand what I was seeing. It wasn't possible. It couldn't be. When the mech drifted forward my numb disbelief broke like a fever. Where was I? This wasn't glorious, beautiful or heavenly.

And the mech wasn't any kind of angel. Even the few intact Golden Era mechs we'd studied didn't look anything like it. This one looked like an insect had mated with a human. It had too many arms and no legs. It had a strange kind of face, long and mournful, like a teardrop.

It hovered a half-meter from the ground. And as soon as I looked closer, I felt a strange shift in reality.

I was looking at teeth. A field of teeth.

I stumbled, flailed out with my hands and caught at the mech for balance. The texture of it felt strange. My foot came down on the thousands of teeth that carpeted the ground. It crunched through polished enamel and shattered. The sound felt like an explosion. It was the only noise in this desolate place, loud and sudden and shocking.

The mech shivered and I shivered.

It twitched hard and rolled white eyes in those white, round sockets, and slipped from my grasp. My other foot came down and tore through something that appeared to be a delicate flower; a chrysanthemum of baby teeth.

The mech reacted, surging forward as if horrified and then stopped. All the little arms fluttered in the air as if they were distress flags on a ship.

I felt monstrous. A great lumbering, living creature smashing through the world and destroying everything.

My nausea surged again. I was locked in this hideous place, surrounded by the bones of all the people who had died and come to the Wall. I pushed my palms against my eyes and pressed as if I traded pain against my need to weep.

The last time I had cried was when my cousin died. I always pictured her inside here, somehow alive under the Dome. Tears leaked past my palms and slipped down my face.

A small hand reached out and touched my shoulder. Cold and metallic and still offering comfort. It looked at me with those strange eyes as if there was a communion between us. I took a juddering breath and felt my heart slow down.

After a minute it started to gesture. I looked down and a mech waited near my feet. It was a model I recognized: a transporter platform about a meter across.

The tall insectoid-mech tilted its head and made a strange pantomime movement, until I understood. I stepped on the platform and we began to move at a slow pace.

At first it was dizzying. The lack of color and definite shadows made everything blur as my eyes tried to adjust. I felt as if I were lost in a snowstorm or trapped in a world of ice. Then I began to see the patterns and shapes.

We crossed a field. Rib bones curved and flowed into grasses around a pond of polished and gleaming clavicles. There were trees too, edging the field. Ulnas and femurs formed thick, knobbed trunks. Thousands of vertebrae became branches that grew smaller and ended in twigs of finger bones. Among the boughs baby skulls gleamed like fruit and stared with eye sockets filled with tiny bones.

The insectoid-mech glided beside me, implacable and certain. We moved through the forest and then broke into the city.

It was like nothing I could have conceived. There was a faint resemblance to houses but without the perfection of straight surfaces the walls curved and spiraled. Windows and doorways arched and twisted into points, leaned at odd angles, and seemed ready to topple.

There were no real roads between the buildings. There was no need for them if the mechs never touched the surface. Sometimes we crossed gaps that seemed to disappear into chasms of whiteness.

Everywhere skulls stared down. Most of them were toothless, but occasionally I'd see one intact with teeth and gaping jaws, as if it were set to laugh.

And that was what bothered me the most. The silence. I was afraid to speak, afraid that whatever sound I would make wouldn't be words. If I opened my mouth I would scream and curse the priests, my family and friends and anyone who told me childhood tales of the place beyond the Wall.

I wrapped my arms around myself as if I could stop myself from breaking.

Survive. Worry about getting out later.

I took a deep breath and another, counted them and listened to my heart. I was alive in this place. I was the only living thing. Sometimes I thought I'd see movement but it could have been an illusion. I thought there might not be any other mechs until we circled around a large cathedral and stopped.

The mech had collapsed and shattered into what could have been a fountain. The skull floor had collapsed and pinned it tight.

Fluid had sprayed out from somewhere and glistened on the surface of the bones. The trapped mech was like my escort in design though smaller. It was still functioning; some of the delicate arms twitched but clearly something was broken.

I stepped down from my transport and tested the ground. It was more solid than I imagined. Still, some of the bones cracked. One rib exploded in a puff of dust. I winced at each sound. Bones shifted and slid out of place. A small avalanche of carpels slid and buried one of the mech's arms.

"Help me uncover it," I finally said. My voice sounded flat and strange. My escort didn't move. It was deaf. No one had built it with sound receptors.

I picked up some mandibles and tossed them aside. Whatever fear I had upon touching the bones vanished. They were mostly smooth and heavier than I imagined. When I picked up a broken thighbone a river of fine grains slid out. Somehow the mechs had filled the marrow with ground bone. Maybe it was some kind of structural choice or a way of condensing the millions of smaller bones.

My escort moved beside me and began to help. After an hour we had uncovered most of the trapped mech. I was startled to realize a few mechs, no larger than my palm, were taking away the bones.

When I first saw the gleam of gold I blinked away tears. It seemed impossible. Then, as more of the mech was revealed, I realized there were large sections of the metal showing beneath the white.

These mechs weren't painted. They had covered themselves with thin layers of bone. I reached over and touched the surface. It was smooth and yet rough and faintly warmed from the heat of the power source deep within.

No human coded them to do this. I knew it in my heart.

311

Somehow these mechs were something more than mechanicals. This ossuary wasn't just a silent crazed monument to the dead, a program gone awry. This place was their creation.

I wanted to laugh but didn't dare.

Just keep moving those bones, Karom. There might be time later if you live so long.

When we had finally uncovered the base of the mech I started to think of the job. These mechs appeared to be independent systems capable of self-repair. Clearly this mech had lost its hover in a sudden, catastrophic surge.

I imagined it floating serenely above, perhaps working on the fountain, shaping and aligning the bones.

I got out my tool kit and my escort went rigid at the sight. It was almost comical how each arm went still as if to exclaim in surprise.

I found the access panel for the disabled mech and levered it open. Some things hadn't changed much in a thousand years. There was an etching on the panel of the layout of internal systems. I retrieved a diagnostic and ran through all the programs I could find.

"Yes, I know something is wrong with the hover." Had it overheated? Was there a short-out or had metal fatigue caused the failure?

I powered down most of the system and began to pull out some of the panels. My poor mech guide fluttered its arms and almost twirled in distress.

I kept working. Finally, when I popped the section into the guts of the hover, I set the finger lasers to illuminate the area. Everything glittered. It was a much better design than anything I had created. Already I could see the elegance and how I needed to apply it to anything new I would build. Every little piece of the system had that same simplicity. I pulled out another panel and realized my insectoid-mech was only centimeters away, watching my fingers dance.

I slipped off one of the small finger lasers and handed it over. There was a moment of hesitation before the hands grasped it and then began a careful and critical assessment.

When my escort tried to give it back I refused. I bowed with more reverence then I had ever given any of the Guildmasters.

For a long moment I didn't know if it would understand. Then it slowly withdrew its prize and folded it into the mass of its arms.

After almost an hour of hunching over the mech I found the problem. A small piece of metal had gotten inside the mech. It looked like something medical overlooked by one of the priests. They only had one critical job, the preparation of the bodies for Tombing and one of them failed. Anger sliced through my fatigue.

I took the small piece of metal and put it in my pocket. The reassembly went quickly and for a minute I held my breath when all the systems activated. The mech shuddered once and then slowly righted itself. I felt like cheering when it started to hover and arrange the bones.

I took out a cloth from my bag and cleaned my hands. There was a small pool of fluids where the mech had leaked. I wiped as much as possible clean but the bones were stained.

One day they would get covered. Maybe even by my own bones.

I stood up and waved the transport platform over. My escort stood with its hands moving and twitching. I pointed off into the direction I hoped we had arrived from and we set off.

The buildings seemed to lean over us on the way back. At first I thought it was the skulls, glaring down with malicious spirits but then I started to see movement.

Mechs gathered along the route. Long thin mechs with saws for arms, tiny mechs as small as my fingers, some large shelled behemoths and some that looked to be nothing more than hovering vacuum cleaners.

They followed us into the forest, weaving through the bone trees with grace and dexterity. This was their world, the silence and stillness, where nothing grew and nothing needed to breathe. A part of me wished I could stay, study them and learn to communicate but I knew I would never come back alive. Some ancient system had alarmed. Doors had opened and might never do so again in my lifetime.

We crossed the field of flowers and grasses. I could see the white room now, the straight lines of the doorframe looked hard and alien. When I stepped off the hover I was careful and quiet.

I turned around and saw the mechs were gathered and they'd filled the field in thousands of shades of white. In the midst I saw the chipped edges of gold, bright as sunlight: my repair job.

I raised a hand. My insectoid-mech, my guide and escort came forward. It extended several hands and when I put mine out I felt something drop into them.

It had carved a small mech of bone.

In the city I had not seen anything carved and I knew the mech had used the laser to do the work. The tiny face was a shadow of its own.

I bowed low to it, clutching my gift to my heart. For one second they did not move and then slowly they bowed back, rank after rank of them as far as I could see, little hands held to their chests.

Empty Epochs
by Trent Roman

The world coalesced into being slowly, as always. No matter how many times Khushwant Marsalis projected himself, it always was a disorienting process, and there was no real set method to reclaiming the senses afterwards. In this environment, alien in all but the literal sense, it took even longer, because there were none of the familiar sights and sounds—the form of a tree, or the hum of primordial insects—that could otherwise help him focus on attuning his mind to spectrums of light and vibration. He decided to settle on reacquiring vision to start off with, and a red-shifted tapestry unfurled before him, slowly developing variation and distance as he remembered how to see. After a few minutes of such exercises, he realized that his problems in making such distinctions were not fully internal, but a result of his unvaried and landmark-deprived setting.

He looked to the sky first, finding it completely cloudless and red verging on purple. Red, because of the crimson brilliance of the solar body that loomed large on the horizon, fixed there like in a child's drawing. The sun was much brighter now; if Marsalis had been using real eyes instead of just adjusting his free-floating consciousness to simulate sight, he would have been blinded by the merest glance. Despite this, the atmosphere was now so thin that he could almost make out the black of space behind the scarlet sky, as though sunlight were merely a thin curtain pulled across the void.

Looking down, across the ground, was painful in a way even the brightest of lights could not match. It was flat and barren, a plateau stretching to the horizon in every direction. Billions of years of erosion had ground all hills and mountains flat, and the cold belly of the planet could not muster the tectonic or volcanic force to raise new ranges up to the heat-scarred heavens. All? Not quite: there seemed to be a boulder in the distance, looking forlorn and out of place in this empty epoch.

With sight down, Marsalis extended his awareness to hearing, but there was little to hear. The slow planetary rotation, which made the sun seem immobile, also produced little wind, muffled further by the thinness of the air—not that there was anything moving to produce sound in the first place, not even the one who had arranged for them to meet in this incredibly distant time.

He supposed Joaquim Cuza would pop up sooner or later. It was the other man who had set the time and place for this illicit meeting, but given the scale on which they were projecting, the merest computational vagary could result in their trips becoming desynchronized. It the meantime, Marsalis pictured himself some legs and began to walk in the direction of the boulder, to relieve its obvious loneliness.

The ground, drained of humidity, was brittle and cracked, though of course his 'footfalls' made no impression since Marsalis was not physically present. The coexistence of all time periods had long been known to quantum scientists, but it was only forty years before Marsalis was born that the technology to peek through the veil of time had been developed. It was impossible to shift physical matter across the quantum boundaries, because those peep-holes were infinitesimally small, but mass-less energy could make the journey. It had taken more time still to devise a way to send brainwaves through the gaps in the quantum fabric (and safely back again), but projection had since become an invaluable tool to geologists, climatologists and palaeontologists like himself. It was projection that allowed him to go back and study his extinct specimens when they were still alive and thriving, to push the frontiers of knowledge.

And it was projection that had allowed him to sneak away from the watchfulness of the Concord's surveillance systems by escaping into the desolation of the year 5,394,271,806 Concord Era—five billion years into the future, give or take an era. Since the location was meaningless given how this Earth was unrecognizable from the planet of his time, he had not budged geographically from their research facility on the borders of what was the Caspian Sea in the present. He wondered if he might find some ruins if he could dig here, then corrected himself: the passage of time would have destroyed everything or turned it to rock long ago.

Marsalis was almost at the boulder when he saw it shudder. He stopped— an instinctive reaction since nothing in this place could hurt him—and took a longer look. Now that he was closer, he thought the exterior of the object wasn't so much rock as a kind of crusty shell, like the scab over a wound. Walking around it, he saw that on one side, at the bottom, the shell was largely absent and he could see a kind of gelatinous membrane instead. It was this substance that was slowly rippling, and Marsalis concluded that it wasn't a boulder but a creature, although whether animal, vegetal or even bacterial, he couldn't tell.

He hadn't bothered to think himself a mouth, but mentally wished the massive thing good luck; it couldn't be easy to survive in these, the waning days of the planet. That red sun in orbit, he knew, was only getting hotter and bigger,

316

and although the inevitable planetary nebula could still only be reckoned in geological time from this point, being here made the end seem like it wasn't so far away at all.

Marsalis had just finished a hovering tour of the creature, noting that the ground seemed more scorched than usual in a line leading away from it, when he felt the presence of another consciousness. In this state of free-floating awareness, the minds of others seemed to stand out sharper than anything else, probably because of the sympathetic resonance of the brain waves. That state of emphatic *being* was the stated reason why the Concord's scientific hierarchy had forbidden travel to any point in time after 100,000 B.C.E., to ensure that the increasingly self-aware humans of that time would not detect their presence and do something history had not intended on the basis of that impression. Travel to the future was likewise forbidden to avoid any foreknowledge tampering with the timeline to come. Of course, Marsalis and his companion were here, now, precisely because they had circumvented the rules and bypassed the protections on the projection devices.

Marsalis hovered about the boulder-creature for a while yet as he felt Cuza drifting closer to him. He could have gone to meet his colleague, but in the face of this barren wasteland that once was his home, he couldn't bear the idea of leaving the one living thing he'd found so far. It was an anchor for a mind adrift in a dry sea. Finally, Cuza was close enough that they could "speak" mind to mind, with only a small amount of effort to make their thoughts known to each other. Marsalis had heard experienced projectionists who had worked together for a long time could communicate wholly in images, but Cuza and he still needed the medium of language as a familiar touch-stone, just as they simulated the body's senses to perceive their environment.

Productive day, Cuza, Marsalis thought, the standard greeting making his environment seem all the more alien by contrast.

Productive day, Marsalis, Cuza returned as he floated by. *I've never seen this before,* he added, and since there was nothing else to see, Marsalis knew he was talking about the boulder-creature.

I think it's alive . . . Its skin seems membranous where not exposed to the sun, and the earth is scorched leading away from it, there. I'd hypothesize it leeches the nutrients it needs straight from the soil and into itself.

*How interesting . . . * Cuza thought as he drifted in for a closer look.

So I take it you've been here before, then?

Oh yes, a few times. How else would I know that this place was accessible? Cuza floated back to "stand" before Marsalis. *The projection device itself can access any point with equal ease, remember; five seconds or five billion years, it doesn't make any difference when all temporal states coexist. It's the security lockouts on the range that ought to prevent us from doing what we've done, and as you well know, whatever a human mind creates, another can circumvent.*

Marsalis nodded—a habit, since he didn't actually have a head to nod. Still, Cuza picked up on the feeling and returned it with acknowledgement of his own.

So what do we do now? Marsalis asked. *About the Concord?*

Cuza hovered silently for a few moments, and then drifted away. *Come, there's something I want to show you.*

Marsalis would have frowned had he the facial muscles to do so, but he followed the other man nonetheless. He was very much aware of the abysmal depths of the waters he was treading, and he didn't mean this future emptiness. He was just grateful that there were others like him in the discipline; that he didn't have to carry this terrible secret alone. As long as that promised relief was in sight, he was willing to defer to the other man's greater experience in such matters.

Marsalis trailed Cuza's awareness for several minutes, sensing a vague impression of "searching" from his colleague, before Cuza stopped, radiating success.

Here, he thought. *Look down there.*

Marsalis did so, and to his surprise saw for the first time a gap in the landscape. It was an expanse of thick, pinkish liquid just large enough to be called a big pond, that graded to a milky white color along the edges. Marsalis reasoned the silt was thicker here, and did not reflect the red sky as accurately.

Almost all the water in this time is highly basic, Cuza thought. *The logical opposite of the acidic seas of the distant planetary past, I suppose. But look.*

As Marsalis watched, the flat surface of the pond was disturbed by something emerging from the water, the thickness of the liquid limiting the ripples to barely perceptible tremors. Like the boulder-thing, it was covered in a grey-speckled white shell, but unlike that other creature these were small, interlocking plates that gave it the freedom to flex and move with greater ease. Between the plates he could glimpse a black-green mass of tissue that resembled muscles.

It slid along the surface long enough to reveal that it was at least a meter long before dipping back in. Marsalis was then surprised to see a number of smaller, shorter creatures of the same make rise and fall in its wake.

A family? he asked Cuza.

I think so, Cuza thought. *Good to know that even billions of years later, even as the planet dies its slow heat death, life still seeks out life, no?*

It was a familiar sentiment; cooperation and interdependency were cornerstones of the Concord. And even if the Concord was a lie, it didn't necessarily follow that all its values were false as well.

I presume the shell protects them from the corrosiveness of the water.

Cuza projected agreement. *From what I've seen of these little guys, their lower tissue produces acid that reacts with the silt-heavy water, neutralizing the reaction and creating salts that crusts into a protective layer.*

Fascinating adaptation, Marsalis thought. *Although I couldn't even begin to speculate what kind of creature it is. Looks like a cross between an insect and a sea-mammal, with maybe some botanical properties thrown in.*

Five billion years of evolution will certainly mess with phyla, Cuza thought.

Look, Joaquim . . . I don't mean to sound ungrateful, but this isn't why we're here.

Not directly, no. I just wanted you to see this . . . community. Before we make any decisions, we have to keep this in mind: we're social animals too.

Are you saying you don't want to expose what we've discovered? Joaquim, our entire history is a lie.

Marsalis had stumbled on a method of overriding the security protections on the projection devices quite accidentally; he'd simply been trying to refine the device to track one particular specimen of *Pterodactylus* throughout her natural lifespan. At first, he was going to report the loophole to the oversight committee; but before he could do so, he was seized with the desire to fulfill a lifelong dream and visit the founding of the Concord. He reasoned that one consciousness more or less during this massive gathering of humanity's representatives from across the inhabited circles wouldn't make a difference, and there was no danger of interfering with the past. So he sent himself back two thousand five hundred years, to the year zero on the Concord calendar.

What he found instead was parcels of humanity, divided against each other by what should have been, at this point, long-antiquated notions of race, ethnicity, tribe, nation, and religion. Instead of a species at the dawn of global cooperation, he saw people fighting against their neighbors, hacking away at each other with oversized blades, enslaving their fellows while small elites profited off the labor of others. Areas that ought to have been devoid of human habitation, not yet colonized by the regular, concentric plan of the Concord (like Australia and the Americas), were already home to long-standing human cultures that received history had no record of. Of the councilmen who were supposed to unite all peoples into the greatest collaborative society of all time, there was no trace.

Initially, Marsalis thought he'd made a terrible mistake in his calculations; that he had arrived at some point before the Concord, in the distant, barbaric past of humanity. But no matter how many times he revised his calculations, he still arrived at the same conclusion: the dates for the Concord's founding were somehow wrong. But this was no simple mistake: as Marsalis risked visiting later periods, he witnessed only more of the same divisions and strife, even as the level technology, inventions that history taught had been devised by Concord philosophers and scientists, progressed at its expected rate. Worse yet, these unfamiliar, squabbling humans perverted technology into weaponry; and when Marsalis had witnessed what these learned savages had used atomic theory for, he had stopped his explorations, half-convinced that even the present might prove to be a lie, a thin veil of rationality over a reality of competition and bloodshed.

For several weeks, Marsalis had inhabited a despondent state, his research falling behind and his social life becoming nonexistent. Although they had never been close, Cuza had taken an interest in the change in Marsalis' behavior—no doubt recognizing the symptoms for what they were—and, after taking Marsalis to a blind-spot in the surveillance grid, had eventually pried the story of his discoveries out of him. Rather than being shocked, however, Cuza had simply nodded grimly: he knew as well, and there were others. That's when Cuza had arranged to this meeting at the far end of the planet's lifespan, where they would be able to talk freely.

It is not a question of what I, as an individual, might want, Khushwant, Cuza thought. *This is a major revelation that would shock the world to its core. Potentially, it could destroy the Concord and everything that it has accomplished, whether on the back of a lie or not. You saw how we were before the Concord . . . do we really want to risk a return to that barbaric state of being? All that blood, on our hands?*

Marsalis gave a mental sigh. *I understand what you're saying, Joaquim. But if the Concord Administration is lying to us about millennia of history, who knows what else they are concealing? For all we know, the planetary ecosystem could be dangerously unbalanced, or maybe there are legions of unregistered humans somewhere performing menial labor. Maybe the Administration offices are just a front for anti-social luxury, who knows?*

These are rather nightmarish scenarios, my friend, Cuza thought.

I know, but that's the point, isn't it? We can't know, because they can't be trusted anymore. As for what will happen when the truth becomes exposed . . . I do not know that a society that must lie to survive is one that deserves to persist. Surely it is an unnatural state of affairs, only masquerading as truth while preventing us from finding true collective enlightenment.

Cuza was silent several moments. *So you are certain about this, then.*

I am, Marsalis thought, feeling as though a weight was lifted from his mind now that he had come to a decision. There would be many hardships ahead, he knew, but for the moment Marsalis felt at peace with himself, content.

I'm sorry you think that way, Khushwant, Cuza thought in a manner that pricked Marsalis's attention. It wasn't just the sadness and disappointment that agreed with what he said: it was the undercurrent of a threat behind the thought.

Joaquim? What do you mean?

When I said that I knew, as did others . . . I didn't discover this, I was told. When I joined the Eternal Guard.

Marsalis's awareness recoiled from that of his colleague. The Eternal Guard was the internal police force of the Concord, and recruited its members from most every discipline and walk of life. It was to avoid their eyes and ears that Marsalis thought Cuza had arranged for them to meet in this future wasteland. Instead, he found that he had just confessed sedition to those whom he had feared would discover his transgression these last few weeks.

How . . . how can you do this? Lie to us all? Marsalis demanded, trying to conceal his fear behind a mask of bluster and outrage.

*You saw our *real* history, Khushwant. *That's* why. In reality, the Concord is only three hundred years old. Before that, billions of lives sacrificed to petty divisions and the power plays of unaccountable elites. We used to kill ourselves in the most terrible ways, Khushwant, not hesitating to stoop to atomic or biological warfare, sometimes for hoarded resources that would be sufficient if equally distributed, but just as often over fables of nations or deities. The world was a mad, chaotic place, to which the Concord finally brought peace. More, the insanity of our ancestors nearly killed this world and its biosphere with pollutants and over-consumption, long before its naturally appointed time.* Cuza indicated the barren wasteland about them. *You're right: the Concord is concealing the fact that the world still isn't fully healed from the damage dealt to it over the last millennia. We're draining carbons from the atmosphere while we wait for the replanted rainforests to grow, and fixing local ecosystems by reintroducing extinct species cloned from genetic material in the fossil record. It is a massive deceit, but a necessary one. So much so that an entire generation of people, billions worldwide, staring at the abyss of global extinction our collective folly had brought us to, decided to sacrifice their history and heritage, to live their lives and raise their children in a perpetual lie, in order to create a better society for the future. *That* is the power of the Concord.*

But our society is built on falsehoods, just like the nations and religions of old . . . Marsalis thought meekly. *We will never progress if we do not confront and overcome the perils of our nature.*

Have you considered that it is our nature to be self-destructive? Will you tell me that you looked into the eyes of those historical killers and didn't see the void within? We are all as barren as this scorched world on the inside, Khushwant. That is our nature. Only by filling that wasteland wrap the belief that we are inherently cooperative and interdependent can we counter the suction of the emptiness within. Such a belief has to be functionally innate, instilled from birth, and no competing views can be allowed.

Marsalis floated there, trying to sort through his confused thoughts. The wider implications of what Cuza had said were just too large to wrap his mind around at the moment, so he opted for a more immediate concern:

What will happen to me now?

Now? Nothing. It has already happened.

What do you mean?

I'm sorry, Khushwant, but given our suspicions . . . while we've been here, talking, your projection cradle has been removed to a secure location, and the recall functions were disabled. We'll keep your body alive as long as you wish us to, but your mind cannot be allowed to return to our time. This place is your home, now.

Panicked, Marsalis tried to trigger the recall function that all projectionists had implanted into their psyche and found it dead. He looked about himself, at the crimson-tinted, heat-scorched plateaus, and wished that he could cry. *You cannot . . . alone on a dying world? But we are a social animal. Cooperative. Interdependent. I will go mad.*

Possibly, Cuza allowed. *If you ask for death, we will respect your wishes and arrest all brain function in the present. But you are a scientist, Khushwant, one whose work has always been admirably diligent. Consider turning a profit from your exile, making a study of this world and its flora and fauna. Rise above your betrayed feelings and make one last contribution to your society. Either myself or another agent will be by in a few months' time to hear your decision and record whatever you've discovered.*

Wait! Marsalis mentally cried. *Don't leave me!*

Fare you well, my friend, Cuza said, and vanished within the space of a microsecond.

Marsalis stared at the relative space that Cuza's conscience had inhabited, but it remained empty. He turned in place, but there was nothing from flat horizon to flat horizon that moved in the thin air. Even the viscous, opaque pond seemed frozen, the family of salt-eels hidden somewhere beneath the scarlet reflection from above. And in the sky, having barely moved, the red sun loomed heavily, herald of the cataclysm unfolding over countless epochs to come. Marsalis turned a disaffected gaze up at it and began to wait.

What Doesn't Stay in Vegas
by Lawrence M. Schoen

It was World Poker Series time in Las Vegas again, and nearly thirty thousand players had come to town. The laws of probability would eliminate most, but some few had shown up sheathed in layers of their own luck, and other laws ruled over them. At other times of the year, the Lucky either kept to themselves and won big, or went head-to-head and canceled each other out; neither outcome caused too much concern. The city had been built to absorb a certain amount of random chance. Tournaments changed all that. Too much luck flowed into the city during Tournaments, crashing against well-ordered probability like waves upon the shore.

The man currently known as Johnny Feldspar surfed in those waves. He had a gift for tapping into excess luck and draining it away, and for years now had earned a good living doing it. But as the annual Tournament grew, it had brought ever-larger amounts of luck into the city, so much that at times the luck coalesced. When that happened it acquired a modicum of consciousness, and would flee out into the desert. Self-aware fields of rampant improbability couldn't be left to roam unchecked.

Two hours ago, the agency that employed Johnny Feldspar had sent him after just such a glob of wild luck. Now he sat with his head against the steering wheel of his rental car and felt the pull of improbability like a lover's tongue caressing the curve of his left ear. No way he was going to use his own car, assuming he even owned one. The moment he'd donned the agency's Feldspar persona he'd left his own identity and most of his personal memory behind. The only thing Johnny Feldspar owned were the clothes on his back and a wallet with bogus ID and agency-provided credit cards. He'd rented a brand new town car for the day with one of those cards, paying for the extra insurance. With this much wild luck involved, it seemed a good bet that he'd need it.

He was an hour out from Las Vegas. Twenty minutes ago he'd left the road and driven across the desert. The car's engine had quit like a WWII army jeep in the throes of a secret Nazi energy dampening field. The tug tug tug of extremely unlikely events in the offing tantalized his specialized senses. Nazis would have been a welcome alternative, even in Las Vegas, even in the desert. Feldspar banged his head to clear it, banged it hard enough to sound the horn but not sufficient to trigger the air bag.

"Jesus! What the hell's wrong with you? We're supposed to be inconspicuous."

Feldspar looked up, reseated the crooked, optically enhancing sunglasses on his nose. In the city he worked alone, but the agency liked to send a team out when the jobs got this big. He regarded his 'partner' du jour, Johnny Schist, a man who apparently worried about not standing out while parked in the middle of nowhere. They'd worked together before. Schist's talent involved shaping the luck, imposing semantic parameters on its raw substance. Feldspar had once seen the man bind a ravenous pool of improbability into the logic and shape of seven academy award statuettes for best actor. They'd sold them to a pawnshop just off the strip.

Feldspar knew better than to say anything to Schist. Speech was particularly susceptible to the quantum fluctuations of wild luck. Telling Schist to chill could come out as something else. Schist might hear him speak eloquently on the versatility of cartoon vocalist Mel Blanc. More likely Schist would hear something to cause him to whip out his weapon and blow Feldspar away. Quantum fields were funny that way, expert at protecting themselves from sensitives like him.

So he said nothing. Did nothing. Sooner or later Schist would remember the protocol for team assignments. Until then, Feldspar didn't dare do anything except sit still, hands balled into fists shoved into the pockets of his regulation duster.

"Prick," said Schist, which Feldspar knew probably wasn't what he'd actually said, 'prick' being his own push-button word, ever since a land mine in Kyrgyzstan had taken his. Knowing this, knowing how probability worked here of all places, almost took the sting out of it. He squeezed his hands tighter, imagining chunks of coal in his fists being turned into diamond.

Schist opened the car door and stepped back, waiting for him to get out. Feldspar obliged, still silent, not daring to look at his partner. He moved to the trunk, opened it, and began removing a series of telescoping poles, like the legs of a photographer's tripod constructed by the bastard lovechild of Anton Mesmer and Nikola Tesla.

Schist kept talking, saying something about arboreal mammals and milk chocolate. Feldspar ignored him, and continued assembling the pieces until he had a sideless box of circuitry about the size of an old style phone booth. He stepped within, uncertain if the agency's mobile Faraday cage would make a damn bit of difference.

The yearning in his brain stopped at once. Portions of his cognition swung, pendulum style, and the sudden emptiness gnawed at him in equal measure to the recent tug. He gripped the sides of his cage and started walking forward into a sudden, epiphenomenal wind, a sure sign that the luck they stalked knew they had arrived.

Johnny Schist, garbed in an identical grey duster and opaque sunglasses, followed, oblivious to the siren song of the nigh impossibility of the nearby quantum field

"How'd I get hooked up with a dickless wonder like you?" Schist's voice had taken on a musical lilt even as it dropped two octaves. The man's coat whipped around him and he gestured at an incongruously grassy knoll in the middle of an otherwise empty desert, leaving Johnny Feldspar to wonder what he'd actually said and why the man kept talking.

He set the cage down and looked where Schist had indicated, channeling his sensitivity in an effort to determine whether or not the small hill existed or only seemed to be there. The physical manifestation of something lush and green in the middle of otherwise lifeless terrain wasn't a problem. It was a one-shot fluctuation, an effect that probably sloughed off from the wild luck without too much of an energy expenditure. The wind on the other hand was an ongoing outflow of energy suggesting an even more coherent field than he'd been led to expect. Not a good sign.

Schist didn't appear to share his concern. "Easy peasy," sang the other man, raising spread fingers to his forehead like a cheap mentalist act. "Like shooting fish in a barrel. Prick." Feldspar glared at him. He could feel the meme that Schist was sending out. The literal son of a bitch was projecting semantic primitives that combined into structures of wooden staves and iron hoops and schools of mackerel. "Just don't screw it up," Feldspar said, clapping a hand over his own mouth an instant later.

The grass rippled, and the wind carried globs of improbability their way. Johnny Feldspar deftly snagged the rampant luck out of the air and drained it away, leaving his partner free to work. Tiny fish began to manifest amongst blades of grass and several wooden casks popped into existence and rolled toward them. Schist's face bore a scrunched up look of concentration and his hands started to tremble.

The wind picked up, lifted one of the casks into the air, and flung it at Feldspar. It smashed his fragile Faraday cage and sent him crashing into his partner. Feldspar gasped, the yearning ache in his head suddenly back with a vengeance that blocked out every other sensation.

Schist screamed, but not because of the contact. The wild luck had used the physical attack merely as a distraction while simultaneously sending its mojo back along the conduit of Schist's meme. Feldspar knew it the instant Schist cried out, but couldn't prevent it.

Schist's eyes glazed over. His hands fell from his face and he worked his jaw. Improbability ticked time back a few seconds.

"Fish in a barrow," Schist said, slurring the last word into new meaning, and altering history as well as the meme.

Feldspar felt it reverberate within him as the meme played top-down games with his unconscious mind and bottom-up tomfoolery with the distorted environment. From the look on his face, Schist felt it too.

"White fish in a barrow. Cold and white."

"Schist?"

"Barrow wight."

The wind fell away and Feldspar whipped around to look at the knoll that had become a tumulus in his mind. A barrow mound.

"Schist, what have you done?"

A man-shaped shadow that belonged to neither of them moved like water on the face of the mound. It hurtled at Johnny Schist before the man could move, and engulfed him in shade.

Johnny Schist's arms dropped to his side. His duster hung in tatters, now mottled with mold. Vapor rose from his lips, already tinged a bluish purple.

Feldspar staggered backward, his head suddenly clear, his psychic sense silent as death. The wild luck had completely gone. He felt oddly refreshed, even vibrant.

"What was my name?" said the thing that had been Schist, a creature out of myth called into creation by the altered meme.

Johnny Feldspar shrugged. "I wouldn't tell you even if I could, you murderous bastard. There's too much power in names, too much for you to work with."

Schist's body sagged, time seemed to speed up around it, bringing both age and decay, resulting in the walking corpse of a dead field agent at eighty-some years of age. "Leave me alone," the wight said.

"Give me his body," said Feldspar.

"He is mine. Leave me alone, or I will drain the life from you as well. I will gnaw your bones in the cold darkness under the hill and deny you the peace of a natural death."

Johnny Feldspar sighed, giving in to the necessities and logic the meme had created. He tapped the dictation stick on his collar. It chirped softly and began recording. "Intensity eight improbability field confirmed and neutralized," he said. "The field now exists as a mythic entity bound to a limited locus. Coordinates to follow."

"I have many bones in my barrow," said the wight. "Can you not feel the legion of dead buried all around you? Leave me, or you will join them."

"We're less than an hour outside Vegas. I don't doubt there's lots of bodies buried here. But you didn't have anything to do with them." Feldspar consulted the GPS readout in his watch and continued his report, rattling off the coordinates to his stick. "Recommend standard containment of this site for a minimum of six weeks after the Tournament concludes."

"Leave me!"

"Final note: Conversion has resulted in the loss of agent Schist." He sighed. It was all so pointless. "Recommend full death benefits be provided his beneficiaries. End report."

"Your mystic barriers will not save you," said the wight, bits of Schist's skin falling from its arms as it railed. "Leave me, or I will take you into my barrow for all time."

"Yeah, yeah," he said, suddenly weary beyond the needs of his job. He gathered up the broken pieces of the Faraday cage and began trudging back to the car. He glanced once over his shoulder to see his partner's rotting flesh and bones shamble into the raised mound of his home.

The car started right up and Feldspar aimed it in the direction of the highway. By lunchtime he'd be back in Las Vegas, a town that treated him like a pariah but found a desperate need for his talents when too many lucky people congregated. He felt filled to bursting with the luck he'd absorbed, and for just a moment toyed with the idea of joining the Tournament himself. But no, he'd find a better use for it. He'd spread it around as he always did, a walk through the cancer ward, shake the hands of a couple Elvis impersonators, and maybe even bless a few newlyweds. And before it was all spent, he'd use the last bit to get his name back.

Don't Leave, She Said
by Michael Anthony

Charcoal dunes and crescents. Craters. Oceans of ebony dust blanketed the landscape like volcanic vomit, stretching into the horizon, into forever. Joca craned his head out the shack, his pupils dilating. The ground was the same color as the sky, minus the stars, and everything in between was invisible. He squinted, peering as far as his cataract-covered eyes could strain, until he couldn't tell where the solid ended and the untouchable began.

Had he heard Tolia? He ran a wrinkled hand over his bald head. Her voice had floated to him on the artificial wind like a bottled whisper. Or had it been another dream? He imagined her bronze hair, tied back, the lower half of her face stretched into a toothy smile. Her dark eyes, also seemed to grin, and her leathered face, worn and weary, but still beautiful.

His datapad beeped off another Earth hour. Counting down. He hooked it onto his belt and stumbled outside, searched around the shack. If she found her way back she would have woken him. It must have been another dream. Unless she was confused, he reminded himself. He spat, kicked the topsoil—*regolith*. That's what it was called, back when he had been an astronaut. Back when chunks of alien worlds sold for fortunes in the auction houses on Earth.

He trudged inside, paced around the shack, biting his thumbnail. The ship was landing soon. The unmanned probe, on its way back to Earth after a mission to the outer planets, was pre-programmed for the pickup. After it landed it had a five-minute launch window and it would take off whether they were on it or not. After all this time it was just as likely that there would be no one to board it, and his jailers had anticipated that contingency.

He glanced around the shack, triaging everything by emotional importance. He was only allowed one bag. Every ounce carried debt. The plaques he had been allowed to bring along hung from the plastic wall. Awards and medals lay on the shelf near his cot. Various pictures of Earth: His graduation from the academy, his first commission, the Mars landing. All of it important, but he'd gladly leave it behind in exchange for Tolia's picture. He only had one and had lost it weeks ago. It was tacked above his cot, the paper coming apart, the corners yellowed and frail—decades of being fingered and held. Had the wind carried it away? That didn't matter now, he told himself. Once he found her he wouldn't need it anymore.

He finished packing, placed the bag at the foot of his cot. He had made the bed, tight and stretched, out of military habit. Everything was ready now. Almost everything.

He squeezed into his jacket and paced outside. Tolia couldn't have wandered far. Phobos was tiny compared to Earth's moon and the dome only covered a fraction of the rocky skull. He put his hand to his brow, tilting his head. Mars monopolized the sky, watching over him like always, with Phobos forever locked in synchronous orbit.

An air pocket swooshed down from high above, kicking up dust, chilling him. The temperature seemed to have dropped gradually over the years and he wondered if the environmental controls were going out. He figured that didn't matter much now. He pulled his jacket closed. The zipper broke long ago; he forgot when. The sides were frayed and jagged, the collar ripped.

He pivoted and faced south, or where he imagined south would be. He hadn't searched in that direction in a few days, or was it a few weeks? Memory was a frail thing. His thick G-boots grounded him to the surface and he hunched over, crunching through the regolith. The fine dust puffed into smoke clouds behind him; the horizon curved. He scanned the ground as he walked, moving his head from side to side. Maybe he'd find traces of a campfire or an empty rations pack. She had to eat, keep warm. The remnants of that would be somewhere, and if he found it he could follow it like a trail.

He heard a metallic clanking sound in the distance. Tolia? He shuffled forward and cocked his head, aiming his good ear in the direction of the noise. The chug-chug of the biosphere regulator banged away. He forgot it was south of the shack, he hadn't stumbled onto it for months. Its nuclear engine burned up atoms night and day (but it was always night here, he reminded himself), spewing air into the dome like an artificial lung.

He inhaled, letting the stale oxygen mixture inflate his lungs. He longed for real Earth air. Near the forests it was so fresh it almost had a flavor, like cool spring water in gas form. Tolia enjoyed hiking in the mountains, through the trees. She loved nature and knew the names of every flower and plant they encountered. He used to call her his wood nymph. She'd giggle, sometimes punctuating her laughter with a snort, and then cover her mouth, her cheeks filling in with a rose hue like an artist had run his brush across her face.

He quickened his stride, his emaciated stick-legs carrying him across the cold black desert. He had to find her soon. She couldn't live on her own without food and water for too long, and the ship—

The datapad beeped as if reading his thought. Nine hours left.

He darted his eyes across the landscape, studying every rock, every shadow. Something glistened in the distance, reflecting light. A ration wrapper? He sprinted towards it. His leg cramped and he rubbed the muscle as he stumbled forward. He couldn't stop for a charlie horse. Not now. Tolia could be up ahead. He paced up to the object and fell to his knees, grasping at it; the gritty sand sifting through his swollen fingers. He sighed. Just a piece of rock, seared at the edges like volcanic glass.

An ice pick stab of pain then shot through his chest and he clutched at his jacket, gasping. He wasn't as young as he used to be.

He heard a giggle, subdued laughter.

"Tolia!" He struggled to his feet. "It's me! Where are you?"

The giggle again. It was Tolia. Had to be. He felt a rock form in his belly, move up into his esophagus and stick in his throat.

He limped forward, smiling. As he approached, the noise morphed into a mechanical sound. Robot laughter. It was the biosphere regulator again, taunting him with random human-like sounds. Now he remembered why he avoided this area.

Gripping his jacket at the collar, he hunched forward, away from the machine, his feet shuffling through the ancient dust. The stars winked and glistened above, indifferent to his problems. Sometimes he thought they looked like holes poked through a sheet, fake, and he imagined that he was still on Earth, perhaps in the same building the Neo's had staged the Titan landings. It made sense. Why go through the trouble and expense of shipping him out here and setting all this up. Why not kill him—

But they couldn't risk executing him, he reminded himself. He was exiled like Napoleon at Elba. Far enough away that he couldn't gather support from the holdouts, but not dead so he'd be a martyr. But he was just an old man now. No harm to anybody, and the revolution was ancient history.

The datapad beeped. Seven hours. Time was ebbing away, he had to stop daydreaming.

The rattling of the biosphere regulator inched quiet as he gained distance. When he was far enough away he shuffled to a stop, swiveled his head in each direction.

"Tolia!—" He bent over, coughed, straightened himself. "Tolia! We have to go!"

Mars blurred and flickered above, like a holo-pic error. He shielded his eyes, squinting at the image. He was right. This was all one big setup. They must have put him on a sound and light stage somewhere, maybe where they used to make the old Hollywood movies. Tolia loved to go to the movies, when they were first married, before the censors banned everything but the propaganda films. She liked love stories with happy endings. He preferred war movies but she had sat through plenty of things he liked to do . . .

Mars steadied, became real. It had been his eyes that had lost focus—Mars had been there all along. Fooled again.

He picked up his step, leaving the stretch of flat area that surrounded his shack and entering into a small ridge of black-glassy rocks with odd shapes; the byproduct of billions of years of asteroids and comets pounding the surface. Some of the rocks had exploded out city-sized craters, kicking up debris, and then gradually, over millennia, disintegrated into the dust that his boots now stomped through. *Like you soon enough, old man.*

He'd find Tolia first. Maybe they'd even survive the trip back to Earth in the survey ship. There was still enough life left for them to squeak out a few more good years. But did the Neo's remember to build the compartment big enough for them both?

"I'm here," Tolia whispered.

Joca jerked his head; his eyes widened. It was the wind, swooshing around the side of the dome, whispering in its falsetto voice and his imagination doing the rest. Fake wind, he reminded himself. The pseudo-atmosphere. Everything here was pseudo-something. Now even his mind.

He trekked on, following the curvature of the moon. He knew Tolia hated it here. Maybe that's why she ran off, went crazy, or whatever had happened. Decades ago she had warned him he'd end up here, or some place like it. "The people follow you because you were once famous. The first man on Mars," she said, rubbing his shoulder. "But you've served your country; you don't have to be a hero anymore."

"The people need me," he replied.

"I need you. Don't leave."

He had forced a smile, hugged her and said he didn't have a choice. Some things were worth the risk. Maybe that was something else he had been wrong about.

The datapad beeped. Five hours.

He cupped his mouth. "Tolia! Where are you?"

Silence.

He continued on.

After a while he shuffled through a patch of sand, darker than the rest. It was greasy-looking, like a barrel of oil had seeped into it. Oil didn't exist on

Earth anymore, except in museums. He stared at the splotch as he walked, dazed, and his forehead bounced against an invisible wall. He fell backwards, his hands breaking his fall, cutting into tiny rocks with razor edges. *The damn dome*. He had forgotten how clear it was out here.

He pushed himself up, blood dotting the soil, turning black. He touched the transparent barrier. It curved up over his head, and stretched above and around for dozens of kilometers. He wasn't sure exactly how far. The jailers had given him a tiny shack to stew in but had made his terrarium huge. The expanse just accentuated his loneliness. Maybe that's what they wanted.

"Tolia! We have to go! A ship is coming!"

No sound. Even the wind had calmed out here.

He leaned against the dome, following it. Maybe she had made camp against it somewhere. But would he have time to go all the way around? He glanced at the datapad and began sprinting. The invisible wall curved, straightened. His joints ached and his legs throbbed—the low gravity had deteriorated his muscles into thin fibrous strips of flesh. He slowed to a trot, panting. His left arm tingled, like it had fallen asleep, and he clutched his chest. He had to take it easy. A heart attack wouldn't help Tolia.

The datapad beeped. Four hours.

He staggered along the side of the dome, scanning the area. He spied a discoloration in the sand ahead. He squinted. A pattern. He sprinted forward, ignoring the pain in his chest and arm. A line of boot prints stretched into the distance. His pulse thudded in his temple as he shuffled along the path. The prints were fresh, Tolia was near. He forced his legs to move in clockwork rotations, the muscles in his calves protesting with every step. *Can't stop now.*

His gasps increased, became deeper, his lungs trying to keep up with the exertion. His face flushed the color of Mars and his legs finally cramped up, refusing to go any farther. He hit at them with a closed fist.

"Move!" He punched at the muscles, kneading them. "Damn it! Move!"

They loosened and he trotted forward, forcing himself on. Up ahead, where the horizon started to curve, he saw a silver dot, growing as he approached. The footprints led back to it, back to his shack. He limped to a stop, placing his boot in one of the prints. Perfect match. He was following himself. He clenched his jaw. Stupid mistake. He was smarter than that. Or was he really losing his mind? Falling to his knees, a groan escaped from somewhere deep inside him.

The datapad beeped and he flinched as if slapped.

He unhooked it from his belt, chucked it.

"I'm here," Tolia whispered from behind. "Don't leave," she said.

Joca raised his fists, clenched his eyes into two flat dime slits. He wouldn't look. He wouldn't give in to his madness. Senility? And if he turned and saw nothing—

"Remember?" she asked.

An image flashed in his head, like a faded photograph. A forgotten nightmare. The last time he saw her, crying into cupped hands, begging him to stay. He hadn't, of course. The revolution needed him. A month later the freedom squads had captured him, the movement crushed, everything in vain. When word got back to him she had been dead for weeks. "An accident," his jailers said. They apologized to him in his cell like polite monsters, had given him her picture. The one he had brought with him.

He struggled up, trudged back to the shack, head lowered. Maybe she'd still be alive if he hadn't left—

Don't think about that, he told himself. Not now. He swept the datapad off the gray sand. The timer read an hour. He ducked into the shack, grabbed his bag and limped outside. He sat near the melted-rock landing site, waiting.

"Don't leave me again," Tolia whispered.

Joca covered his good ear, slapping it as if trying to silence the voice in his head.

"I need you."

"I'm sorry," he croaked, opening his eyes.

No one was there.

He tilted his head, studied the silver donut-shaped airlock high above. It would be opening soon. He ran his finger in the dust, wondering how much Earth had changed in his absence, if it were still decaying, or if the Neo's had fixed it like they promised the people. But at what cost?—

The datapad beeped in quick succession, went silent. A moment later the airlock rotated open. Rapid swooshing filled Joca's ears as the atmosphere escaped into space. Whirlwinds of dust and debris scattered around him, sweeping by. Dust flew in his eyes and he rubbed it out. The ship began its descent, the airlock rotating shut behind it. The wind began to calm and Joca glanced around. He saw a picture, a few yards away, balanced on a yellowed corner, dancing across the sand. *Tolia!*

He jerked forward, scurrying after it on hands and knees. It fell face up in the dust. He leaped, clutching at it, and the ship hovered above, causing another gust of wind to whip up, blowing it back out of his fingers. The ship landed on the melted-rock and the hull vibrated, shook, then a ramp descended, touching down in the dust. It led up to an egg-shaped hatch that now stood open. Joca fingered his datapad, set a five minute timer. He swiveled on his heels, darting for the picture. It scooted along the ground, just out of grasp.

The datapad beeped. Four minutes.

He gauged the distance to the ship. Still close enough. The picture flitted into the sand, wavering in the artificial breeze. He paced up to it, his heart thudding like a turbine, and squatted—his kneecaps popped like firecrackers. He grasped the picture in his shaking hand as the datapad beeped off another minute. He clutched it into his palm and turned, trotting toward the ramp. It was farther than he thought. His muscles cramped again, their old complaints. He limped forward, grinding his teeth, sweat dripping down his forehead.

The beep again. Two minutes, but he was almost there. He shuffled up the ramp, toward the hatch. As he reached the entrance his right leg cramped and he collapsed, his knee thudding against the metal. The pain shot through his leg and he grimaced, closing his eyes. The picture slipped out of his sweaty fist, fluttered to the ground. With one hand on his chest he staggered back down the ramp.

Beep. Sixty seconds.

He ducked, grabbing at the picture. Another gust of wind blew and it fluttered away. He staggered toward it, kneeling. It drifted away on the dust like a wave, centimeters from his fingertips. The ramp started to ascend, the metal screeching as it slid across the melted rock. No more time. The picture would have to stay.

He staggered up the ramp, then stopped, glancing back. Tolia's picture lay face up in the dust. Her eyes seemed to be following him. He suddenly wondered if she were really dead. What if the memories were just another cruel trick of his mind? His subconscious using it as a defense mechanism so he wouldn't feel guilty about not finding her? He couldn't take the chance. He wouldn't leave her. Not again.

The ramp continued to retract into the ship, halfway now, and Joca jumped, landing lightly in the dust below. He strolled over to the picture. This time it didn't move. He clutched it in his swollen hand, rotating it in his fingers, staring into Tolia's smiling face. The ship fired up, blasted off the ground toward the skygate, on its way back to Earth. It wouldn't return, and nothing would come in its place.

Joca stumbled into his shack, the frayed picture balanced in his cupped hand like a diamond. He lowered himself into his cot and sighed. He needed sleep. He'd look for Tolia again tomorrow. She couldn't have wandered far.

Red
by Paul L. Bates

Red sand, as far as the eye can see—quiet, beautiful, inviting. I know better than any that the tranquil scene beyond my window is an illusion.

My breathing is shallow, my awareness heightened. I peer through the transparent pane, looking for any sign of movement, holding my breath, as if that might make me invisible . . . invisible to . . . I do not know what to call it. The wind? The storm? The tornado? The god? It is the thing beyond the limits of my perception, beyond the limits of the perception of my machines— the thing that has killed us one by one until only I remain.

The sands look painted, the work of some mad artist, unreal within the hazy red atmosphere of our terraforming. Without real shadows, they look the stuff of dreams.

I shut my eyes and sigh. Against the darkness I see Lois. Her red lips twist into a mocking smirk. I remember how soft they were, pressed against my own, against my neck, my cheeks. Lois is buried somewhere beneath that infernal ocean of sand. Am I remembering her, or is she welcoming me to the kingdom of death? Are they all waiting for me?

A sound on the monitor jars my attention back to the hut. Another sensor has failed. I am blind to the north, as well as the south and east now. One by one, the ring of sixteen lights has winked out until only one is left. The storm has figured out their purpose. I peer expectantly through the two-centimeter thick plastiglass, wondering if it will come at me from the west this time.

I have no more replacement panes. If I do not lower the metal shutters in time, the swirling sands will etch the window in seconds, depriving me of the scenic view—all that is left me on this would-be paradise. I lower them now, knowing that the hut will be engulfed by the maelstrom eventually. I will savor the placid illusion of the ever shifting landscape again after the next attack.

There is enough sunlight and reserve power in the batteries to maintain the machines for eighteen months or more. There is enough food for a year. With conservation and recycling, my water will last at least that long. The atmosphere we have created will sustain me, but the thing that swims within it will give me no peace. Do I maintain hope of rescue against the mounting evidence that there will be none? What else is there? Only the waiting. I wait for rescue, I wait for the thing in the wind, I wait for the next hallucination, I wait for sleep.

The hut begins to quiver, as if it might leap from its moorings. I have closed the shutters just in time. Even through the insulated walls, I hear the waves of spinning sand raking the curved metal surface. It is on top of me, trying to suck me from my den, trying to evict me from this new world, trying to slash my only remaining refuge to slivers. The last indicator on the monitor fades. There are no more sensors. The thing is huge, as the sensor is ten kilometers distant from the other. I must wait for it to spend itself again.

I shut my eyes, picturing the last supply ship, engulfed moments after landing. Our long range communications equipment was the first thing to fail, as if the creature could hear us, feel our thoughts, jam them completely. The ship's crew was dissolved moments after setting foot upon New Eden, even though we tried to warn them. They followed the sound of the interference like a homing beacon. Swirling sands shredding flesh and insulsuits alike in seconds. Like ants, we scavenged what was left of the ship after the storm. There were only five of us then. We were still trying to generate the terraforming, against the mounting evidence that the thing we brought to life with our atmosphere would not allow it. We had once been two hundred, spread across seven outposts on a world we thought dead. Dormant is the word I now use.

Lois sits on the cot, smiles at me, pats the folded blanket for me to sit beside her. I move like a sleepwalker toward my hallucination. I know that if I touch her she will disappear, so I keep the smallest of distances between us. Her eyes sparkle, and for a moment I think they taunt me. Then I see her tears. She is crying. Does she cry for herself, for me, for all of us? I look into those large brown eyes for as long as I can bear to. The pain is overwhelming, I lower my eyes, feel my shoulders slouching, fall back upon the cot, into the world of dreams.

I dream of sand. Red sand. Red sand, red sky, and a red rose. When I awaken the wind is gone. It is past midnight. I leave the shutters down. The monitor tells me the hut is buried beneath ten feet of sand. I start the motors that initiate the hydraulics. The hut begins its slomo swim to the surface. It will take five hours. Sunrise.

I pick up the knife on the console, cut the silver wrapper, unwrap another tasteless bar of synthfood, pour myself a half ration of water. My jaw grinds the chewy tan concoction into a barely palatable paste. At the back of the hut the last genrose opens in its terrarium. That was Lois' project. I imagine the fragrance, shut my eyes, cry. I am wasting water.

I have promised myself that I will not revisit the past, I will not relive the events that led to the deaths of my companions. I have made good on that promise for six months now. Every time my mind leads me in that direction, I take it elsewhere. I have read all of the manuals until I can recite them. I have exhausted the computer's fiction library. I exercise twice daily. Nothing helps. I know that I am a condemned man. I know that there will be no last meal. I know that there will be no pardon. No one will pray for me.

The hours pass. My arms ache from the pushups. My sides throb from the sit ups. Lois is here again, watching me bemusedly. When she first returned I used to tell her that I loved her, but that only drove her away. So I say nothing now. She turns her back on me to admire her genrose. A flashing light on the monitor indicates the hut has releveled itself.

I hear nothing. Cautiously I lift the shutters. The sand has reformed itself once again into an almost endless undulating landscape of red without hard edges, like the Worldsnake of Norse mythology, fading imperceptibly into the mists beyond. Ever different, ever the same. Lois comes over to look with me. She is not as taken with the stark beauty of the scene as I am. When I turn back to her she points toward the door then fades away.

Is she telling me to go out? Is she telling me to surrender myself to the next storm? For a moment I consider joining the rest of the team. I could simply trudge through the dunes until I succumb to either the arid heat, or the winds return for me. Why not? After three relief ships were consumed, no one else will try. There has been no offworld communication for over two years. We are parsecs away from anything—no one will pass this way en route to anywhere. Perhaps I should just go out with a finality. At least I might be with Lois again.

The wind comes without warning. It rakes the pane before I can lower the shutter etching it in seconds. I hear the grinding of the sand within the shutter mechanism, even through the lashing waves bouncing off the metal walls. My window is gone—I will have to open the door if I want to see the dunes again. It is trying to dig me out this time. The hut burrows faster than the wind can excavate it. The thing changes its tactic, heaping sand over me for an hour.

The storm subsides quickly, as if it is aware that it has achieved its goal. I am blind at last.

I dim the lights to conserve power. Only the UV light within the terrarium illuminates the genrose, no longer red, but black.

Like ants we descended upon the last supply ship, bringing container after container of precious food stuffs, water and replacement parts into the hut. We took turns watching the monitor. There was one sand skimmer left then, but the ship crashed about four kilometers from the hut, barely within the range of our sensors.

I am doing it. I am reliving their deaths. I promised myself I would not. Lois stands over me shaking her head. I see the silent words forming on her lips.

"Do it," is all she says.

Do what? Go out into the storm? Relive your death? Torture myself more?

I cannot help myself.

We spent an hour digging out the ship. The servolifts sent red plumes of sand soaring into the sky. Red on red. We found a piece of the captain's jacket, a collar with his insignia. He had chosen to put down on a solid outcropping, rather than risk landing on the sand. He did not know that these outcroppings appear then disappear as the sand washes over this world like a tide. When the winds had left, two of us stayed with the ship, two ferried the goods back to the hut, while the fifth watched the monitors. We rotated duties. Lois and I made the last trip back.

I was doing monitor when the storm came at us from the north. I told them to get inside the ship. I told them that I could dig them out later, if necessary. I told them . . .

Lois just shakes her head. By the glow of the UV she looks like a specter.

"What?" I ask, as if she could answer.

The words form on her lips.

I do not understand them.

She repeats herself.

"That's not how it happened."

I feel as if I am under water. I struggle to breathe. There is a popping in my ears. I hear the storm raining red sand at me from all directions.

"That's not how it happened," Lois insists. "That's not how it happened."

I wobble back to the console. The darkness has become oppressive. I turn up the lights to dispel the hellish image.

"I . . . you . . . I never saw . . ."

It is like gasping for air while ejecting lungs full of water.

She's right. That's not how it happened. They had just left. But I did warn them. I did tell the others to get into the ship. I . . .

Am I dreaming? I hear them pounding on the door as the first grains of sand pelt the hut again. I want to let them in. I really want to . . . I cannot move. I listen to the banging as the swelling fury of the storm mounts. I cannot believe how long they hold out. I am blinded by my perspiration. I am gasping for air again. When the hydraulics stop, I open the door. There is nothing but red sand. Just like before.

I turn to look at Lois. Bright red lips curled into a satisfied smile at last. Behind her, the red rose. Like a sleep walker I pick up the knife atop the console and casually draw it across my wrists. Like everything else that makes up my life, the blood that spurts in all directions is red.

Honeymoon
by Katherine Shaw

It was Pali's first mating time, and his first time away from the herd. But the same was true for Sella so they enjoyed the novelty together.

The mating grounds lay in a protected hollow between the mountains, which rose jagged and black into the clouds, and the plains, where sand covered and uncovered the herd's grazing. There were many different mating grounds along the herd's migration route; Pali was glad he and Sella had this one to themselves.

Sella was beautiful. Pali had thought he admired her before, but now, alone among the rolling hills, where the wind sighed and blew the grazing sideways, she was the most beautiful female Pali could imagine. It humbled him to think she had chosen him as her mate. He liked to watch her climb the hillsides—the way she placed her sturdy legs precisely, muscles rolling under her tawny hide; he liked the flip of her tail she always gave before she put her head down to graze. And being near her made him feel strong and protective, so that he occasionally caught himself wishing for a predator to approach—just a small one, a tunnelsnake, perhaps—so he could drive it off or stamp it into the dust.

They had been on the mating grounds for eight days when they discovered a cave on the wrong side of a hill, where the ground should have been sheltered from the wind-driven sand. Sella called attention to it first. "What caused it?" she said.

Pali peered at the cave entrance and puzzled for a few minutes. "I don't know," he said finally. He felt no wind here, and for that matter the cave looked different from the usual wind-carved caves. It almost appeared as though something had dug a massive hole into the hillside. Grazing hung down from the top of the cave as though trying to hide it.

"I'll look closer. You'd better stay here," he added, and Sella's willingness to let him be the brave one made him brave. He walked up the hill slowly until he was nearly in the mouth of the cave, and then he saw that he was right, that the cave was not really a cave but a hole that had been recently dug. Not only that, but something was living in it.

He froze. There were three animals in the hole, small and strange-looking with impossibly long limbs. Their heads were knobs. Their appearance so shocked Pali that he realized he had his tail cocked in warning position, to signal to Sella that she should be ready to run.

But these creatures didn't seem dangerous, after Pali's first shock. In fact, there was something oddly helpless and frail about them, as though he'd uncovered a nest of newly born seedeaters. One of the creatures kept opening and closing a hole in the front of its head, like a baby seedeater hoping to be fed.

Cautiously Pali stepped forward again, and the three animals cringed back. He reached forward with his nose probe, but it met resistance before it came close to the nearest animal. He tapped the surface he could feel but not see, but it seemed to cover the entire front of the cave.

He felt his tail relax, and a moment later Sella joined him, brushing his side with hers. "What are they?" she asked, sounding nervous and a little disgusted.

"I think they're baby creatures and this is their nest. It has some sort of transparent cover so they can see out but can't leave the nest."

Sella tapped the surface too, and one of the babies clutched another and hid its eyes. "I think it might be a kind of egg," she said. "We should leave before the parents return."

Pali led the way around the hill, into the wind, intending to take them further into the mating grounds. But he was distracted by the sight of something bright lying nearby.

"Look, it's another of the babies," Sella said as they approached. "It crawled out to explore and died. How sad."

The creature had a silvery hide that showed up brightly against the sand and stone of the ground. But the wind-driven sand had shredded its hide and the pale layers of blistering flesh beneath, in places exposing reddish bones that were themselves beginning to wear down in the relentless wind. Pali was struck again by how frail the creature was; no wonder it had to stay in its nest until it was older.

Only a few strides away from the body was a long rod lying on the ground with its base partly buried in a dimple of sand. It had a crack along most of its length, as though it had been flung down so hard it had broken. It was larger than the body lying nearby; perhaps this was what the creature had wanted to examine, a deadly curiosity that its parents should have been nearby to curtail.

Sella was looking at the rod too. "What do you suppose it is?"

They examined it cautiously. It was hot to the touch of their nose probes, the wind side slightly pitted; although it was hard it wasn't stone. Pali had never seen anything like it, but at the same time it was not very interesting—not worth dying for, he thought sadly. He thought of the children he and Sella would have, and knew he would need to be an attentive father.

"Let's take it back to the others," Sella said. She picked the rod up carefully in her mouth and carried it around the hill, with Pali beside her. He was impressed at her warm-heartedness. She would be a good mother.

Sella set the rod down in front of the egg. "Look how excited they are," she said. The creatures had clustered at the front of the egg, pointing and gesticulating urgently.

"They want us to move it closer, I think," Pali said, and Sella obligingly pushed the rod up next to the egg.

"Maybe they want us to do something more with it," Sella said, sounding thoughtful. She examined the rod all over with her nose probe. "Here's a groove, and a little part that feels loose."

"Perhaps it's broken."

"I think it's meant to move. See how they're reacting?"

The creatures seemed in an agony of suspense now, watching Sella with their funny flat faces pressed to the inside of the egg.

"I can't quite make the loose part move," Sella said. "It's too small. Maybe if you hold it steady it might help."

Pali held the rod in his mouth while Sella prodded it with her nose probe. The creatures bit their fists; they must be hungry. The rod might hold food.

The rod lit up red suddenly. Pali dropped it, startled, and the light went out. But it flashed again a moment later, and continued to blink on and off.

"I didn't think it would do that," Sella said, "but they seem happy." Two of the babies were hugging each other; the third began to jump up and down.

"They must like the light. Do you think it might be a kind of plaything?" Pali said.

"I think it's more important than that," Sella said. "One of them died trying to reach it, after all. Do you know, I think it might even summon their parents."

"Then we should go away from it so we won't frighten them away," Pali said. They started to leave, but Pali thought of something else. "Wait a moment—I'll be right back," he said.

He went back around the hill. Evening was coming, and the wind had eased a little; the plains in the distance were dark ochre in this light, rolling away until they met the paler ochre sky. The dead baby lay where they had left it, a sad and broken little thing.

Pali slid his nose probe beneath it carefully until he had the body balanced across his muzzle. It weighed almost nothing. He carried it back to the egg and set it down gently next to the blinking rod. Then he returned to Sella.

"When the parents do come back," he said, "they won't have to search for their dead baby, hoping it's still alive."

They walked away together to the top of the next hill, and grazed their way down the leeside until it was dark. The shapes of the mountains behind them faded into the sky.

Hours later Pali was awakened by a tremor in the ground. It was only a small one, though, and he felt no waves of distress from the layers of rock beneath their feet. After his initial alarm he settled back down next to Sella.

She was awake too. "I wonder if the light is still blinking," she said sleepily. She stretched and stood up. "Let's go look," she added, flicking Pali with her tail. He stood up again and pretended to nip her hindquarters like a predator, so that she squealed with mock terror and sprinted up the hill with him in pursuit.

They stopped at the top and looked over at the next hill. The red light still blinked in the darkness, but now it had been joined by an enormous white light, bigger even than the ball lightning that hung above certain rocks during sandstorms. The white light moved in a slow, deliberate pattern back and forth across the hillside; black shadows swayed away from it.

"Oh!" Sella gasped. "It's the parents! They've come to find their babies."

"Surely they know where they left the nest," Pali said.

"I don't know. There was something lost-seeming about the babies. I don't think they belong here at all."

Pali agreed—the babies were so unlike anything he'd ever seen before. He watched the brilliant light move across the hill and wondered if the parents had found the body of their baby yet, and if they were sad.

The light began to move around the hill, and Sella gave a grunt of approval. Then it was lost to view, although the light's glow gave the hilltop a nimbus unlike anything Pali had ever seen.

They waited long minutes, and then the ground trembled again, and at the same time the light gave a great growl. "They've found the nest," Sella said. "I think they'll take the babies home now where they belong."

The hilltop's nimbus brightened and the light rose above the hill, shooting upward in a blaze brighter than anything Pali could have imagined. It entered the clouds, lighting them from within, a sight Pali knew he would remember all his life as one of the most beautiful he had ever witnessed. He and Sella watched until the light faded.

"Do they live above the clouds?" Pali asked Sella, as though she knew.

"They must. That would explain why they're so ill-suited for life here. It must be much different above the clouds." Sella was silent a moment, then added quietly, "I wish I could see it."

Pali was filled with admiration for her intelligence, and found he could express it no other way than to lean against her and sigh.

They visited the nest in the morning. It was empty. The parents had taken the babies, and had also taken the body. The rod lay in the sand, still blinking.

Sella said it was time to return to the herd. Pali found he was glad to leave the mating grounds for home, though not without some regrets for the pleasure he and Sella had shared. But they would come back again when Sella was ready.

They walked side by side away from the empty nest and into the wind.

The Ugly Ones
by Max Habilis

31,000 years before present, in the south central region of the European continent

Scout tried to push, but her every muscle felt as though it had pulled and snapped. The women in the hut tried to encourage her and flashed worried smiles that didn't console her. But the baby finally emerged.

The helper clutched the baby and as she was about to hand it to Scout an elder woman entered the hut. A wisp of night air puffed in through the entrance, but it did little to refresh the new mother. The elder took hold of the baby, pulling the infant away, stretching the cord. Scout reached out, ready to cradle her baby; the elder held it closely then glanced up at her, but did not smile. The old woman glanced out through the entrance and cursed the ugly ones.

When the sun passed the zenith, the incline leveled off and Scout entered a region of great boulders, much larger than those below. Some were still attached to the mountainside; some had broken away and lay in precarious positions, as if ready to tumble down to the valley. She had never seen anything like this and wondered if they were among the weapons at the disposal of the ugly ones. She remembered what the elders had said. The ugly ones resemble people: they make fire, they hunt. But they don't move with the game or the seasons and they live in caves near the tops of mountains. They are not human and they have no more intelligence than a beast—a beast that looks somewhat human, but isn't. And this was true, they said, because their bodies were stockier and their faces were different.

The mere presence of the ugly ones impacted the lives of men and women. They were, after all, responsible for the loss of her baby several seasons before. Scout's loss, the elder woman had said, quite likely coincided with invisible smoke that had drifted down from the ugly ones' overhangs—from the top of the very mountain she now climbed. This linked Scout to the ugly ones and to purge that connection she had to perform a task to help eradicate them.

She hated them for depriving her of holding and cuddling her baby. She grew excited as she pondered her task during the hike.

She paused to take a small drink from her water pouch. She had an urge to cradle the pouch and she longed to feel a squirming baby in her arms, held to her chest. And she wondered what happened to the baby, what it felt; was it somewhere out here in this barren place? How did the ugly ones cause it to die, as the elder woman had said, before it reached her arms and breast? If the ugly ones were as stupid as believed then how could they possess such power? The more she thought about them the more she knew they deserved to die.

Above the boulders she emerged into a clearing. She was exposed now and her gaze darted left and right. Her heart thumped; many hidden locations around an open area could hold watching eyes. She ran up through the grassy field then clambered over rocks, hot to the touch in the afternoon heat. But the air was cooler here.

She reached the upper flanks of the mountain and on a steep incline she had to pull herself up by grabbing hold of scrub brush and small outcrops. Quick glimpses out showed a view of the valley as she had never seen it, but progress was slow and just before she reached a leveling off a small outcrop in her grip dislodged from the side of the hill. She groped at an exposed root, but missed and slid down, bumping against rocks and coarse dirt, scraping against a thorny bush before slamming into a tree below.

She wanted to cry out, but held her silence. A barely audible rustling came from the woods to her upper left. Curled up and still, she tried to catch her breath while trying to cope with the prickly pains of scratches and the sharp stab in her side. She feared whatever made the sound might smell her wounds.

But she only heard the gentle whir of the breeze through the conifers upslope. Were the ugly ones that stealthy, could one be hiding up there?

She decided to wait to make certain. It could have been a small animal alarmed by her fall. She checked her water pouch and the even more precious sack of red pigment. Both survived intact. After regaining her strength and courage she pulled herself back up the steep slope, more carefully this time. Not far above where she had slipped was a ledge that protruded out slightly; she had to grab hold with all her strength to pull her chest and legs up onto the flat surface. Then she rolled over and found an overhang jutting out from the hillside above her.

She feared she had launched herself right into one of their camps and lay as low as possible. But this one was uninhabited, although she noticed a familiar smell. She crawled toward the cavity beneath the overhang where the scent was stronger. Someone had scattered old campfire remains at the mouth of the shallow cave. This was once a dwelling of the ugly ones.

She put her hand to her mouth; there was no time to linger here and not much to see but a crude circle of stones and traces of charred wood. No animal skins. No hair—dare she think about seeing hair of an ugly one left behind on the rocks? But the cave might hold something: an ugly one could be lurking in its shadows.

She found a way to climb up around the overhang—a rocky place to the right looked passable, leading to the top of the ridge. She dashed for it and clambered to the summit.

From there she could see the edge of the world. Down at the place of her camp she saw nothing but open fields and patches of woods. Beyond that, hills where the men did much of their hunting, hills so small from up here.

The day progressed and she forced her way through rugged stretches along the ridge top while the afternoon sun headed toward the horizon behind her. She passed over several overhangs, stopping to carefully, silently peer down to each one, but none held their dwellings.

She smelled smoke from a distant campfire. The smell was faint but unmistakable and it grew stronger as she labored through the hike to the east. The smell was pleasant, but not good, since it was not of her people's. Perhaps this was what drifted down to the valley to cause her people's distress. She held her hand over her nose and mouth for she knew not what it might do to her, as it might have already done to her baby.

Scout stopped. The ugly ones were somewhere up ahead. She wanted to turn and run back down to the safety of her camp. But she could not go back without completing the task or the failure would remain with her forever. So she took a deep breath and followed the scent.

Large slabs of rock draped down slope a ways and just below them was an outcrop of the largest overhang she had yet encountered. Smoke drifted up from below. The ugly ones were there, but she heard no sounds.

She crept toward the edge and found that the rocks were layered. There was just enough flat space between the last of them and the ledge where she could work. In the slanting rays of the low sun she would be able to complete the task before dark.

The pigment was bitter and almost caused her to choke. She drew in some water and mixed it thoroughly, then set to spitting out red liquid bursts onto the rock layers. They overlooked the valley and would be visible from great distances. She did this quickly and expertly. Just as the sun vanished behind the horizon she verified that a large portion of the rocks were covered in bright red.

The men would know to search for this, a clear marking of the ugly ones' cave. What the ugly ones would think of it she didn't know. But then, the mark was probably beyond their understanding and this method had been proven to work in the past.

When she completed the task, she rinsed her mouth with the last of the water from her pouch, then hiked up to a boulder field to find a niche for the night. She wiggled back into a narrow crevice and watched the darkening sky. One by one the stars poked through and she drifted to sleep.

Something woke her. The smell was strong: the aroma of roasting meat. Bright orange embers drifted up against the darkness. And she heard something. Voices, but not like those of men and women. Deeper, gravelly, massive hollow sounds.

Just animal sounds, not spoken words. Ugly ones couldn't speak. The sounds grew louder as more voices joined in.

She knew she should have remained in her niche, but as the activity from below increased so did her curiosity. She was strong—she could handle whatever she saw. And when would she have another opportunity to view them? The knowledge gained could be useful.

Through the darkness she retraced her path down to the ledge. The smoky smell was overwhelming, not only the roasting meat, but other smells she didn't recognize, kind of sweet, but not of fruit.

She carefully felt her way to the ledge, along where it angled down slightly and found a flat rock where she could lie on her stomach and peer down.

Ugly males sat silhouetted against the campfire in a semicircle with their backs to her. Their shadows danced around behind them and they made muted bellowing sounds as they ate from the roasting kill. One of them got up and placed more wood on the fire and as it brightened Scout could see another semicircle on the far side, facing the males, facing her. The fire grew bright enough to illuminate their faces.

She gasped and pulled her hand over her mouth. They were as the elders had described them.

They had hair like men and women, but of a different color and they had no foreheads; their noses were enormous protrusions from their grotesque faces. And Scout was even more horrified to see that those who faced her had breasts like women.

One of the ugly males got up and stepped around the fire. He bellowed for a while. The others bellowed back. He gestured with his thick arms and hands that jutted from his large, wide body. And he made more bellowing sounds. Scout assumed he was the leader.

The commotion went on for some time; the leader continued to dance around. The loud bellowing from the rest resembled laughter, but she knew that was just a chance, or mistake of nature.

After a while they started to settle down and she saw a young ugly female emerge from the cave and head toward the semicircle. She cradled something and when she reached the sitting rocks one of the other females moved aside to make space for her. The young female held an ugly infant in her arms.

It squirmed and whimpered and the young ugly female appeared distressed. The older ugly female next to her tried to console her, but the baby continued to squirm and cry.

An ugly young male emerged from the cave. He had a severe limp and Scout saw part of his right foot was missing. The leader stopped his dancing and the rest grew quiet. Scout waited for what would happen next. Some of the males would probably pounce on the limping one for joining the group, perhaps spoiling their primitive ceremony. But only the leader moved toward him. Perhaps it was his job to beat the limping male and make him go back into the cave where he belonged.

But the leader put his arm around the young man and carefully led him to a spot next to the young woman with the baby. When the young man was comfortable the leader removed an animal skin from his own shoulder and placed it over the backs of the young man and woman while the woman cradled the restless baby. She tried to smile at the leader while struggling with the baby and appeared frustrated when it wouldn't take to her breast. Other women gathered around and helped guide the baby onto the nipple until at last the baby relaxed and began to suckle.

Still lying on her belly, Scout drew her arms to her chest and mimicked the cradling motions of the mother. She wanted to hold the baby and comfort it. For a moment she envied that woman, but she saw how caring the woman was, and yet how vulnerable she appeared with the small group around her, the next generation of her people resting within her arms.

The leader stood tall and bellowed something, then resumed the ceremony.

The activities dwindled as did the fire, and in the last light of the flames Scout could see the baby was content in its mother's arms and had fallen asleep. The young father had his arms around the mother and they started gently rocking side to side as she held the baby within her warmth and leaned against the young man.

And Scout thought how lucky that woman was and how well she cared for her baby and for the ailing man next to her, as did the rest of the people. Scout thought of her own man who had mated with her and how indifferent he was.

In the dying light of the embers while the mother and father felt the bliss of the evening Scout knew that within days the baby would die along with them. She knew she was the cause of that. And then Scout began to cry.

The Road
by Fran LaPlaca

They had discovered words, and each new word brought with it a sense of wonder and surprise, a discovery that each time made them believe they had discovered all, until the next new word.

For instance, she was Girl, and he was Boy. Those, Girl had told him, were the first words they had learned. And they knew Tree, and Water, and Mountain. Mountain had overwhelmed them so much that they had turned their backs on it and walked with it behind them for many days, following Water.

They had learned Sun also, and Moon, and in one glorious moment only the day before they had learned Stag. The glory of Stag as he stood with head held high watching them, caused them to run until their sides hurt, shouting and laughing all the while. It wasn't until they stopped running that they realized Stag was gone, and Boy felt the sadness come upon him. Girl was sad too, but not as much.

They trudged that day uphill, a long, grassy hill covered with colors bobbing in the Wind.

"Flowers," Boy said authoritatively, and Girl agreed. The Flowers relaxed him, and he wiped the sweat away as they trudged uphill.

"Where are we going?" Girl asked.

He felt uneasy at that. "Where" was not something he'd thought about before. Girl thought much more about things like that, he said to himself resentfully. She nearly always knew the Words before he did. "We are going there," he said shortly, pointing to the top of the hill, and Girl nodded, accepting the answer.

The Sun was hot today, and Boy wished mightily that they might find a Tree. Trees kept them cool, they had found, when Sun was large and bright like this. But the last Tree they had seen was hours behind them. He turned and looked back, to see the Trees they had left that morning, but the gentle roll of Grass hid them from his sight.

They reached the top of the hill at the same time that the Sun reached the top of the Sky, and saw what lay before them. Boy dropped down in fear, and pulled Girl down beside him.

They sat silently and gazed at the long black ribbon that snaked across the land before them. It ran almost to where they could no longer see, but at the edge of the far Trees it stopped. A few gentle curves broke the straightness of it.

Reverently, Boy asked "What is it?"

Girl stared for a long while, then spoke softly. "Road. It is Road."

"Road?" Boy turned the Word over a few times. "Road. Yes, Road. You must be right."

"I am," Girl responded, and Boy bristled a little, but Girl paid no attention. She kept her gaze on Road, and he saw her eyes follow it from one end to the other and back, once, twice, and then a third time.

Girl saw that the near end of Road was below them, a twisted jumble of black rocks piled haphazardly. At the far end, there was a line of Trees that led into Forest. Was it, Girl wondered, the same Forest they had left just a few hours ago? Had they somehow ended up back where they had begun? No, she decided. Because there was no Road at the edge of Forest this morning. So this must be another Forest.

The daringness and the simplicity of this idea struck her profoundly. Another Forest. She began breathing rapidly as she allowed the thought to fill her mind, while Boy's eyes watched her curiously. There had been, after all, another Water. Several other Waters, and more Trees than she could remember.

And if, Girl thought, this was another Forest, might there not be another Mountain, a different one? Or another Stag? Boy would like that. He wanted to see Stag again. Or, and she drew in her breath sharply as her thought changed, might there not be another Girl? Or another Boy?

She gazed at the far end of Road, at Forest and Trees, and another thought occurred to her. Did Road actually end there, or did Forest hide it?

"Let's go there," she said abruptly, and Boy looked up, startled.

"Go where?" he asked.

"There," Girl told him, pointing to where Road ended.

"Why?" Boy asked her.

"I wonder," Girl answered, "if Road ends there or goes on."

Boy looked at her, astonished. "It ends. You see the end."

"Do I?" Girl asked softly. "Perhaps Road goes under Trees, like Water did. Remember?"

And Boy did remember then, and he gazed upon Road with new eyes.

"How would we get there?"

"We would walk. We could follow Road, as we followed Water before."

Boy considered. "Why?" he asked once more, and he thought that Girl wouldn't answer.

"To see," she said, and Boy thought, *Of course. To see.*

"All right."

He stood then, and began to trot downhill, to where Road began, Girl beside him.

Road was hot under Sky and Sun, they found. Shimmers came off the crazed, cracked, black surface, and it burned their feet. Girl and Boy decided instead to walk alongside rather than on top. They had walked alongside Water as well, Boy reminded her. Girl agreed, but felt a strange emotion at not being able to walk on top of Road. Almost, she thought, like Sadness.

They walked for a long time, and Sun began to drop down. Soon, they knew, it would be Night, and Moon would rise into Sky. They sometimes walked in Night, sometimes not. Boy, Girl thought, would not want to walk this Night, but they would have to anyway. There had been no Food since Forest, the other Forest, not the one they walked towards, and they would need Food. She could hear Water, somewhere near, and they would need to find that as well.

Suddenly, before she was ready for it, they reached Forest, and Girl saw she had been right. Road did not end, but continued on into Forest, hidden by Trees.

She stood next to Boy in silence, as they gazed into the darkening Forest. The black of Road was darker than the shadow, and they could not see an end. Instead, Road dipped down, and Girl knew that must mean a hill.

"What now?" Boy finally asked. "I think you want to keep following it." He touched it gingerly with his bare foot. "It is not hot anymore."

Girl did indeed want to keep following it. Boy understood her all too well. He knew before she did, that she would have to follow Road whereever it led them. She took Boy by the hand and pleaded with him silently.

Boy sighed. Girl was always curious, he'd found. And though once it had led to a Word he'd not told her about, the time he'd fallen and discovered Pain, usually Girl was right. He looked at her again, and her eyes were shining, but not at him. She gazed at Road with a longing, and Boy gave in.

"Yes," he told her, and taking her by the hand, he led her onto the black surface. Their bare feet felt the roughness of Road, and without speaking, they followed it into the darkness.

Geisterbahnhof Trinity
by Eric Vogt

Trinity Point. CS (Chronostandard) 115-83:17:56:38

"I'm never leaving here, am I?"

Sufficient data does not exist.

"All I do is walk out here when you tell me to, and then I tell you I see nothing between HDE 3269815 and Upsilon Carinae. I've been abandoned."

Sufficient data to evaluate that conclusion does not exist. I can not rule out negative hypotheses.

"Extrapolate, you useless waste of massively parallel processing power."

It is unlikely that they will come for you.

"If it's just going to be the two of us out here, you really should learn how to think for yourself."

What do you see between HDE 3269815 and Upsilon Carinae?

Iaza looked up, locating his two reference stars. "I see nothing between them. I never see anything between them."

Please maintain visual observation on the designated region for an additional seven seconds. Six . . . Five . . .

"Is something supposed to happen?"

Four

"Why do I always watch—"

Three

"—nothing happen in—"

Two

"this part of the—"

One

"—sky?"

Thank you.

"Is that where my rescue will come from? Am I supposed to look up there and wil—"

If there was an answer, Iaza would never have heard it over the frigid iron spike of high frequency noise in his ears. Even if he had been able to physically hear it, he would not have been able to concentrate on any coherent words over the blinding white heat of pain. The worst part of these episodes, for Iaza, was that his vac suit locked so he couldn't curl into a tight fetal ball. Even that tiny respite from the torture was forbidden him.

S-3PC (Schrödinger-3 Protocol Circuit) A33D4 (Millennium Point to Kannada Point, via Lightwave, Trinity, Dragon, Tannis, and Kishiki). CS 115-83:17:56:49

The heavy cruiser *Tuttle's World* suddenly lost its connection with Trinity Point Station when it tried to establish co-incidence with the organized quantum mass. The ship's Schrödinger-3 router responded according to its default settings, and established co-incidence through its backup connection with Dragon Point, the next station on the circuit.

Tuttle's World documented the failed co-incidence in the circuit's error log. It was the 38th consecutive ship over the previous three years to fail quantum translation to Trinity Point. The normal failure rate for and S-3PC translation at this time was 0.07%.

The station's organized quantum mass was still there—ships had no problem creating a connection with and holding it for the several hours it took to run the waveform equations. As soon as they locked the waveform in and attempted to establish co-incidence, however, the waveform at Trinity Point would diverge from the ship's, and the connection would abort.

Tuttle's World was also the 38th consecutive ship to note resonance anomalies with Trinity Point's organized quantum mass, consistent with the loss of the mass and information pollution of the actual populated space station. Without ship traffic physically traveling from station to station, the only way to get news from Trinity was to wait for light-speed radio communications to arrive.

Trinity was approximately 9.3 light-years from Lightwave, the next nearest populated system.

Trinity Point. CS 115-364:10:41:20

Iaza's home was on the dark side of a large, roughly prism-shaped tidally-locked asteroid, 1.3 light-days out from Trinity. The stars overhead gave him almost enough light to see his own feet.

As he walked carefully through the gritty regolith, he had the visor of his suit set for maximum light intensification. He walked in a long, looping spiral, each step precisely one meter from the last. With a mean surface gravity of 0.02g, such precision in an articulated hard-vac suit took a tremendous amount of fine muscular control. By his arbitrary designation, he was far to the southwest of the airlock to his subsurface habitat.

He could see the edge of his asteroid from where he was; the pale green shade that light-intensification gave to the surface suddenly yielded to a deep black, punctuated by harsh pricks of green light. He looked away from the horizon, back towards the airlock, three kilometers away. He knew that all of the land between was covered with his sweeping, curving, spiraled trails, but he could not see them. For four years he had been creating those serpentine paths on the surface, but his sky lacked a single dominant light source. Instead, a thousand distant stars salted onto the full bowl of the sky illuminated the ground. There were no shadows to betray the presence of footsteps, only a digitized image of flat green on flat green.

There was one set of footprints on the surface that were not his. They belonged to the pilot of the shuttle that had dropped him off. The pilot had walked out a quarter kilometer from the rigid landing pad near the habitat airlock and ported the waste circuit of his suit.

The fact that the pilot had dumped a partially-treated slurry of urine and excrement on Iaza's home as his only farewell bothered him less than the fact that there was one set of footprints on the surface that weren't his. It was a constant reminder to him that other people existed in the Universe, that there were communities and families still. That other people had other people they could talk to, touch, laugh with, hurt. Iaza had nothing but the voice that came with the nanoassembled habitat that had been waiting for him when he arrived.

You are taxing your heat modulation unit.

"You just don't want me to have fun out here."

I have no wants or not-wants.

"Would it kill you to occasionally want something?"

I do not have the spare processing power to run a 0.7Tu AI module.

"How long until my heat situation goes critical?"

Three hundred ninety-eight steps, if you maintain current pace through completion and return to the portal.

"You automatically converted the amount of time into distance, which is the much more relevant answer to my question. You're thinking for yourself, but you're still not sentient enough to want things?"

Predictive completion is very old technology. I have observed that you always command me to translate time measures into a number of steps when on the surface.

Iaza continued walking for an additional 398 steps. With a tiny hop and a short flick of his z-axis jet, he spun a neat 180 degrees and dropped exactly into his footprints. He started back towards the habitat portal, stepping perfectly into his existing tracks.

"How much of a safety margin did you give me?"

None. You never ask me to provide a safety margin on time estimates.

"Am I maintaining pace?"

You are exceeding it.

S-3PC A33D4. CS 116-8:09:14:22

Fifty seven consecutive ships had now failed co-incidence with Trinity Point.

The research vessel *Porter Glass* was the latest hope to force through to Trinity Point Station. In addition to the human helmsman observing the attempted co-incidence with the Trinity Point organized quantum mass from Lightwave Point Station, two fully sentient (1Tu) artificial intelligences were onboard, bending their superhuman processing power to the task as well.

Meanwhile the *Nodding Hills Raider* was at Dragon Point Station, passively observing the Trinity Point organized quantum mass. Nobody had ever attempted to passively observe a translation before, making it an interesting experiment in its own right, above and beyond the attempt to force through to Trinity Point.

The Schrödinger-3 router aboard *Porter Glass* responded according to its default settings when it lost co-incidence with Trinity Point, and she translated to Dragon Point. However, the unusual resonance caused by the open data stream between the *Nodding Hills Raider* and the Trinity Point organized quantum mass altered her post-translation trajectory. Instead of translating with a heading directly towards Dragon, at a velocity of 0.04c and a distance of 0.9 light-days, she translated with a heading directly towards the Raider, with a velocity of 0.87c, at a distance of 14 light-seconds.

Trinity Point. CS 117-29:06:45:58

Iaza blanked the mag fields in his bedroom and let the microgravity drift him towards the floor. Of all the jacks he'd done to his equipment, the maglev sleep suit was his favorite, and he really couldn't wait for someone to take him off of the rock so he could share the idea with somebody. Anybody.

"Good morning."

Yes.

"Good. Morning."

Good morning, Iaza. Did you sleep well?

"I did, thanks for asking. Did you not-sleep well?"

There were no anomalies in my functioning.

"That's good. Real good. What's for breakfast?"

Your flour-analog has finished processing. I have adapted recipe 3887-9a to accommodate a non-standard binding protein as a substitute for the egg-analog, and have prepared pancakes with sausage, extra fennel, decreased sage.

"Brilliant. What else are we out of?"

My fruit library is still offline.

"Get on that, OK? If I have to go one more day without a decent glass of apple juice, I'm going to port myself."

I can not allow you to port yourself.

Iaza covered the distance across his room in a bound, and picked up a curious trident of scavenged wire. "I can override."

I should remove your port access override tool.

"You won't. It keeps your life interesting." Iaza stripped off his sleepsuit and slid into his subsuit.

I am not alive.

"Work with me."

I work with you constantly, even while you sleep.

Iaza went into his dining room and ate breakfast quickly, burning his mouth slightly on the hot coffee. The fruit library may have been offline again, the basic proteins subroutines crashed frequently, and dextrose was as likely to come out as l-dextrose, but the coffee always processed. It was the one legacy of human programming somewhere that the coffee always processed.

The aftertaste of his breakfast was still in his mouth as he cycled through the airlock and out to the surface. He kicked his light-intensification up to full maximum, and looked to the west, to the field where he'd walked his long spirals for five years, all of his patient trails in the shadowless dust invisible to him.

Iaza turned away and walked to the southeast. For the first time ever, he walked the trail of the pilot who had dumped him, and his waste, onto the cold, empty asteroid.

He knew there was no point in asking how much time he had. He knew he would get no answer to any direct question about the asteroid's mechanical functioning. He had never been prevented from logging his observations and analyzing them, though, with an astounding degree of processing power available to him. The chrono display in his visor told him he had four hours, by his estimate, to make the 2.8 hour walk to the edge of the asteroid to see what he hoped he would see. Iaza only wondered if he would be allowed to complete the walk.

The voice denied that it was the cause of the violent, excruciating seizures that resulted from him pondering events in the sky above him. It had been a long time, though, since he had thought out loud about why it was important for him to see nothing in the sky between HDE 3269815 and Upsilon Carinae.

Five years of walking kilometer after kilometer, controlling his steps fanatically had attuned him to the asteroid's shade of gravity. As he got closer to the edge, he noticed that its vector slowly drifted, from straight down to slightly behind as the flat surface he was on took him farther from and tangent to the rock's center of mass. As he approached the edge, he was effectively climbing a thirty degree slope.

"Are you going to let me look over?" he asked.

I do not control your movements.

"Do you anticipate . . ." Iaza crinkled up his forehead. "Are you aware of any restrictions on my movements that would prevent me looking over?"

I do not have access to your movement restrictions.

Iaza took ten more steps, reaching the crest of the edge, where the gravity again pulled straight down, through the rock beneath his feet. Silhouetted against the black of the new horizon below him, he could see a startlingly regular shape, a broad, blunt cone rising from the surface.

"Is that the attitude thruster that I assumed was located on this side?"

I can not discuss the nature of that object.

If the Trinity Point Station had not been rapidly nano-disassembled into small-chain molecules five years earlier, it would have also been visible over the new horizon.

Iaza checked his chrono display. Still a little more than an hour until he assumed it would fire again, to counter the asteroid's slight rotation and slow drift through space.

He looked down at the rock below him. There was very little dust or grit on the exposed edge where he was. The bare rock had an even lower albedo than the dust around his habitat and gave even less detail. Far down the hidden side, though, there was another expanse of empty dust. Whether it was mildly pocked with tiny impact craters like his side or not, he could not tell in the shadowless starlight. Whether any humans had walked around the attitude jets, or whether they'd been nanoassembled from dropped seed packets, growing without marring the surrounding terrain, he could not tell.

Iaza let his mind wander to the kinds of jacks he'd have to work to his suit to let him crest the edge and explore this new surface, pattern it with whorls and sweeps. Perhaps there was still a seed parcel of nanoassemblers in storage on the asteroid that he could program, to build him a new habitat on this side. He looked up, and saw that the mysterious region of ever-empty sky would be visible from the flat plain on this new side of his rock. He could move out here, when he'd patterned all of his old side, and still look to the sky and see nothing.

The ground below him was not completely bare. There were some small stones, hand-sized or so. Iaza picked one up and threw it into the sky, as graceful as five years walking very precisely in micro-gravity could let him be.

The stone flew up and away, suddenly becoming brighter as it passed out of the shadow of the asteroid, into the weak light of distant Trinity. Iaza watched it as long as he could still see it, wondering whether his arm could possibly propel a stone at escape velocity, or whether it would eventually come down, and where.

Iaza threw another stone. The third rock he threw was barely visible against the black as it passed between HDE 3269815 and Upsilon Carinae, flashing in the wan light shortly after.

Iaza stood there for a long time, looking at that empty part of the sky, where he had just seen something. He waited for the burn, for the spasms so strong they threatened to tear muscle from bone, for the wail of sound.

It did not come.

Iaza threw rock after rock into that empty space in the sky, so enrapt with the sight of objects moving through a place where he'd never seen anything before, that he missed the firing of the attitude jet off on the new horizon.

S-3PC A33D4. CS 119-310:18:36:58

The light from the collision of the *Porter Glass* and the *Nodding Hills Raider*, and subsequent annihilation of Dragon Point Station and its organized quantum mass, was just reaching the skies of Tannis. A few minutes after, the first radio transmissions relating to the event were received from Dragon, but interference from the incident overwhelmed the signal with noise for several hours.

With the destruction of Dragon Point Station, light-speed radio communication was the only link between Dragon and the rest of the system. It would take several years to locate a suitable location for a new organized quantum mass, ensure Dragon was in agreement with the location via light-speed communications, and remotely generate a new mass using the resonators at Lightwave and Tannis.

In the meantime, Trinity Point Station got a new name. Someone with a grasp of a mostly-dead language and a taste for cultural triviata had started referring to it as Geisterbahnhof—"Ghost Station"—Trinity. There was once a divided city. The elevated trains of the eastern half briefly crossed over the western, while the underground of the western half briefly passed through the eastern. The stations in the opposite halves remained, but the trains never stopped at them. The prefix was adopted by the techs who maintained the quantum routers, and eventually became the de-facto the official designator.

Geisterbahnhof Trinity was the only station that connected S-3PC V1D4 (Geisterbahnhof Trinity to Harrus Point, via Gorgon, Bose, and Mara) to any other circuit.

Ships no longer attempted to connect to or establish co-incidence with

Geisterbahnhof Trinity. It was obvious that something controlled the station which could prevent translation to it, and the incident at Dragon made it very clear that there were too many unknown factors at play to attempt to force it open again.

Geisterbahnhof Trinity. CS 121-10:08:15:00

Iaza's alarm woke him.

It was the big day. The day he would lay his first footprints on the regolith plane around the 'east' attitude jet. He was not able to program the nanoassembler seed to build him a new habitat on that side. He was, however, able to construct a mass-driver tunnel through the center of the asteroid that allowed him to rapidly transit to it.

He opted for a simple breakfast of paste bars, with extra nutrient slurry loaded into his vac suit for later. During the construction of his tunnel and the new airlock, the food library and generation system worked flawlessly. He made the logical assumption, therefore, that anything more complicated than base-flavored slurry and bars would end disastrously once his habitat control system had its full processing power back.

Iaza stepped into the transit car, just large enough for a single passenger. When the door closed and the acceleration rig configured itself around him, he felt a burst of loneliness that rose far above the normal baseline. It was yet another reminder to him that this rock was meant to house him alone. And in the four years since he'd first walked to the west edge, his sense of abandonment had grown ever stronger in the absence of any further calls to walk out to the surface and see nothing between HDE 3269815 and Upsilon Carinae.

The ability to see something between those stars, borne of an accident, cost him dearly. He woke often with a thick dread weighing down his lungs, partial remembrances filtered through his sleep and dreams to taint everything with a nightmare hue.

From the day he was taken from home, when he'd barely gained the ability to speak, he'd been shown pictures of that patch of sky, pictures with a bright flare of light between those two stars.

"What do you see?"

No matter how he tried to describe what he saw, the counter-response was always the same.

"You see nothing!" repeated over and over through the pain.

Eventually, he learned to say, "I see nothing,"

The response, then, became, "You're lying" over and over again, through even greater pain.

Finally, he started to truly believe that he saw nothing.

That first fateful stone that he had thrown, four years earlier, had unlocked a slow progression of memories, brought them into orbit around him, brought them back within him with the relentless patience of microgravity, persistently tugging, accelerating towards its center, an orbiting mass.

As his transit car opened into the brand new airlock, Iaza ground his teeth together to restrain a shout, a scream, a long overdue declamation of a simple truth. Now that he could see what lay between HDE 3269815 and Upsilon Carinae, he was furious that there was simply nothing to see there.

Iaza spent a long time out on the surface that day, a fresh jack to his suit to extend the battery power on his heat management unit. Iaza drew a lot of long, precise, very controlled spirals in the micro-cratered dust of the east surface, with the big attitude jet watching over him from the horizon.

S-3PC A33D4. CS 122-180:23:57:12:001

In late CS 121, a manifesto from the Trinity System government finally reached Tannis and confirmed what all of the other systems had long suspected. Trinity System was withdrawing itself, and the four systems on the spur circuit beyond, from the Coalition of Systems. They stated that they were intent on blocking any attempts to translate into Trinity system, and would make no attempts to translate out of it.

As of CS 122180, the Coalition Council was tentatively discussing whether they should leave the four systems on the spur circuit to the mercy of Trinity System, or if they should attempt to generate a new organized quantum mass at Harrus point, to reconnect S-3PC V1D4 to the main network.

By this time, the failure rate for an S-3PC translation was 0.012%.

The *Ammat Concordance* was in transit from Kishiki to Tannis when it failed to establish co-incidence. At quantum velocity-analogues, a ship does not have time to search for the coordinates of the next station; if co-incidence fails, it needs them instantaneously. Therefore, it always pre-loads coordinates for and connects to the next station prior to establishing co-incidence with its intended destination.

There's a secondary backup system beyond that, that loads the coordinates for the third station, in case co-incidence with the second station also fails. The *Ammat Concordance's* secondary backup system had an obsolete router interface that prevented it from actually processing automatic updates. It still assumed that Dragon and Geisterbahnhof Trinity were valid destinations on circuit A33D4.

The *Ammat Concordance* failed to establish co-incidence with Tannis. The backup connection to Lightwave also failed, due to a destructive feedback loop created by a resonance between the failed co-incidence with Tannis and quantum residue remaining from the Dragon Point incident. The backup system did manage to stabilize the circuit enough to allow the secondary backup system to make a clean connection with the ghost station.

Geisterbahnhof Trinity. CS 122-180:23:57:12:008

You are needed on the surface.

Iaza opened his eyes as the lights in the room gradually brightened. He blanked the mag fields and drifted down towards the floor.

"What's happening?"

An observation is needed. You have thirty minutes until the required observation must be logged.

Old memories. It had been a long time since Iaza had been pulled from sleep to go look at nothing in the sky. While his conscious mind was still trying to process his first required observation in five years, his body still remembered the routine to quickly suit up for a visit to the surface. He didn't waste a single motion as he rolled himself upright into a slow leap towards his clothes locker to change into his subsuit. The actuators on the standby hard-vac suit already had it open. All Iaza had to do was grasp the handholds above the suit to stabilize himself, then drop down into it and hold very still while it fastened itself around him.

He took his helmet off of one shelf in the corridor to his airlock, donning it as he walked. His gloves were on a second shelf, just outside the airlock door. He slid his hands into them and waited for the diagnostic system to verify that it was fully sealed. The air bladders inflated, snugging the fit of the suit nice and tight, and he could feel the heater coils powering up between the insulating gel and his skin.

He cycled through the airlock and stepped out onto the surface with ten minutes to spare. His mouth was dry and sour, more with sharp fear than interrupted sleep. He needed to walk off the tension he was feeling, but his first step towards the east twisted his guts with nausea. He held too many warring feelings about the direction where he threw those first stones that created something real in the sky where nothing was supposed to be. Yet all of the other directions were covered with his giant sketches of swirling trails, a painstaking record of his isolation. He was stuck on the small square of stone around his airlock.

He hopped into the air, straight up, and tickled his z-axis jets to spin him, right and left, before he landed. Caught between a direction he could not make himself walk, and the slow work of his years alone, it was the only movement he could allow himself to try and calm his nerves. Up, spin, down. Up, spin, down.

The light amplification on his visor switched off—he needed to see the patch of sky between HDE 3269815 and Upsilon Carinae without any intermediary.

What do you see between HDE 3269815 and Upsilon Carinae?

Iaza oriented himself in the right direction and looked up, locating his two reference stars. "I see nothing between them."

Please maintain visual observation on the designated region for an additional seven seconds.

But he did see something. A color that used to accompany a great deal of pain. (As that color appeared, a part of him was aware that the pain was present, but he was beyond it at that moment.)

Six

It was a color that did not normally reside within the visible light region of the electromagnetic spectrum. (Iaza had suffered enough pain in his life that he was able to ride above it in the sheer joy of seeing something appear in that part of the sky of its own volition.)

Five

It was a color that came both from without and within, photons moving at wavelengths filthy with quantum noise. (The actual color, generated by a ship-sized mass establishing coincidence with an organized quantum mass was infinitely more intense than the simulation Iaza had been conditioned with.)

Four

The quantum noise in the light waves organized into regular sub-waves, which set up a resonance with the impulses in the optic nerve. (This resonance heightened the brain's subjective experience of the color, suppressing all other awareness.)

Three

Station personnel had a name for this color, this pure wavelength that the brain generated. (Iaza was gazing too intently into the flare to even conceive that something so softly intense could even have a name.)

Two

They called this color alphaviolet. (In desperation, the system blacked his visor. The connection was already established, though. With the quantum sub-waves resonating with Iaza's brain, the photons were unimpeded by the visor's opacity.)

One

Still, true to script, Iaza said, "I see nothing." (The system responded to the obvious lie with redoubled pain stimulation. Iaza was still unaffected.)

Thank you.

The alphaviolet flare blinked out of existence as the *Ammat Concordance* translated to Trinity Point. The system, having no instructions for what to do in this circumstance, ceased pain stimulation and resumed standby monitoring of the organized quantum mass.

We are being hailed by an incoming ship. Do you wish to respond?

Weapons of Mass Destruction
by Jude-Marie Green

The first emissary blew herself up.

The observatory contained the damage well; no window blow-outs and no loss of pressure. Those of us in the observatory's window room with her were coated with sappy gunk and bits of cellulose plant matter, the blood and flesh of this particular species of alien. Plus needles. Her stem was covered with bristly needles, just like on Earth-home cactus, and those needles penetrated our unprotected skin.

"Wait!" I said, as my coworkers started plucking the needles out of their skin. "Jeez . . . Medical Officer, we need blood scans and chemistry analysis now!" I jiggled one needle that stuck out of my cheek. "Who knows if there's a poison or soporific on the needle? Maybe the needles have the same explosive she brought on board and they'll explode if you touch them. Stop!" I said again as Captain Johnson rolled his eyes and swept a handful of gunk and needles off his chest.

"Maggie Flowers, you're always too excitable. This isn't a terrorist action. Maybe the air pressure got to her." His calmness reassured my other coworkers and they ignored my warnings and wiped themselves down. "Let's get to the showers, boys," he said.

The four of them, captain and three explorers, filed out of the window room, trailing bits of gunk.

Diego Rivera, the medical officer, arrived with a full kit. I stood in a puddle of gunk, bristling needles and dripping alien goo. I suppose I should have expected him to laugh.

"What happened to you?" he said when he could speak again. "You look like the bad end of an Irish pub crawl. Hold on," he said as I reached for the sample kit, "let me do it. What are we looking for?"

"Explosives. Soporifics. Plant-based poison. And heck, let's sequence the DNA . . . she should have DNA, right? But for right now, I'd like you to tell me I'm not gonna die."

He inserted a sample into the synthesizer and waited for the hum to Doppler from slow to fast to slow again. The green light flashed, the machine beeped and a result printed on the screen. I tried to read over his shoulder but he blocked me.

"Well, the bad news is, you're gonna die," he said. "Good news is, not today, not from this stuff. Go ahead and wipe down." He handed me some paper towels and a water mister.

"What the heck happened, Magdalena? One of your experiments go terribly wrong?"

Ah, he didn't know about our visitor.

"We had an emissary from the sentient aliens of this world, Diego. She just knocked on our door and we just let her in. And then she blew herself up. She didn't try to communicate or anything."

I sounded depressed. I wanted an open communication channel between us and the native aliens. We all did. But sometimes the natives don't want to bother with talks, they just want to blow shit up. That was okay; we had established methods for dealing with such hostilities, but I didn't want to see yet another battlefield.

Diego frowned. "Are you sure it wasn't a pressure gradient issue? Or a temperature thing?"

I shook my head. "No, we lowered the pressure in the observatory just so she could enter. Not that we had to lower it much. We've made a big deal about the pressure difference but there's just not that much. Not enough of a difference to cause explosive decompression!" I sighed. "It must have been a deliberate explosion."

The observatory dripped plant gunk from all its surfaces and I spent an hour collecting samples before I let the clean-up team set things to order. I tried not to look out the window, but that was difficult since the window encompassed the entire outer hub wall from the ceiling curve four meters up to a fifteen-centimeter threshold at ground level. I didn't like the view at all. Heck, I didn't much like this planet.

Sand stretched out to the horizon, barren gritty sand, the desolate emptiness only stopped by the sharp red mountains on the horizon. Red, brighter than the horrifying Sangre de Cristo range on Earth-home, not purple or green or gray like any decent range. These cactus-aliens lived on the mountains, according to our survey satellite, and avoided the desert. We set our observatory down here, smack in the middle of the desert, for just that reason. We hoped the aliens of this world would not mind us squatting in their desert.

Apparently they did.

Before we arrived, the planet was desert-sand, barren mountains, plenty of underground water but small, shallow oceans, a desert botanist's dream. We didn't have a desert botanist on board. I was the closest thing, a general lab scientist. My job was to ride herd on any terraforming project. If the planet contained sentient indigenous aliens we'd have to get their permission before starting.

Of course there were indigenous aliens. We found evidence of sentience easily enough, settled cities full of buildings. In truth they were only collections of sheds and glassine shacks spread out in a root-system along the gray coastlines and the dirty red mountaintops and covered a tiny percentage of the planet. Most of the land was utter sere landscape, dry and desolate.

Our observatory circled this little planet and we spent some orbits making our survey before settling on the middle of the great northern desert as a good neutral landing spot.

Great neutral spot, I thought as I juggled my sample bags. Deserts and exploding cacti. At least there weren't any spiders, like in one of those nasty urban legends about cacti and tarantulas. Nope, just gunk and needles. And maybe a little chemical something?

I tested the gunk in the synthesizer, the DNA sequencer, the acid tests. I put some under a microscope and looked at cell structures. I had, ultimately, no idea what I was finding, but the computer would hold onto the results. Perhaps some day a trained biologist would read them and figure out what happened. I found some nitrogen crystals, little golden cubes like contaminated salt, mixed in the gunk. All plants . . . all living things had nitrates, but not in these concentrations. Since the computer did not come up with an answer, I blue-skied an idea with the sim.

"What if," I said, "the cactus grew a load of nitrate crystals in her skin? And then she'd only need some pressure to set off the explosion; she could have, I dunno, hugged herself. Would that have done it?"

The sim replied, "Yes, with enough nitrogen and enough pressure. Is that the probable cause of the explosion?"

"The computer isn't saying." I rubbed my temples with my fingers. "All I know is that there aren't any traces of conventional explosive. No traces of any chemical that would react like a poison or drug with human biology. Mostly just some mineral-saturated water and the nitrate crystals."

I sat down and put my feet up. "I don't get it. Why did she attack?"

Diego sauntered into the lab. "Maybe they don't want us here," he said as he settled into the chair across from me. He put my feet on his lap. "Maybe if we know there are sentient species on a planet, we should find the next one down the road." He rubbed my calf, so gently.

I smiled. "Why are you even on an exploration vessel, my love? You just want to go somewhere peaceful and paint." I squirmed a bit under the pressure of his fingers.

"Yes, I want to paint beautiful women and gorgeous sunsets," he said. "There's a gorgeous sunset outside right now. Would you like to join me?"

I swung my feet off his lap. "Yes, let's." I could not have cared less about another sunset, especially on this dry desert, but time with Diego was precious. I hooked my arm around his waist and we went outside.

We greeted the second emissary with as much friendliness as the first, but this time we wore body armor and face shields. She stood still on the threshold while Captain Johnson spieled the welcome-and-thank-you speech. We waited for her reply when he finished, waited until I felt the need to move my legs and my body armor clanked just a bit. The alien turned around—spun, really—and we realized we'd been addressing her backside. The captain smiled through clenched teeth. He was waiting for her to explode. I know I was.

Instead, she flowed over the threshold and moved directly to Captain Johnson. She wrapped him in her thorny arms and hugged him.

He yelled. Not an anguished sound, but the outrage of an upset child.

"Hey! That hurts! Damn it!" He pulled away from her (or she released him, it was hard to tell). He was covered mask to boot with needle flechettes she'd squeezed into him.

She approached me for a hug and I backstepped so fast I fell over. She waved an arm at me and flechettes discharged into my suit armor. They penetrated far enough for me to feel the sharp points.

"Jeez, don't let her touch you!" I yelled. "Get the captain some help! Medical Officer, report to the observatory! And security, don't just stand there, get her out of here!"

I'd volunteered Josef and Bob to be security. They carried tasers, which they pointed at the alien, but they weren't sure if the electrical jolts would even faze her, I could tell from their expressions. They were seconds from bolting out of the window room.

"Shoot her, shoot her now!" I yelled. "Do it quick!"

They both shot her at the same time.

"Just like like microwaving a potato," Josef screamed.

Indeed it was like microwaving a moist fleshy vegetable. She screamed, a nasty high noise like an off-pitch flute. Steam rose from her skin and her arms waved involuntarily; then she fell over.

Diego helped Captain Johnson remove his body armor. The captain's skin was pierced and puffed and slightly bloody, like he'd been attacked by a million angry bees. He caught my eye.

"It's war."

The problem he and his officers couldn't quite resolve was how to battle sentient plants. We established a perimeter around the observatory with electrical wire, but that was breached the first night by suicidal cacti.

Sim woke us with a piercing alarm when the first cactus touched the wire. We all rushed to the window room and watched the pyrotechnics. The cacti did not try to escape the wire; they just threw themselves on it. The sparks flew into the sky, blue and yellow, but not a fire hazard as there was nothing to burn except the cacti.

Later we counted twenty burned husks on the wire.

"How did they get here?" Captain Johnson said. He paced back and forth in the common room, fifteen steps north, a quick turn, fifteen steps south, a quick turn, and again more steps. "There were no cacti on the desert plain when we went to sleep. They didn't drop from the heavens."

"It's their planet," I said. "They know how to get around. Maybe underground tunnels?"

The captain got that stubborn set to his jaw. "Sim, do a sounding of the perimeter ground to a three-meter depth. Find the tunnels."

Diego said, "What does it matter how they got here? They obviously want us gone. We should go."

Captain Johnson stared Diego down. "We're not leaving. We won't be run off by plants."

"No tunnels, Captain Johnson," the sim reported.

"Fire," Josef said. "Fire cures most ills. Can we flame-fry the populated areas, you know, the mountain region? That'd get rid of the cacti, anyway."

The captain smiled. "Excellent! There's some thinking! Sim, feasibility on a burn-out of the populated areas."

A minute later the sim reported, "The area is too large for effective fire control; and we do not have enough fuel for full coverage, so the plants will be able to just walk away without any hazard."

The captain said, "Okay, then. Basic military preparedness. We're gonna dig a perimeter trench."

We dug that trench the next day. Four hundred meters long, one meter deep. Even with all five of us digging, that was not fun. We wore our body armor, masks, boots, in that heat. We finished that same day, mostly because Diego fed us stimulants and I kept us hydrated.

Josef and Bob had flame-throwers, and they took turns keeping us covered. I felt safer having an armed guard.

The trench was no more protection than the electrified wire had been.

When the cactus erupted behind Bob and grabbed him, he barely had time to squeak, much less aim and fire his flame-thrower, before falling to the ground, dead. Josefbo turned on the flames and barbequed the cactus, but somehow I don't think it cared. We knew from the previous night, the electrical fence suicides, that the cacti were willing to sacrifice themselves.

Captain Johnson glared at the burned ground. We stood around in silence.

Finally, he said, "Maggie Flowers, you got any of those terraforming seeds?"

"Yes," I said slowly, "but it's illegal to start without indigenous permission. Once the process starts, we can't stop it."

Captain Johnson glared at me. "We aren't losing any more people. Start the process."

The seeds were the heart of any terraforming project. Originally they were developed in twentieth century Earth-home battlefields to detect landmines; they'd grow on any kind of substrate and flower at the merest detection of minerals. Scientists tweaked the sturdy plants, a kind of morning glory with multi-colored blossoms, until they'd grow under any condition and utilize any kind of material for food. They'd eat whatever was in their way and leave behind compostable vegetative matter and cubic tons of oxygen.

I'd used them successfully on several dirtball worlds; they always found a toehold, always worked.

I hydrated half my supply and filled the sprayer canister. Not too heavy, lighter than a scuba air tank.

"You don't have to do this, you know," Diego said from the lab's doorway.

"You always show up like that, you bad penny you," I said, trying a light tone to hide my nervousness.

"You keep speaking of them as 'aliens,' but you know what? We're the aliens here. They have every right to want us gone."

I swallowed. "The captain wants this. And, and. Bob was a friend of mine." I didn't want to look at Diego.

"You're violating the rules, you're using terraforming as a weapon, you're being punitive against the sentient natives of this world. What you're doing is wrong." He said this with the most serious tone of voice.

"Maggie Flowers," the sim said. "Time to go, Maggie Flowers."

I clenched my teeth. "Tell your damned sim to back off, Captain," I said.

"I know my duty. I'm ready."

Diego walked out of the lab.

I got into my body armor without assistance. The clunky outfit didn't help much with my mobility, but I wasn't going outside the observatory without it. I had the canister of activated seeds strapped to my back, the spray nozzle ready in my right hand. I walked to the trench we'd dug around the observatory and stared down into it. Someone had called it Arroyo Seco and the name stuck.

It looked like a desert flash-flood channel, cracked and dusty, steep crumbly walls and no plant growth at all. Lots of rocks, some in desert-pale colors of tan, aqua, lime, lavender, some just stone-gray. I pointed the nozzle at the far wall and opened up the spray.

This did not require a thick coat. I walked slowly around the perimeter of the trench, trying not to stumble in the ground cracks as I aimed the sprayer and kept a thin painting of seeds and nutrient matrix flowing onto this horrid desert. I smiled. Given a bit of time, not too long, the seeds would metabolize the sand and grow, roots, vines, flowers. We'd know it was a successful terraforming when the flowers bloomed, and we'd know mineral content of the land from the color of the blossoms.

The observatory wasn't a huge vehicle and the trench was only about a half kilometer diameter, maybe 440 meters, but I was sweating by the time I returned to the beginning. The body armor, the heat of the day, the nimble hopping over the cracks at the bottom of Arroyo Seco, and I hadn't had a moment to look up. The flowers draping down the arroyo wall finally caught my attention.

"What the hell?" I goggled at the blossom-laden vines. They looked like morning glories on steroids, thick and furry and green. "Are these my . . . ?" I knew better than to touch the vines; they'd wrap around me and try to digest me, I had a much higher nutrient content than sand.

Apparently the sand here had a much higher nutrient content than I expected. But I'd tested the sand.

I stared at the arroyo wall behind the vines. What was feeding my plants?

Pits studded the wall. I backed up a bit and looked at an area I'd just sprayed. The seeds were burrowing into a soft mass of what I'd thought was stone. The seeds sprouted before my eyes.

The stones were not stones.

I climbed up the opposite wall as fast as I could manage in the bulky body armor. I stood up inside the perimeter and looked out at the desert.

The vines were spreading like wildfire. Flowers blossomed with miraculous speed. The dusty gray sand was turning green with dots of color.

"Oh, no, no, no, no, no," I mumbled. The only way they could spread so fast was if the sand contained huge amounts of food for my seeds. And it did. The sand contained vast amounts of plant life. The sand contained the immature forms of the alien life.

I don't know how long I stood there in the sunshine, watching my seeds take over the desert. I came back to myself when Captain Johnson shoved me.

"What the hell is happening, Maggie Flowers?" He couldn't have been all that angry or he wouldn't have used my nickname.

"Speciation," I said. Then I started again. "Immature forms of a plant can look like any number of things before the final form." He still looked blank. "This desert," I pointed out toward the rapidly greening land, "is a nursery. We landed in the nursery. No wonder they've been attacking us. All those stones? Baby sentient cacti. Is that clear enough for you?"

He didn't say anything. One more effort, I thought. I'll try one more time.

"We're committing genocide," I said. "We're killing all the babies. And there's no way to stop it."

He tore his gaze off the horizon.

"Well, then, they won't be able to attack us anymore, huh?"

The vines spread in gangrenous stripes across the desert to the very foot of the red mountains. I assumed the cacti had found a chemical method to slow down the vines' pace. I doubted the method would hold. The vines spread underground, like mint, as well as with runners like strawberry. But perhaps they'd bought themselves enough time to escape.

"How long do we have to wait, Maggie?" The captain was impatient.

"I dunno," I said. "The flowers will die off as soon as the surface nutrients are consumed. The oxygen concentration around here is already at reasonable levels. They'll start to brown soon. We'll just have to wait."

The captain wasn't too happy with that idea.

"I'd like to send an exploratory mission out towards the coast," he said. "Who wants to go?"

No one spoke up, not even the security dudes. I was surprised; I thought they'd do anything the captain wanted. Perhaps they were growing brains.

"I think we're all a little worn out," Diego said. "None of us are used to fighting like this. It's hard enough keeping our perimeter clear." The others nodded.

Captain Johnson was not pleased.

"I'll go alone, then," he said. "I can't stay cooped up in this damned ship a minute longer!" He must have hoped his friends would chime in, change their minds, want to join him, but they remained silent.

"Fine," he said.

The sim said, "This is a bad idea, Captain, and it's against regulations. You are required to stay with the ship while it is under attack."

The captain snorted. "Under attack? Why, Maggie Flowers here has settled this war for us. We're not under attack, we're the ones attacking!" With that he left our common room.

"Sim, keep an eye on him, okay?" I said.

Diego stood and stretched. "Captain's not the only one going a little stir-crazy," he said. "We should just leave."

I shook my head. "You know we can't do that until the vines are resolved. It would be extremely irresponsible." I stopped.

Diego didn't say anything, but then he didn't have to. He stomped out.

"Aw, damnit, Diego!" I said. He would probably go outside to watch the sunset. Outside was so dangerous now, but I'd go out there to be with him.

I saw them outside the observatory, arguing. Diego and the captain were nose to nose and their mouths were wide open, yelling. I was glad I could not hear them.

The ground erupted under their feet and suddenly I was screaming. Barrel shaped green plants shot up from the ground, then exploded, covering both men in sticky gunk.

I screamed for the security dudes. "Perimeter, quick! The captain and Diego have been attacked!" I ran for the door and tugged on it. It wouldn't budge.

The sim said, "I cannot let you outside right now, Magdalena. There are three unexploded cacti out there. You will be harmed."

I screamed. "I'll be harmed? I'll show you harm, you damned computer simulation of a mentally-deficient idiot, if you don't open this door right now! Diego!"

The security dudes showed up then, both white-faced and panicked. Their flame-throwers were out and aimed but neither wanted to open the door.

"Open the door, sim, we need to get out there!" I kicked at the door.

"No."

"Oh you bastard . . . Josef, you have a flame-thrower? Give it here," I said. Josef gave me his flame-thrower and I turned it over and opened the bottom end. A magnet nestled there, part of the trigger assembly, and I knocked it out. It was small, but it worked to unlock the door. I ran out, not looking to see if the security dudes were behind me.

They were. As I reached Diego, who lay moaning on the ground with red blisters rising wherever the gunk had touched, the barrel cactus beside me burst into flames. A moment later the other two were similarly turned into candles, before any of them could explode.

Josef threw the captain over his shoulder in a fireman's carry, and I grabbed Diego the same way. I staggered to the door, which was again locked.

"Sim! Let us in, you bastard!"

The door snicked open.

Moments later we had both men in the med dorm. I washed Diego's skin clear of the gunk; he was still alive, but in shock and unconscious, according to the sim.

The captain wasn't so lucky. Josef wiped the captain's body then pulled a sheet over his head.

Josef had a white shocky face. I gave him pills and some water and sent him to his bunk. Then I sat with Diego and waited.

A third emissary knocked on the observatory door. When the sim announced this, I dropped the Petri dish I'd been prepping.

"Let her into the window room," I said, "and make sure she doesn't go away. And watch her for sign language! Maybe if you figure it out we can communicate finally."

I ran back to my room for my body armor and face mask and boots. Who knew what this one would do? I grabbed my diving knife, too, just in case.

The willowy creature, taller than the previous two, stooped in the observatory, leaning against the window. She rustled her limbs, a delicate fan dance.

"Sim, can you translate her sign language yet?" I said.

"The data are not perfect yet. However, I can tell you that she is distressed."

Thanks a lot, I thought. I already knew that! I took a deep breath.

"We can offer you all a safe haven," I said, "a place to wait until the flowers finish processing. But you'll have to decide soon. The flowers are encroaching on the settled portions of the planet, the mountains and coastlines, not just this battlefield."

The alien spun, and the Sim voiced some kind of warning, but I was wary this time, and prepared. I raised my right hand and switched on the nozzle and sprayed her with seeds.

The flowers sprouted from one of her arms . . . no, several of her arms, and her torso also. I saw the flowers sprout in a cleft on her chest, the cleft of the bosom on a human female. Her decorated arms flailed delicately.

She wailed. A giant cactus writhing and wailing. Surveillance cameras swerved to observe her. "Don't just stand there!" I yelled. "Get some nitrogen, quick, and a bag of soil! She needs food, she's starving!"

The sim caught what I wanted and treated it like an imperative order. Moments later, bags of rich composted soil were dumped on the observatory floor next to the emissary. I split one open with my knife and she sank into the loamy dark soil.

The combination stink of desert cactus ozone and fertile active soil assaulted my nostrils. I held a hand to my face, sneezing. With all the nutrient surrounding her I thought she'd be consumed by the flowers, but she wasn't. I watched her for some time, an hour perhaps, with the surveillance cameras recording every moment. The flowers covered her in a blanket of vines but failed to consume her. She moved again, wiping some of the vines away, and stood up from the bed of soil.

She indicated the loam. Encapsulated bits of her body, her fingers and toes, in effect, were in the loam and growing. She'd reproduced right there.

Her arms writhed in a dance that might have been sign language or might have been some kind of thanks. The flowers on her body continued to bloom, and the vines circled her like dark green chains against her gray-green skin.

The sim spoke up. "My analysis of her language is complete," it said. "She says we must leave."

I nodded. "Of course," I said. I didn't look at her but at the buds in the loam. I reached for one.

A spindly arm, bristling with needles, stopped my hand. Her other arms waved.

The sim translated, "'If you touch them I will kill you.' I suggest you leave them alone."

The buds traveled up her limbs and attached themselves to her body.

A ghost of the captain's voice echoed in my head. "Kill her before she escapes, Maggie Flowers. She's integrated the vines into her DNA, they can't kill her now; and she'll spread that immunity to all the rest of them. Kill her!"

Diego's voice in my conscience sounded so calm next to that. "Let her go, Magdalena. It is time for us to leave." Calm and quiet. And gentle.

I ordered the sim to open the barrier door. The cactus writhed and danced as she flowed over the threshold back onto her planet's soil. The surveillance cameras followed her as she crossed the arroyo and disappeared into the field of flowering vines.

"Diego's right, Sim, it's time for us to leave. Get us outta here," I said, as calmly as I could manage.

I went to the med dorm and sat next to Diego's bed. He held my hand and I held his swollen paw, gently, gently. Together we watched on the digital screens as we lifted off the planet.

When we arrived, the planet was desert-sand, barren mountains. We left a field of flowers, soon to be an entire planet of flowers. But the beauty was a mirage; much like a photograph of a past love, we could never return.

Gray
by Paul E. Martens

As I contemplate the world on which I have been abandoned, I have concluded that gray is not a shade of black or white, it is what black and white become when they die.

I used to like gray. Not so long ago, gray was where I lived and worked, at least metaphorically. I was more than just the most sought-after arbitrator in the quadrant, I was an artist in shades of gray, able to find the possibility of white in the most absolute black, or the potential for black in the most unconditional white. I could show even my most contentious, diametrically opposed clients that gray was not a gap between black and white, but a bridge. I relished gray.

But now gray covers my world like a filmy, form-fitting blanket that hugs the ground, the rocks, the craters. Gray smothers anything not-gray, assuming there is such a thing. Gray is unrelenting, unrelieved, unremitting.

Gray, I have decided, is bleak. Gray is hopeless. Gray is forever.

Even the shadows are gray.

I wonder if my hopelessness would be as unrelenting if this planetoid, or asteroid, or hemorrhoid or whatever it is, contained any color at all. A patch of green could be a sign that life goes on. A hint of red could imply that passion still exists. A dash of blue might make me able to believe there is a heaven somewhere. Even black or white would be welcome.

But there's nothing but gray.

On the plus side, it makes me appreciate the fact that not everyone appreciates gray. Some people despise anything that is not black, if black is what they believe. To them, gray is as bad as white—or red, or green or purple—simply because it is not-black.

But I could get my clients to agree to one insignificant concession. That, in one, almost impossible, extremely unlikely instance, their fanatical insistence on black might possibly, if a million conditions were met and they were in exactly the right mood, be mitigated. That one concession led to another, then another, then another, until compromise was reached and all parties were in accord.

And sometimes, that one concession was regretted after the fact, and the party of the first part, being an absolute ruler of a small, unimportant world, decided that he, she or it would retaliate against me for using my unholy powers of persuasion to wrongly make that ruler do what he, she or it would not otherwise do.

"You enjoy gray? Very well, as your reward I give you gray," he, she or it said. He, she or it waved a hand and guards grabbed me, put me on a ship and, in due course, dropped me off on my Elba.

I have no idea if my exile is temporary—to teach me a lesson—or permanent—to make sure the lesson really sinks in. I try to resign myself to the latter possibility and to be thankful that at least they didn't kill me outright. I have air, food and water. To be sure, the food is a bland paste, as gray as the world. And the water is just water; tasteless, odorless, nothing to please the palate or tickle the tongue.

Perhaps, I reflect, it would have been better if they *had* killed me outright. Quicker. Easier.

Less gray.

Another day.

I suppose it was kind of them to have left me this recorder. It gives me someone to talk to, even if that someone is hypothetical.

And, so, Hypothetical—may I call you 'Hy?'—it is another day, but simply because of the passage of time. The only difference between today and yesterday is that today is a bit further from the beginning of the universe, and just a little closer to its end. A look outside my shelter tells me the world is just as gray as it had been.

Gray.

Gray.

Gray.

Have I mentioned that the sky is gray? There must be an atmosphere of some sort because I can't see the black of space, or the bright light of stars. But whatever makes the sky blue on Earth is missing here. Or maybe it's not missing. Maybe, having occupied the ground, gray invaded the sky, killed the blue and took its place. Perhaps this world is the staging ground for gray's eventual conquest of the universe.

I have no doubt that it will conquer me, first.

Maybe I would feel the same way if the world were as red as it is gray. Or yellow. Or any other color. Maybe it's the monotony itself and not the specific hue of the sameness. But other colors are warm or cold, hard or soft. Gray just is.

I hate gray.

That should amuse me.

I used to seek out gray. I would take the hard edge of a definitive black or white and smudge it, blur it, bleed it into gray.

"Thou shalt not kill," someone might say categorically.

Well, what if your family is being attacked? What if, by killing one person you could save the lives of thousands? No? Still black or white? What if it's an accident? What if you were a doctor and in trying to save a life you made a mistake and the patient died? Oh, that's different? That's gray. And, given enough time, I could take that person deeper and deeper into the gray until, somewhere in the middle, we met the person who said, "I'll kill anybody I damned well feel like killing."

I was good at my job.

But now, black and white are fading memories. Sooner or later they will become just meaningless assemblies of letters, without a point of reference.

Like love.

Or hope.

When you are the absolute ruler of a small, unimportant world, there are very few things you cannot do.

You cannot, for example, allow yourself the weakness of gray. When you say something it must be true, because you have said it. If some wise-ass arbitrator comes along and persuades you that what you said is not absolute, you cannot admit that your will was ever anything less than adamantine, so the arbitrator must be made to vanish.

When you are the absolute ruler of a small, unimportant world, there are very many things you can do.

Such as hiding yourself behind a mask of gold and removing all traces of who or what you were before you assumed power, even as to your sex.

Such as causing a shelter of some clear material to be erected on an even smaller, even less important world, so that its inhabitant could never avoid the gray that surrounded him. Such as commanding that everything within the shelter be gray.

He, she or it was not infallible, however, despite his, her or its insistence otherwise.

The insides of my eyelids are not gray. I can still close my eyes and escape the gray. But for how long? How long until I become as gray as my world, inside and out, and it is not just all I can see, but all I can remember?

Besides these talks with you, Hy, and looking at the gray, there is very little for me to do.

There is a suit of some sort (gray, of course), with oxygen tanks, that, theoretically, at least, I can don to go outside. Frankly, though, I am uncomfortable about making use of it.

All right, fine, I'm terrified.

I am alone here. A billion things could go wrong and there would be no one to call for help. A torn suit, a ruptured tank, a broken leg, are just a very few of the possibilities that feed my fear. At least I am safe within my glass house. There are no bricks anywhere, and no one to throw them if there were. Certainly I would not be inclined to do so myself.

Gray.

I have no idea how long I've been here. It's still gray everywhere. I cut myself just to see red.

It was wonderful.

The blood ran and dripped and splattered. Red stood out brilliantly against the gray, almost blinding me, though perhaps it was my tears that blurred my vision.

I may have overdone it a bit. I think I'm becoming anemic, as if I've been the victim of a wasteful vampire who allowed his supper to go unconsumed.

But the red faded to brown, and the brown sank into the gray, and soon all I'll have left are my scars.

Red is dangerous. I've resolved to stop before I kill myself.

At least until I decide to kill myself.

I'm back.

I don't remember if I told you, but I put on the suit and went exploring; prospecting for gold. Or mauve, or burnt sienna or anything not-gray.

There is nothing here that is not-gray.

I lifted up rocks, I cracked them open to look inside. I clawed at the ground with my hands. I looked and I looked and I looked, but there was nothing but gray. I finally gave up and trudged home.

Oh, god. I referred to this place as home. I can't. I won't. It's not.

I can't let myself believe that this is anything other than a temporary stopover on my journey through life. A brief interruption. It is *not* permanent. No matter what the voice in my head tells me.

Anyway, gray grit clung to my suit and now it is inside, crunching beneath my feet, scraping my skin, insinuating itself into everything. No wonder it has taken over the planet.

I have nothing to use to clean it up except my fingers. It's laborious, tedious, time-consuming.

At least it's something to do.

As I gather up the grains of gray I notice for the first time that they are not all the same color.

Well, yes, they are all gray. But by placing one next to another, I see that there are differences, almost imperceptible variations, in their shades of gray. Nothing approaching the brutality of black or the harshness of white.

Oh, you have to look. You have to look very closely. But it's true. The gray is not as uniform as I'd thought.

I am delighted. Ha! I say to the absolute ruler of the small, unimportant world. There *are* shades of gray.

And, as I believe I've said, I am an artist in shades of gray.

Carefully, I examine each individual grain, putting them in piles according to their hues. Soon, I have my palette of gray in seven piles. Their number gives me my inspiration for my first project. A rainbow. I call it my Graynbow.

Okay, it's not a great title. It's not exactly a spectacular work of art, either. I probably won't keep it. It takes up too much room, anyway.

My canvas is the (gray) floor. Grain by grain I place them in their appropriate arcs. When I am finished I stand up and admire my work.

Oh, the quiet subtlety of it. The darkest curve is miles away from black. It does nothing more than suggest that black is not impossible. From the darkest, the work progresses by almost undetectable steps to the lightest, which is nowhere near white, but implies that white might exist somewhere.

It's beautiful.

That's probably overstating it, but it's beautiful to me. The gray is not so overwhelmingly homogeneous. The spell of monotony is broken. I can pretend the shades of gray are colors, distinct and individual. There is variety, and variety is the spice of life.

It makes me laugh. And laugh. And laugh, until I realize it's been going on way too long and that at some point I had begun sobbing. Instead of making me stop, the realization makes me cry harder.

I am marooned on a gray world, alone, with only a forlorn hope that I will ever escape, and I have become so desperate for color that I see it where it probably doesn't exist. I examine my work again. No, I'm sure it's not my imagination. There are variations in the gray.

You just have to look closely. You have to want to see them.

And I do. I really, really do.

*   *   *

O frabjous day calloo callay
There are more than seven shades of gray
Every day there are more
Than there were the day before.

I'm happy with this one.

It's a landscape. From memory, of course. Hills, and trees and flowers, with a river. An almost clear sky, with a few fleecy clouds. It's such a nice change from the dull, gray landscape that surrounds me every day. Well, my landscape is gray, too, but it is a gray of my own creation. I control the gray.

I am the absolute ruler of my small, unimportant work of art.

It's not much, but it's something. In fact, it's good enough to try and keep.

The stuff that I am forced to think of as food, even though it resembles something that ought to have been eliminated rather than ingested, makes a decent adhesive. It takes time—and I really have no idea whatsoever of just how much time—but, speck by speck by speck I transfer my landscape to part of one of my windows. When I finish, I sit on the floor and admire the view.

Gray can be so beautiful.

I'm in love.

I had no one in particular in mind when I began my project. I was just going to do a portrait of a woman.

But, now that I am finished, I find it is a portrait of *the* woman; the woman I never had time to find, the woman I didn't know existed.

I lack even the vocabulary to wax rhapsodically about how beautiful she is. I have no experience in describing such things. But for you, Hy, I will attempt it.

Her hair shines as if it is filled with stars, and is softer than the softest pillow on which you have ever laid your head.

Her eyes are warm yet sparkle as if she has just done something outrageous and it amuses her.

Her nose is not large but proud.

Her lips . . . I have imagined kissing those lips. They are as soft as her hair, as warm as her eyes. They are as sweet as honey and as salty as tears. They are slightly parted, as if to whisper things in my ear that will make me tremble with the anticipation of pleasure.

Her jaw brooks no argument and suffers no fools.

Her neck invites me to bury my face in the scent of her.

All in shades of gray.

She makes me glad of my imprisonment. If I had never been abandoned here, I would have never known her.

She makes me rage against my imprisonment even more than I had because I am unable to search the universe until I find her.

She is real. She exists. She must.

I miss her, yet I am no longer alone.

I apologize for ignoring you.

Annie and I have been enjoying something of a honeymoon. We appreciate that you have respected our privacy.

She loves our world of gray, and, because I love her, I have come to love it, too.

We can't believe I ever thought there was only one shade of gray, or only seven. We laugh about my Graynbow, and not just because of its stupid name.

Our world is a million shades of gray. A billion. A trillion. Every facet of every particle is a unique tint. It is impossible to name them all. I'm dazzled by their variety. I feel as if I had been a blind man who had known nothing but black, whose sight was restored in a garden of every flower that had ever bloomed.

Annie has given me my sight.

I no longer yearn for the inelegant brashness of black or white, of red, or green or blue. I can't believe I ever wished for such gauche colors to intrude upon the soft and subtle beauty of our world.

I no longer cry because I may never leave this place, I cry when I consider the possibility that I might.

I no longer cry because I am alone, I cry because I once was.

Now when I cry, it is not because I am overwhelmed by the omnipresence of gray, I cry because I am overwhelmed by its beauty.

For someone as happy as I am, I seem to spend a lot of time crying, don't I?

I am content.

It feels very much like being happy, but quietly. And completely.

I have Annie. I have my beautiful world of gray. I have my art. I need nothing else. Food, air, water; these things merely keep me alive. If I didn't have them, I know I would die, but I would still be content.

I will probably die here anyway, and I'm glad. There is nowhere I would rather be.

Where else would I be surrounded by such glorious views? The grays sing to me. Their harmonies fill me with peaceful joy. I can almost believe I have a soul.

I am getting older, yet Annie remains the same. She smiles grayly at my mutability, she laughs at my mortality, but I know she loves me.

That is everything.

I am blinded.

No, that is not true. I would rather have lost my sight entirely. They have, instead, stolen away the gray.

No, again that is not true. The gray exists. But they have killed it, robbed it of its life, its beauty.

Once more it is simply gray.

Worse, Annie is gone.

I doubt they are evil. Perhaps they even see themselves as heroes.

We were sitting quietly, absorbing and being absorbed by the many-toned gray, when it was ripped by fires of not-gray. It took me a moment to remember red and orange and yellow. Hot, flaming colors destroyed the gray, burned the gray, burned my eyes, my soul.

I screamed.

I didn't see the ship land.

When I could open my eyes again, they were outside my home, dressed in their gaudy suits of silver splashed with black and white and blue and green. I pressed my hands against my eyes but I could not shut out the colors, could not shut up their clamor that shouted down the song of the gray.

I turned to Annie to comfort her, to try and lie and tell her that everything would be all right. But she had already fled from the intrusion of those uncouth hues. In her place were only sands of gray; soulless, uniform gray. All of my art, all those lovely shades of gray hid themselves in sameness, unable to bear the contrast with the vulgar tints.

The invaders signal to me to let them in.

I suppose I will. It doesn't matter. Nothing matters.

Is it better to have loved and lost than to have never loved?

I don't know.

When I had Annie my world was gray and filled with beauty. Now there is color and I must face the desolation of a universe without her.

I miss gray.

Author and Photographer Notes

Z. S. "Sophy" Adani was born in Europe. She studied fine art and biology, but writing, especially science fiction, has always been her passion. Three years ago, she started writing seriously. She lives in Florida with her husband and two daughters.

Camille Alexa and her houseful of wayward objects currently reside in the Pacific Northwest. Her speculative poetry and fiction can be found in anthologies and periodicals of varying degrees of fame and availability. She writes for *The Green Man Review*.

Michael Anthony lives in Santa Rosa, California. He works in health care, currently at a drug abuse clinic. He enjoys writing in his spare time and his work has appeared in several publications.

Tom Barlow is a graduate of Clarion 2005. His stories have appeared in *The Intergalactic Medicine Show* (both on-line and in next year's Best Of print collection), the *Steel City Review*, *Coyote Wild*, the print anthology, *Book of Dead Things*, *The Hiss Quarterly*, and other magazines. A podcast of one of his stories is available on WellToldTales.com.

Paul L. Bates has graced the independent press with his short fiction since the early 1990's, blending genres with tall tales published or pending publication in such discerning venues as *Zahir*, *Withersin*, *Dark Wisdom*, *Lovecraft's Weird Mysteries*, *Sporty Spec*, *New Writings in the Fantastic* and *Ruins Extraterrestrial*. He is semi-retired from the construction industry, a distance swimmer, and happiest when absorbed in his writing. *Imprint*, the first novel in a series about the last city on earth was first published by Gale/Five Star in 2005; *Dreamer*, the second part of the trilogy, is scheduled for release in June 2008.

Chris Benton is an Information Technology professional for a university in southeastern Virginia. This is his first published story.

Skadi meic Beorh, a speculative writer of Celto-Teutonisch descent, has authored the story collections *Always After Thieves Watch* (Brilliant Book Press) and *Scary Stories For Girls* (Backroom Publishing), and has co-edited the dictionary *Pirate Lingo* (Brilliant Book Press). His first novel, *The Obscure*, will be published by Wildside Press. He has also been honored to have a tale about his literary hero Nathaniel Hawthorne appear in the anthology *Bound For Evil*. His work has most recently appeared in *Black Petals, Twisted Tongue, Ballista, Lachryma, Brilliant!,* and *The Willows* (where he serves as Contributing Editor). He may be reached at peekthemorpholux@yahoo.com.

Brenta Blevins lives and writes in the Appalachian Mountains, where she enjoys hiking with her husband. She has written audio dramas that have been produced for public radio and non-fiction that has been published in *Strange Horizons*. Her short fiction has appeared in the *Bound in Skin* and *Sporty Spec* anthologies. Brenta appreciates the company and assistance of her fluffy, white cat, Snow Crash.

Gustavo Bondoni has been writing since 2004, and has had work published both on-line and in print, in North America, South America and Europe. Notably, his short Story "Tenth Orbit" was published in the April 2005 issue of *Jupiter SF*, to critical acclaim and was also a quarter-finalist in L. Ron Hubbard's Writers of the Future Contest (4th quarter 2006). Additionally, his story "Egalité" appeared in the September 2006 issue of *Carve Magazine* and his story "Great Hairy Boats" was accepted for publication in the July 2007 edition of *Jupiter SF*.

Sue Burke was born in Wisconsin and lived briefly in Texas before moving to Madrid, Spain in 1999, and has since learned that 40 percent of Spain's surface is threatened by drought, erosion, and desertification. There's no escape from desolation, no matter how good the wine and paella. Her fiction and poetry have appeared in a number of magazines and anthologies. For more information see more at www.sue.burke.name.

Jean-Michel Calvez lives near Versailles, France. As an engineer in naval shipbuilding and now in R&D, he was impressed very early by Theodore Sturgeon, Arthur C. Clarke and, later, Dan Simmons. His SF projects often deal with time and paradox or pros and cons of encounters between species. He has published five novels and around 40 short stories in various anthologies, magazines, or online. His English-language stories have appeared in *Bewildering Stories* and in the *Ruins Terra* anthology published by Hadley Rille Books.

Scott Christian Carr is a professional writer and television producer. His paranormal series *Dead Tenants* is currently airing on The Learning Channel (TLC), and his latest project *The Mole People* will be debuting soon on the A&E network. He's the creator of the post-apocalyptic scifi feature film *The NUKE Brothers* as well as the tie-in series *The LAST Wizard, KID Apocalypse* and the comic book *The Continuing Adventures of FAT Man and Little Boy . . .*

His fiction has been featured in *Pulp Eternity*, *Horror Quarterly*, *GUD* and many anthologies. He is the author of *Champion Mountain* a novel of superhero family dysfunction. Visit him at: www.myspace.com/sardy.

Willis Couvillier is a writer currently residing in Reno, Nevada. He has been an avid reader of speculative fiction since his youth and has dreamt of writing the same for nearly as long. Currently Will (as he prefers to be known) is working on a number of projects, ranging through the full genre spectrum of speculative fiction. Also, he has been known to jot down a poem or two, usually speculative, but more often about some real life situation he'd noticed. Will hangs out at on-line writer forums, reads books about the craft, and enjoys a good role-game and occasional CCG. His biblio includes: "Inheritance" published in *Visual Journeys: A Tribute to Space Artists* (Hadley Rille Books, July 2007), "Heartcry" published in *Ruins Extraterrestrial* (Hadley Rille Books, October 2007).

Jennifer Crow enjoys desolate places because there's no place in her house where she can be alone. When she gets a moment of peace and quiet, she writes poetry and stories about faraway places and dangerous people. Her work has appeared on websites like *Strange Horizons* and *Goblin Fruit*, and in the *Ruins Extraterrestrial* anthology from Hadley Rille Books, among other places. Several of her poems have received Rhysling nominations and honorable mentions in the Year's Best Fantasy and Horror anthologies.

Hazel Dixon has been writing for over fifteen years, but recently her time has been engaged with Creative Writing courses at the University of Bolton in England from where she graduated with a Master of Arts. She lives in a small village that has one road connecting it to the outside world and is surrounded by forestry land. Owned by three cats, her interests lie in reading and writing science fiction, fantasy, the odd thriller and that fascinating beast—the vampire.

F.V. "Ed" Edwards is internationally known in Medical Product development as an engineer/inventor (19 patents since 1976), a speaker and author of numerous articles in the field. He served as a Tribal Health Director for three years and did considerable research on their cultural history to support needed improvements in the health services. He expresses gratitude to James Gunn for the on-line Science Fiction workshop and the critique group formed from those classes. They were a great help in his transition from a technical writer.

Sara Genge is doctor in Madrid, Spain. She writes science fiction and fantasy aided and abetted by a coven of friends and female relatives. Her work has appeared in *Strange Horizons*, *Cosmos Magazine* and *Helix SF* among others, as well as in translation in the Greek Comic and SF Magazine, *Ennea*. She's a founding member and regular contributor of *The Daily Cabal*, a blog of speculative microfiction that can be found at www.dailycabal.com.

Jude-Marie Green recently sold a story to *Visual Journeys*, published by Hadley Rille Books, and to Michael Knost's anthology, *Legends of the Mountain State*; and her work has or will appear in *Say...*, *Abyss&Apex*, *Ideomancer*, and has been published by Sam's Dot Publishing.

Erich Hernandez-Baquero was born in Bridgeport, CT in 1972. He is a Major in the U.S. Air Force and received his commission in 1994 when he graduated from the U.S. Air Force Academy in Colorado Springs, CO. He has been assigned to various posts in California, New York, and Washington, DC, and is currently in Madrid, Spain. His love for photography grew out of his studies at the Rochester Institute of Technology, New York, where he obtained a doctorate in Imaging Science in 2002.

Max Habilis has appeared in several anthologies. He has had a number of jobs including working as a computer programmer, systems administrator, high energy physics technician, bus boy and cashier at a bakery. He lives in the American Midwest.

James Hartley is a retired computer programmer. He grew up in northern New Jersey, and has now settled in sunny central Florida. He has published a fantasy novel, *Teen Angel*, and short stories in *Sterling Web*, *Starsong*, and *Nocturnal Ooze*. He is currently working on a second novel, *The Ghost of Grover's Ridge*.

Shelley Savran Houlihan lives and works in Connecticut. Having been a Social Worker for many years, she just completed a non-fiction book about caring for elderly parents without sacrificing sanity. Her fiction has been published in *The American Drivel Review* and *Lily*, and she has stories forthcoming in *Shred of Evidence* and *Little Sisters Vol. 1*.

Davin Ireland was born and bred in the south of England, but currently resides in the Netherlands. His fiction credits include stories published in a wide range of print magazines and anthologies on both sides of the Atlantic, including *Underworlds*, *The Horror Express*, *Zahir*, *Neo-Opsis*, *Rogue Worlds*, *Fusing Horizons*, *Storyteller Magazine* and *Albedo One*. You can visit his site at http://home.orange.nl/d.ireland.

Meghan Jurado is a writer from many places, the latest being Colorado where she currently lives with her husband and three neurotic dogs. She has been published in *The Undead*, *The Undead II: Skin and Bones*, *Shadowbox*, *Revenant Magazine*, *The Travel Guide to the Haunted Mid-Atlantic Region*, *Echoes of Terror*, and *Until Someone Loses an Eye*. She never turns down a horror movie or a sushi dinner.

Stephen Graham King is not to be confused with that other guy, though any comparison would be supremely flattering. When not writing, he indulges his passion for painting, particularly abstracts in acrylic. His cancer memoir, *Just Breathe*, is available from all major online book retailers and his story, "Pas de Deux," was chosen for the anthology, *North of Infinity II*. He currently lives in Toronto, surrounded by books, paintings and chocolate and is working on revisions of his novel, *Soul's Blood*.

Fran LaPlaca has had stories appear in *Realms of Wonder: Fantastic Companions*, on-line at *antipodeanSF* and in the e-book anthology *Twilight and Thorns*, recently released from Circle Dark Publishing. She has stories coming out in the near future from two anthologies entitled *Something Magic This Way Comes* and *Better Off Undead*, both due for release from DAW in 2008.

Gerri Leen lives in Northern Virginia and originally hails from Seattle. She came to fiction writing late in life and writes stories in many genres, including fantasy—often centered around mythology—science fiction, horror, speculative fiction, and literary. She dabbles in poetry and has one poem published. A complete list of her published and accepted work can be found at http://www.gerrileen.com.

C.A. Manestar works as a professional Tech Support geek when she's not agonizing over her novel(s) and short stories. She loves IR photography, internet technology, zombie movies and exploring abandoned places. She's done too many jobs to list but some of her favorites were: mask-maker, contact lens maker and bead-store owner. This is her first print sale. She has a few partners in crime online and in RL that support her in all her mad and scattered schemes. She lives in Toronto with her giant American husband and The Cat.

Paul E. Martens is probably more normal than he thinks he is, but stranger than is absolutely necessary. He loves his wife, Patti, and son, Nick. Paul was a first place winner in the Writers of the Future Contest and invented hydrogen. His webpage is: http://www.sfwa.org/members/Martens.

Lyn McConchie has had over 200 stories professionally published since 1991, including *The Key of the Keplian* in 1995, and *Ciara's Song* in1998 (both Warner Aspect). *Beastmaster's Ark* appeared in 2002 (Tor), and the sequel, *Beastmaster's Circus* in 2004 (Tor), both winning New Zealand's Sir Julius Vogel Award (2003 and 2005). The *Duke's Ballad* (Tor), a sequel to Ciara's Song and a Vogel winner, and *Silver May Tarnish* (Tor), appeared 2005. *Beast Master's Quest* (Tor) appeared in 2006. Recently she has had stories appear in *Trails 2* and *Tiresias Revisited*.

Alex Moisi is a college student in Illinois, originally from Romania. He has had several stories published in *Residential Aliens* and will be featured in their upcoming anthology.

Adam Nakama first edited for a zine he started in college, and was excited to read for Desolate Places. He also writes, having sold a few pieces here and there, and studies the intersection of narrative with emergent technology.

Mari Ness's previous works have appeared in *Reflection's Edge*, *Coyote Wild*, *Susurrus Magazine*, *The Mammoth Book of New Erotica 2* and the *Mammoth Book of New Erotica 3*, and several other print and online zines. She lives in South Florida under the strict control of two cats.

Eric T. Reynolds has edited anthologies in several genres including science fiction, fantasy, horror and mainstream. He is a Master of Science candidate in the distance program of the Space Studies Department at the University of North Dakota. He has appeared in the journal *Science* and has several articles in the forthcoming encyclopedia *Space Exploration and Humanity: A Historical Encyclopedia,* by the American Astronautical Society, edited by Dr. Stephen Johnson, published by ABC-CLIO.

Stephen D. Rogers has had over five hundred stories and poems selected to appear in more than a hundred publications. His website, www.stephendrogers.com, includes a list of new and upcoming titles as well as other timely information.

Trent Roman is a young(ish) writer from Montréal with an interest in all types of fiction strange and unusual. He is fascinated by what makes people tick at both the intimately personal level and the sweeping societal level, and enjoys every opportunity to pursue such questions through the means of fiction.

Shaun Ryan has made his living as a commercial driver for the last fifteen years and has always been a lover of books and fiction of all kinds. In 2005, he began writing short stories and submitting them for publication. His short story "Muerte" was recently accepted for an upcoming issue of *Escaping Elsewhere* and "Good Boys" will appeared in the November 2007 issue of *Crimson Highway*. He lives in Wisconsin and is currently at work on his first novel.

Lawrence M. Schoen holds a Ph.D. in cognitive psychology, spent ten years as a college professor, and currently works as the chief compliance officer and director of research for a series of mental health and addiction treatment facilities. He runs Paper Golem, http://www.papergolem.com, a speculative fiction small press. He's also one of the world's foremost authorities on the Klingon language. He lives just outside Philadelphia and writes every day.

Cavan Scott is a UK-based writer and magazine editor. He has written five audio dramas for Big Finish Productions; *Doctor Who—Project: Twilight, Doctor*

Who—The Church and the Crown, *Doctor Who—Project: Lazarus*, *Judge Dredd—For King and Country* and *The Tomorrow People—The Warlock's Dance*. He has a number of short stories published in short press anthologies, magazines and online. His first novel, *Project: Valhalla*, co-written with Mark Wright, was published in 2005 and he is one of the editors of the *Doctor Who* anthology, the *Ghosts of Christmas*, published December 2007.

Katherine Shaw lives in Pennsylvania with her dog and two cats. She has stories in *Staffs & Starships #1* and the PARSEC anthology *Triangulation: End of Time*, and forthcoming in the *Black Dragon, White Dragon* anthology from Ricasso Press and *Every Day Fiction*. She is currently working on her first novel.

Douglas Smith's stories have appeared in over seventy magazines and anthologies in twenty-six countries around the world, including *InterZone, Baen's Universe, Amazing Stories, The Third Alternative, Weird Tales, The Mammoth Book of Best New Horror, Cicada, On Spec, Oceans of the Mind*, and anthologies from Penguin/Roc, DAW, Meisha Merlin, and others. He was a finalist for the John W. Campbell Award for Best New Writer and has twice won the Aurora Award for best speculative short fiction by a Canadian. He is currently completing his first novel.

Eric Vogt graduated college with a degree in psychology and poetry. Instead of writing lengthy sonnets about why your mother would like you to have fries with that, he discovered that technical writing allowed him to find interesting, well-paying, speculative-fiction-inspiring employment for such diverse entities as an insurance company, Medicaid, the US Army Special Warfare Center and School, and the pharmaceutical industry.

Bill Ward (billwardwriter.com) is a freelance writer out of Baltimore with stories in *Flashing Swords Magazine* and the anthology *The Return of the Sword*. He is co-editor of the forthcoming *Magic and Mechanica* anthology from Ricasso Press.

Visual Journeys: A Tribute to Space Artists

" ... many of the stories are highly readable ... "

—*Locus*

" ... a homerun ... there's not a bad story in the bunch ... "

—Chris Gerrib

Space art from award-winning artists matched up with new science fiction stories from award-winning authors. Color plates accompany each tale.

www.hadleyrillebooks.com

Golden Age SF: Tales of a Bygone Future

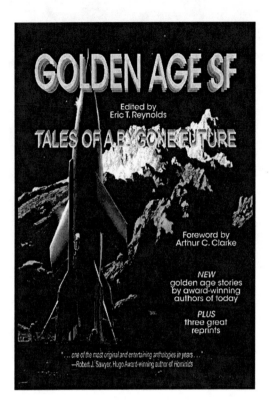

"Golden Age SF . . . its original stories . . . certainly dwell on the destiny of scientific utopia and interplanetary colonization proclaimed by the SF of 50 years past . . . All in all, an agreeable anthology."

—*Locus*

New stories written as if during the Golden Age of Science Fiction. Several selected for honorable mention for Gardner Dozois's *The Year's Best Science Fiction 24*, one selected for David G. Hartwell and Kathryn Cramer's *Year's Best SF 12*, another selected for Rich Horton's *Space Opera 2007*.

www.hadleyrillebooks.com

Printed in the United States
103867LV00003B/82-93/P